Ardgour's Daughter

Fiona Robson

Platform One Publishing

Published by Platform One Publishing

978-0-9927422

First published in Great Britain in 2013 by Platform One Publishing

Platform One Publishing is part of Paddington Associates Ltd Reg. No. 7893770

A CIP catalogue record is available from the British Library

Paperback ISBN 978-0-9927422-0-1

In memory of my father George Clark, who loved Ardgour and Morvern.

Acknowledgements

This book would not have been published without the constant encouragement and tireless help provided by my husband Simon, who also edited, proof read and published this eBook. Thanks also to my three children for reading extracts from 'Ardgour's Daughter' in various stages of its preparation and offering their very useful opinions as to how it could be improved and for being so patient and understanding when Eilidh Ruadh seemed to be getting more attention than they were. Thanks in particular to my eldest son for so painstakingly and willingly proof reading the document and helping with the production of the front cover. I would also like to send my heartfelt thanks to my mother for obtaining local information to aid me with the background research for this book. Finally I would like to thank those friends of my parents who were so willing to provide material to assist with this project.

Table of Contents

Prophesy[1]

The Selkie is enchanting
Her boundless joy enthrals
The Selkie is entrancing
Her beauty never palls

Dragon lurks in danger
Feared by everyone
Enemies surround him
The fight is not yet done

Selkie's in the water
Dragon's dared the tide
True Sight has Seen
Legends still abide

The Selkie is elusive
Whoever can she be?
A promise must be kept
A ring will hold the key

The Selkie she is hurting
Trapped in history
A gift must be redeemed
Before she be set free

The Selkie she is dying
Caught in mystery
Fire must consume
Dragon choose her destiny

---

[1] Extract from an ancient Cornish manuscript.

The Curse, 1780

Hot air brooded, heavy and humid, menacingly poised above elaborate drapes; whilst the smothering scent of incense enveloped all in its coils, spiralling sinuously upwards.

In the centre of this boudoir, engulfed on one side by dense luxuriant hangings, an enormous bed languished.

Nearby, a solitary candle quivered bleakly, abandoning the exquisite pictures and intricate tapestries which lined the walls to obscurity amidst the shadows.

Silence suffocated the room, distorted only by an occasional stifled cry from the occupant of the bed who lay there exhausted, determined.

Long ash blonde hair draped across a pillow, unbound, tangled, damp with sweat.

Enormous brown eyes swamped a face, deathly pale, etched stiff with revulsion; as mouth pinched tight, she battled to keep in the screams that threatened to rise, the screams that once released she feared would never stop.

At her side, as if on guard, there sat, fiercely upright, a tall gaunt female of indeterminate age bearing a harsh, inscrutable expression, except when she glanced at the woman on the bed when it would soften, become almost doting.

As her thoughts drifted, unbidden, to the source of her torment the woman on the bed grimaced, bitterly, 'Was it not said that to carry ill was a warning of the probable birth of one of the monsters? And of a certainty she had been so very unwell these past few months!'

'It had not been thus with her other two children' she reflected resentfully. 'She had revelled in the bearing of them, relished the feeling of triumph she experienced when she carried her lord's heir; in the satisfaction of knowing that in this at least she had succeeded. And then when the first was found to be a boy...' she gasped as the pain came upon her again.

'It was too early! The child was not due for another two months. But this also was a sign.' Her face twisted as she mused cynically 'A child carried in distress and discomfort and delivered in pain with long travail! Yet He rejoiced. He rejoiced at these signs, rejoiced at the prospect of the birth of this travesty! A monster such as his twin had been. Rejoiced, even though he knew that such a birth could cause her death!'

For a moment she almost hated him. 'But no, never that! Not when he had rescued her from Hell. She had been prepared to accept virtually any offer of marriage, and so when he had so unexpectedly, so flatteringly offered for her she had not hesitated. Some might have quibbled over his reputation, but what did she care if he had ten thousand mistresses! Had not her own father preferred his paramour to his wife much to her mother's intense and bitter humiliation! But that would not have distressed her. Not when marriage to him meant that she could get away, meant that she could escape...... not when he was so charming, so handsome, so very, very wealthy.'

Abruptly from the garden below there intruded a penetrating peal of merry laughter and the clamour of vibrant childish trebles ringing with excitement,

"Selkie she must marry ere she's twenty one
She must choose aright else the angel of death will come
Choose! Choose! Choose! Selkie choose!
Tinker, tailor, soldier, thief, butcher, baker, shepherd, chief,
dragon, doctor, sailor......"

As the chanting paused a pleasant baritone joined in.

"A Sailor! - No! No!
Dragon has not won!

The Selkie she must die
For the curse is not undone
Hear Dragon's frenzied cry!
Weep as the spell anew is spun!
Alone must dragon ever fly
To prey on each and every one.
Run away! Run away!
Dragon's coming after you!"

Then the confusion of loud screams, the clatter of scurrying feet, as attended by his deafening roar the frenzied dragon pursued its terrified quarry.

The woman on the bed clenched her fists tight, finger nails biting into the soft skin of her hands as she sought to block out the clamour of her children playing.

The sound of their childish game upset her for they recited a rhyme she hated, abhorred, and their laughter and loud screams grated on her already fractured nerves. She would have sent them away but *he* was there. *He* was joining in their play!

She was gripped by another contraction, stronger than the last. 'Ye gods, the other two births were as nothing compared to this, not even the first and she had thought that overlong!' The pains were coming faster, more furious. But she swore she would delay this birth as long as she could, delay the arrival of the aberration. For the longer the birth was delayed the less the chance of the creature surviving, especially a seven month child as this was, they rarely lived - not even the monsters!

'His twin sister had been one of *them*. Their mother had died giving them birth! She had heard the servants' gossip, heard them say that sometimes it was the changeling child that died, but more often it was the mother who was lost as she struggled to give birth to the miscreation. They thought she did not hear but she did!'

'She had heard the servants babble, heard them talking about the curse that followed the family down through the generations. But never did she discover why the girl had died, what she had died of'.

'His twin had lived for eighteen long years but he never mentioned her, would not talk of her. Neither would he have her picture put away. He refused to have it removed from his bed chamber, refused to banish it to the gallery where it could hide amongst all those paintings of all the other freaks, all those other monstrosities.' She shuddered again 'So many pictures of the changelings, century after century, all wearing that same face! Never now did she enter that long corridor were their pictures hung, nor could she ever bear to even glance at that picture of his twin sister that perpetually haunted his bedroom wall.'

'He would not speak of her; but the servants did, they whispered at how he had gone wild after she had died, been inconsolable. No,' she thought, 'if she had known about the family legend, about the sister, she would never have accepted his offer, not even to get away, she would have waited..., waited..., would rather......'

Her contractions came upon her once more and she cried out, not with pain but with fury for she knew that her time was upon her; and that just as all those who are born must eventually die so must the child in the womb come forth, unless death intervened first.

A thin wail pierced the air.

Then silence returned.

The woman slumped back against her cushions exhausted, defeated, vanquished.

11

The tall gaunt female, who had remained so patiently and tenderly at the bedside side throughout that long travail, bent down to murmur comfortingly to the woman on the bed before approaching the third occupant of the room and handing her a small cup of liquid. "Give her Ladyship this to drink. It will help calm her nerves," she ordered before declaring harshly "heaven help you should her Ladyship come to any harm!"

"Yes ma'am," the other woman gasped, hands pressed tight against her ample thighs to hide their tremor, her wide frightened eyes belying her round comfortable exterior.

"When you have made certain that her Ladyship is comfortable and is resting quietly you will ensure that this chamber is spotlessly clean. The Marquis will wish to see her Ladyship immediately he learns that she is well enough to support a visit." After issuing these instructions the tall gaunt woman walked over to the small crib, picked up the tiny damp occupant and said curtly, "I will take *this* to the Crypt. It would only distress her Ladyship if it were to remain with her further."

She started to wrap the tiny baby in sheeting. Inadvertently she looked at the infant's face. 'Those strange eyes,' she thought. 'It wasn't natural. It was almost as if they looked right through you, straight into your heart.' She shuddered. Quickly she pulled the sheet tight over the infant's face and head, and draped a blanket over the top of this to further muffle any sounds. After putting the bundle into a bag, which she hung over her shoulder, she walked towards the door.

There she paused and turning to the plump, pallid woman, who stood forlornly at the bottom of the bed, the glass of liquid still clutched tight in her hand, and said harshly, "Do not under any circumstances allow anyone to enter the room. Say it is on my instruction. I will warn the Marquis that things are not progressing well and that her Ladyship is resting. I shall tell him that if he values her life she must not be disturbed. We will not inform the Marquis that his daughter was stillborn until later this evening, by which time her Ladyship will have had time to compose herself. Is that understood?"

"Yes ma'am." The other's voice trembled and the sweat flowed more freely down her ashen, furrowed brow.

Then without glancing further at the other occupants of the room, the gaunt woman opened the door and went out.

The Crypt, 1780

The Marquis was extremely striking in appearance. He was just over the average height, slim with the swordsman's graceful gait; but it was his beautiful melting brown almond shaped eyes, his mane of auburn hair streaked with blonde, the contrasting olive skin, tanned dark by the warmth of the summer sun that caught one's attention and made him such a memorable figure. He was still entertaining his children when she found him.

As soon as the Marquis became aware of the presence of the tall gaunt woman he made his way towards her, his eyes full of laughter, and a question. Eyes that darkened with worry on being told that his wife's travail was going ill, that this third birth was not progressing as smoothly as the previous two had done.

He acquiesced quietly to the woman's request to have the children's help in collecting fresh herbs for their mother; ignoring their urgent pleas to continue their game or return to their nurse. Then head down and with a heavy heart, he made his way slowly to his study to seek consolation amongst his books.

The boy was about 8 years old, and though of different colouring he had the look of his father. The little girl, slightly younger, was exceptionally pretty and resembled the woman who lay suffering in the bedroom. Both were big blonde children with large brown eyes, but the boy looked the more sensitive of the two, with his thin pinched face and high cheekbones.

After a few moments the boy exclaimed "This is not the way to the gardens!"

"We are not going to the gardens."

"Where are you taking us?" There was a touch of defiance in his voice.

"To the Crypt. You will remain there the rest of the day so that you may devote your time to praying for the health of your mother and the safe arrival of your new brother or sister."

"Not there Annie! Please, we haven't done anything wrong! Mother whipped Louis and me last time we were bad rather than leave us in the Crypt," pleaded the little girl.

"Indeed Annie, we would far rather have another whipping than be left there," the boy asserted fervently.

"I told her Ladyship that whipping the both of you, so near her time, would bring the birth early," Annie declared malevolently. "I told her that I could thrash the pair of you as well as she could," she hissed. "But her Ladyship would have it that it must be she and she alone as had the chastising of you!" Then, barely pausing for breath, her voice rising sharply, the tall gaunt woman continued her rant. "I told her that if she refused me the leathering of you, she should send you to the Crypt, and leave you there a-thinking on your sins. 'They will learn more from a stay in that Crypt than from a whipping that is over too soon and as quick forgot,' I told her." Annie glared manically at the children. "Pray that your wickedness, which caused your poor mother to give the both of you that beating, is not what made her birth the baby so early! Pray that it does not die. Beg the Lord in all his mercy that your foolishness has not killed your mother!" She said this last in a fierce whisper, not to be overheard.

The children ceased importuning her further and instead edged closer together; while the little girl raised her chin higher and a mulish look of defiance came over her face, though her clutch on her brother's hand tightened.

Before they had walked much further a small ornate building came into view.

Beautiful carvings of numerous different fish and other sea creatures were cut into the exterior stonework of this memorial. As they approached nearer the edifice, they could see a statue of Neptune and that of a mermaid standing on either side of the entrance, as if to welcome them.

Annie opened the door.

Once inside it could be observed that the interior walls were covered with exquisite paintings of creatures and artefacts of the sea. A beautifully sculpted statue of a large grey seal graced the centre of the room, and from a window set high in the roof light streamed down, illuminating the head of the seal as if in benediction.

A small door was located inconspicuously in the corner of the chamber, and towards this Annie now strode, with the children following reluctantly in her wake. Taking a large key out of her pocket Annie unlocked the door and then led the way down a few small steps and from hence into a long dark corridor.

They had only one small candle with them and the children, holding tight to each other's hands, stayed close together while they silently followed the woman as she marched along the shadowy passage. Through their ill lit journey stray glimpses of the wall showed that here also the artist had left his mark, for the walls were covered with mementoes of the sea. Many small doorways were situated on either side of this passage, and next to every door there stood a different carved statue of a sea creature.

Upon reaching the large door at the end of the corridor they halted.

Engravings of hermit crabs, lobsters, sea anemones, sea urchins and pretty shells adorned the door, while ribbons of seaweed draped themselves rapturously above the archway as tiny sparkling fish leapt and danced amongst their tangled strands.

On each side of this entrance, standing like sentinels, there prevailed a statue of a grey seal.

The woman took another large key out of her pocket and unlocked the door.

Unwillingly the door opened, as if reluctant to reveal the treasures within.

Dominating the centre of the room, its lid ajar, was an enormous ornate rectangular box.

The darkness did not permit the inscription on this sarcophagus to be deciphered, neither did it enable a clear vision of the ethereal paintings that shrouded the walls; rather it but served to expose the ghostly spectre of the assorted statues grouped around the room.

The children stood at the doorway and watched as Annie placed the bag, which she had hitherto carried, down in a corner where the shadows grew longest. They watched as she turned and walked quickly back the way she had come.

As Annie reached the door she glanced fleetingly at the children; then after ordering them to go inside, but on no account to go near the parcel, she left the chamber, locking the door behind her. Leaving the three children interred within.

The boy and girl huddled together.

"Never mind Linnie," said the boy, "Father is home. They never leave us here long when he is home. He will expect us at dinner time."

"Not tonight, not if the baby comes. He will dine with mother," said the little girl seriously.

She suddenly moved closer to him and pointed at the bag that the woman had left with them. The boy looked. It was almost as if it moved, and into the dismal silence in the room, quiet sounds could be heard coming from that direction. He took her hand and tugged her away.

"Come Linnie, come away, she said not to go near!"

The little girl clutched his hand tighter and, after giving another fearful glance in the direction of the package, followed him to the other side of the chamber where some smaller statues stood. They played for a while quietly, casting furtive glances in the direction of the disturbing object from time to time.

The movements and noise that came from the corner of the room where the woman had placed her bag gradually grew less and less and after some time the little girl turned and stared in its direction for a few moments, before suddenly standing up and stating defiantly "I don't care! I am going to go and see what it is that she has left there."

"Don't Linnie, she will whip us if she finds we have touched it," the boy pleaded.

"I don't care!" the little girl repeated stubbornly.

She marched resolutely towards the bag, hesitated for a moment, then lifted out a small object wrapped tight in blankets. The little boy had come over too, but hesitantly keeping to one side.

The girl began to unwrap the blanket more and more eagerly. Then suddenly she thrust it away, screaming.

"Hush Linnie," the boy said urgently "she'll hear!" He leaned forward to look.

He saw the little stiff arm and the tiny cold face. Momentarily he stilled. Then face averted he calmly picked it up and quickly and methodically rewrapped the parcel, and replaced it carefully back into the bag; while the little girl looked on weeping silently. Quieter now, but with abject horror in her eyes she watched.

He took her hand gently and led her over to the open coffin and helped her climb in. Inside were some rough blankets but no cushions nor a mattress. It was getting cold and the two snuggled together close, not just for warmth. The little girl trembled, not just with cold. The boy moved gingerly, careful not to scrape the healing scabs on his back as he tried to get comfortable, to comfort his sister. Lying there, holding her, he pledged an oath, silent, but no less fervent, that to the end of his days he would do what he could to protect her from harm, from any hurt, that he would never leave her and as her tears began to flow he held her close and kissed her tenderly.

The Birth, October 1802

A golden eagle screeched aloud his fierce pride and joy as, revelling rapturously in the warm air, he soared heavenwards to survey the splendour of his domain.

Balanced precariously on high rocky outcrops or roaming far and wide amongst the heather were the wild black goats with their rough coats, regal heads and magnificent horns.

Nearby, indolently luxuriating in the glorious autumn sunlight majestic red deer congregated; while far below, grazing lazily amongst the shaggy highland cows, the stocky garrons rested from their work, surrounded by numerous noisy birds warbling happily in the surrounding trees.

Nestling peacefully at the foot of the heather clad hill, a large comfortable house basked sleepily in the sunshine.

This house was conspicuous in that most homes in these parts were of a more modest size, containing only a couple of small rooms in which a dozen or so folk would live and laugh and love and die.

From its grounds one could behold the grandeur of the high peaked mountains, wherein there yet nestled pockets of last winter's snow. Below these magnificent crags vast sea lochs reposed, holding within their bowels another world teaming with life and beauty, whose peaceful waters sparkled in the sunlight like multitudes of diamonds.

Indeed, and it was a grand spot for the Laird to make his abode!

Into this idyllic scene a horseman came galloping, weary, travel worn. As he approached the door of the house, he slowed sharply, dismounting before his steed had halted. Not waiting to tether his horse, pausing only to nod at the lad who came rushing to meet him, he ran up to the front door.

The door opened before he reached the top step.

"Mother!" the rider exclaimed.

Noticing the mewing bundle in his mother's arms the rider stated, "I..., I see I am come too late." Then urgently added "Linnie. is she well?" He noted the affirmation on her face.

"God be praised! I..., I came as soon as I could. I would not have stayed over or gone so far if I had known, if I had thought... What brought the bairn so early? Was Linnie ill? Did some accident befall her?"

"Alex, come on in and sit yourself down," his mother urged. "I will explain all in a moment. But you look tired, worn to the bone!" She looked down at the infant she held in her arms before adding quietly, "You have not yet asked after this wee bairn. Will you not come and give your blessing upon your youngest daughter?"

He struggled to keep his disappointment from showing on his face. Then he stilled momentarily before saying urgently "Linnie! I must go to her! She will take this ill."

"Wait!"

He stopped in mid step, chilled by the unusually shrill note in his mother's peremptory request, then looking intently at her troubled face, stated quietly, "There is something that you have not told me."

His mother nodded unhappily before beginning hesitantly to explain, "Linnie, she is not well, overwrought. The birth was not easy and then when Ceitidh brought her the babe..., Linnie..., well, she..., she began to scream and scream and would not stop! We had to send for Dr Maitland. Fortunately he was in the village. Old Maisie is unwell again..., it is to be feared she will not last the night. Poor Sheoras will be so lost without her......" She sighed and then continued tiredly, "Dr Maitland, he came and gave Linnie something to calm her. She is sleeping quietly now."

The young Laird looked at his mother silently for a moment as if digesting what he had heard, before saying, "She knew mother, she knew that I would not blame her, that a girl child is no great sadness to me. I wished for a son, an heir, but the blame is as much mine, if it be anyone's, that it is yet another lass. It was too soon, too early, but she would have it that she must have another bairn, that she must have a son, and I feared..., well, no matter, it will not happen again. I at least will not be responsible......" He murmured this last in a lower voice almost to himself. Then with a set look he met his mother's eyes as he stated soberly, "Another bairn too soon after this one may be the death of her." Then anxiously he asked again "She is well otherwise is she not mother? Dr Maitland is happy that Linnie will make a full recovery?"

"Dr Maitland suggested much as you yourself have just said, that Linnie should wait some time before having another child. He maintains that she will suffer no lasting harm, but that it may be some months before she recovers her full health and spirits. He believes that her hysterical behaviour was caused by a combination of her having been so unwell these past few months, the shock of the bairn coming so early with such a long and difficult birthing, and then after all that, the bitter disappointment of being blessed yet again with a daughter rather than the son that she so desperately desires. He thinks that she will probably feel less distraught when she has seen yourself and hears from your own lips that you do not blame her for it."

Alex made no reply. His kind eyes rested on his mother and the tiny bundle she carried, their worried look not a whit abated.

22

"Come Alex, eat, get washed and changed," his mother urged. "You will be of more use to Linnie when you have supped and rested. I will have Ceitidh come for you when Linnie awakens. Only…, only…," she paused and then her face crumbled and her distress showed in her voice as she continued "Linnie swears this babe is not hers! That it is a changeling! She says she will not have it near her, will not have it in the house."

They had walked into a small comfortable room wherein a large welcoming fire blazed. Alex slumped down onto a chair next to the fire and sat with his head, already spotted with grey, in his hands for a few moments; then raising his careworn face he said tiredly, "Perhaps she will see things differently in the morrow after she has slept, when she has had some time to think."

"Meanwhile," his mother said more sharply, "this bairn must be fed. It is a wonder she is still breathing; thrust thus too early into the world, unwanted, rejected."

The man looked up suddenly alert, a slow smile suffusing his face, banishing for a time his careworn look.

"Not unwanted. Here give her to me."

He sat with his tiny baby in his arms just looking at her for a few moments, and then held her close; almost it was as if he needed the comfort and warmth she gave as much as she needed his care and succour. He looked into her huge brown eyes. It was as if he could not look away, then a look of pain passed across his face. He glanced at his mother looking grim but saying with infinite compassion, "She has the Sight poor little scrap. When I 'Saw' that Linnie's time had come, I thought I saw this too, but was not sure, hoped that it was not so…"

"Say not that, my son!" The old woman smiled and her eyes lit up. "It is a blessing surely and brings much honour on our family. I have prayed that one of the children would have it - a

23

lad I had hoped, but she will do just as well. What will you call her?"

He hesitated for a moment, looking at the baby carefully. Then smiling gently, still holding her tight he affirmed, "I will call her Eloise, after her mother's father, who she has a look of; and Catriona after you mother dear: God grant she may be as kind and true. But for herself alone I will call her 'Eilidh'[2], for thus she will be, 'bright one', and he bent over and kissed his newest daughter on her head. "Take the bairn to Lachlan and Mairi, mother. Ask that they take her, just for a day or two. Mairi's bairn was born not three days past, so I heard tell. She will perhaps have milk enough for two."

"Mairi! She will not wish to take her in," his mother stated categorically, "not when this is her first, not when she has waited so many years for a bairn. I heard tell that it is a son that she has borne. It is not right Alex, to spoil thus her moment of triumph, to intrude on her happiness."

The strained look had returned and he sighed as he replied, "You are right of course, but what else can we do. Our little Eilidh is born too early and will die if she has not milk soon. Take her to them. Say that I ask it of her. Lachlan will, I believe, be able to persuade his wife to accept the lassie - for a time at least."

"The poor wean will imbibe bitter milk," stated his mother dryly, "but better that than none at all. I will do as you say."

Alex smiled ruefully, "Perhaps Linnie's failure to produce a son and her own success will reconcile Mairi to the imposition." He stood up. "I will now do as you advised mother, and wash and change into fresh attire, after which I will go and see my other daughters. It is almost the children's mealtime. I will eat

---

[2] Eilidh, Gaelic for Helen; pronounced *'ay-lee'*.

with them in the nursery and visit Linnie as soon as she awakens."

His mother watched anxiously as he left the room, saddened at this further trouble cast on her son's already overburdened shoulders. As she sat tiredly by the fire fretting over her son's worries and the necessity of leaving this tiny baby with her son's blood brother Lachlan, and Mairi, that sharp bitter woman who was Lachlan's wife, she wondered anew as to why her son was so secretive as to the identity of his wife's family.

She remembered only too well the day that Alex had unexpectedly returned home, bringing with him his young and dazzlingly pretty English wife. She remembered how surprised they had all been at her sudden arrival, and how perturbed they had all felt when he had adamantly refused to disclose whence she had come from or what her name and station had been before she had wed him. He had assured them that she was nobly born, though that had been hardly necessary as Linnie herself had made it abundantly clear that she was accustomed to living in a much grander house than the one her new husband had provided for her.

Lachlan Beaton, her son's blood brother, had also returned with a wife, a small dark haired woman who was said to be Linnie's aunt; though she and Linnie were about the same age as each other and most dissimilar in looks. Neither Lachlan or Mairi his wife, nor Alex and Linnie would discuss further the connexion between the two women; though Linnie made it quite plain that she perceived Mairi to be her social inferior. She supposed that would make Mairi great-aunt to this tiny bairn, but she feared that the relationship between Linnie and Mairi was such that this would cause Mairi to love little Eilidh the less rather than more.

25

She sighed and turned her attention back to her newest grand-daughter, talking to her softly whilst gently rocking her; and then she looked into her eyes, those beautiful enormous brown almond shaped eyes and thought wonderingly that it was almost as if she saw right through you, as if she could see into your innermost heart.

The Sight, January 1819

The night was wild, the wind screamed and moaned relentlessly, yelling its rage to the world. Lightning whipped through the clouds, lashing the night air, tormented, in tune with the angry voice of the thunder: while the rain wept torrents.

Into this cacophony stalked a creature dark as the night itself, ears pinned back, teeth bared, hooves wary, eyes rolling. As remorseless as the storm he strode out to greet.

Accompanying this apparition there paced a cloaked furtive figure as out amidst the raging tempest they fled; intent on the execution of their desperate race.

On and on they travelled, away from the coast, out from Fife. On and on they travelled barely stopping day or night as they maintained their driven march into the Western Highlands of Scotland.

On and on they travelled, tarrying only briefly for the occasional hour to snuggle together in the shelter of a tree as they attempted to gain some small respite from the continuous onslaught of the wind and rain. Past Loch Lomond they rode and then on to Crianlarich; unremittingly, interminably, endlessly pursuing the wind, battling the torrential rain as they chased through Bridge of Orchy before hastening onwards to traverse the desolate, majestic wilds of Rannoch Moor.

Though taking little in the form of sustenance besides a quick drink from a passing stream the rider was ever assiduous of the care of the dark stallion; while this steed, contrary to his malevolent looks, remained constantly willing, seemingly untiring, meticulously attentive to the simplest requests of his companion. Almost it was as if the two were one, united in purpose, in understanding, in spirit.

They approached Kings House, but not for them the welcome that had for centuries been offered the weary traveller, instead like dark wraiths they passed by that homely dwelling to continue their eternal progression.

Forsaking the dark, bleak, merciless paths of Glencoe they climbed up and over the Devil's Staircase where the lightning struck anew.

Now they battled onward with renewed vigour and replenished strength, barely hearing the cry of the wind or the loud call of the thunder; for at long last, they had caught the scent of home and with the banner of lightening ever visible to their eyes they advanced.

They traced the oft trod trail down into Kinlochleven, their sure footed progress as unwaveringly indefatigable as the remorseless tempest they rode within. Then onwards through the familiar but unacknowledged hills that led down to the waters of Loch Linnie. While the storm raged incessantly.

At the Corran narrows they halted.

The thunder and the lightening had stilled, even the wind had ceased its wailing, but the rain continued to weep.

Pausing only for a moment to survey the stretch of icy water before them, undaunted and with renewed urgency they plunged in to dare the Corran narrows.

To traverse the Loch thus was not in itself unusual, for cattle had been swum across here for countless centuries. What was unusual was to cross in midwinter in full flood in the aftermath of a storm.

If there had been anyone watching they would have feared for the safety of these weary travellers. If any had looked closely they would have seen the exhaustion etched on every line of the proud stallion's body; while the rider sat like one of the hero's out of the lays of Ossian[3], face impassive, head high, eyes wide and desolate as they looked over to the lovely land of Ardgour.

If there had been anyone watching they would have seen that the pair were not wholly alone as they struggled against the tempestuous waves that sought to draw them further down the Loch, down indeed into the very depths of the mighty waters.

Seals, kin to those faithful friends of sailors, the dolphins, came and surrounded them, gently aiding them to the shore. There, shivering and dripping, both horse and rider paused to give thanks to their attendants before dragging themselves achingly onward. The stallion's legs were trembling from exhaustion as well as the cold, but valiantly he struggled on, uncomplaining, as in haste they scrabbled up the stony shore before turning right to hurry along a track well known to the two of them in former times.

A short journey along the loch side and they were no longer alone.

It was said by some that the ruins of an old kirk lay here at Cille Mhaodain; one of the seven churches built by Ailean-nan-Creach to atone for committing murder whilst in a place of worship.

But it was not for the sight of these remains that they had come. It was not for the shame of a sin committed by some old chief of a family not their own that they had travelled.

Not one head raised as the pair passed by as spectres unnoticed in the gloom, while the mist came down and the rain fell and the eyes of all were lowered.

Silently but surely they advanced forward.

---

[3] Warrior and bard in ancient times. Ossian was the son of Fingal; Fingal was King of Morvern and Chief of the Feinne (Bodyguard of the Kings of Ulster).

At the rear of the company they halted, stern faced and stiff. They heard the minister speak.

They saw the clod of earth fall onto the ground wherein lay The Maclean of Ardgour. For the Maclean of Ardgour was dead.[4]

Then the piper sounded the wail of the lament and slowly the mourners made their troubled retreat from the burial ground of The Maclean.

The pair stood still as statues.

As the procession withdrew many glanced up quickly, furtively at the newcomers, but not one person chose to approach, deterred perhaps by their bleak and desolate aspect, unwilling to intrude on the raw wretchedness and despair that shrouded this strange and unexpected manifestation.

Only one, a woman supported by a large group of family members, who appeared to be the principle mourner, gazed askance at the late arrival. The widow was beautiful, that much could be seen despite her veil, and she evinced not only surprise but also consternation, revulsion at this unsolicited presence.

Only when they were alone did the rider dismount, and then as always the care of her mount was her first priority. She unsaddled him, rubbed him down, gave him a few oats, then set him free to graze; before casting herself onto the damp earth that newly covered the grave, distraught, too anguished even to weep.

---

[4] Alexander Maclean of Ardgour, 13th Chief and Laird, Colonel of the Argyllshire Militia was born on the 16th April 1764. He married Lady Margaret Hope on 10 July 1793 and died on the 8 September 1831. His son Alexander Maclean, born 11 February 1799, became the 14th Chief and Laird. (The Landed Gentry: Great Britain). The fictitious character styled The Maclean of Ardgour who features as a character in this story was born in 1761 and died in January 1819. His wife and children and all their actions as they appear in this story are also all wholly fictitious.

How long she remained thus she could never afterwards recall. She lay there frozen until nuzzled to consciousness by her companion.

From hence she made her way to her old cave near Salachan, where she slept soundly for the first time since the wild storm had brought her Sight of her father's death.

As the tempest had brought warning of death so the easing of the rain and the quietening of the storm brought with it a fresh Sight: a face unknown whose mocking smile brought ease and sleep free of torment.

Chapter 1 Looking over at Seal Island, January 1820

Dawn was breaking. Over distant hills the sun arose huge, blood red, come to paint the ice blue carpet it rode upon a similar hue. New Year's Day heralded in with the shepherd's warning.

The black of the night fell away making visible the small islands close to the shore where, surrounded by the clear peaceful waters of Loch Linnie, seals yet slumbered grey fat content, unconcerned with portents for the future preferring instead the certainty of the present.

Perched high on the cliffs a lone figure sat, much as the ancient Ossian would have done so many centuries before. Watching, watching over the seas below. Waiting for those ships which would not come. Remembering their dead whilst fearing their future.

Unlike the long dead Ossian, all of whose kin had died and whose wraiths and memories were many, most of this watcher's kin yet lived, excepting those most beloved; and the wraith that haunted her now was a vision from an unknown future rather than the remembrance of deeds and heroes long dead.

As she sat, wrapped tight in her plaid[5] for warmth, on this fiercely cold morning, her thoughts drifted back to that day when she had first returned to her ancestral home: the day she gained her first memory of her mother.

---

[5] After the battle of Culloden in 1745, when the Jacobite uprising had failed, the wearing of Highland dress and the carrying of weapons had been forbidden. This edict had been rescinded in 1782 but even that short time had been enough to change the habits of generations.

She had walked with her father into a room, large and comfortable with age, and had immediately noticed the great fire roaring in the hearth; for bitterly cold it was that day and their journey had been long. As she started to run towards its welcome warmth she had suddenly become aware of the horror struck gaze of the previously unnoticed occupant of the chamber.

Even now she could remember how she had just stood there and stared; for never before had she seen anyone so beautiful. The woman had hair the colour of new wheat and huge glorious brown eyes.

Those eyes, so like her own, had stared back at her: but their gaze had been chillingly malign. Transfixed she had heard the woman, in a voice as icy as frost, demand to be told the identity of the strange child, and heard as if in a dream her father's reply: that she was their seventh daughter just returned.

She could still remember, as if it had just happened, the sound of her mother's cold, frightened voice as she insisted that 'the changeling' be sent away. She remembered seeing her mother lift up the babe she held in her arms, to show it to her father, and the sound of her mother's voice rising and rising and her father's voice calm and weary as he tried to reason with her. She remembered turning and running. Running to get away from the voices, running and running to escape from the fact that here too she was unwanted.

After some time, worn out by her wild tempestuous flight, her steps had begun to falter and she remembered stopping and just gazing all around, overwhelmed by the sheer magnificence of her surroundings, by the strange scents and sounds. That was when she had noticed the thin white line high up on the hill.

Mesmerised by the sight of it she had just stood and stared, then sharp voices forgotten she had started that long, long scramble up the hill to get to the place where the rainbows dwelt.

She smiled as she thought of that spot, for it remained one of her favourite refuges, a place where she would go when she wanted to think, to dream, to escape - Maclean's Towel[6].

But it was not however this waterfall, not even her mother, nor yet the wild black goats with their huge horns that she had met as she wandered over the hills, that she remembered that day for. She remembered that day best for quite another reason.

She had sat full to overflowing with delight and exhilaration, on a rock near the top of the waterfall, panting from the effort of her long, hard climb. Spread out before her were the sparkling waters of Loch Linnie, and beyond this lay the majestic snow covered mountains of Glen Nevis, while next to her the waterfall known as the Maclean's Towel, frolicked and gambolled its way down the hillside. She had sat there completely captivated by the sight of the water frisking and cavorting over the stones, fascinated by the way that the wet pebbles sparkled and the water droplets shone a myriad of different colours as the sun's rays joined them in their dance. Then suddenly a small sound had alerted her to the fact that she was not alone.

It was love at first sight.

Nearby was the tiniest little woman she had ever seen, with the kindliest face and brownest eyes of that same almond shape as her own, sitting on the other side of the waterfall slightly higher up. She wore clothes of green and brown so that it was easy to mistake her for part of the hillside itself. The woman

---

[6] Maclean's Waterfall

had smiled and the child she had been then had responded automatically and scrambled eagerly up towards her. All that afternoon woman and child had walked the hills hand in hand looking at the flowers and the wild animals as they made their way back to the woman's little bothy[7].

It was only many years later that she fully appreciated how agonizing that journey must have been for the woman; for when she was a very young child Kai- Ying's feet had been bound tight so that they would remain forever small and 'beautiful', so that now, even with the aid of her stick, she could walk the hills only with great difficulty. She had once asked Kai-Ying how she had come to be there that morning and had been told simply that she had felt that she was needed at the waterfall and so had gone.

It was many years also before she understood the anguish her father had suffered that day in the hours that he spent searching for her. She had at the time been but five years of age and did not then possess the means to convey who she was or from whence she came, for as yet she had never been known to speak.

Her father, when he had eventually discovered her, had decided to leave her in Kai-Ying's protection for the summer months, but every year just before the commencement of the harsh winter weather he would make the long journey south to return her to her milk mother Mairi and her family in Fife. So it was that she had not been here on that dreadful night just under a year ago when she had Seen her father's death.

Sombre memories of the death of both her father and, barely 6 months later, of Kai-Ying who had been mother to her in all but blood, were what now occupied her mind: that and the nagging anxiety as to what the future was to hold for her.

_____

[7] Small dwelling place.

She had shed no tear at the death of her father, nor since. Rather a knot had gathered in her stomach, a knot that never left her though the initial intensity of the pain had dulled as the weeks and months had passed slowly by. After Kai-Ying's death the knot had grown even larger. Suddenly she longed for the comfort of those arms, for her warmth and common sense, for her laughter and quiet wisdom and for her father.........
Loneliness washed over her anew and the knot tightened.

It was not however her intense wretched grief at the loss of these who were so very dear to her that had caused it to be preferable to sit on these cold rocks sooner than risk sleep. Rather it was the vision which had eased her to sleep on the night of her father's funeral that now returned to torment her night after night, leaving her sleepless and distressed.

The mocking face which had erstwhile served to bring her peace, pleasure and at times amusement had on the night of the funeral of Kai-Ying her foster mother transformed into a nightmare that returned to haunt her more and more frequently. Where before she had believed him to be a figure from her imagination, sent to ease her loneliness and despair following the death of her father, now she felt more and more that the personage was real and that the dreams which disturbed her sleep were a warning, but of what she knew not for she was sure she had never seen him in life.

A twig cracked, the girl turned and her hand went unconsciously to the knives that she had secreted about her person.

In these wild places even the Laird's sister would not feel herself safe, especially when she lived so alone. Those who knew Eilidh Ruadh[8] would know her reputation with her knives and know also that there was no one more accurate with a gun

[8] Gaelic for red-haired; pronounced 'roo-ah'.

hereabouts. Those who did not know would see instead only her youth and beauty and forget to think: for even wrapped in all those clothes you could tell she was most lovely. Even with her hair plaited so strictly about her head like a crown and then covered in a scarf so none of its colour could be seen you would somehow know she was quite exquisite. Try as she might to disguise her looks, her form, nothing could disguise the fire within, which showed itself in her posture whether still or moving, in the expressions that danced across her face, in the radiance in her eyes.

Poised, alert in case it was a stranger who approached, she as suddenly relaxed. "Joe! I did not know you were back. Why travel north so early? When did you arrive?"

"Bliadhna Mhath Ur[9] Eilidh Ruadh! I sought for you long last night Eilidh. You were much missed in the New Year celebrations!"

"Bliadhna Mhath Ur Joe. Better is the New Year now for the bringing of you with it. Who else has come? Is your father come? How went the business down south?"

Laughing now he strode over her to her in long strides and sat down facing her.

"So many questions! Only myself and Will returned." He looked stern for a moment before continuing grimly, "The others will return later. In plenty time for the wedding."

"There will have been much jollity last night at the house of Will and Elspeth then. Your sister, Joe, was she there too?"

"Aye and the little one, along with Iain Mor, 'twas a good night, lacking only yourself Eilidh." He looked at her hungrily for a moment before continuing, "I sought ye long Eilidh. Ye were no at your bothy, nor at your cave. Liath Macha[10] was there unconcerned, so I knew ye were not far."

---

[9] Happy New Year.

37

"Last night I needed to be alone. To remember this past year. Then later I could not sleep. So, as you can see, I came here."

"The nightmares again?" he asked, concern written across his face.

"Yes they get worse, but no matter. What news do you bring?"

"We go south with Lachlan, Mairi and Ewan after the wedding. Father says you are to come too. Your mother has agreed; indeed she has been writing to Mairi to arrange it. For what purpose you go I know not. But is it not good news Eilidh? I wished to be the first to tell you. Are you not pleased?" Joe could hardly keep still he was so obviously delighted. "It will be just like old times when you, I and Ewan would accompany your father down south. Only it will be more work as Lachlan wishes to take some of the young stock south with us and stable them at Sam's. I am to remain in London Eilidh when everyone else returns home. It is arranged that I will stay with Sam and Sarah and train our young horses and some of Sam's. He will of course continue to help with the sale of them, as he does now. We should get prime prices for them," he continued excitedly. He paused for a moment, then suddenly anxious he asked, "You do not answer. You are pleased are you not?"

"Pleased and relieved Joe. You know how much I have been praying for this. After mother is married she will not wish me to remain here, and I had been worrying..." she trailed off. She smiled, then the smile fell away and she turned to him suddenly

---

[10] Liath Macha (Grey of Macha). Two of the horses of the legendry warrior, Cuchullin, were born on the same day as was Cuchullin himself. These were Dubh Sainglainn (Black of Sainglainn) and Liath Macha. Dubh Sainglain was the name that Eilidh gave to the twin brother of her stallion Liath Macha.

anxious. "Joe you should not be here! Not at this time, not alone. I would not have folk talk. You know how they are!"

"What matter when we shall both be soon gone? What matter what folk say?" Joe retorted sharply.

"Indeed and it does matter Joe. I would not have my father's memory tainted by talk of the ill-considered behaviour of his daughter."

Joe did not reply, merely continued looking thunderous.

"I had a mind to leave with the tide today, take Cuchullin[11] away, as I did after father died. I would see the islands one last time", she smiled. "I would fain sail Cuchullin to the 'Isle of Mists[12]'."

"On your own? Don't be foolish Eilidh. You are no longer a child to dream that you are Scathach[13], that…"

Her eyes danced, as she said teasingly, "Ah Joe, but at least it was not her sister Aifa[14] that I used to pretend to be!"

Joe flushed

Then she continued more seriously, "It is true that I am no more a child, yet still do I long to visit Dunscathach[15], to once more sit high up on that rock where her castle was built and look out to sea, just as she must have done all those years ago, and try to believe that one day I will be as free as she."

Joe looked unconvinced.

---

[11] Eilidh's sailing boat named after the great hero warrior Cuchullin who is known well in both Irish and Scottish poetry and legends.

[12] The Isle of Skye: some say that the Cuillin Hills of Skye were named after Cuchullin as he and his wife Bragela were reputed to have one of their homes on Skye. Some sources name his wife as Emer.

[13] Scathach was a warrior princess who trained Cuchullin as well as many other warriors. She lived on the Isle of Skye.

[14] Princess Aifa, Princess Scathach's sister, became one of Cuchullin's mistresses, and was said to have born him a son called Connla.

[15] Dunscaith Castle; legends says that Scathach once lived there.

Sensing his continued disquiet Eilidh sought to reassure him. "Really Joe there is no need for you to worry. When I am out at sea sailing Cuchullin I am never truly alone, the seals are always with me; they will ensure that I am kept safe. I do not intend to be long away. Indeed I plan to return in time to see February in." Then she asked tentatively "Are you staying with William or Iseabail?"

"Will," he replied abruptly and then continued roughly. "I suppose you will be wishing for me to look after the bothy for you, and Dawn[16] and Liath Macha[17] also?"

"If you would, though of a truth they can shift for themselves. If you could mind Ginny though I would be grateful, the calf's due early March and it's her first. Luath[18] can bide with Alex."

He turned to leave, saying over his shoulder bitterly how it was a good thing he had caught her now or else he would have missed her altogether. He walked off, but before he reached his tethered steed he turned back regretting his acrimonious leave-taking.

There was no one to be seen.

The only sign of where she had gone was an ever widening circular ripple of waves in the otherwise still water below. Unable to repress an involuntary shudder, he turned and walked quickly away, angrily kicking a stone as he went.

As he moved to mount his horse he was hailed by a voice.

"You there! Have you seen Eilidh Ruadh?"

He didn't answer, merely continued the task of mounting.

---

[16] Eilidh's chestnut mare.
[17] Eilidh's stallion, the son of Dawn.
[18] Eilidh's old hound, who used to belong to her father.

40

The other fellow, obviously the gentleman, a handsome young man dressed in an almost dandyish manner, demanded again "Did you hear me? I asked if you had seen Eilidh Ruadh."

Joe looked up without answering.

"Is that Joe?" said the voice suddenly more polite. "I had not heard you were returned. Do you know where Eilidh is?"

"I do not," Joe replied dourly and began to ride off. Then he appeared to think better of it and turned and glowered at the other man. "What is it that you would be wanting with her?" he demanded abruptly.

The other looked sheepish for a moment then took from the inside of his jacket a newspaper.

"I have brought her this edition of The Scotsman newspaper. It contains a report of the Strathnaver Clearances[19]. She said she would like to read it. She was very annoyed at the reports that were written recently refuting the brutality of the recent evictions in Strathnaver."

"Aye a bad business that!" Joe replied. "This is what trying to copy those Sassenachs[20] does for our chiefs, makes them forgetful of their duty. Sheep instead of people! What do they think they will do when they want to call on their tenants to fight for them? Dress the sheep up in the tartan and give them a bayonet to hold!" He laughed dryly then continued, "I heard that not content with burning their homes they forbade others to give them succour. How many of them will die in the townships I wonder, and how many will die on the ships on

---

[19] In Strathnaver in Sutherland the people were forcibly evicted from their homes, on the instructions of the Duke of Sutherland. The land was cleared and the people were replaced by the more profitable sheep. This particular Scotsman article was published at the end of December and referred to an eviction that occurred in May 1819.
[20] English.

their way to America away yonder?" He pointed out over the Loch way beyond the seal islands.

It was said that if you looked out to sea and had good enough vision, then one could see America itself from here. Maybe that was false, for who had such eyesight, but he knew that the maps he had seen did indeed tell him that the birds could fly straight there from these shores without hitting land. Joe sighed, lost for a moment in thought, wondering how long before those that he knew would also be compelled to leave as the economics of sheep made the landlords forget their landed, their birth right duties. The sudden sight of his companion rekindled his anger.

"And you Fergus, how long before your family turn out your tenants in favour of sheep? Your soon to be stepmother I'll warrant will never say nay to that which will increase the contents of your family's coffers!"

"You have no love for your late Laird's wife then?" returned Fergus. "She is still very beautiful and it is said that few can resist her charms."

"Your father never could, that much is clear, even when she was lawfully wed to another!"

It was Fergus's turn to look annoyed. "What is it that you are implying?" he asked indignantly.

"Only that which is common knowledge! If it was her youngest daughter that you were courting, then there are some who might advise that the Church say ye nay!" With that Joe began to ride away, but Fergus followed angrily after him.

"Joe Lovell, you forget yourself! The old Laird treated you as a son, but that gives you no right to insult your betters! How dare you insult my father, my soon to be mother and sister?"

"You too forget yourself, you have lived so long south you forget that in the Highlands all men are equal as men, just some have different fortune and responsibilities. The Clan Chief forgets this at his peril, for now the people forgive his harshness as his right but they will not forgive his negligence. With regard to your stepmother to be I do apologise for what I said, it was wrong, but only in so far as it damages the honour of the old Laird." He bowed slightly, "I should not have said what I did, my anger loosened my tongue, please accept my apologies."

Fergus Campbell, of an easy disposition, quickly accepted his assurances and the two young men rode off together conversing amicably.

Chapter 2 Beside the Loch of the Crannog

The Castle Lochan[21] was thought to have once been the habitation of a crannog[22], an ancient dwelling place of some long forgotten chief. It lurked amidst numerous small scrubby trees, surrounded on all sides by high rushes, leading those few who ventured near to be wary of the promise of treacherous bogs.

This was a place feared and shunned by local folk. There were reports of strange sparkly lights being seen above the Lochan. Indeed many held that it was bottomless and that it housed some unearthly hidden secret. Moreover until very recently there had been an additional, a more tangible reason for people to avoid the Lochan.

On the banks of the Castle Lochan there had dwelled an old woman who had long been believed to be a witch. Only the gravest need would cause anyone to venture along the pretty avenue that led to her home. But come they did, in fear and with great trepidation they came, for there was no one quite like Kai-Ying when it came to the setting of broken bones, rescuing a birthing that was going ill, or calming a fever.

Aid was always given by Kai-Ying, but if her intervention failed, as happened on occasions, she was cursed and even

---

[21] Small loch (or lake).

[22] Crannogs were homes built over water, usually on a small loch. Surrounded by water the people inside would be more secure from the ravages of wild creatures such as the wolves that roamed those parts long ago, and from the predations of hostile strangers. Situated thus the occupants of the crannog would have the added advantage of a constant plentiful supply of fresh water and the continual presence of fish and sea birds readily accessible to fill the empty cooking pot.

when the cure was successful she was still feared and reviled. However when she effected a healing, to show their gratitude, the villagers would venture forth with offerings of food and herbs, which they would leave at a certain spot not far from her abode.

Many there were who remembered her arrival but few knew where or how she had dwelt hitherto.

One day, when the previous Laird[23] had been young, he had arrived home unexpectedly, bringing with him a very beautiful Sassenach bride. It was said to have been a love match and that the laird had stolen away with his bride against the wishes of her family, and that because of this her father had disowned her, and no more was her name mentioned in her father's house.

No one would tell where exactly the Laird's southern wife had come from, nor who her family had been: though the airs and graces she gave herself led some to suppose that it was a great family she had hailed from.

Kai-Ying had been with the Laird and his bride on the day they arrived home that first time.

It was whispered that the laird had found Kai-Ying starving by the wayside and had felt pity; that it was his insistence that she accompany them home and his subsequent care of her which had caused the ever-increasing coolness between the Laird and his exquisite wife. For not content with housing her, the Laird spent many a long evening in Kai-Ying's company and from far and wide he had parcels fetched for her, parcels said to

---

[23] Although this story uses the background and location of the Macleans of Ardgour, all the main characters in this story are fictitious. Alexander Maclean 13th Laird and Alexander Maclean 14th Laird did exist historically but not in the guise they are portrayed in this story. Although by all accounts they were both honourable men.

contain music and various manuscripts: but manuscripts of what ilk was a question asked by many.

As suspicions grew, great apprehension was felt even for the very soul of their beloved Laird.

It was widely believed that this witch, Kai-Ying, had cursed the Laird's young wife so that she would bear only daughters. Eight daughters she bore before the long awaited son was born and that was only after the Laird had gone south for many months to bring home his seventh daughter. This changeling child, whom his wife had rejected, was given into the care of old Kai-Ying. What unearthly bargain had been agreed? His ugly changeling daughter in exchange for a healthy male heir!

Kai-Ying, already frail, had not lasted six months after the Laird's death and her ashes had secretly been buried near to his remains. The Changeling now lived alone in Kai-Ying's old cottage.

Chapter 3 Kai-Ying's Cottage

It was cold this bright New Year's morning but the fire inside Kai-Ying's Cottage burned most cheerily in the hearth. Cooking on the griddle were the bannocks whose enticing aroma filled the cosy room, while on either side of the hearth were shelves on which lay an array of cooking utensils. Next to the griddle, a kettle was steaming away merrily.

The room was small, but very tidy, containing the few chairs and small table that would be expected in such a dwelling. What would not have been expected was the harpsichord in the corner, the myriad of pictures on the walls, the books and parchments in every possible nook and cranny, and the beautiful, ornate clarsach which sat next to the harpsichord.

There were only two other rooms in the cottage: a tiny chamber where the food was kept in which lay a huge array of herbs drying or neatly stored away, and a little bedroom which Kai-Ying and the Changeling had shared.

Outside were various outhouses, namely a byre where the cow sheltered alongside the occasional equine companion and which also sufficed as a temporary home for a variety of sick animals and birds in differing stages of recovery. Attached to this was a small barn where the animal foodstuff and other such essentials were kept.

The Changeling sat close to the fire on an old comfortable rocking chair, clearly struggling with some needlework, whilst in front of the fire there lay an old hound sleeping.

Suddenly two small boys burst in upon this homely scene.

"Eilidh Ruadh! Eilidh Ruadh! Guess what, guess what?"

The girl looked up grinning and put down the sewing in evident relief, while the younger child looking expectantly at the bannocks baking on the griddle, complained "Eilidh, I'm so *hungry!*"

"Oh and it is hungry you are, and that after one of Sandra Beag's meals! It is I that must be going to see her with some posit if she is so unwell that she is not able to cook properly for you."

The boy grinned back at her engagingly, "Oh, but I finished that ages ago and now I'm hungry again! Besides, no one makes bannocks like you." He looked up at her, eyes wide and hopeful.

"Flatterer!" Eilidh said laughing as she took down a good few bannocks, put them on a plate and began to butter them.

The older boy had been eying the operation keenly and now asked for lots of honey on his, apparently forgetting his exciting news at the more immediate prospect of food.

The younger boy, whilst trying to force as much into his mouth as humanely possible, didn't forget the obvious message from the dog, and rewarded the beseeching look, after a sideways glance at his sister. Eilidh however was looking at the older boy.

"Well?" she said.

He looked back confused. Then his face cleared. "It's mother! She's set the date of the wedding!"

Eilidh stiffened slightly but said nothing.

The boy continued, "It's to be the 15th of March. She said that this should satisfy propriety or something like that."

"Who's propriety Eilidh?" the younger child mumbled, while the older boy looked suddenly superior.

Eilidh sighed and said tiredly, "Propriety is anyone who takes too much of an interest in everyone else's business, Hugh."

Hugh glanced at his older brother, daring him to laugh. "Oh you mean it's not a person at all."

She laughed, and then continued more seriously, "In a way it is Hugh, for it is people who make the judgments, decide what behaviour is correct and what constitutes good manners. Propriety is what society thinks of as suitable, acceptable conduct. Mother means that she can marry Archibald Campbell quite happily on the 15th of March knowing that no one will accuse her of being heartless as it will then be over a year since father died."

"I wish she wouldn't," said Hugh, "because she will go away now won't she and leave us behind? She says you will have to go too Eilidh, but you won't will you?" he asked anxiously. "You aren't to be married?"

"No Hugh, I'm not, but you know after the wedding I must do as mother bids - until I come of age that is. She is unlikely to wish me to stay behind when she goes." She stood up suddenly, "But let's not worry about that now. Who's for fishing?"

Both boys cheered.

Then the older boy said, "Oh, I've just remembered, John Boyd said to remind you that you need to decide what to do about Malcolm MacLeod. You know," he giggled, "the stable boy that Adrianne says tried to kiss her." He continued scornfully "As if everyone didn't know that he is walking out with Norah McInnis; and who would want to kiss Adrianne anyway!"

"Aonghus Ban did! He did! You told me he did Alex!" cried Hugh.

Eilidh looked suddenly grim, "Looks like I had better have words with young Aonghus."

"But I promised not to tell!" said Alex quickly.

"Good thing you did tell. Poor Malcolm is in trouble even though he almost definitely didn't kiss Adrianne, think of the trouble Aonghus would be in if anyone else found out that he really did! Alex tell John Boyd..., no don't worry, on second thoughts I'll write him a note instead."

Then she smiled reassuringly and changing the subject importuned, "Come on then, go and give your ponies some hay and check they are comfortable and leave some hay outside for Ginny too. I'll just pack some food and then we can be off."

The boys turned immediately to carry out her request, but as they reached the door she called "Wait a minute. You have both finished your lessons haven't you?"

Alex groaned. "Yes, two pages of Greek translation, and then mathematics. When is the new tutor coming Eilidh?"

She laughed. "After the wedding, John Boyd is arranging it. Old Thomas is just great for the basics but I think you will enjoy your lessons better when James Marriot comes. Yes and you, little rascal!" she said to Hugh with a grin.

"Eilidh it's our riding lessons with you that we prefer," Alex declared, and then asked anxiously "Who will teach us when you are gone?"

She looked worried for a moment, then sighed, "You will just have to wait until Lachlan and Mairi return, but, no matter, you have the colts to keep you busy. Just remember to be kind, firm and consistent. Try to make them your friend, but an obedient one. If you do your work well then by the time that Lachlan comes back they will be very quick to train." Her face brightened suddenly. "What am I thinking of! Duncan's eldest son William is staying behind. I will ask him to help you both, he is almost as good as his father and there is not much Duncan does not know about horses."

By the time the boys had finished their tasks, Eilidh, her bag packed, and Luath[24] the old hound, were standing outside

---

[24] Luath was the name of one of Fingal's dogs. Another was said to

waiting for them. "Alex, I want you to have Luath now," she said as soon as they approached. "He will be quite happy with you. He was father's and so is used to living up at the Big House," she smiled. "He can wait with old Padraig, the seannachie[25], while we are fishing and then go home later with the both of you."

Alex was delighted and immediately ran over to the old patient dog and began to pet him but Hugh looked anxious and asked "Where are you going Eilidh, you will be back won't you?"

"I'm taking Cuchullin out for a few weeks. I thought I might sail around the islands, maybe go to the Hebrides; you caught me whilst I was waiting for the tide to turn. Just think, much later and I'd have been gone and no honeyed bannocks for the pair of you!"

They ignored the beautiful avenue of young trees, choosing instead to go straight down to the path below. It was a steep brae that led down to this track, a few scrubby trees grew on the slope and it was thus covered in old brown leaves left over from autumn. The three with the casualness of long practice cast themselves to the ground and rolled all the way down the brae landing at the bottom laughing and covered in leaves. Eilidh saying she'd race them, first ran up the hill again to fetch her bag, and then ran after the giggling pair overtaking them with ease. The path they took brought them between two small lochs. They followed the edge of the smaller of the two, Lochan na h'Eaglais until it took them to Camas Aisaig, by the shores of Loch Linnie, near to the Corran Narrows where Eilidh and Liath Macha had swum across the Loch on that wild stormy morning almost a year ago.

---

have been called Bran.
[25] Story teller.

No sad thought today seemed to cross the mind of the foursome, for Luath too raced alongside despite his great age. Moments later they came flying into the path of that same seannachie who they had earlier said they would leave Luath with whilst they went fishing.

"Have you all come for the party then?" asked the old man.

"Party! What party?" cried the boys.

"Any food?" demanded Hugh, then, "Oh there's Gordon. Gordon, we're going fishing with Eilidh!"

"What about a story first, and some of Ceitidh's' cake? It's a lassies party and some of them were hoping to see young Eilidh here. Would you mind stepping in Eilidh, just for a few moments or so? I'll entertain these two young gentlemen. I've got a couple of other lads here already. Now what story is it that you would like?"

"What about 'The Battle of the Birds'?" suggested Eilidh, as she walked with them into the cottage. "I for one haven't heard that for some time and it's one of my favourites."

"Aye that's a good one to tell. Come on in, come on in. Eilidh, all the lassies are in the back room with Ceitidh."

The seannachie, as they called him, had an unusually large house for the area. This he shared with his oldest daughter Ceitidh and her husband and their youngest daughter Ada.

His main occupation now he was so old was to tell stories to the children, and to the adults, in the long winter evenings. For everyone loved a good story and he knew many, for they had been passed on from father to son for generations. However, when he had been a younger man Padraig had been the head gillie[26] for the Macleans of Ardgour and it was said that none knew the hills as he did. Though he would claim that if anyone

---

[26] Someone who helps with deer stalking or fishing expeditions and may also act as gamekeeper.

else was as canny in the ways of the hills as he was himself it was young Eilidh. Even now, despite his age, you would often see the two of them walking together over the hills as in past times he had walked with her father.

As soon as the door opened the boys rushed inside and made for the main room of the house where they expected to find their friends, Padraig's grandchildren.

Eilidh, who knew this house almost as well as she knew her own, quickly made her way to the small room where she knew she would find Paidraig's daughter Ceitidh, and more than likely his grand-daughter Ada and a few of the other young women of the village also.

Chapter 4 A Lassies Party

As she neared Ceitidh's room Eilidh could hear the loud buzz of people talking.

She knocked on the door. The chatter immediately hushed.

A pretty little brunette, who looked to be about fifteen, opened the door. "Mother, it's our Eilidh!"

"Failte[27] Eilidh, failte," came the voice of an older woman. "We were all of us just saying that it was you as we needed to speak with."

Eilidh smiled at the girl who had opened the door, "Thank you Ada." Then she turned to the girl's mother, "Aye, so said your father Ceitidh. We met him just as I was about to taking my brothers fishing in my wee row boat. I fear that they are at present demolishing all your baking!" she added apologetically.

Ceitidh laughed "That Hugh, he is forever hungry! It's right good to see a young lad with such a healthy appetite, a pity my Ada does not follow his example!" She looked kindly at her daughter. "However, it is Norah MacInnis here as is a needing a word with ye lass, for she's fair out o' her mind wi' worry o'er that foolish young man o' hers!"

Eilidh looked now at the other occupants of the room. It was only a very small room but so comfortably and prettily arranged. A tiny but cheery fire burned fiercely in the hearth and there was a petite dresser on the back wall alongside a little table which was at present packed with scones, cakes and other tempting victuals. On the walls were numerous small tapestries, a testimony to the skill and artistry of the women in the house. The cushions on the numerous chairs that were set around the room were similarly anointed with needlework of various designs. Eilidh knew all six of the young women who

---

[27] Welcome.

were present very well and noted with pleasure that one of them had brought her baby with her. All of them gathered around a pale young girl who looked to have been crying.

"It will be all right now Norah," said a very pretty red head. "Eilidh will sort it out if you just explain it all to her."

Eilidh walked forward hesitantly, and then halted as she asked the pretty red head "Ealasaid, is your father at home just now?"

"Yes he is talking to Norah's father just now, which is why she is so upset. Norah's father has heard that Malcolm is in trouble, that Adrianne has accused Malcolm of making up to her. He is threatening to withdraw his permission for Malcolm to wed Norah." As she said this Norah, who had dried her eyes as Eilidh entered, started to weep again more openly. Ealasaid Boyd nonetheless calmly continued her explanation. "Norah's father says that he wants her to wed a decent, sober, sensible man, not one whose head is easily turned by a pretty face. You know how he wasn't right happy when Malcolm and Norah started walking out, says he is too independent minded. He is worried that Malcolm will lose his job now and that he won't be able to get another if it gets out that he has been malarking around with the old Laird's daughter."

Eilidh looked at the girl who was weeping so unashamedly and asked, "Norah, is that why your father is up at Kiel farm talking to John Boyd just now?"

The girl choked back her tears and managed to nod, before turning away, her face red and blotched from so much crying.

"They arrived at our house about fifteen minutes ago; I brought Norah down here, thought it might cheer her up seeing some of the other girls, but as you can see...," Ealasaid indicated the clearly miserable girl hunched up in the chair.

Eilidh smiled, "In that case I don't think that you need worry Norah. I am sure that Ealasaid has told you how well her father thinks of Malcolm. He will be just fine. There is no likelihood of Malcolm losing his job. He will have to be punished of course."

"But he didn't do anything! He swore to me he didn't do anything! He says he has no liking at all for…, for…," Norah stopped suddenly, realising who she was talking to, realising the implication; that she was accusing the old Laird's youngest daughter of lying, of making false accusations, and she was telling this tale to the girl's sister; or so she claimed to be……

Eilidh hesitated too before saying gently, "Norah, we all know that Malcolm would never be false to you, he is a right nice lad. Once John Boyd has spoken to him I am sure that Malcolm will explain it all to you. I can assure you however that he will lose neither his job nor the good will of John Boyd, so there is not the slightest need for you to worry. I am sure that John Boyd will be reassuring your father as to that at this very minute." Then Eilidh turned to Ceitidh, "If you will just excuse me for a moment I have just remembered a letter I should have delivered to Ealasaid's father at Kiel farm. I will be back before you have had time to make us a hot brew." She glanced impishly at the older woman, smiled at the other girls and then quickly departed.

When she was much younger she might have eavesdropped for a few moments out of curiosity for she knew from experience that people always talked about her as soon as she left a room, sometimes even before! That was how she had learned of the mystery that surrounded her own birth.

That piece of gossip, accidentally overheard, which had explained why she lived with Kai-Ying, rather than at Ardgour House with the rest of her family, had sounded fantastical. Indeed when she had later confronted her father as to its veracity he had dismissed most as pure nonsense; but the truth had been, if anything, even more incredible.

Kai-Ying and her father had both always advised her to try not to listen to gossip, for once it was heard it was difficult to forget. She understood now that people sometimes said hurtful things to each other, or about each other, in the heat of the moment; perhaps hoping that this would temporarily ease their own pain, or pay back something hurtful that had been previously said to them. Even things heard that were favourable or flattering were equally likely to be untrue. Flattery, she had learned, whether inadvertently eavesdropped on, or said directly to her face, was often false; uttered for reasons untold, for undisclosed motives.

She now realized that when she overheard someone's opinions that these were not necessarily that person's true beliefs at all but said only to impress, to curry favour, or perhaps uttered in order to conform to the views which they believed others to have, because of fear, or a wish to be accepted or thought better of; often did not really mean what they said, nor did they appreciate the possible long term effects of their unguarded speech.

Usually there was no way of ascertaining the truth or otherwise of the rumours or opinions stated, but still in some subtle way they affected ones feelings for both the teller and those who were told about. So Eilidh left quickly so she would have no chance to overhear.

She gave a short whistle and then mounted the fast black arrow that came galloping down the hill to answer her call.

Chapter 5 The House of the Seannachie

When Eilidh returned to the seannachie's house barely half an hour later, after having completed her errand, she was met by a stony faced silence which was broken by Iseabail, the pretty dark haired young matron who was Joe's older sister.

"I hear that you think yourself too good for my brother, that it is a young lord that ye prefer to wed," she declared loudly as Eilidh entered the room.

"Iseabail, who told you that May tale?" Eilidh replied looking amused.

"Beitidh Livingstone says Adrianne is telling everyone that you are in love with some Lord or other," she cried accusingly.

"What does Adrianne know of me, we hardly ever speak and even then there is little civility," Eilidh returned calmly. Then she turned to another of the women and asked "Magaidh, can I hold your baby? He's just gorgeous. I love them at any age but this age is delicious."

"Mind he's a bit grouchy now, it's his teeth you know!" said the proud mother while passing the baby over eagerly enough.

"Do you realise that it is because of you that I am to be left all alone while all my family go south?" interjected Iseabail hotly.

Eilidh looked at her a moment silently before replying quietly. "William and Elspeth are remaining here and I am sure your parents will return just as soon as they can. Your mother will not wish to be long away from your and William's bairns. They are going south, as you well know Iseabail, for two reasons. One of which is to establish Joe in London with the aim of expanding your family business. Then when your parents return to Scotland, rather than immediately come back here, they will stay in Fife for a short while minding my brother's estate there while Lachlan and Mairi settle Ewan at Oxford. Neither of these arrangements have anything whatsoever to do with me."

"Joe would stay if you'd wed him," Iseabail retorted, but in a more subdued tone, a look of pleading on her face.

"Maybe yes, maybe no," Eilidh answered sadly. "Though I myself believe that he would still wish to live in London and work with Sam. You must have seen how excited he is about the opportunity. Why is it that you bring this up now Iseabail? About my wedding Joe I mean. You know that was all settled long ago. I love Joe dearly, but as you do, as my brother. We would not suit."

The baby had become anything but grumpy while Eilidh held him. Soon he was cooing and smiling.

"Even the younger ones fall in love with her," Cairistiona commented sourly.

Iseabail interrupted again "What are we going to do now when we need help with a birthing or when folk are sick or injured?"

Eilidh looked at Padraig's motherly daughter Ceitidh and smiled, "Ceitidh here and her daughter Morag manage very well when I am not here." Then she looked at Iseabail searchingly "Are you in the family way again?"

She nodded, "And I'm right feart an' all as to what will happen if you're not there Eilidh. Can't you wed my brother anyway?" she begged beseechingly.

"I can't Iseabail it would be most unfair to him. Don't you be worrying about next time though second babies are a lot easier that the first, you will be just fine with Ceitidh here. Though if you feed the little one more often yourself the next time, instead of farming him out to Iain's sister, there might be a bigger gap before another one arrives."

Iseabail looked unconvinced.

Then Magaidh, the mother of the baby Eilidh was holding said, "If ye wed Joe you would have some of your own bairns to cuddle."

"The bairns are best had with a man that one loves enough to accept the pain as well as enjoy the pleasure," Eilidh returned seriously. Then she gave the little boy she was holding a hug before handing him back to his mother.

Magaidh replied softly, "The bairns themselves give pleasure enough even when you get none frae yer man."

"Aye perhaps," she sighed and then before she could continue a quiet voice at her elbow said hesitantly.

"Eilidh, Dhughall and I have fallen out!"

Eilidh turned to look at the pale girl in the corner as she continued.

"He kept talking and talking about you. I got that jealous! I told him to take you for his sweetheart instead if he thought so much of you."

Ealasaid turned to her in scorn. "Surely Cairistiona you know that they all feel that way for our Eilidh, they can't seem to help themselves!"

"It's very well for you," she retorted in turn. "Your sweetheart must be the only man that won't want her, seeing as he's her milk brither." She startled as everyone else laughed.

"Didn't you know? Even Ewan wanted her but she wouldn't have him," Ealasaid countered.

Eilidh interrupted. "Cairistiona, are you going to the Ceilidh at Hamish Cameron's place?"

Cairistiona looked slightly bemused, but nodded to affirm that she was going.

"I am going away for a few days now, but if in the meantime you and Dhughall practice a couple of songs with Joe, I'll endeavour to return in time to play for the two of you so that you can sing together at that Ceilidh. The both of you sing very well. Say I asked it and then apologise for being so hen witted." Eilidh looked at Cairistiona, her eyes laughing as she continued "Dhughall will never refuse, he's right proud of his singing voice! By the time I'm back there may even be another wedding on the cards!"

Cairistiona blushed and muttered her thanks, while the other girls continued to tease her kindly.

The atmosphere in the room was now more relaxed and Eilidh noticed with pleasure that Norah, although she was still rather subdued, was looking happier.

After she had drunk her tea Eilidh stood up and went over to Ceitidh, who was hosting this impromptu party, saying that it was time she went.

Iseabail overhearing, looked concerned, "You've had nothing to eat Eilidh, bide a while longer."

"I want to set off in Cuchullin as the tide turns and I promised those two urchins, my brothers, some fishing before I leave," Eilidh replied with a smile. "They will never forgive me if I delay too long here and they don't catch their fish!"

Ceitidh asked apologetically "Do you think perhaps I could have a wee word before you go?"

Eilidh acquiesced immediately and, after saying her goodbyes to the other young girls, followed Ceitidh out of the room.

Chapter 6 A Tale o' Three Bairns

Eilidh followed Ceitidh into a pretty little bedroom which, like the room they had just come from, had the walls covered in numerous cleverly worked tapestries. On the bed there lay a beautiful counterpane painstakingly decorated with intricate needlework. Two large and homely chairs occupied a space to one side of the bed and on one of these Ceitidh made herself comfortable, automatically picking up some darning which was lying nearby as she did so.

As soon as Eilidh sat down, and without any prevarication, Ceitidh got straight to the point. "One of my good friends was at your sister Caroline's bed when she died."

Eilidh hesitated before replying and then said sadly, "You don't know how much I grieve that my mother's prejudice against me prevented her allowing me to assist at the birth. I might have saved her Ceitidh!"

"Maybe, but she was always a sickly one Eilidh. My friend, she saw the baby, said it was a seven month bairn for sure, and from what she said it's eyes and hair were like as yer own. She told me that the delivery went very ill and the babe was dead at birth. You were lucky Eilidh, for your poor mother also had a terrible time with your birthing; perhaps on account of your being the seventh child."

Eilidh shrugged, "As you know it is often those who have had many bairns that have a bad time of it. Sometimes later deliveries go ill as the muscles of the womb itself get too tired from over much usage, and the women are exhausted and worn long before the bairn is born. So you are right I was very fortunate, am very fortunate, to be alive!" She smiled. "Though from what I have heard my mother did have an easier time with Adrianne, Alex and Hugh."

"I can vouch for that," Ceitidh acknowledged. "However, what I wanted to tell you was something that our Alice overheard. You know that she works at the Big House. Well, she says that she heard your mother talking about the babe Caroline lost, and that your mother said that Caroline's 'seven month monster' was a sign that the Curse of her family was following her still."

Eilidh looked puzzled and then said slowly, "I've not heard of any curse connected to our family, father never mentioned anything. Perhaps he didn't know."

Ceitidh gazed at Eilidh thoughtfully for a moment before continuing abruptly, "Caroline herself was never the seven month babe your mother claimed she was, nor was Adrianne. I was there at their births as I was at yours; myself and old Martha were both there. You were just a wee scrap o' a thing when you were first born. Why none of us thought that you would survive a week ye were born that early; but with Caroline and Adrianne it was different. I warrant that the both of them had stayed their full term in the womb. I'd wager also that the old Laird, your faither, he knew, though the neither of us let on to him what we suspicioned. He knew well enough that we never would say ought about it to any other body; only now, now you are to go..." She stumbled to a halt embarrassed, at a loss for words.

Eilidh said quietly, "Don't worry Ceitidh, I know; father told me long ago, but my thanks anyway for your honesty and loyalty."

Ceitidh hesitated, then went on awkwardly. "There was something else Eilidh, and this is something that all the village talk about, not openly of course, so you may not know, unless your faither mentioned."

Eilidh went still and attentive.

"It's about Adrianne; the talk is that she's Campbell's get, not your faither's. I'm sorry Eilidh but we thought it best that you knew. We wanted Joe to tell you, but he refused." She looked carefully at the girl and then said dryly, "You don't look surprised. Something else your faither confided in you about? We need not have spent all that time worrying whether or no we should tell you."

Eilidh said slowly, "I didn't know about any family curse, though father did tell me once of a family legend that he believed some of my mother's family misinterpreted, perhaps that is what she was talking about. I am really grateful that you should care enough to tell me all this and appreciate how difficult it must have been for you. I ..., I'll never forget your kindness Ceitidh."

"That's all right lass, you know most of the women of my age in the village gave ye suck when you was just a little thing, no bigger than a doll ye were, we all feel right motherly towards you, your own being worse than useless and that Mairi well I'd like to give her a piece of my mind I would. Young Iseabail there was right about one thing though," she continued, "it would be a real good thing if you would wed Joe or some other lad. Even young Campbell has his eye on you, not but that they all do, an' that's the truth o' things! It's not right for a young lass like you to be talking so cool about love."

The girl remained silent so the motherly woman continued. "What about her suspicions as to your wishing to marry this Lord? You could you know! What, with your birth and your looks!"

Eilidh stayed quiet for a few moments longer before saying slowly, reluctantly, "Ceitidh, with my father dead and my mother still set on denying me it would be foolish beyond measure for me to wish such a thing. If any lordling married such as me it would bring him social ruin. You see Ceitidh, I am not so much heartless as realistic."

Ceitidh still looked concerned. "It worries us to see you so alone, and now with your mother said to be sending you away..." She hesitated before continuing. "When your faither was alive and old Kai-Ying, you were usually with either one of them, but now... It's not good for a young girl to live all alone as you do, to have no one to confide in or discuss things with. Padraig, Alasdair and I, we see how you keep yourself to yourself, how you try to keep all the young men at a distance and the lassies an' all. You don't attend the parties or such like or if you do its only to play your music or tell one of your stories. What you need is a good man to be a companion, a marriage such as Alasdair and myself have. I'll warrant young Campbell wouldn't care for any of that nonsense such as your mother speaks about you Eilidh, and him a gentleman an' all."

"Fergus is a good man, Ceitidh but he's not for me. He does not realise it at the moment but it is unlikely that I would make him happy."

Ceitidh continued doggedly "A right good lad he is for all he's a Campbell! As for happy, you won't get me to believe that you would not make a good man such as he is, happy."

Eilidh laughed, "However I have plans quite other than this for my dear brother to be, which he is as yet unaware of. Now Ceitidh stop worrying, I will soon be travelling south with Lachlan, Mairi and Ewan. Duncan, Joe and Hamish will be with us too for a time. How could I be lonesome when all of these will be with me? Besides, I'm never really alone Ceitidh; I've always got Liath Macha, unless I'm away sailing in Cuchullin, and even then there are always the seals nearby to keep me company. If I didn't have them then, yes, I might feel alone, though on the hills or out at sea somehow one feels closer to

God. Sometimes I almost feel I can hear or see those angels which father used always tell me were all around protecting us." She paused for a moment as if reliving a memory and her face lit up and she turned shining eyes to the older woman. "I know it sounds fanciful Ceitidh, but it is all so beautiful, so peaceful, with the cry of the wind, the calls of the birds and the animals, and the sounds of the sea in all its different moods. And I have to leave it all!" She said the last under her breath. "Then though," she continued with an upward tilt of her head, "when I leave, and wherever I go, I shall still have Liath Macha, and so long as I have him I'll never feel lonesome." She grinned across at Ceitidh as she maintained, "And of course there will always be all those angels too!"

"There was one thing though that I wanted to mention to you before I left," Eilidh continued more soberly. "Iseabail, once she has had this next bairn I think she would enjoy being trained up as a midwife like you Ceitidh. Despite what she pretends she finds looking after the house and her bairn rather boring; she needs something else. While Morag, I think, would prefer to spend more time at home with her man and her bairns instead of being out assisting you. Oh I know she never complains, she never would, it's just sometimes you can see what it costs her."

The older woman looked thoughtful, "I know what you mean, only I hadn't really thought of it before as it's what all the women in our family do, we sort of pass it down from mother to daughter."

"I know, that's why she would never complain. She would never willingly do ought to hurt you. Iseabail though, if she really took to it, I feel sure that her father would teach her other things. She's really clever and quick and I'm sure Duncan knows more than many an old Saw Bones! What do you think?"

"I think it is a very good idea, especially with you going. I was wondering how we were going to manage. What will they do for the horses with Duncan and you away? Lachlan I've heard won't be back for a good year?"

"Will is staying. He and Elspeth will look after his parent's old house and he will run their business from this end while they are away. Will is almost as good with the horses as his father Duncan. All he needs is a bit more confidence. He is so very self-effacing! Young Hamish is to stay with their parents in Fife and help them with our estates there when he and Duncan return from our journey south. You must have heard, especially as Iseabail is so upset about it all!"

"Just checking Eilidh!" returned Ceitidh with a twinkle in her eye.

Eilidh laughed, "I might have guessed! Well I'd better drag those boys away from your scones."

Ceitidh stood up and came over and gave her a motherly hug. "We will all be praying for ye Eilidh."

Eilidh had also stood up to make ready to leave, and as she hugged Ceitidh in return she said warmly, "My thanks Ceitidh for everything, give my love to your men folk too, and say my goodbyes to all the girls."

She left quickly, whereupon Ceitidh returned to her chair and picked up her sewing again, sitting thoughtfully alone for a few minutes before returning to the young women who were awaiting her return, full of curiosity.

Chapter 7 Archibald Campbell Talks to Joe

Eilidh and her brothers spent the remainder of that afternoon on Loch Linnie in Eilidh's old rowing boat, fishing. As was always the case when they went fishing with Eilidh, the catch was plentiful and it was two very tired and happy little boys that drew up alongside Eilidh's little sailing boat Cuchullin, which was anchored in the bay at Corran, just before the tide began to turn.

Eilidh had noticed a group of people above the shoreline who were looking in their direction. To these she now drew her brothers' attention. "Look! Alex! Hugh! There's mother, Adrianne, and yes I do believe it is our future step father, come to see where you have got to. You had both better make haste and not keep them waiting," Eilidh urged her brothers cheerfully.

She and the boys waved to those on shore and then Eilidh, after first handing the oars to Alex, climbed aboard Cuchullin, leaving the boys in the rowing boat alone. Before her brothers set off to meet those awaiting them on the shore, she reminded them to ask Joe to look after the boat and their ponies, for Joe also was standing on the shore alongside the others of the welcoming party, and she knew that her mother would expect her brothers to return home immediately.

The boys very proudly rowed the remaining few yards to shore where they toppled merrily out into the water. Not forgetting to hold fast to the little boat, they splashed unconcernedly the remaining few feet to dry land, calling vociferously for all come to look at their catch.

Instead of the hoped for praise and admiration, they soon heard an angry voice demanding of them why they had left their lessons, run away from their tutor and been out all day without permission.

"Oh, Eilidh made sure we had done our lessons before we came out," declared Alex nonchalantly, quite unfazed by his mother's criticism.

"Now do come and look at my fish, I've one here that is quite enormous," demanded Hugh.

"One of mine was even bigger," boasted his brother. "It was so big......" he said holding wide his arms, "only...," his voice changed, "that one escaped...... Eilidh said."

"I have no wish to hear what that creature said," his mother retorted. "Now come here at once, we have visitors tonight. MacDonald's boys will arrive soon and you are not fit to be seen!"

The boys, complaining bitterly, did as they were bid.

Joe came towards them as they made their way up the shore, saying that he would see to the boat and reassuring them that he would deliver all the fish to the kitchen at the Big House where they and everyone else could go and admire them at leisure before the fish were consigned to the pot. He also, after hearing Eilidh's missive, promised to see to the dog and the ponies.

The elder Campbell overhearing this, volunteered to accompany him and help bring the ponies down. Joe whilst cordially thanking him for the offer assured him that there was no need.

The older man however was most persistent in his offer despite the boys' mother complaining that if he did this it would make him late for their visitors.

Guessing that the offer was not all it seemed Joe got one of the watching lads to help him with the small boat and then left him with instructions for the disposal of the fish and the

69

cleaning of the craft. Only after ensuring all this was done did he set off with the impatiently watching gentleman.

Archibald Campbell lost no time in getting to the point. "That girl, I understand you know her well."

"If you are talking about Eilidh Ruadh, we have been friends since she was a wee bit of a thing, only five years old she was when first I saw her."

"The old Laird so it is said, treated you like a son, paid for you to go to the University?"

Joe nodded his head but said nothing.

"Yet he refused you permission to marry that girl just as he refused my son."

Again the young man nodded silently.

"Well, I will be honest with you. You see, I have a problem. You are probably aware that my son, young Fergus, remains set in his determination to wed that girl, while my affianced wife is totally against the whole notion of it. From all that I have heard of her I do not myself believe that she would make him a satisfactory wife. However I neither want to give offence to the one nor refuse the other. He's my heir, the only son I have and I do not want to alienate him, nor do I wish to run the risk of him running off with her. Now I want your honest opinion. If he offers for her will she accept? To be sure, it is in her best interest to do so, but I've heard she's a funny lass and unwilling to go against her late father's wishes. If I know for certain that she will refuse him then I can give Fergus my blessing."

They had got to the bottom of the brae that they would have to climb before getting to the cottage and Joe stopped there to look at the gentleman he was walking with. They were in sharp contrast to each other. The older man was obviously the landed gentleman and despite his age, was extremely good looking. He dressed expensively and fashionably but not in the florid manner of the dandy which his son was prone to affect. He was of medium height and build, and there was just the hint of spreading corpulence. His expression was that of one unused to being denied his own way and showed just the slightest trace of petulance.

In contrast Joe was lean of build, just below medium height but with the step and gait of the athlete, one would presume that he would be an excellent swordsman. His clothes were plain, serviceable, working clothes, but of such good quality and worn with such an air that if you had not known him you would find it difficult to place which strata of society he belonged to. If you had engaged him in conversation, you would have found him strikingly erudite and well-spoken and suspected a well-educated younger son. However you would have been wrong if you suspected him to be the younger son of a gentleman, he was the younger son of a gentleman's gentleman, for his father Duncan had been all things to his Laird and above all a devoted servant. The old Laird had indeed treated him as a son, and educated him as such. The main contrast however between the two men was their countenance. Joe's face was not handsome as was the other man's, and although there was just the touch of dourness about his expression, this was counterbalanced by such an air of honesty and trustworthiness, that he could be assured of being universally liked and relied on.

He now turned thoughtfully to the older man before replying. "By rights I should say that this is none of my business and something between Eilidh herself and your son. Indeed, as your son's rival for Eilidh's affections I wonder that you should ask this of me when I have such a definite bias. However on this instance I will answer and tell how I see the land lies, as I feel sure that Eilidh herself would be anxious that no trouble come about on her account between your son and yourself. As such I can say with no doubt or hesitation that she will of a certainty refuse him."

"Are you positive about this? There is no vestige of doubt in your mind?"

"Quite sure! She knows that her mother will never agree to her stepping, as it were, into her shoes on your death."

"I had not heard she was ever over obedient to that lady."

Joe grinned, "No, 'tis true, but she would not wish to put herself in the way of increasing any contact between them either." He continued more soberly, "But more importantly she will in no way wish to go against any decision of her father's."

They had now reached Eilidh's bothy. The older man was openly curious but Joe refused his request to look inside. He did however have a good look around the byre and barn, and expressed his astonishment at the neatness of it all, and at the contents of the little room off the side of the barn which was furnished with many bookcases and contained a number of tables upon which were arrayed numerous intriguing objects. He asked if they had belonged to Eilidh's father and was answered in the negative.

Archibald Campbell was silent for a few moments before inquiring hesitantly, almost despite himself, "I noticed that the lassie's boat was leaving its moorings as we made our way here. Have you any idea where she might be headed?"

"She talked of the Hebrides," replied Joe.

"Who goes with her?"

"None but herself," Joe answered shortly.

Archibald Campbell looked disbelieving. "A boat that size! I am no expert but I do know that it takes two strong men to manage a craft of that ilk, and not a mere lass. It's not the Hebrides she will be sailing to, not with the weather and the seas she will meet in those parts!"

Despite Joe's own misgivings about Eilidh's plans he was quick to refute Campbell's assessment. "I know none better sailor than our Eilidh, she is as home on the sea as you yourself Sir are at home on the land. She knows those seas well, oftentimes before she sailed them with her father and she has been there at least the once that I know of since his death, and that time she sailed alone."

"It is a strange girl so they say she is. If what you say is true it almost persuades me to lend credence to some of the other tales that I have heard," returned Campbell. "Do you know when she plans to return?"

Joe shrugged his shoulders, "She will return when she wills. However she has promised to be home before the date that your old mare is due to foal."

Archibald Campbell looked suddenly suspicious, "What reason would she have to be returning for that time? It was that Black Devil of hers that did the mischief in the first place and if she dies as a result I will personally shoot the vicious brute. Anyone could see that the mare was too old to have any more foals," he continued angrily.

To which Joe coolly returned, "I doubt Liath Macha was over concerned with her age when he found her left outside, unattended and willing. However Eilidh feels responsible and indeed she is the best chance that the mare and foal have of survival."

"I will have no women near any of my animals, still less one reputed to be a witch child," Campbell retorted. "My old mare is valuable; besides which I am fond of her. She has been with me many a long year."

"You are a fool if you believe of Eilidh other than what her father maintained to be the truth," Joe replied bluntly. "Furthermore, if you think to deny her access to your mare it is likely that you will lose both mare and foal. The mare is old, as you have said, and she is not carrying well. The foal, if it survives, is likely to be valuable; she is a fine old mare and Liath Macha's other progeny have been, though I hate to admit it, better than both himself and his extremely well favoured twin."

"My own groom will suffice. There is no need for other interference," Campbell returned curtly.

"Not so, he told me himself that he had no liking for midwifery, that he was no expert. My older brother would have been able to help, if it were not for the fact that he is to set out early next week to journey south again to join Duncan our father. They are not expected back until the week before the wedding. I myself have not their skill."

Joe had been catching the two ponies and tending to the young heifer whilst he had been talking. Now he curtly gave the ponies' reins into the hands of the other, saying brusquely, "I have plenty other business to finish this evening. If you are still of a mind to return the ponies of the young Laird and his brother back to their stables, I will be off and attend to my other duties. My thanks for the company and the offer of assistance. Good day to you."

Joe then departed without a backward glance, leaving the other man holding both ponies and looking rather nonplussed.

Chapter 8 A Family Interlude

She sat near the top of the hill, arms wrapped tightly round bent knees, gazing out across Loch Linnie where far in the distance majestic mountains towered over the landscape. Cascading down next to her, full and fast flowing, were the beautiful waters of Maclean's Towel. A quiet contentment filled her as she watched the waterfall frolicking its way merrily down the hillside. This was one of her favourite places. A place she felt linked to, connected to by a long line of her forebears.

Legend claimed that the day this waterfall dried up there would be no more Macleans in Ardgour. The very fact that the waterfall was now at its height, full to bursting as it rushed sparkling over the rocks, caused her to feel utter delight.

Down below stood Ardgour House and gardens, her ancestral home; though she could remember but one occasion in which she had entered any part of that house other than the servants' quarters. That was the day she had toiled all the way up here all alone, the day that her father brought her home from London for that very first time.

London, she had missed not going there this autumn. Her father owned a part share in a London livery stables, and every year she had been want to accompany him on his annual visit there. During her time in London she would always live with Sam and Sarah Lyon, who held the other part share in the stables and did the day to day running of the business. But where her father resided during this time she had never discovered. Invariably though he would visit her at the stables every day, and some days he would take her out with him around the City and the outlying countryside, when he would delight in explaining to her London's ancient history and the various legends it held.

Only one year had he failed to visit her on their sojourn in London. She had seen him but briefly that summer and then her feelings of hurt and rejection had almost blinded her to the dejection and almost desperate worry etched across her father's face and imprinted in every line and movement of his body. To this day she had never found out what had been the root of his torment. He had never spoken of it except to bleakly inform her that the problem had been resolved.

When her father had died he had given his share in the stables to Joe's father Duncan and it was at these London stables that Joe planned to reside when the rest of them returned to Scotland. She felt a flicker of excitement at the thought of seeing them all again, especially Sam and Sarah's daughter Helen whom she loved as a sister. She wondered idly whether Helen and James's baby was born yet. No doubt she would get a letter before long.

She had been told that as a very small child she had spent more time in their home than she had in the house of Mairi and Lachlan who she had been fostered with. It was a shame that Helen's sister Katherine disliked her so much.

Her hand brushed against the chain that she wore around her neck and she smiled as her thoughts leapt to the giver of the ring that hung from it, of the goodness, the love that could be found in the strangest of places. The ring had never left her neck since the day he had given it to her.

A movement caught her eye disturbing her silent reverie. Two small figures hurrying up the hill. Her eyes lit up. It was two of those whom she loved most in all the world. She scrambled to her feet and raced to meet them. But before she had gone far she was almost bounced to the ground by four hairy feet, a furry face and a very wet tongue! She collapsed on the heather laughing. Moments later she was enthusiastically pounced on by two more small warm, laughing creatures.

"Eilidh Ruadh! Eilidh Ruadh! Luath told us you were home. He insisted on us coming here!" cried her brother Alex excitedly.

"It is a clever one that he is," she replied as she rubbed the upturned abdomen of the ecstatic dog; "and you two, am I right in supposing that you have informed nurse of your whereabouts this early morning?"

Hugh giggled, while Alex replied seriously, "Eilidh, Luath was most insistent that we come. Besides we knew that nurse could do with a rest, she was only telling us yesterday how tired she was feeling. As soon as she hears that Cuchullin is back in the Bay she will know where we are."

Eilidh laughed, "Rascals! Well, what shall we do today, and what shall we do for food, as I confess I have little in to feed such hungry urchins as you?"

"Eilidh can we go to Inversanda with the ponies?" asked Alex. "Then we could show you some of the things we have been practicing."

"Yes! Yes!" Hugh agreed enthusiastically, "And Sandra Beag will make us a huge picnic if she knows we are going with you Eilidh. Joe will bring it to us if we ask. He can come too, he also is quite good at the riding tricks," he said kindly.

Eilidh laughed. "Sounds like as good a plan as any - and of course nurse and your tutor will get the day off and so everyone benefits."

Unaware of the mild irony in their sister's comments, they rushed down the hill with her laughing and chattering. Then the children ran on to the Big House to wheedle a picnic out of their kind cook while Eilidh rounded up the ponies ready for the ride to Inversanda.

It was while they were practicing standing up on their ponies' backs as the ponies walked, trotted and then cantered at a spoken command, that Eilidh noticed a party of riders approaching.

Hugh, more of a natural athlete than his older brother, was delighted to discover that for once he could do something easier than him.

Alex, rather annoyed, decided to show that he was really the more skilled of the two.

"Look at me! Eilidh look at me!" Alex cried as he tried to do one of the summersaults that Eilidh did with such ease. Predictably he ended flat on his back in the sand with his brother crowing with laughter. Indeed he laughed so much that he himself fell off just as the small party of riders came round the corner.

Eilidh bent down and murmured something to the two boys who were back on their ponies and off in the opposite direction in a flash.

Then Eilidh gave a shrill whistle and seconds later her Black Stallion was there looking as menacing as ever.

The riders had picked up speed and were approaching quickly and so rather than following immediately after her brothers Eilidh waited for the company to approach.

"Eilidh I'm sorry, they asked..." It was Joe looking rather sheepish.

"How many times have I told you that I do not want my sons taught those awful tricks? Don't you know how dangerous they are?" interjected a woman who was seated elegantly on a very pretty chestnut mare.

The woman's voice was beautiful, low and melodic, despite the fact that it oozed rage and disdain, and the face and form of the speaker was equally lovely. Caroline Maclean, or Linnie as her friends called her, widow of Alexander Maclean, 13th Laird of Ardgour, the woman who Eilidh believed to be her mother, rode as she did everything else, with grace, style and authority.

Accompanying her was Archibald Campbell, to whom she was betrothed, and also his son and her youngest daughter.

Before answering her mother, Eilidh first turned to the final member of the party, he who had spoken first, and said. "You did right Joe to answer thus. Don't worry! Would you mind though taking that food to our picnic place for us? I have no doubt that my brothers already believe themselves to be starving!"

Joe left immediately to carry out her request and as he rode past her he quickly and quietly murmured, "You are needed at the stables, I'll look after the children."

She nodded but made no reply, turning instead to look at her mother, who was impatiently waiting for her answer.

"Madam, it was the express wish of our father that I should teach them what I could. He maintained that the gaining of such expertise was worth the risk. Though indeed Ma'am the sand is so soft here that a fall is almost a pleasure."

"Their father is dead, and I say that you are to leave them alone, that you are to have no further communication with my sons. It is my wish that you immediately travel down to Morvern and the other outlying districts with invitations to our wedding." She looked fondly at the man by her side before continuing, "Thereafter you are to stay away from the children and I expect you to be gone from this area by the day after our wedding. Lachlan and Mairi have their instructions for your disposal. Is that clear?"

"Yes indeed Madam. However I had previously engaged myself to attend a Ceilidh the night after next so will be unable to leave before this."

"My orders take precedence over a mere Ceilidh."

"Moreover," Eilidh continued steadily, ignoring her mother's dictate, "I would be grateful if Adrianne would grant me a few words in private before I set out to deliver your letters Madam."

"There is no need whatsoever for you to speak to Adrianne," replied her mother shortly.

"I have agreed with John Boyd that he will deal with young Malcolm, and that I would myself talk to Adrianne about the situation, delicate as it is."

"It is not for the likes of you to talk to Adrianne about anything, John Boyd can tell me how the boy has been punished and I can then reassure Adrianne that the boy will cause her no more trouble."

"However I have some things of a personal nature that I need to discuss with Adrianne. If you wish John Boyd may be present also but she might find that rather embarrassing," countered Eilidh.

"John Boyd will discuss the situation with me. There will be no need to involve Adrianne."

"Madam, might we discuss this somewhere more private? There are those listening who you might not wish aware..."

"I have the utmost confidence in both Mr Campbell here and his son," interrupted her mother. "Mr Campbell and I will discuss the situation with John Boyd and you will proceed immediately to Morvern. That is my final word on the matter."

Eilidh walked over to where her mother was standing, first telling the stallion to wait. She looked straight up at her and said gently, "Madam, I do beg your pardon, but you must know that until the day that you are wed it is John Boyd and Lachlan Beaton that have joint guardianship of myself, and not you. Moreover it is in Adrianne's best interest to talk with me about this matter."

Eilidh then turned to her sister and addressed her directly. "Adrianne, I will be in Father's study from six o' clock tomorrow night. I would be honoured if you would spare me a few moments of your time. Please feel free to bring others with you, such as you feel would lend you support. If you choose not to come to see me at that hour then I will apprise John Boyd of my concerns and ask that he and his wife discuss the issues with you on my behalf." She bowed slightly. Whereupon her mother pulled her horse round sharply and rode off, indicating furiously for the others of the party to do likewise.

The younger gentleman however did not immediately follow. He waited, watching while Eilidh jumped on her horse and galloped swiftly away in the opposite direction to that which the two children and Joe had gone.

Chapter 9 In the Study

What immediately struck one on entering the chamber was how homely, comfortable and peaceful it felt. That it was also a work place was perceived only secondary.

Around the perimeter of this large room, from floor to ceiling and wall to wall there were books: books of all shapes and sizes. A huge fire flickered merrily in the grate, and on either side of this there resided a comfortable, well-worn chair. Nearby was a games table, accompanied by four neat stools, while in the centre of the room, facing the door was an old much loved wooden desk attended closely by a couple of stout ancient cabinets containing an assortment of documents and other papers. While at the window there stood a plain, austere vase in stark contrast to its abundant vibrant, sweet smelling occupants.

There was a knock on the door.

"Come in!" responded a bright cheery voice, then, "Put the papers on the games table please Mary."

As the person busy working at the desk looked up smiling to give thanks for the documents that she was expecting, her eyes widened in surprise as she saw that the individual who had just entered was other than the one whom she had awaited. "Why Sir, this is an unexpected honour, what can I do for you?"

As she spoke she rang a bell that had lain on the desk. A young girl came in hurriedly, casting a quick anxious glance at the unexpected visitor as she did so.

"I've brought what you asked Miss."

"Thank you Mary, just put them over on that table if you would be so kind and would you then please ask Edith to come in. It would seem that I am in sudden need of a chaperone." As she said this she glanced across at her visitor and smiled, then stood up and approached him.

"I hope I am not disturbing you Eilidh," he said diffidently.

"You are indeed Fergus, but that does not make the interruption unwelcome! I was in any case getting tired of these figures. I am expecting John Boyd in the next half an hour to go through some of them with me."

"Perhaps it would be better if I came back another time and left you to finish your work, though if you are setting off for Morvern so soon..." Fergus trailed off disconsolately and stood looking rather despondent.

Eilidh laughed. "Oh don't worry! I've been through them all before and am now only rechecking it all. You see I am quite determined to leave things in order for young Alex."

"Do you really do all the management of the estate?" Fergus asked curiously.

"Only until mother gets remarried, then Lachlan and John Boyd hold it in joint trust until Alex comes of age."

"But you are not of age yourself yet."

"True, but father," Eilidh hesitated, "father involved me in all the decisions, so when he died it seemed natural for me to continue to help with the running of the estate, though really it is John Boyd who does all the work. He dislikes the paperwork however, and as I am leaving he has tasked John Beag[28], his eldest son, with the learning of it over the past few months. John Beag does not really like it much either, preferring to work outdoors! He is doing very well with it though."

An old woman had entered. Eilidh turned to her and smiled as she asked "Ah, Edith, would you mind taking your usual

---

[28] Beag is the Gaelic word for small. John Beag was called this as a child to distinguish him from his father John, and the named had stayed with him as he grew older.

seat?" The old woman nodded dourly and then proceeded to walk slowly over to a rocking chair which had been placed inconspicuously in a corner of the room and after sitting down carefully upon this seat she took up her knitting with the comfort of much familiarity.

Eilidh then said to her gentleman visitor "Now, won't you take a seat?"

"I had hoped to talk to you in private."

"I am sorry Fergus, but father was very strict about such things," Eilidh said apologetically. "Edith is very discrete you know," she flashed Edith another smile which brought a glimmer to the older woman's eyes as she continued stoically with her work.

"Eilidh," he paused.

She smiled encouragingly as she sat down on a chair near the fire indicating for him to take the other.

Seated, he began again, "Eilidh, you must know why I'm here." She said nothing and he continued.

"You seemed to be avoiding me and then I heard from Joe that you spent an hour or two in here most mornings. At first I didn't credit it, but then when you told Adrianne that you would meet her here this evening..."

"Why should you not expect to find me here?" Eilidh asked lightly. "Don't you believe women are capable of running an Estate? Many do you know, when their husbands are too idle or have other concerns."

"No it wasn't that." Fergus hesitated again before continuing awkwardly, "I understood that you were forbidden to enter this house." He stopped embarrassed.

Eilidh laughed, unconcerned. "I am. That is why father had his study and library moved down here to the servants' quarters. Mother never comes near here, she does not even go to the kitchen; Sandra Beag goes upstairs to see her to get the orders for the meals, as do all the other staff when they are required."

"Eilidh," he continued without further preamble, "my father has given me permission to marry you if you will agree."

"But my father did not! If you remember he refused categorically."

"Eilidh, your father is dead. The situation is different now. He is no longer here to protect you, and you can have no idea of the future your mother has planned for you. I love you Eilidh," he said urgently, "and wish to offer you that protection which you no longer have. I wish to offer you my name, I wish you to have the position in Society that is yours by right and has so long been denied you. Your mother will not wish to embarrass my father by continuing to deny your birth when you are wed to me."

Eilidh was silent for a few moments before answering. Then she looked up at him and said gently, "Fergus, you cannot know how immensely grateful I am for your love, your offer, your thought and concern. Indeed there is no one that I know whom I would rather wed; but the answer is still no. Things have not changed that much since when you first sought permission of my father. I would still drive you mad within a year! Neither is my future quite as desperate as you might think. Lachlan has still some say over what happens to me, it is yet a year until my mother and your father get full guardianship, by which time I will be the grand old age of eighteen. Who knows what will happen in a year!"

"Lachlan will not help you. It is his mother-in-law who is supposed to take you in and, and to have the educating of you," Fergus said with obvious discomfiture. "I have heard them talk Eilidh."

"I would not think that even my mother would wish me to undertake that particular occupation," she refuted, sounding amused.

Fergus looked doubtfully at Eilidh for a moment then, as if unable to help himself, blurted out "Then it, it is true what they say! You refuse me on account of the Earl of Hindley!" he cried. "It is as I feared."

"Who!" she exclaimed, looking puzzled.

"The Earl of Hindley, do not pretend not to know him. I myself have seen his likeness; drawn by your own hand it is said!"

"The Earl of Hindley," Eilidh said slowly. "I have of course heard of him, read of him in the papers, in magazines. However to my knowledge I have never seen him."

"Adrianne carries with her a painstakingly detailed sketch of his countenance; she claims it was you who drew it," Fergus said accusingly.

Eilidh stilled suddenly, then rose, walked to the desk, took something from a drawer and handed it to him and resumed her seat. "Is this he?"

"Yes, that is his likeness, his companion I have also seen, although I hesitate to mention this in front of a lady."

Eilidh paled. "I..., I had hoped that he was only a dream, imaginary," she said slowly, "only lately, lately I have feared otherwise, and now... Are you positive that it is he?"

"Indeed I am quite sure. I was up at Oxford with him. I did not know him well, but well enough to recognise. Now he is quite infamous of course. Everyone knows him, or knows of him. It is he for sure Eilidh. Do not tell me you did not know who he was when you sketched that drawing."

"Then," Eilidh murmured as if to herself, "then I have been right to fear."

86

She rose suddenly. "You may rest assured that it is on no account of his that I refuse your most generous and kindly made offer. I am not unconscious of the difficulties you have gone through to obtain your father's permission and I truly value your regard. It's just Fergus that I know that you and I would do much better and love each other much longer as brother and sister rather than as husband and wife. Now, was there anything else you wish to discuss as I am expecting, as I previously mentioned, John Boyd in a matter of minutes?"

"If you have never seen Hindley how did you come to draw his likeness so accurately?" Fergus demanded tightly.

Eilidh shrugged, "I have the Sight. He has haunted my dreams since my father's funeral. I had hoped he was only that, a dream."

"All the women in London Society are reputed to be in love with him, he is quite the rage! Why should you be any different?"

"I would imagine he would be, however..."

"Adrianne is quite determined to marry him when she is Brought Out next Year!"

"Mother intends to take her to London does she; and your father?"

"He is agreeable to this plan. I do not believe Eilidh that you are as indifferent as you maintain."

"If he is as I imagine a rake and a gambler then what possible interest would I have in him. No manner of other attributes sporting or personal would tempt me to consider any type of liaison with such as he. Anyway..." she looked at him, her eyes full of laughter, "what type of fool do you think I am to imagine that even where I head over heels in love with him that he would even notice me?"

"Everyone notices you Eilidh!"

"True." She smiled so sweetly that his heart turned over and he almost forgot to breathe. Oblivious she continued lightly, "But as my mother has made clear her position with regard to my standing in the family, it is not his Name that he would offer such as I," she said quietly. "Now..."

"He is also a murderer!"

"That I find less easy to believe, unless of course he killed someone duelling."

There was a knock on the door.

"Miss, Eilidh..., John Boyd is here to see you."

"Thank you Mary. Would you ask if he would mind waiting ten minutes or so?"

"Miss, that might make you late for Miss Adrianne. They say your mother and Mr Campbell are intending to come also."

"Thank you Mary, I'll bear that in mind."

The door closed. "As you have just heard Fergus, I have a busy evening ahead of me." Eilidh went quiet for a moment then continued, almost reluctantly, "If as you say Adrianne is, ah..., interested in this Earl maybe you had better tell me more about his unsavoury reputation and how you seem to know so much about it!"

Nothing loathe Fergus commenced, "As I mentioned, I was up at Oxford with Hindley. He and two friends, they were always together, kept themselves to themselves. All three of them had the reputation of being very intelligent, quiet, studious students and indeed Hindley was even intending, so it was said, to stay on to do his Fellowship. Then his parents were murdered. He was accused of having murdered both them and a young girl who lived on one of their estates. The day before he was to go to the gallows they set him free. The young man whose sweetheart Hindley was said to have killed had been found dead, apparently he had shot himself. It was thought by most that Hindley's maternal grandmother, Lady Holden, The Dowager Countess of Freeme, bought, bribed, or blackmailed one of the servants and a man from the local village, to say that they had seen this young man run away from the scene of the murder. As a result Hindley was granted a reprieve from his execution; however no one truly believed him innocent. They say he toured the continent for a year after this. When he came back he was ostracised, not allowed into any of the clubs. He came back changed; cold, hard, an expert athlete, swordsman, nonpareil whip. It is reputed that he has won, by means of his gaming, the fortunes off many a young buck. He is said to be quite heartless as well as having the luck of the devil. Nor is he to be trusted where women are concerned. All love him, but he loves none, or only as it is convenient to him. The duels he is reputed to have been involved in are infamous. Now, despite his reputation, despite the fact that all continue to believe him guilty of his initial crime, he is welcomed everywhere, sought after by all."

"Not everyone believed him guilty. I remember the story now, father talked of it. I do not know why, but father always maintained him innocent," Eilidh said lightly before continuing carefully, "Fergus I thank you for your information regarding the Earl of Hindley but let us not discuss him any longer, there is another matter more close to my heart that I wished to mention to you."

He sat up and looked at her intently, even hopefully, as she spoke.

"Your sister Fergus, is she to come for the wedding? I would like very much to meet her before I leave. She will after all be a sister to me also when our parents are married and I would very much like to give her a gift."

Eilidh looked at him anxiously, while Fergus, surprise evident on his face, gave her his assurances that he would arrange such an interview.

"There was one more thing Fergus which I wished to talk to you about," Eilidh continued. "I did hear that your father would prefer an alliance for you other than that which you have so kindly proposed today; that your father wishes you to wed the youngest niece and ward of one of my father's good friends, Cameron of Lochiel."

Fergus looked awkward, but Eilidh, choosing not to notice, continued with what she wanted to say. "Iona Cameron is quite my best friend, you know. She and I often used to play together when we were children while our fathers talked. She would make you a fine wife and I believe she could do a lot worse than be wed to you!"

"You'd let your friend have that which you choose not for yourself?" Fergus said bitterly. "Besides", he continued slightly sulkily, "it is reported that she is not over pretty!"

"Iona Cameron is a fine girl, none better, a staunch friend, kind, brave, true, an excellent horsewoman with plenty of sense and a very good education. She may not be a beauty but she has an excellent figure and is far from being plain. If she would have you, then you would indeed be a very lucky man."

"If she would have me!"

"She will have heard of some of your goings on......, she would not wish to be wed to one who spends too much of his time and money on the muslin[29] company!"

"Eilidh!"

She grinned. "Don't worry! I'll reassure Iona that it was only the experiments of your calf time and not indicative of an incurable degenerate character." She stood up. Fergus copying

---

[29] Courtesans

90

her did likewise, realising despondently that this was definitely all the time he was going to be given.

"When Ewan arrives, why don't you, Joe, Ewan and myself take a trip across the Loch in Cuchullin and pay Iona a surprise visit?" Eilidh suggested. "As you know, I travel up to Morvern after tonight's Ceilidh on business of mother's. I will not be back until after Ewan arrives but I can ask Joe to make all the arrangements. Shall we say the morning of my return?"

The bell was rung, Mary arrived and was sent to summon John Boyd, and the only reply Fergus received to his attempted remonstrances was the reassurance that Ewan was always up for any kind of caper and not to worry as to his agreeing to come, and somehow Fergus found himself outside the room and Eilidh and John Boyd inside.

He was left wondering what exactly it was that he had just been inveigled into doing and even more worrying; however was he going to get her to see sense about her future?

Chapter 10 Second Visitor to the Study

John Boyd received a warm welcome from both Eilidh and Edith when he entered the room, and as he seated himself comfortably on the chair just recently vacated by Fergus Campbell, he asked with an amused grin "What did that young fellow want then?"

It was Edith who answered, "Still mythering our Eilidh to wed him. What would she be doing with the likes of him? As if she couldnae do better than a Campbell! Though he must be dullard indeed if he thinks that Madam would let the match go ahead!" She cackled, "Madam won't want our Eilidh stepping into her shoes!"

Eilidh grinned back. "You think that Archibald Campbell is in for a shock then?"

"Nothing but what he deserves, what with carrying on behind your faither's back Eilidh, whilst he was alive, and returning to haunt the place again afore he was cold in his grave! They are welcome to each other I'd say!"

John looked at Eilidh carefully, and then said, "It would be a sensible step you know to wed the lad. He is no fool and a kindly, sober, decent fellow for all he's a Campbell."

"He's a right nice lad considering the stable he's come from, I like him very well, but not as a husband. I think my dear old friend Iona would suit him much better," Eilidh declared.

"Locheil's niece?"

"Yes."

"I'd heard rumours, that Campbell Senior had hopes that way, but everyone knows that Fergus has eyes only for yourself."

Eilidh changed the subject. "What about Ealasaid, and my milk brother?"

"That young rascal," John Boyd's brow clouded. "You know my opinion on the matter. He is a spoilt, worthless young ne'er do well."

"Ewan's not that bad! He's just thoughtless. He has very good prospects you know John. His grandfather has left him a very fine estate for when he comes of age. He and I have often been there to visit."

"Only if he survives a term at Oxford."

"True, but even he should manage that. Though I shouldn't think that he will stay much longer than the term. It is not that he is stupid, he is quite clever you know."

"Just damnably lazy and feckless. Nor do I like some of the stories I hear about the company he keeps. Not exactly faithful to my little Ealasaid is he? Nor can I see that changing."

"True, but with a good wife..."

"You are much easier on your milk brother than you are on your sister Adrianne," John Boyd said harshly.

"Perhaps," Eilidh sighed. "It's just that I know that there's not a smidgeon of harm in Ewan and I am quite certain that he will somehow always manage to land on his feet, but about Adrianne I am not so sure. Also the world will condemn such antics in Adrianne where they will be much more forgiving of my rapscallion milk brother."

"Why do you not wed him yourself then rather palm him off on my poor daughter?"

Eilidh grinned impishly. "If I did your Ealasaid would surely come up in the night and murder me and Mairi would happily aid and abet her. She might even strike the blow!" she giggled. "You wouldn't really wish me on Ewan would you?"

"Ewan's father would."

"That is only because Lachlan worries too much, and not just about me. He is worried about my brothers also. If I were betrothed to Ewan then he and Mairi would be able to be back here the sooner and thus look after me and my brothers both."

"The boys will be fine with me for the time being," retorted John shortly. "I've engaged that tutor you advised Eilidh, their nurse will of course remain. You have ensured that the estate is thriving and Johnnie and I will maintain it thus until Lachlan returns. He need not worry."

"You know Lachlan, he always worries," Eilidh sighed again. "The other boy, young Malcolm, have you dealt with him?"

"Yes, he is at present at Kiel Farm doing the dirtiest jobs I could find. I will have him back working at the stables here when Adrianne leaves to join your mother at her new home. Malcolm doesn't really enjoy the work though Eilidh. He is too independent by far!"

"Yes I know for it was that independent streak that got him into trouble in the first place. He wants to be free, to decide for himself what and when he does things. He does not like to be constrained, to do only that which is asked of him, and the sea is in his blood, it sings to him. Working on the estate is no life for such as he, not when it is the sea he hankers after. He is just like his father."

Eilidh went silent, and then after a few moments she continued quietly, "John, I would like for Malcolm to have Cuchullin after I am gone. I..., I saw his mother yesterday and talked to her. She has agreed to my leaving Cuchullin for him. I think that this incident with Adrianne has shocked her. She knows in her heart of hearts that Malcolm wants the freedom of the sea, but she has lost husband and brothers to the sea and fears to lose her son thus also. Now though I believe that she fears more the possibility that he will choose to join those that have been forced off the land by the sheep, that he will wish to sail to foreign shores to seek his fortune. If he has Cuchullin for

94

his own he may be able to wed Norah McInnis the sooner and she hopes that this will constrain him to settle here, will curb the restlessness. John, once I have gone, could you tell Malcolm that I wish him to have Cuchullin and ask that he teach young Alex and Hugh how to sail and take them to the herring fishing an' all. Please John!" she looked at him appealingly.

"Why don't you tell him yourself?" he asked gruffly

"It would come better from you. Also I don't want anyone to know, especially Adrianne, until I am long gone. She will probably claim that I am rewarding Malcolm for his misdemeanour."

"I'll tell him the week after the wedding, and don't you be worrying about Ewan and Ealasaid. If Ewan returns from England in good form I won't stand in their way."

"I know," Eilidh smiled. She passed him the keys. "I won't be requiring these any more. Edith will lock up after I've finished talking with Adrianne." She gave the old woman who yet sat on the rocking chair, busy with her knitting, but listening intently to every word, a smile before continuing. "I'm off to Morvern tomorrow and will be back the week before the wedding, but everything is all straight in here, ready for you and Johnnie to make it your own until Alex comes of age." She stood up.

John did likewise but as he stood he asked "You will have heard on your travels that King George III has died?"

Eilidh sat down again and John nothing loathe also resumed his seat.

"No," she said slowly, "no I had not heard. I am so sorry! Though," she continued thoughtfully, "perhaps I should not say thus for perhaps it was rather a blessed release, since the poor King has been mad for so many years. To be insane and shut away like that, frightened and unable to know what is real and what is not would be terrible for anyone, but for someone like His Majesty who has been used to having his every word obeyed it must have been an even worse torment. I wonder how the poor Queen feels?" she mused. "I heard it said that he even turned against her towards the end."

"His son, Prince Edward the Duke of Kent, died just a few days before," John Boyd continued grimly.

"Oh the poor Queen," cried Eilidh. "To lose husband and a son within a week of each other! How she must be feeling. The Duke of Kent was recently married was he not?"

"Yes, and he leaves behind an infant daughter. I believe she is called Victoria."

"'Tis so sad," said Eilidh softly. "Now the little Princess Victoria will never know her father, not hold any memories of him." Eilidh sat silent for a few moments, thinking of what she had just heard. Then all of a sudden she looked up and quietly stated, "The Princess Caroline, she will be distressed at the old King's death for 'tis said that he treated her better than does her own husband, the Regent, or should I now say King George IV."

"It is a sorry going on," John agreed. "With regard to the Princess Caroline however, I would imagine that she is little worse off now than she was before her father-in-law died. When her daughter Princess Charlotte[30] died so tragically in childbirth, Princess Caroline lost even the status of being the mother of the future Queen. Though I suppose," he mused, "her situation is little worse than the fate of most of our late

---

[30] Princess Charlotte, Princess of Wales and only legitimate child of King George IV. In May 1816 she wed Prince Leopold of Saxe-Coburg-Saalfeld. She died in November 1817, a few hours after giving birth to a still born son.

King George III's daughters; condemned to spinsterhood by their own father."

"At least they are accepted by Society, or most of them anyway, and they have each other. Perhaps things will improve for them all now that their brother is on the throne. However, who does Princess Caroline have who cares for her now her daughter is dead? Her husband is now King, but he does not want her," Eilidh stated quietly. "Though strangely enough the people seem to love her, although they love not our new King, have no respect for him. Are you worried John that the death of King George III will just add energy to the talk of the Insurrection?"

"You have heard then?" John replied, relief in his voice.

"Ruairidh[31], he writes to me often. John I am sorry. I know you would wish..."

"I know lass," said John reassuringly. "All my poor son can ask of you is your friendship. I would expect nothing more and he will realise it himself."

Eilidh looked despondent for a moment, and then looked up and admitted, "I..., I, wrote and asked that he return for the wedding. I will talk to him then. See if I can make him understand that there are other ways, better ways, I..., I had thought at first it was just the ideas of the young, that it was all talk, so I did not worry. Now I am not so sure and I fear..., what with things being so bad on the Sunderland Estates, and the increasing poverty of workers such as the weavers, and the unrest spreading elsewhere, the increased uneasiness over the question of suffrage and now with the old King dying..."

"So fear I, for as you say our new King is not loved!" John agreed. "His profligate spending while his people starve, his gambling, his debts and his loose ways with women, added to

---

[31] Gaelic name for the English Roderick (Rory)

his ill treatment of his wife, all mean that he is not popular with the people. My Ruairidh, he is a good boy, he means well but he is over fond of the writings of such folk as…, as … Who was that lad as wrote that infernal pamphlet that Ruairidh goes on about?...'The Rights of Man' or some such nonsense!"

Eilidh grinned at this, "Thomas Paine, I think you mean, and not all he says is nonsense, or so I think, though I must admit that I do not agree with all the ideas which he upholds. The government is however, or so I believe, over cautious to forbid his writings."

"That is as may be, but if it is filling my son's head with dangerous nonsense, I for one cannot help but agree with the government on having that pamphlet banned; for Ruairidh will pay no heed to what I say and I hesitate to call him home for good. He is a clever lad and doing right well at the University. It seems to suit him all this learning."

"Aye," Eilidh said thoughtfully, "Ruairidh is clever and compassionate, that is why he has got so involved in these plans, so excited about the thought of reform, why he attends all those meetings. It would be wrong though to take him from the University. Besides he would not stay here if he believed he would be better elsewhere. He is neither stupid, nor over biddable," she added ruefully. "I am sure however that when he has had time to think fully on the damage the French Revolution has caused in proportion to the benefits that have ensued, and when he thinks about the effect the '45 Rebellion has had on the people of the Highlands; I am sure he will not fail to realise that revolution is not the best way to effect change in the long term."

"It changed things in France. That is what he will argue," rebutted John.

"For how long? Do they not have a monarchy again? How many people got hurt and had their lives ruined by the excesses of that revolution and its aftermath? I'll warrant that the lot of the people, the lives of those that the Revolution was fought to improve, at least in theory, are no better. Ruairidh is right, change must indeed come; but by peaceful means not by way of uprisings and bloodshed. I will talk to him when he returns, as I know will you and Ann. Perhaps he will listen. Though I very much fear that many of his friends will not."

"You are a good lass Eilidh. Your father would be right proud. It is sorry I am that you are going."

"So am I, but it is time to go, I know that now. I have a feeling though that I shall never return, or at least never return for good," she said sadly. "I had thought that I could stay here forever. However when Joe told me that I travel with them when they accompany Ewan on his journey south to attend the University at Oxford, I knew it was right that I should leave. I have been getting restless these past few months and the nightmares have been getting gradually worse…, perhaps they will disappear when we depart."

"You are still getting them?"

"Yes, most nights, sometimes so bad I don't sleep. I've taken to spending the nights in the old cave down by Seal Island, which seems to help for I can always swim over to join the seals if things get really bad. Mother believes that she is upsetting me by sending me away on her errands just as Ewan is due to arrive, but to tell the truth I am pleased for it means that I get to visit all the old familiar places. I will be especially happy to travel through Morvern with all its memories of Ossian and his people. I mean also to cross over to Mull and then on to Iona; Father and I went there often and I long to go there one last time."

99

"Eilidh, you know you are always welcome at our home whatever, whenever," John said warmly, and then he paused, before asking "You will not be at the wedding will you?"

"No, mother has forbidden it and requests that we are gone the morning after or she may forbid me to go south at all," she smiled. "However I shall make especially sure that I come and see you and Ann before I go. I have so much to thank you both for. I will try and catch Ealasaid also - if she isn't too busy saying her goodbyes to Ewan that is!" she said with a grin.

"See that you do then Eilidh. I know how you are about goodbye's. God bless you!" And with this he left the room.

Chapter 11 The Third Visitor

As soon as John Boyd left the room Eilidh turned to her companion saying, "Edith, I understand that my mother intends to accompany Adrianne when she comes to talk to me this evening. I thought perhaps they would be happier in the Library than in here as it is much less formal and certainly more comfortable."

The kindly older woman nodded in agreement, and although she said nothing her eyes spoke her concern, her understanding of the difficulties inherent in the forthcoming meeting.

After a few moments, hesitantly, Eilidh spoke again, "Edith, I..., I probably won't be returning here for some time. I would like to say thanks for, for everything..." she stopped, unable to continue.

"Lassie, it's been a pleasure. I'll see that no one else has the key to this here study, only my grand-daughter Mary will come in to clean, she's a good lass knows how to keep mum she does. You'll be fine Eilidh. You're your father's daughter."

Eilidh came over and gave her a hug. No more able to speak, she left the room quickly.

The chamber that Eilidh next entered was library only in name, more like a parlour, laid out with comfortable chairs and settee grouped around a fire bigger and brighter than the one in the preceding room. It contained books enough to merit the name of library, but the main focus of this room was the enormous pianoforte, which was standing open at one end of the room. Eilidh now walked over to this instrument, sat down and began to play; even to the ignorant she was no novice, the music was quite exquisite.

So indeed was the woman who only minutes later burst unannounced into the room. Everything about her cried out to be noticed from the tips of her delicate beautifully shod feet to the top of her elegant head. She was built on generous proportions, some would call her majestic, and none could deny her appeal. Love her or hate her, all acknowledged that Caroline Maclean was a captivating, fascinating woman whose glamour few could resist. One of those most obviously smitten was the gentleman who accompanied her, and he was almost as handsome as she was. He had been at her side in some form or another nearly thirty years. Caroline Maclean was forty five years old but you wouldn't have supposed that she numbered even five and thirty. Still less would you believe her to be the mother of ten children, all of whom but the eldest were still living. Her eldest daughter had died but recently, only hours after giving birth to her second child.

There could be no mistaking whose daughter was the girl who followed her so reluctantly into the room. It was said that Adrianne possessed all the looks that her mother had as a girl. It was also mooted that she lacked almost all the charisma that the older woman exuded.

The musician at the piano was allegedly Adrianne's full sister, although in appearance they were most dissimilar. Despite this the musician also bore a strong resemblance to their mother, not in looks, but in the way she moved, in the assurance of her manner, in her sheer vitality. For both possessed 'The Glamour' and wore it as an invisible cloak, unconsciously.

The music stopped as soon as they entered. Eilidh rose, vibrant, beautiful, and advanced towards them smiling.

"Madam, Sir, Adrianne, thank you for coming. I will try to take up your time for as short a period as possible." She turned to her sister. "I understand your reluctance to discuss this matter with me Adrianne but, considering the delicate nature of the complaint, I felt sure that it was better that I rather than John Boyd talk with you."

"He could have consulted myself, or Mr Campbell and thus rendered your impudent interference unnecessary," retorted her mother.

"Madam, I agree that he would have been more than happy to have communicated with you in person the details of the punishment Malcolm has received for his misdemeanour. However it was not principally to appraise Adrianne as to the manner in which Malcolm has been chastised that I wished to meet with her. He has, or so I believe, been dealt with satisfactorily and has learned a valuable lesson from the affair. I wished rather to discuss with Adrianne her future plans."

"Those are no concern of yours," stated her mother icily. "In which case we shall depart at once, and look to John Boyd for our information. Come Adrianne!"

"Madam I beg you reconsider," said Eilidh anxiously. "At least listen to what I have to say." She turned to her sister pleadingly, "Adrianne, father asked that I look out for you, he said that one of his deepest regrets was that he did not get to know you as well as he would have liked. I asked to see you as I believed that father would have wished me to speak to you on this issue."

Eilidh then looked at her mother before continuing, "I was not confident Madam that you would feel it necessary to talk bluntly to Adrianne about the possible repercussions of the type of allegation that she made about Malcolm," she said apologetically. "That was what I wished to discuss with my sister."

Her mother looked furious, and was about to speak when the third member of the party spoke.

"Linnie, we are here already. I understand fully the impertinence of this person's behaviour, and agree with you that she has no right to concern herself with the matter. However I confess to a slight curiosity with regard to the manner in which she conducts herself. It is important to the success of your little scheme that she does nothing that will disgust the gentleman whose attentions you are hoping that she will command. Indeed Linnie I must confess that I am quite fascinated to observe a living copy of those pictures that lined your father's walls. Quite, quite fascinated Linnie! If I am satisfied with her demeanour this evening I could almost feel that your plan could work."

The woman looked doubtful, but her anger seemed gradually to be evaporating. "Of course it will work," she snapped. "How can you doubt me?"

"Come, Linnie. To please me. Remember I too wish to be revenged."

Eilidh's mother appeared as though she were still about to refuse, then she shrugged and said indifferently, "As you wish," and turning to Eilidh said coldly, "Mr Campbell it seems wishes to ignore your impudence and is agreeable to hearing what it is that you have to say." She looked again at Mr Campbell, smiling now, "Well, shall we be seated? If we are to talk then we may as well be comfortable."

"My thanks," said Eilidh quietly. "Would you like me to send for something to drink, some refreshments?"

This was refused.

Eilidh's mother now made her way to the chairs by the fire and sat down, motioning for Adrianne and Archibald Campbell to do likewise, but before they could follow suit Eilidh made to address her sister "Adrianne are you sure you wish to have Mr Campbell with us for this discussion?"

Her mother interrupted quickly, "I have asked that her *step* father accompany us, so that he may hear what you have to say and get some first-hand experience of your lies and deceit."

Without further argument Eilidh settled herself on a seat some distance from where the others had made themselves comfortable, but where she could see all three of them at once. Without further preamble she came straight to the point.

"Adrianne, John Boyd and I have investigated your allegation regarding the stable lad Malcolm. We understood that you claimed that he tried to kiss you when you came out to the stables to see your mare. Malcolm has denied that the incident occurred in the manner that you related and instead asserted that it was you who made the advances to him. He claims that you got annoyed when he refused you and that you made the accusations out of pique."

"The boy is obviously lying. I want him whipped and immediately dismissed," demanded the girls' mother.

"Unfortunately, it is not for you to make that decision," Eilidh said apologetically. "However Malcolm has been punished, but not for the crime he has been accused of."

"That is infamous. I will not have it so. I demand that you send for John Boyd at once so the matter may be dealt with properly."

"He was here about fifteen minutes ago Ma'am, during which time he informed me that the lad has been reprimanded and already begun his punishment. He has been transferred to a more menial position at another location and will not be returning until after your wedding. In future whenever Adrianne is at home Malcolm will be transferred to work in some other place."

Eilidh turned again to Adrianne, and asked her gently, "Adrianne, did you not know that Malcolm Mor's heart was already bestowed elsewhere, that he is betrothed to Norah MacInnis? Your accusations almost cost him his betrothal as Norah's father was most concerned when he learned of your allegations."

Eilidh's comments were met by a stony faced silence, but she continued undeterred with her explanations. "You may not have noticed Adrianne, but for some time now all work on your horses has been carried out by the older men, or myself when I am available. All the stable boys have been instructed to vacate the area when you are known to be in the vicinity. This practice was enforced in the hope that it would prevent the occurrence of any incidents or allegations such as that which you made with regard to Malcolm, or worse, an incident such as what happened, or should I say what nearly happened in the barn between yourself and Seamus, if Johnnie Boyd hadn't been passing at an inopportune moment."

Adrianne glanced quickly at her mother as she heard this but could discern no reaction on her parent's face.

Eilidh observing this, calmly went on talking. "Yes Adrianne, that is why Seamus is not around. He too has been temporarily sent away, much chastened and very unhappy, for Seamus, unlike Malcolm, did fall for your charms. He is now nursing a broken heart and is lucky to have escaped a breakage someplace else, as from what I heard his father was none too happy when he learned of the doings of his heir. Malcolm Mor was punished, not for the disrespectful behaviour you accused him of Adrianne, but for disobedience. Malcolm believing himself immune to your various wiles and ah..., other attractions, mistakenly considered that this rendered the orders given with regard to yourself unnecessary, so far as he was concerned. He has had to learn the hard way that he may not always be in possession of the full facts as to the reasons behind any instruction that he is given. In future he will ask permission before he disobeys an order." She stopped and looked at her sister, waiting for her response.

The reaction to her comments came from elsewhere.

"It is lies! All lies! How can you tell such lies?" cried her mother. "How dare you! It is due to jealousy! Jealousy of my youngest daughter who has a place in my household such as you desire to have and who is a thousand times more beautiful than you are! Lies told for spite and revenge because you wish to have what she has. My late husband mistakenly gave you to believe that you have a right to his name and now when you find yourself about to be reduced to your correct situation in life, you use the authority he should never have given you to try to gain revenge on an innocent girl!" her mother exclaimed furiously.

Eilidh looked at her mother calmly for a few moments, before replying sadly, "You are right, I too must accept some of the blame for the situation, but only in so far as I did not earlier explain personally to Adrianne why John Boyd and I had decided to put in place the measures that I have just mentioned. If I had discussed my concerns with her sooner then perhaps that in itself would have rendered the measures unnecessary. Adrianne may have felt able at that point to amend her behaviour and none of the unfortunate incidents with Malcolm and Seamus would then have occurred and we would not be sitting here today. I confess that at the time I was too much aware of the awkwardness of the situation and felt great reluctance, as in truth I feel now, to discuss the subject with her." She turned now to her sister and said sincerely. "I am truly very sorry Adrianne for my neglect. This omission grieves me the more as father especially asked me to look out for you

Adrianne. He always felt he should have spent more time with you and that your lack of confidence was somehow his fault."

"Lack of confidence!" cried Adrianne. Shaken at last out of her silence.

"Yes, why else should anyone as beautiful as you seek to gain the attentions of any and every man or boy available, if not to bolster her self-confidence?" Eilidh looked at Adrianne openly admiring. "I have never met, nor seen a more beautiful creature than yourself, apart from our mother of course!"

"How dare you!" interjected their mother angrily.

Eilidh ignored their mother's interruption and merely continued to address her sister. "Adrianne, our mother chooses not to see that which is before her eyes and hence she refuses to correct your behaviour. It therefore falls to me, in accordance with our father's wishes and with the hope that your future behaviour neither lends disgrace to his memory nor ruins your reputation, to advise you as to what is a more acceptable form of behaviour. It is for this reason I have asked you to come."

"And if I refuse to listen to your presumptuous advice! Indeed why should I listen to a filthy changeling peasant?" cried Adrianne furiously. "How can a whore advise the daughter of a lady as to the correct mode of behaviour?"

"Any God fearing individual could give you sound advice on how to act in due modesty as behoves a Christian maiden. However I am not come to lecture you on the morality of chaste behaviour, but to discuss your future ambitions. I understand that our mother is proposing to take you to London next year and have you presented at court, with I suspect the purpose of your making an advantageous marriage," Eilidh answered tranquilly, no whit put out by her mother's fury or her sister's vitriol.

"So you are jealous," retorted Adrianne with evident satisfaction. "I knew you would be. I will get the man you have been dreaming about all these months!"

"Incidentally, Adrianne," replied Eilidh curiously. "How did you get that picture?"

"I saw you drawing it as we came out of church. Remember you jumped up when you saw me and tried to hide the pictures. I knew you were coming back to the house and when I heard you playing I saw the study open, you had left the pictures on the desk. I only took one, in case you should miss them," she said smugly. "Now, I get to meet him, and it is you he will not even look at as you will not be fit to be admitted into polite society."

Eilidh looked amused. "I never did, nor do I now, have any pretensions to be admitted into polite society; our mother has made sure of that. However if you Adrianne do have any intentions of beguiling this Earl of Hindley into matrimony then you needs think very carefully about your behaviour. Beauty, which I confess you have in abundance, will not suffice on its own. A gentleman such as he is will want to be quite certain that his heirs are fathered by himself and not by some other known or unknown individual. Any hint of immorality on your part will make him, or any other, keep well away. Unfortunately Adrianne, whilst it may be acceptable for a man to play the field, society will censure such behaviour in a seventeen year old debutante."

"What does such as you know of the preferences of Earls?" Adrianne spat contemptuously.

"You forget that father frequently took me to Edinburgh and to London in the guise of his nephew and as such I met a number of interesting people and heard a lot of gossip. I understand that the Earl of Hindley is one of the Corinthian Set and that he is quite infamous, but although I may have heard his name mentioned in conversation I confess that I do not recollect ever having seen him and one would think with such a physique he would be a memorable sight."

"So you do find him attractive!" Adrianne exulted triumphantly.

"I should think anyone would," Eilidh replied lightly. "Though his way of life, if reports are true, I find less admirable. If you were successful in obtaining his love Adrianne I would wish you well, but the chances of anyone being happy with such a one are slight. Fergus, I would imagine, has told you his opinion of his character and itemised his faults as he understands them. However it was not my purpose to encourage or discourage you in your pursuit of any particular personage, only to advise you that liaisons with stable boys, and such others who you can have no matrimonial interest in, will not promote your ambitions; indeed will do the reverse. I suggest that you minimise your contact with all such persons, in order to reduce temptation."

Eilidh now turned to her mother and future step father, "I would advise you Madam and you Sir to keep a watchful eye on your daughter to her good benefit. For indeed," and here her voice filled with admiration and warmth, "I have no doubt that if her undoubted beauty and intelligence are coupled to good sense and chastity, Adrianne will not fail in her ambition and before long the society papers will report that Adrianne has contracted a very beneficial alliance. Indeed I hope and pray that will be the case."

She stood up and turned once again to her sister, "I suspect Adrianne that our paths are likely to cross but little in the future, please be assured of my best wishes for your every success."

The older woman remained seated. "You may have finished with us, but I have not finished with you. Sit down."

Eilidh obediently complied with her order.

Her mother then turned to Adrianne and said harshly, "Pay no heed to her lies, they are due to ignorance and jealousy." Then she transferred her attention back to Eilidh and in a voice oozing with malice she purred, "It may have escaped your notice that in less than a month I shall be remarried. Under the terms of my late husband's will you will then pass into the joint care of myself and Lachlan Beaton, rather than that of Lachlan and John Boyd as you are at present. You will from this point on have no further interest in this Estate, which belongs to my eldest son. A year after my marriage you pass into the joint care of my husband and myself. Indeed if you fail to obey Lachlan in our plans for you in this year you will fall into my and Mr Campbell's care prematurely and Lachlan will no longer have any jurisdiction whatsoever over your future. You were aware of all this were you not?" she demanded.

Eilidh nodded her head.

"A strange will," murmured Mr Campbell.

Eilidh smiled at him and answered, "Father felt that it would look odd if the woman he claimed was my mother did not have guardianship over me, but he decided to transfer it slowly to give us both a chance to get used to the new situation." She glanced quickly over to her mother, who was glowering impatiently at her interruption.

"I understand that you have not as yet been informed as to the details of our plans for your future," her mother interrupted stridently. "I had intended that Mairi tell you of them at a later date but since you are here then it might be better if I explain them to you myself. Mairi and I have been in discussion over the winter and we have come up with the following

111

arrangement. You will leave with Mairi and Lachlan the morning after the wedding; I understand they are travelling south so that Ewan can go to Oxford. It is their intention to visit Mairi's mother for a few days on their way there. When they depart to continue their journey, you will remain behind with Mairi's mother who has agreed to supervise your training."

"My training! My training for what?" Eilidh asked quickly.

"Are you so stupid that you have not yet realised what occupation Mairi's mother used to have? One has only to look at her to guess," she replied derisively.

"She is indeed very beautiful despite her great age, but that in itself need not suggest any profession which she may have undertaken in her youth," Eilidh retorted calmly.

"Well I suppose," her mother admitted contemptuously, "it may be that Mairi did not tell you. She is after all ashamed of it, and well she might be as her mother stole my grandfather. She was nothing but a common whore who kept my grandfather away from my grandmother by God knows what lures, allurements and tricks. Then she induced him in his dotage to leave some estate or other and such money that was not entailed, to that equally worthless grandson of hers!"

"Ewan is very conscious of his good fortune in having a grandfather so well disposed to him," Eilidh acknowledged with a fond smile, before retorting, "However Madam I am at a loss to understand of what possible concern all this that you say with regard to his grandmother, could be to me. You can surely not wish for me to learn the arts of the Courtesan?"

"That is precisely what I do mean."

"But Madam, consider!" Eilidh cried, for a moment her calm visibly shaken. "You cannot have considered the dishonour to my father, to our whole family, if I undertook such a position. I understand that you feel it cannot affect yourself as you claim

112

that I am not your daughter, but father claimed otherwise, that Adrianne and the other girls are my sisters, that Alex and Hugh are my brothers! It would be shameful for them!"

"I have considered carefully," her mother replied maliciously. "You will of course realise that down south, that in London, none in Society will know you. There are none who will gainsay me when I claim that you are none of mine, that you are a fraud intent on claiming name and position that you have no right to. I have my reasons which I neither wish, nor need, to divulge to you. I demand this of you to the benefit, not to the detriment of my interests." She smiled malevolently.

Eilidh, calm again, looked at her mother carefully before replying. "You may not realise Ma'am, but Mairi's mother dislikes me almost as much as you yourself do and would never teach me. Indeed she could never bear to have me long even in the same room as herself; she maintained that my presence grated on her nerves."

"I believe that Mairi did make mention of that small detail, but she also assured me that her contacts are such that she could easily find some other woman to train you and to…, and, ah…, what is the expression? Yes that is it, she would with very little trouble to herself, find an 'Abbess' who would manage things for you, put you in touch with the right people when the time comes …"

"By the right people I assume you mean rich gentlemen," interjected Eilidh now looking amused.

Her mother was visibly irritated by this lack of seriousness. "What else! What with your alleged riding skills I have suggested that you would fit very well among those 'Pretty Horse Breakers', or whatever it is they call themselves."

"I had thought that ladies were supposed to know nothing of that sort of female," Eilidh fenced lightly.

113

Her mother ignored this, merely asserting, "I will be very much displeased if I hear that you are causing any trouble or are disobedient to my orders. I have told Mairi the name of the particular gentleman whose interest I am most set on you gaining, but I will settle for any other of reasonable stature and importance. If you are not successful it will be the worse for you. There is a very nice little asylum that I have in mind whose proprietor owes me a few favours," she smiled unpleasantly. "Your arrogant treatment of myself and Adrianne today has made it certain that if my plan fails then things will go very ill with you, very ill indeed."

Eilidh looked at her mother calmly. "I knew when I decided to talk to Adrianne that it would count against me when I was eventually under your guardianship. This plan though that you and Mairi have put together..., I must suggest that it will not do. I have no argument with doing the training, such as will not involve me in dishonour. Indeed it might be amusing to learn how to wear the pretty dresses and to dance the lady's part in all the dances rather than the gentleman's. However Madam, though I honour you greatly I love and honour God more and will go willingly into no man's bed excepting that of he to whom I am lawfully wed."

"What respectable man will marry you when you have neither fortune nor name?" retorted her mother derisively.

"I never expected nor wished marriage Madam, I had other plans. Indeed Madam, I have never had any interest in beaus or such like," replied Eilidh quietly.

"Indeed you will never marry," her mother sneered. "For I will never sanction any marriage and I have no doubt that you will be dead long before you come of age; though if needs be you will spend those last few remaining months of your life in an asylum. Now what is it to be, go south with Lachlan and

Mairi and do what you are told, or agree that the pact is broken and you are in my sole guardianship and I will have my debt off the asylum proprietor paid?"

Before Eilidh could answer Mr Campbell interrupted. "What is this of the girl dying? Has she some disease? Why was I not told of this?"

"The Changelings always die young," replied his betrothed in a voice full of loathing. "None gain their twenty first year. If they survive at all!"

Eilidh looked at her, confusion in her eyes. "What is this you are saying Madam?" she asked. "Do you realise that by ascertaining that there is something in my heritage that you thus know, you are indirectly acknowledging my legitimacy and for this indeed I thank you."

"Much good it will do you since none here will repeat it in public. Now how do you answer?" her mother demanded.

"I will go with Lachlan and Mairi and I will receive whatever training that will not conflict with my beliefs. Other than that I cannot promise," Eilidh answered quietly.

"Good, I thought you would see sense." A pleased almost gloating, expectant smile crossed her face. "Now we shall see who laughs longest!" and the man and the woman exchanged triumphant glances and stood up.

Eilidh stood up also and bowed. "My best wishes to yourself and Mr Campbell. I hope that you have a long and very happy marriage." She turned to her sister. "Adrianne, I do indeed wish you very well. Do remember what I have said to you this afternoon." She looked again at her mother and Archibald Campbell and said quietly, "Please excuse me, I have a ceilidh to prepare for before I set off on that Morvern trip that you requested of me. Be assured Madam that I shall be ready to leave with Lachlan and his party the morning after your wedding."

Her mother and sister looked at her frostily but silently.

Mr Campbell however spoke, albeit hesitantly, "I understand that I have you to thank for the fine colt that my mare birthed last night."

Eilidh's face lit up for a moment. Then she gave an impish grin as she replied, "That would be Liath Macha you should thank for that!"

Archibald Campbell laughed, "Let us hope the colt has inherited his temperament off his Dam and not his Sire." Then he asked tentively, "You are to be at the Ceilidh tonight?"

"Yes, I had intended to be there."

"My son has been trying to persuade me to attend. He tells me that it will be entertaining."

Eilidh smiled, "If you come I will recite for you the Lay of Diarmed," and with that she left.

Chapter 12 Adrianne Maclean Attends a Ceilidh

The clamour of swathes of loud music could be heard reverberating joyfully out of Hamish Cameron's barn. As they drew nearer to the source of this merriment, Archibald Campbell, his son Fergus and Adrianne Maclean could see small groups of people standing around laughing and talking. The conversations quietened as the threesome approached but none greeted them other than with a quick nod of the head before looking quickly away. The elder of the three tightened his mouth but walked on resolutely, while Adrianne only noticed that as they moved away those loitering outside the barn turned again, this time to stare.

This pleased Adrianne. She was used to being stared at. She had not at first enjoyed coming to the local ceilidhs, not until she was older, not until she realised how pleasurable it was to be so unreservedly and universally admired. She did not doubt that it was at she they were staring, did not notice the less than friendly looks.

It must be over a year since she had last attended a ceilidh, Adrianne mused, not since her father had died. There had been no one who would take her. Her mother had not approved of her attendance at what she called 'those uncouth gatherings of the unwashed and unlettered, the ignorant and the vulgar.' Indeed her mother had opposed her daughters' attendance on each and every occasion that her father had suggested that one or other of them accompany him to a ceilidh or any other such gathering, declaring that although *he* might enjoy low company that did not mean that his daughters should be subjected to its unhealthy influence. Why her mother had wasted her breath she had never understood, for despite being the most unassuming of men her father invariably achieved what he wanted. Despite her claim to better breeding, sooner or later she would find she had to accede, however reluctantly, to her husband's requests.

Similarly he, usually the gentlest, kindest, the most indulgent of fathers, would react with unjust severity to any act or comment from his children which he deemed to be undermining of the local people; whom he regularly required them to meet, no matter how poor or ill those individuals might be. He would explain that though these people may have had the misfortune to be born into less wealthy families than their own, this did not make them inferior, nor did it mean that they could be treated with less respect. If their good Lord Jesus washed the feet of his brethren, he had been want to say, the least they could do was treat any and every individual they came across with kindness.

As a small child she had been terrified that he would one day insist on her washing the feet of the filthiest beggar he could find. For a time it had made her extremely circumspect in her behaviour, at least whilst he was watching, all the while resolving that never, never would she be forced into such a disgustingly repugnant task.

Adrianne remembered how her father had insisted that it was their duty to treat well those who looked to them for employment and those that held land on their estates, because these people were dependent on them for their very livelihood.

Her mother had disagreed, had indeed argued the antithesis; maintaining that the common people needed to be shown who was superior, that if you allowed them any familiarity they would abuse this by laziness and insolence. When she had attempted to explain this to her father however, he had proved stubbornly, immovably, unreasonable. He had avowed that she would only be treated with disregard if she were not worthy of being shown respect, stating adamantly that respect had to be earned, that it was very different from fear, which he suggested she had confused it with. Her father had seemed quite unable to grasp the fact that they were owed this respect due to their greater gentility and intrinsic superiority and that it was extremely important that the commoners be brought to appreciate this for their own general improvement.

Her mother taught that servants and those of their station in life expected to look up to their betters, that they would be confused if they were shown undue familiarity. Her father however refused to countenance either this idea or her mother's stated view that it was as much the lot in life of the poor to serve, as it was the right of the rich to be served.

Eventually she had learned that it was useless to argue thus with her father if she wished to continue with her privileges. Indeed he had threatened to make her work in the stables for a week with 'that girl' he called her sister, if she did not show more respect for 'the commoners'. So she had complied and ceased to argue with him, but secretly she had continued to hold to the same opinions as her mother. She had watched the elegant way her mother behaved with the servants and seen how they were so much more respectful of her than they were of her father. Why some of them behaved as if they were his equal! True, they never disobeyed an order, but there was that in their manner that was just too overfriendly. They were never so with her mother. She would ensure they were never so with her either.

The door opened and they were met with a sudden influx of heat and noise. Gradually the clamour died away as first one and then another noticed who it was who stood at the entrance.

At that moment four boys rushed towards the doorway, almost colliding into them. One of these boys stopped abruptly and a strident voice pierced the silence. "What are you doing here Aidie?" was the vociferous demand.

On hearing this someone laughed and gradually the noise and buzz of chatter resumed.

"Don't call me that…, I might ask the same of you. Does mother know that you are here?" Adrianne demanded indignantly.

"Nurse brought us," Hugh returned smugly. "Eilidh is to sing and tell some stories and we are to perform a play. We have been practicing and practicing. I am to be Donald Maclean, you know…, the 1st Laird! Have you come to listen to our play or are you come to see Seamus? He's not here you know. Eilidh sent him away!" He said this last comment with decided satisfaction.

"Just wait until Mother hears about this!" Adrianne threatened, annoyance in her voice, but her brother had already disappeared, after a sideways glance at the elder of her companions.

She had hoped that Seamus would be here. He at least admired her, listened to her, considered her to be clever as well as beautiful. Of course she did not really like him, he was too common, but she was so bored.

For the thousandth time Adrianne bemoaned the unfairness of it having been the Changeling whom her father had taken everywhere, told everything to, let help with the running of the estate. She too wanted to travel, not be stuck in this boring bog. Had he never thought that she, as well as his precious Changeling, might have wanted the opportunity to attend the University? No matter that she had not a head for Latin and Greek; and as for music and maths! That freak had nothing better to do than read those boring things - if she really did!

Well change was coming, next year she and her mother were going to London and then it would be she, Adrianne, with the adventures. It would be she who had all the admirers. It would be she who was held to be important, who people came to when a decision had to be made.

Quite why she had come here tonight she did not know. It had not been to see Seamus, though his presence would have made the experience more bearable, for she knew that she would be unable to see him alone here. Perhaps it was that afternoon's mention of her father, perhaps this had caused her to feel some nostalgia. Also Fergus had particularly urged her to come. There couldn't be any harm in encouraging attention from him. He was quite eligible, not quite as handsome as his father, but he dressed much more elegantly. Some said he was a dandy, but she knew that that was just due to jealousy.

They had arrived just in time to see three lads dancing the Highland fling. One of Duncan Lovell's boys was playing the bag pipe.

It gave Adrianne an odd feeling to see Joe play rather than his father Duncan. For as long as she could remember Duncan had been there. When her father was alive Duncan had never been far from his side. Now Duncan also was leaving. John Boyd himself had told her this. He was leaving to oversee her brother's estate in Fife. Lachlan usually looked after this, but Lachlan and Mairi were travelling down to England to settle their son Ewan at university there.

Adrianne Maclean liked to keep abreast of all that happened on the Estate; liked to feel she knew all the happenings in the area, and beyond. Did not her mother say that information gave one power, that you never knew when a seemingly worthless, uninteresting bit of news would be useful.

Suddenly Adrianne saw *her*. For once she was on her own and she was seated beside a clarsach. 'The clarsach that should by rights have been mine', fumed Adrianne, 'for it had belonged to *my* grandmother, not that creature's'. Adriane had loved her grandmother intensely and could remember so very clearly the day that she had been told her grandmother had gone to live with the angels. She remembered the rage she had felt that the angels rather than she should have her beloved grandmother. How she had hated those angels. They had each other and all those other people who had gone to live with them, while she had no one. Her father was more interested in that Changeling, and after the boys were born even her mother did not give her much attention.

She was never sure quite how much she loved her mother, or indeed if she loved her at all. She was so very beautiful, but she could also be very frightening. She had even heard it whispered by the maids how her father had ordered them to go straight to see him 'if they saw Madam being too severe with her children'.

A sweet sound suddenly tore through the air, drawing Adrianne's attention away from her memories and back again to the clarsach and the girl who sat next to it.

The instrument was beautiful, a small harp, delicately made, encrusted with jewels and intricate carvings. Its age was a matter for conjecture, its history unknown. It had come into the family with her grandmother, and so was not an original Maclean artefact.

The girl who sat next to it was as delicate and beautiful as the instrument she tuned. She wore a long simply made skirt and her rough wool shirt was fastened high up about her neck, covering her arms down to her tiny wrists. She displayed neither ornament nor jewel about her person.

The severity of the musicians dress was in marked contrast to the sparkle in her eyes, the merry curve to her mouth and the light, joyful way she carried herself. If the blithe figure and lovely countenance hadn't been sufficient to catch one's attention, then the colour of her hair would undoubtedly cause one to pause and stare. That hair so strictly bound and controlled, almost as if to hide its glory, was made up of strands of auburn red and corn gold which glistened in the light like a halo around her head.

While most folk stared and admired, Adrianne stared in scorn. To her it was further evidence that the girl was no sister of hers but the Changeling that her mother claimed her to be. She watched as Joe Lovell, the young man who had just been playing the bagpipes, walked over to talk to the girl. Adrianne looked on disparagingly, she knew that Joe wished to wed the creature, and she knew also that her father had refused to give his consent to the match but that irrespective of this Joe still doted on, was mesmerised by her. 'It was witchcraft', so her mother said, 'taught her by the witch Kai-Ying whom she had lived with.' Adrianne shuddered. 'Not that the Changeling needed witchcraft to attract any man. She at least had no difficulty in understanding why all the men found *the creature* so fascinating! She would have plenty of opportunity to encourage them, living as she did in that cottage all on her own, or in that disgusting cave. And she dared to censure her, Adrianne! When she herself was guilty of far worse behaviour! Despite her pretence at always having a chaperone before seeing a man on her own! Still,' Adrianne admitted to herself, 'she supposed that there was some truth in what the Changeling had said. If she wanted to marry well she would have to be more circumspect. She most certainly did not to wish to damage her chances due to a bit of harmless dalliance.'

Adrianne watched as the Changeling plucked another note on the Clarsach.

As the clear sound pierced the air the musician looked up and surveyed her audience as expectantly, the cheerful chatter hushed. Then she began to speak.

Even Adrianne had to acknowledge that the Changeling had a most beautiful voice.

Chapter 13 Diarmuid O' Duibhne

"As this is the last time for a while that I will be able to attend one of these ceilidhs Paidraig, our seannachie, has permitted me to choose which story I tell tonight."

Eilidh paused, looking to the back of the room to where Adrianne and her two companions were seated, before continuing.

"You will all have noticed that we have surprise guests with us tonight, that my sister Adrianne has brought with her two who have not previously had the pleasure of attending one of our ceilidhs."

Most now turned curiously to follow her gaze to where the two Campbell men sat.

"I am sure you all know that Archibald Campbell is soon to marry my mother. Our other guest is his son Fergus and his father's marriage will thus shortly make him my brother."

There was a half heard comment from one of the audience followed by an audible chuckle from some of the others, as most there knew that young Fergus Campbell wished to claim relationship other than brother with the fair story teller.

Eilidh waited a few moments and then continued, ignoring the friendly banter. "I thought that a story in honour of them, in recognition of who they are, would be in order." She smiled across at the two men who were soon to be so closely related to her by the marriage of her mother.

"All know Clann Duibhne, or Clan Campbell as they are now known, to be descended from Diarmuid O'Duibhne. My own inestimable mother, soon to be linked with this house, will in all probability take their emblem of the Boar's Head as her own. I would like therefore to tell the story as to why the Boar's Head is connected with Clann Duibhne. The tale is particularly apt as it begins with the wedding of the King of Morvern."

Eilidh smiled again at the two men as she said this. Then she began to play:

"Many, many years ago when giants and the fairy folk roamed these Glens and took an interest in the affairs of men, in the days when bards sang tales of heroic deeds, tales of bravery, chivalry, love and honour, tales of men of great integrity who dared to fight for and uphold that which is right, and that which is true. Into that time was born Diarmuid, foster son of Aonghus Og, the god of Love and Beauty.

Diarmuid, was blessed with two quite extraordinary gifts. On his heel was the Ball Dorain[32], such that he could not be killed unless this mole was pierced; while on his forehead was the Ball Seirc[33], and thus could no woman look upon him without feeling love for him welling up within her heart.

Diarmuid grew up into a handsome, brave, strong and clever young man who was much loved and esteemed by all his fellow warriors and companions. In the trial at arms few could best him and many are the songs that are sung and the great tales that are told of his boldness, his valour, and his daring and chivalrous deeds.

Soon Diarmuid came to the notice of that great warrior king, Fingal[34], Righ[35] of our own beautiful Morvern[36], who granted him the greatest accolade of all; membership of his select group

---

[32] A mole.

[33] A beauty spot.

[34] Fingal was called Fionn Mac Cumhail by the Irish or Finn. MacLauchlan of Rissipal published a book containing translations of poems alleged to have been composed by the great Bard Ossian, Fingal's son. He alleged that Fingal had been the King of Morvern.

[35] King.

[36] Macleans had owned land in Morvern for many centuries.

of warriors, the Feinne. *Fingal was the leader of this legendary band and he and his loyal Feinne[37] hunted throughout the length and breadth of these grand wild hills that are all around us.*

Now the Ard Righ[38] was Cormac Mac Art and he had a daughter so beautiful that tales of her comeliness had spread far and wide and many were they who came to beg of him the hand of his daughter in marriage.

However Cormac counted all who came as unworthy of receiving the hand of his beloved daughter Grainne, and rejected all suitors; until the day that Fingal came to eat at his table.

Grainne was young and she was most lovely, with raven hair and cheeks pink with the flush of first youth, skin as alabaster and teeth like tiny pearls, while her lips were red as if brushed with the fresh juice of the berry.

Fingal, when he beheld this vision was intoxicated by the sight and immediately entreated Cormac for permission to wed his daughter. The Ard Righ considered that only one of such renown as the great leader of the Feinne would be worthy of this pearl, his most precious jewel, and so he most joyfully and willingly agreed to their betrothal.

Grainne, the proud and enchanting daughter of the High King, was not so pleased with this arrangement. She had dreamed of a mate young and bonny, one sweet with the breath of youth still on him. She longed for love, for a husband who would adore and worship her and her alone; and Fingal was no longer young. Although time had as yet not touched his vigour, Fingal's hair had been white for many a long year.

---

[37] The Feinne (Fianna), were an elite military order. They were the band of warriors who guarded the High King of Ireland.
[38] High King.

The beautiful Grainne, spoiled and impetuous, vowed that this aged warrior was not for her. Long she sought to discover a way to escape this union that was so distasteful to her. With great sighs and many tears she begged her father to reconsider, to wait a while before giving her to so repulsive a bridegroom.

However Cormac was wrath with the ingratitude and foolishness of his daughter and would not listen to her importuning.

Grainne though was no wit discouraged and seeing Fingal's son, the great Bard Ossian, and sensing his compassion, she begged him, with tears dripping down her beautiful face, begged him to take her away, to rescue her from this marriage which she did not desire.

But Ossian's heart was hardened. He would not steal away his father's bride.

Then came Diarmuid into the presence of his liege; fresh from the hills had come Diarmuid, and the breath of the wind was in his hair, his was the gait of the wild deer and the strength of the boar.

Through eyes that were filled with tears Grainne saw Diarmuid: she saw him, saw the ball seirc on his brow and immediately knew herself to be in love with him. She vowed she must have Diarmuid or die.

Alas for Diarmuid thus to awaken the love of the spoiled and troubled daughter of Cormac Mac Art.

Three times came she unto him, and begged with many tears and professions of love, begged that he take her away, rescue her from this hateful marriage; else she would surely die. Three times he refused.

At last, despairing of ever persuading him to betray his King, unused to having her wishes slighted, she put on him a geas[39] whereby he would have to obey her bidding.

So it was that Diarmuid O' Duibhne stole the bride of Fingal, King of Morvern, chieftain of the legendary Feinne.

Great was the rage of Fingal when he found his bride gone. Great was his fury at the treachery of Diarmuid!

War parties were sent forth throughout the land to find Grainne and kill Diarmuid.

Fingal and the Feinne searched frantically for Diarmuid and Grainne, but to no avail. Far and wide did they hunt for the lost daughter of the Ard Righ, but the cleverness and craftiness of Diarmuid and the aid of Aonghus Og saved them from capture time after time.

Many are the tales that are told of the pursuit of Diarmuid and Grainne.

At first Diarmuid remained true to his King, and treated Grainne only as a sister, but this did not long please Grainne and at length she beguiled Diarmuid into love with her and the fruit of this union was four strong handsome sons.

As the years went by the followers of Fingal greatly missed their noble friend and pleaded with their King to pardon Diarmuid, blaming the wiles of Grainne for his treachery. They urged him again and again forgive Diarmuid, to recognise that though he had been wrong to steal away Fingal's bride, no ill intent towards Fingal himself had been meant.

But the long years that had passed by had failed to assuage the rage in the heart of Fingal. Instead his fury grew ever stronger and there lurked within his heart no forgiveness.

Grainne soon tired of being hunted and pursued. She longed for reconciliation, and as time passed and the search slackened, some of the companions began to visit secretly and dine and while away the hours with Diarmuid and his lady.

---

[39] Spell, enchantment.

Grainne soon grew dissatisfied even with this, she wished to entertain openly, to give and attend grand banquets, to lead again the life she had enjoyed before as the daughter of Cormac Mac Art. She longed for the time when the Feinne could visit freely, when she would no longer be a fugitive.

Nothing however could induce Fingal to acknowledge the couple, and sixteen years went by before Diarmuid could be persuaded to try to effect reconciliation with Fingal.

Then one day, after much coaxing and cajoling, Grainne's wishes prevailed. A banquet was prepared and much feasting and merriment organised.

To this feast Fingal and many of his band were invited. Great was the excitement when it was told that the great chieftain himself deigned to attend.

Wild boar hunting was a favourite sport of these times and as part of the celebrations a boar hunt was planned to amuse the warriors.

Diarmuid himself attended the hunt in full confidence and pride in his skill and his prowess.

But unbeknownst to Diarmuid, the wild boar that they would hunt this day was magic and a geas had been laid on it to kill him.

Before long the boar came upon Diarmuid. However Diarmuid, a master of the sport, was keen of eye and strong of arm. Soon he had pierced the boar clean through with his spear. Yet the boar, its powers magically augmented by the geas, did not die.

Long and terrible was the contest between the foster son of Aonghus Og and the geas maddened-boar. Fast, furious and most awful was the fight between Diarmuid and the boar; but eventually Diarmuid prevailed.

Then in its death throes one of the boar's poisoned spikes pierced the ball dorain on the heel of Diarmuid.

This mole on Diarmuid's heel was his only vulnerable spot. Thus the poisoned gash, from the spikes of the dying, geas driven boar, was mortal.

As Diarmuid lay dying Fingal and his grandson Oscar arrived at his side along with some others of the companions.

Diarmuid, knowing that he would be healed if he drank water from the hand of Fingal himself, asked Fingal to fetch him some water from the nearby stream.

Fingal refused.

Oscar and his companions begged Fingal to save Diarmuid, begged him to give to Diarmuid the water that would heal him.

Fingal refused their pleas.

Then Fingal began to recall their friendship of old, to recollect the gallantry, charm and wit of Diarmuid, to remember the times they had fought back to back in battle, the countless instances that he had experienced of Diarmuid's selfless bravery.

Then it was that Fingal departed to fetch the water, carrying it back to Diarmuid cupped in his two hands.

Returning with the water Fingal knelt on the ground beside the dying man so that he might give him the water to drink.

But as Fingal looked down upon Diarmuid the image of Grainne suddenly rose up before him and smote him sore. So it was that the heart of Fingal hardened anew.

Fingal raised himself to his feet. He stood for a moment just looking down upon Diarmuid. Then slowly he let the water trickle through his fingers down onto the dry ground.

Thus died Diarmuid of the Feinne.

Some say that Fingal felt much sorrow and regret for having let Diarmuid die when he could have saved him, and that he long mourned for him; but others tell of how the four sons of

Diarmuid and Grainne armed themselves ready to avenge the death of their Father, of how Grainne begged them to desist from such foolishness. For she had no wish to lose sons as well as husband, and for her sons' sake Grainne agreed to once again become the bride of Fingal.

However for all the long years that Grainne remained in the house of Fingal she never gained the respect of Fingal's court, for none could forget how she had brought shame upon Fingal and upon her father the Ard Righ, and none would forgive her for causing the rift between Diarmuid and Fingal that brought upon Diarmuid O' Duibhne his doom.

Diarmuid was long mourned by the companions and is honoured down through the ages for his valour, his wit and his daring. For his sake were the noble sons of Grainne protected from the jealousy and wrath of their wronged and cheated chieftain."

The mournful tones of the Clarsach died away then stilled.

Eilidh looked up and gazing directly at Campbell senior said, "Our guest tonight also weds the bride of another. My father however expected this wedding to take place after his death and indeed was happy that his wife would thus enjoy the protection of Mr Campbell. I am sure you would all like to join me in wishing them all happiness and joy in their future life together."

The silence was palpable, though the odd faint gasp, quickly repressed could be distinguished and then slowly the clapping began. As the noise faded away Eilidh, as if oblivious to the mood in the hall, still looking at the elder Campbell continued, "Even the best of men, as was the case of the valorous Diarmuid and indeed even the renowned King David who the Bible tells us God loved so well, were not always above reproach. We all know the story of how King David caused the husband of

Bathsheba to be sent to the most dangerous position in the battle, and so to certain death, so that he could then marry his bereaved wife. Many families have such stories from the past of deeds that their forebears have done that they might perhaps prefer to have forgotten, such indeed is even the case in my own family, that of the Macleans of Ardgour."

"My brother Alex, our young Laird, is in a few moments going to recite one such instance of this: the exciting saga of how our proud and valorous forebear, the first Maclean of Ardgour, obtained his inheritance with the aid of the forefathers of many of you who are amongst us this evening. Our younger brother Hugh and some of their friends will assist him by acting out the tale whilst Alex tells it."

Eilidh paused for a moment, then, with an amused smile on her face she continued, "I rather fear that today, if it were not that his actions took place in an age much different to our own, our brave and adventurous ancestor Donald Maclean would incur our condemnation rather than our commendation." She then glanced over to where Cairistiona and Dhughall were sitting. "In the meantime, while the children are getting ready......"

A bright little voice jumped in and asked enthusiastically, "Eilidh, Eilidh tell us a story of Cuchullin first, or that of Diarmuid and Aonghus Og and the tale of why the boar had the geas laid upon him to kill Diarmuid!"

Everyone laughed and the young brother of the Laird looked suddenly bashful.

"I've had my turn now Hugh. Cairistiona and Dhughall are about to sing, I am only to accompany them on the Clarsach. However I am very much looking forward to seeing you dressed up as Donald Maclean, the first Laird of Ardgour. So the sooner you are all ready, the sooner we will be able to watch your performance."

With no more encouragement needed, the little lad ran off to join his brother and friends to prepare for their act, while the newly engaged couple walked proudly forward to sing their duet amidst much friendly encouragement and all the congratulations from their delighted families and neighbours.

Chapter 14 Maclean's Tale

The lovers left the stage, having sung their songs to a most appreciative audience; while Eilidh moved her clarsach to the side of the building before going to stand amongst the other young girls, rather than with her sister and companions.

Proud relatives waited nervously in anticipation of the commencement of their children's performance.[40]

In the large barn that hosted that night's ceilidh there was now an expectant silence.

Moments later Eilidh's brother Alex, the young Laird of Ardgour, walked forward alone to the front of the gathering, then turned to face his audience, beaming proudly, displaying no trace of shyness or reserve. He was dressed in his kilt and clan regalia. Without any preamble he began to recite:

"In Morvern where the heroes dwell
By glen on hill beside the sea
Where once the Feinne did roam so free
And hunt and fish the streams so well"

"Where water cascades crystal clear through
Sunlight dancing in the rain
As rainbows bring their promise true
To cheer the heart and heal the pain"

"While deer aloud their challenge roar
Defiance to the wind."

---

[40] The idea of children performing their local history came from a CD which recorded the performance given by the children of Ardgour Primary School. The play was written by Fiona Torrie-Maclean, the wife of the present Laird of Ardgour.

Two of the younger children suddenly charged into the room. They raced up and down behind Alex making loud roaring noises, wearing majestic antlers on their heads, before galloping out again.

Their audience laughed and clapped them loudly.

Next an older boy entered the room and commenced a stately march around the length of the barn. He wore a long cloak and was followed by a number of other 'lordly' children. They exited through the same door which they had come in by.

The young Laird continued his recitation:

"This is the land of Somerled[41]
From these proud shores sailed he
With men, brave, true yet dread
To rule this bountiful Isle of the free."

"King of the mountains, the waves, the sea"

Now to the fore there came a different child, also wearing a cloak; but this child was a small and scrawny individual who did not stride forth confidently. Rather he scuttled in, all the whilst looking nervously around. Scurrying anxiously behind him was another small child, carrying a stool.

As this pair reached the centre of the stage the child wearing the cloak somewhat fussily directed the other child as to where to place the stool. He then proceeded to spend the next few moments ordering this 'underling' to place the stool in various different positions. Once satisfied with the location of the stool he turned his attention to its cleanliness, instructing his servant most particularly to dust it and then carefully inspecting his work.

---

[41] King of the Isles.

Eventually, looking extremely self-important, he grudgingly indicated that he was satisfied and sat down very pompously on the stool; while his servant rushed fearfully to stand ready and waiting just behind.

The audience dutifully chuckled at these antics.

As soon as this character was seated, the young Laird continued:

> *"Safe behind stout Castle doors*
> *On Ardtornish's beauteous shores*
> *Sat one of the line of Somerled*
> *Brooding on where his future sped*
> *Plotting how he could gain more fame*
> *Not knowing it would end in shame."*

In ones and twos some other children began to enter the room. These were excitedly talking to each other, and began walking too and fro behind where the child on the stool, the Lord of the Isles, still sat.

> *"Now this Lord of the Isles had his vassals to please*
> *And chanced on a plan which he voiced far and wide*
> *There is land to be had for those that would choose*
> *To dance to the tune of MacDonald,"*

A number of other children entered, galloping frantically around, as if on horses, shouting the news of the offer of the Lord of the Isles[42].

Young Alex gamely raised his voice above the noise and continued:

---

[42] John MacDonald, 4th and Last Lord of the Isles, 3rd and last Earl of Ross.

137

"From far and wide the land hungry came
With their swords at their side they rode and they laid
Down their weapons, and bent their stiff necks
And all for the land of MacDonald"

Child after child came in, sometimes more than once
wearing a different hat or cloak, and knelt before the 'Lord of
the Isles,' bent his neck, took his hand in his, and in return
received a scroll of paper. He would then scramble to his feet
and walk off and another would immediately take his place.

When these were all gone and the 'Lord of the Isles' was
once more alone the young Laird continued his story:

"Oaths had been sworn and the land gifted out
When one came there laggard, with visage fell fair
Bold, fierce and valiant he came with no doubt
Of a welcome from a kinsman with something to share."

"With sixteen fierce followers in a galley so fleet
With weapons a plenty for to fight was their game
Hungry for land, for fortune so sweet
He had braved the rough seas with no sense of shame."

"Come to answer the call of MacDonald!"

The Laird's younger brother Hugh, now stalked arrogantly in,
accompanied by a small group of other children, pretending to
be the fair newcomer with his fierce band of men. A few other
children moved to stand behind the 'Lord of the Isles' as if in
admiration at the picture the newcomers presented:

"Surely 'tis Oscar the bravest of all
Or Fillan perhaps with his visage so grim
Or is it Cuchullin, come with tales of a brawl?

The whispers grew louder as the band entered in."

"Wise Ossian's long dead though his ballads shine bright
'Tis eons since Fingal ruled in Morvern supreme;
Who is there left who will fight for the Light?
And believe and continue their beautiful dream!"

"John of Islay[43] now reigns as Lord of the Isles
And the supplicant is Donald but Donald of where?
His fortune he earns through his cunning and wiles
A kinsman perhaps but to no land is he heir."

"Grandson of Duart and of Kingairloch's Maclean
His father he married the proud daughter of Mar
Yet no Baronet's crown from his Sire can he claim
For his Dam's Kingairloch's daughter, and there's the bar."

"Donald raced over from Ireland to gain a domain
For long had he dreamed of winning power and fame
Wishing to acquire great lands for his sons to retain
Desiring to establish a legendary name."

As Alex stopped speaking his younger brother Hugh, who was acting the part of young Donald Maclean, strode over to the Lord of the Isles, who was still sat on his stool and bowed slightly. Then he raised himself to his full height to proclaim proudly:

"As you can see I am brave and I'm true
I've an arm strong and sure and a sword that is willing
Doughty Boyd's and Livingstone's' are here with me too
Who've seen many a shore and won't faint at a killing."

---

[43] John MacDonald, Lord of the Isles.

139

Alex again took up the tale:

"MacDonald thought for a moment, he liked this man's look
He had need of such followers and misliked to offend
For this was Duart's bold son, if he was not mistook
Who could muster a strong force his liege lord to defend."

"'All the land free is gifted,' he said, and looked steady
'But there is land that is wasted, and a blaggard too many'
He looked at the young man waiting impatient and ready
Said 'His lands yours for the taking if you just go canny.'"

"'MacMaster was insulting at our very last meeting
That chief is a fool and has a reckoning waiting
If your grandfaithers watching he'll no waste time greeting
For Fuich! Fuich!' is his neighbour an' he'll join in the
baiting.'"

"'So away with you kinsman, Falbh - away
You gain Ardgour when you settle this score
Go now and bring that old fox to bay
Deliver a warning none will dare to ignore.'"

Young Hugh Maclean now raised his bright treble voice to
declare:

"I'll away now and punish that snivelling swine
When Maclean's in Ardgour and the Fox gone from his lair
In Kingairloch they'll drink to my good health and thine
But no warning to MacMaster must any rogue bear."

Hugh Maclean, in the guise of his ancestor Donald Maclean,
now galloped around the hall with a few other children
following him, while his elder brother took up the story again.

"He strode out of the hall and in haste mounted his mare
Roaring that they must ride like the Hounds of the Fienne
They must run with the wind to MacMaster's lair
If they were desirous this day their fortune to win."

"They galloped through Kingairloch with their brave band of
horse
Past the deer and the goat that live high with the gorse
And over many a high hill, ever faster and faster
Through the glen, past the lochans as if the deil was their
master."

While the Young Maclean recited, his younger brother and
their friends enacted the gaining of Ardgour by the Macleans:

"He knocked on the door demanding lodging and wine
They must answer at once let them in for to dine.
But there was none there to answer
At the brave house of The MacMasters."

"No one was there though they searched every crack
And the cry went up that a traitor had warned of the attack"

"To the ferry they flew as if there was fire in the wind
And there found The MacMaster a' crying 'Tis too late to go
rind!'
A begging and pleading the ferryman to 'gae faster'
Row across the broad loch tae escape frae disaster."

"No and they couldnae jist wait for the tide
For that cursed yellow dog he will no' bide!
The mad cur sent by yon scunner to punish the jibe
O' the careless MacMaster saer puffed up wi' pride."

"They took him and slew him before he could race
While the ferry man stood by, a smile on his face
And proudly told Donald of the part he had played
How to help the Maclean he had the old Laird delayed"

"Donald looked hard at the false hearted jade
As his hand yet held firm to the hilt of his blade
'So too would you betray me in my hour of need
Let this sword taste flesh let it once more to feed.'"

"'Mete the fate of the Fox to his ferryman true
For thus should all traitors receive their due
Let it be known that such villains labour in vain
If they wish to dwell in these Lands of Maclean!'"

"Now MacMaster's young cub with his Sire did not ride
Deciding instead to skulk and to hide
This young Fox was soon found at bay in a wood
Was dispatched and hung up just as soon as they could."

"In the 'Heights of the Goats' and down by the tide
Now 'Virtue Mine Honour' sounds far and wide
And loud in Ardgour you can hear the proud victor's cry
Altera Merces -To Conquer or Die;"

"Into this proud land of the Fienne
The Macleans of Ardgour now enter in!"

"And from that time onwards until yon waterfall that bubbles so bravely down the hill beside their home runs dry, will the descendants of Donald Maclean make their home in Ardgour, along with the Boyds and the Livingstones that accompanied him on that grand and glorious day that they first entered their ancestral home," finished the proud young Laird of Ardgour.

He stood their grinning as his brother and friends came to join him, including the gory MacMasters and their kin who had been dispatched so cheerfully only moments before, secure in the belief that they would get praise and commendations a plenty; and in the happy knowledge that cakes and lemonade had been brought by Sandra, the Maclean's cheerful and talented cook, to aid the festivities and that even now these were being laid out on tables at the back of the barn.

The children and the older people left shortly after eating there fill; leaving behind the young people, as the ceilidh transformed into what was more like a barn dance.

Eilidh stayed only for the first few dances and though opportuned by many of the young men to dance, including Fergus Campbell, she remained at her harp for the remainder of her stay.

Adrianne, although she would never admit it, enjoyed the evening thoroughly, being quite the 'the belle of the ball', though watched over carefully by her step father to be. Her future step brother was less happy with the outcome of the evening having failed to win conversation with Eilidh; while his father, Archibald Campbell, left the ceilidh later that night with unusually mixed feelings.

143

Chapter 15 Setting Out for Morvern

As she left the ceilidh Eilidh breathed a sigh of relief. On her way out Joe had attempted to detain her, to dissuade her from going alone to Morvern. She understood his concerns, appreciated how he worried, that it was only because he loved her that he sought to persuade her not to go, that he offered to go in her stead. He ought though to have recognised that her mother could as easily have asked a servant to deliver those invitations to the wedding, that she would be wroth if she discovered that someone else had delivered them for her, that she would not easily forgive this further disobedience.

Joe however would not have suspected, as she did, that her mother had sent her away at this time because Lachlan, Mairi and Ewan were expected any day now, that her mother had somehow discerned the depth of the bond between herself and Ewan, guessed just how much she was longing to see him.......

What neither Joe nor her mother would have comprehended was that despite her desire to see Ewan as soon as possible, she yet yearned to visit Morvern, to ride through these lands of her ancestors just one more time before leaving, perhaps forever.

Morvern with it high wild hills, lush glens, its sparkling lochs and its enchanting shorelines had a feel such that she had never experienced anywhere else. There was a strange mystique about the place. Travelling through its breathtakingly lovely glens you could almost believe that you could glimpse through the mists, the ghosts of the Feinne traversing the heather clad hills and the wide grassy valleys as they had done in the flesh so many years before.

As her brother had chanted in his poem, 'this is the land of Somerled', and indeed in Morvern, Somerled's castles still stood proud and tall for all to see. Though in less good repair than of old they were still an impressive reminder of that time when those of Somerled line had reigned supreme.

Very little of the land thereabouts now belonged to the Macleans though long ago Morvern had been a stronghold for many of her clan. Maclean of Drimnin had sold Drimnin a few years before her own birth, to a MacDonald no less, so she had been told, but he had never lived there. However this past year another Maclean had taken up residence there but she herself had never met Maclean of Boreray, though by all accounts was pleasant enough; it was to him that one of her mother's missives was destined.

Ceitidh was right though, it would not be the same visiting Morvern alone and she did miss having someone to talk to. She missed Kai-Ying and her vast knowledge and teachings about herb lore, her tales of all the old legends of the Highlands and those from her homeland; she missed her warmth, her dry sense of humour and her sound common sense advice. Kai-Ying had loved her despite what she was, had loved whatever she did. Kai-Ying had always been interested in her every thought and deed, had never condemned, but had corrected her mistakes yet somehow never criticized. She missed her most dreadfully... and her father! But she wouldn't think of that, not just now.

She had never cried after her father's death, nor indeed had she cried when Kai-Ying died. She had been unable to...... rather there had grown inside her a tight knot of pain that increasingly gnawed at her insides. Over time this had gradually developed into a hollow, empty feeling that grew and grew whenever she thought of them. So painful was it that even after all these months she would think of them but rarely; for fear that this emptiness, her loneliness, would overtake her, encompass her and swallow her up. If she didn't think about them the pain usually subsided, hid somewhere quietly deep inside. Sometimes though the hurt got so bad, became so all-consuming, that it felt as if she would disappear forever inside the well of emptiness; then though she would sing in 'tongues', pray in the 'tongues of men and angels' as had Saint Paul and the apostles, and she would be safe.

Kai-Ying it was who had taught her that this ability to 'pray in an unknown tongue' was a gift of God and she had read later for herself in the scriptures that this was indeed so[44]. Nevertheless Kai-Ying had always cautioned her to remember that the apostle Paul had said that 'though I speak with the tongues of men and angels and have not charity I am like the sound of brass or tinkling cymbals[45].' Kai-Ying, for whom Christianity was not the religion she was born into, Kai-Ying whom the villagers had reviled, had always talked of the importance of Charity, of Love. Not the love between a man and a woman, but of unconditional, compassionate love.

Kai-Ying had told her so very often how Jesus had explained that it was easy to love those who love us in return, that indeed most people love those who love them, but he wanted us to love even those who revile and persecute us. She smiled to herself grimly, she had needed to remember that today, her mother's pronouncement as to her future had shocked her more than she liked to admit. Indeed it had shocked her far more than it should have. She should have expected something of the kind. Had she not received warnings aplenty?

It was not the threat of the asylum that surprised her, but the other. Why did her mother wish her to undertake such a dishonourable occupation, of what benefit could it be her mother? True her mother had disowned her at birth and even

---

[44] Acts chapter 2, verses 1-4; 1 Corinthians chapter 14, verse 14.
[45] I Corinthians chapter 13, verse 1.

now still appeared to despise and detest her. Perhaps she hoped that if she were thus dishonoured then she could be forgotten forever. Though surely incarceration in that asylum that her mother had threatened her with would be a far more secure way of ridding herself of the daughter that she wished had never been born, or at the very least wished had never lived.

However she had got the impression that rather than wishing her to fall into obscurity she instead desired that she become infamous, that somehow her mother wished to use her daughter's thus engendered notoriety for her own ends, to punish someone; but who? It could not be her father she wished to humiliate. Her father was dead and could no longer be hurt by her mother's wiles or tricks. Who was it then that her mother and, if she was not mistaken, Mr Campbell also, wished to be revenged upon? How could her joining the 'Pretty Horse Breakers Set' enable her mother to gain this redress? Who was there left who would care about her disgrace, let alone share in it?

There was no one to talk to, no one with whom she could discuss the matter. She could only pray and hope and wait. She smiled suddenly, almost with relief. But of course, Duncan! When Duncan came she could ask him. He had been her father's friend, most loyal servant; he would not let Lachlan and Mairi carry out her mother's request. She would forget about it until Duncan returned. She would not allow such worries to spoil her last few weeks of freedom. Besides which, as she had told Fergus, she was not herself entirely without other options to which she could turn to if all other support failed. With this decided Eilidh turned her attention to the joys of the journey.

Hers wasn't a nature to stay sad and dour. Hers was one of joy, of happiness. She had been trained to give thanks, to look always for the bright side and now with the beauty of nature all around and her beloved Liath Macha trotting out of the trees to meet her, she determinedly chased away those thoughts and memories that were so hurtful to her and concentrated instead on the present.

She had left the provisions for her journey in her cave down at Salachan; to there she now sped, collecting on the way her mare Red Dawn, the mother of Liath Macha. Dawn's yearling foal she had left in the care of John Boyd. This was no journey for her.

Eilidh's thoughts drifted to the day she had first seen Red Dawn. She had been but six years old and it was the first time that her father had taken her with him when he journeyed south to visit his estates in Fife which Lachlan tended. She remembered how he had brought her out to a paddock at the side of the house and told her that she could have any of the youngsters she wished for her very own. There had been no choice. As soon as she had looked into the filly's kind eyes she had fallen in love with her. She suspected that if Red Dawn had been blessed with three legs and had all the bad points possible she would have still chosen her for that kind look. But Red Dawn, part Highland Garron, part Arab, was beautiful from the tip of her nose to the end of her tail, an elegant dainty red chestnut. She would follow Eilidh everywhere, just like a puppy, as would her son Liath Macha, but there the resemblance ended. Red Dawn was barely fourteen hands high while her son was a good sixteen hands. She had the sweetest nature while Liath Macha was bad tempered and ugly. He was jet black apart from the one small grey area on the base of his mane, and a splodge of grey on his saddle area; hence his name 'Grey of Macha'. He had a white ring round his eyes which gave him a mad look and his ears seemed perpetually pinned back; while woe betides any who came too near or tried to get in his way. Only with Eilidh was he as gentle as a lamb, as playful as a kitten and obedient, loyal; but it went further than that, it was as if he knew what she was thinking without her saying anything. When she went away he knew before she could be seen that she was returning, almost seem to appear before she whistled him. He was, she thought, her very best friend.

She had raised him herself from when he was a tiny foal. Red Dawn had carried twins, had barely survived their birth and had neither milk nor energy enough for two. Dubh Sainglain[46], his twin, was his double in that he was black and about the same height. However, he was a very handsome creature and in temperament took after his mother. They were named after the two horses of Cuchullin who were reputed to have been born on the same day as Cuchullin himself. Their mother was named Red Dawn because of her chestnut colouring and because just as the 'Shepherds Warning'[47] told of bad weather to come, so had the coming of Red Dawn heralded the unwelcome news that her father was to leave her for the winter in Fife with Lachlan and Mairi.

It was some time before the two horses were laden and ready to set off. Liath Macha was piled high with venison, while his mother carried a variety of herbs and other provisions and Eilidh walked untrammelled alongside the pair of them as they began their journey to Morvern.

---

[46] Black of Sainglen.
[47] Red sky at night, shepherds' delight. Red sky in the morning, shepherds' warning.

Chapter 16 Glen Gower

Eilidh, Liath Macha and Red Dawn trekked briskly to the mouth of Glen Gower and from there ambled on through that wild and beautiful valley. As they traversed Glen Gower a sense of deep and utter peace descended upon Eilidh, such as she had not enjoyed for a long time.

They walked on as if in a dream, glorying in the silence and beauty of the Glen. It was a perfect night. The moon was almost full and the sky clear of clouds, so that her old friends the stars could be seen plainly as they strode across the broad sky, while she far below traversed the heather clad glens.

Her thoughts began to drift, as she found they did all too frequently, to the stranger who had disturbed her nights for the past year. During the six long months after her father's death whilst she had nursed Kai-Ying, she had dreamed of him every night, she had seen his cold face mocking his companions, his disdainful look rest on the faces of numerous beautiful women, seen him riding and driving his magnificent horses with ease and noted his careless confidence with a gun at the shooting parties he attended, noticed the way he treated his acquaintances with scarcely concealed contempt or at best disinterest, acquaintances whose faces she never quite seemed able to distinguish. She had been with him, as a ghostly presence, at the races and at many grand balls, watched him at the card tables as he won and then won again with seeming indifference; but then he seemed to do everything with dispassion as if nothing mattered to him, as if he regarded the whole world and everything in it as an irrelevance, as being beneath his notice.

She wondered now if somehow she had inadvertently caused him to haunt her dreams by allowing her thoughts to dwell on him during the day. Perhaps this stranger had filled her dreams since her father's funeral with such alarming frequency simply because she had unconsciously encouraged the dreams to continue so that they might fill the vacuum, assuage the loneliness brought by the death of her father and comfort her in her anguish and despair at Kai-Ying's terminal illness.

She had on occasion wondered if perhaps the face and personage that haunted her dreams was something born out of her imagination rather than being a true vision, something that she had conjured up to comfort and entertain her; though even then she had ruefully thought that if that be the case, it was strange that she had sought comfort in such a guise. However it was only when she had with shock recognised one of the women he was with that she had begun to worry, to wonder as to the purpose of the visions and seriously question who he might be. The woman she knew stabled her horses at her Uncle Sam's stables in London, and her occupation was the same as that which she had just learned her mother and Mairi were planning that she pursue.

Then on the night of Kai-Ying's death those dreams that had so beguiled her nights, and haunted her days, had suddenly turned into nightmares...... Why the nightmares? Why had they begun on the night of Kai-Ying's death?

Now from Fergus she had discovered that he was only too real. She must therefore suppose the nightmares, the dreams, to be some form of warning. But of what? Fergus claimed he was a gambler, a rake; well so much her visions had told her. That he was also a murderer! Her heart told her that this was not so, while her head remembered the duels she had 'Seen' him fight, and she went cold. But still she could not bring herself to believe this. He had been with her throughout the past year, nearly every night had held for her a vision of his mocking face, his ice cold eyes, his distant contemptuous expression until she felt she knew him as she knew herself; knew that underneath the ice there lurked another who wore the mask to disguise...... To disguise what?

Like a fool she had allowed herself, thinking it harmless, to fill her empty heart with thoughts and fancies of a wraith whose face and very being might in some future time confront her not just in a dream but with its actual physical presence. What idiocy, what weakness, she railed at herself, had allowed her to give in to her womanly need to love, and caused her to dream, to think so frequently of this sceptre and endow him with a gentleness, a goodness which he did not merit; so much so that she now died nightly with him in her every nightmare? As he died in every way imaginable many times each and every night it was as if she too died.

For when she awoke, the residual remains of the nightmare invariably left her with the ludicrous lingering impression that his death would render her life null and void; that this final unendurable loss would wholly eradicate her wish to live, bereft her of all hope.

Even now when the manner of his death had become more fixed, when most nights he died the same way again and again and again, she would still wake cold and shivering; she who was never cold. She who was never afraid would fear to return to sleep in terror that the dream would return, while during every waking hour his face would habitually drift into her thoughts, unsolicited, unwanted; and despite herself, she would reluctantly wonder what he did, where he was, who he was with, and a longing would possess her that she had begun to fear almost as much as the dreams.

152

All peace for Eilidh was now banished. The now too familiar restlessness had returned. She had planned to spend the night on these hills, but now she travelled on more quickly filling her mind with thoughts of her plans for the trip ahead as she struggled to force out the thoughts her lonely heart sought to retain, to dwell on, to welcome, to dream perhaps of a future that could never be.

On reaching Strontian she followed the sides of Loch Sunart that led on into Morvern itself.

As she travelled she tried to avoid the small settlements that were situated throughout Morvern, and by dawn break she found herself forced to travel far inland; for the best grazing was near the loch side and around these the communities gathered.

The sun had begun to shine through the rising mist and as she looked around at the rapidly expanding horizon she thought to herself of how strange it was that most of Morvern now belonged to the Duke of Argyle, kin to her own step father to be, where once the land hereabouts had all belonged to the Macleans. The story she had been told was that the Campbells had obtained the Maclean land through trickery, but the truth of this was something she did not know; many such stories changed with time and with the teller.

She was so taken up with her musings that it was Liath Macha who alerted her to the fact that they were no longer alone. She felt him stiffen beside her and then his head went up as he sniffed the wind. Her hand went to her knife as she looked to see who it was that thus disturbed her solitude.

Chapter 17 Rahoy

A lone boy was running. A boy small, wiry, hardly older than her brothers. As he approached Eilidh saw that he was underfed and skinny and wondered at him running as he did so effortlessly over the hills. She waited as he came panting towards her, face stained brown with the smoke from the peat fires, wide eyed and anxious as he stammered out his message.

"Eilidh Ruadh, Mo mhathair[48], mo mhathair she asks, would ye bide, would ye...... ...." He stopped, as if suddenly tongue tied, not knowing how to continue.

She waited quietly.

Then he rushed on, "Mo bhrathair[49], he is very sick, mo phiuthar[50], she..., she died a few days past o...' o' am fiabhras[51] agus[52] am paiste[53], he is unwell. Mo mhathair, she..., she asked......." He stammered to a stop.

Eilidh turned to Liath Macha's packs and drew out a bundle of bannocks, saying kindly, "Peace child, eat these and I will make haste to your home. Though I cannot promise that there is aught I can do to help. Where is it that you hail from?"

"Rahoy," was the whispered reply as the child clutched tight his bannock looking if anything even smaller than he had at first sight, as the relief of delivering his message suddenly brought to his awareness his own weakness.

Eilidh nodded, then called for Dawn to come over. After asking permission, she quickly lifted the child onto Dawn's back, to sit as well as he could up amongst all the other packages.

---

[48] Mother.
[49] Brother.
[50] Sister.
[51] Fever.
[52] And.
[53] Baby.

Then she herself mounted Liath Macha and they cantered off in the direction the boy had come from.

It was some time before they spied the small settlement at Rahoy. The sight of the spiralling plumes of dirty smoke was the first indication of the presence of the dwellings.

Most of the houses hereabouts were so tiny that they contained only one small room, some few boasted two, but inside they were invariably clean and tidy, albeit overcrowded. At least six people would live in one of these small cottages, in addition to whatever animals were brought in from the cold and the chickens that would roost in the rafters.

As she approached the village she saw several small ragged children turn to stare. The small boy jumped down off Dawn as soon as they arrived, impatient to take Eilidh to his home.

An old man, hearing the voices, had come out of one of the houses. He now approached and Eilidh noticed the boy's eagerness die away as he read the message on the old man's face.

"A blessing on you Eilidh Ruadh for hastening, but ye are too late, the bairn has already died," the old man said sadly.

"It is sorry that I am to be hearing that," Eilidh replied quietly. She looked over to where the boy had been and was just in time to see him disappearing into the small house the old man had just come out of. Then she returned her attention to the old man. "The boy, he said...," she hesitated again before resuming, "may I at least see the baby?"

The man, face gaunt and grim nodded and turned back the way he had come, Eilidh following.

Inside the air was thick with smoke, and Eilidh wondered more at the children surviving than not, living in this place. The winters, she mused, must be especially dreadful for it was then dark for so many hours of the day, and so cold. The family and their animals would all stay inside this small house, getting what heat they could from their stubborn smoky peat fire, with little food and few clothes. She guessed that the presence of the animals in the house would help to make it slightly warmer.

This house was no different from the many other such homes that she had visited. It contained a clay floor, and inside was neat and clean, or as clean as it could be with the chickens roosting in the rafters above. There was but the one bed in the room and in this lay the dead child as if sleeping, small as a doll. Next to this sat a woman, tired and wan with empty eyes holding a mewing infant.

Eilidh went over to the woman and knelt at her feet and after talking to her for a few moments stood up and took the infant from her arms. She sat on the other chair and gently examined the baby and after asking the woman a couple of other questions, returned the child, still whimpering piteously, to its mother.

Then she went out to the horses, which some kind villager had already watered and unsaddled, and unpacked a number of parcels of food which she distributed around the villagers before returned to the fire of the house wherein lay the dead child. There she proceeded to mix some herbs into a drink which she instructed the woman to give to the baby. She then gave the woman some fresh herbs and gave instructions as to how to make it so she could give it to the baby over the next few days until the child became well once more.

An older woman came quietly in, and to her she gave the package of venison and other food stuffs that she had brought with her whilst suggesting various ways in which portions of it might be prepared so that the baby might be persuaded to eat some of it.

As the old woman began to busy herself with the foodstuffs, Eilidh walked over to the pale woman who yet sat beside the bed with the mewing infant on her knee; "Drink this Shona, 'twill perhaps help bring back the milk if ye drink this morning and noon, and eat what ye can. Don't think to eat sparingly of it so that others may eat more. Remember that the bairn will more likely survive if your milk returns, but the milk will only return if you yourself eat well and keep returning her to the breast very frequently. Even if you think that there is no milk it will comfort the bairn to suckle, and as you get stronger and eat and drink more the milk will of a surety return."

"I have had nay milk for a week past," the woman replied bitterly. "The poor wain just turns away and greets, for she is fair sick wi' hunger. There is nay use in tryin' further."

Eilidh smiled reassuringly, "With God's help, and some good food and rest the milk will surely yet return if you do as I ask and keep encouraging the bairn to suckle. In the meantime," she asked, "is there no one else who has milk who could feed her for you for a few days?"

"We are all alike here, all are going dry of milk while our bairns starve," the woman replied despondently. Then she said slowly, "Perhaps Anne might be willin', able…," she stumbled to a stop. Anne's wee lad died two days past. He was her first……"

The winter that year had been hard and the food scarce and she did not explain, she did not need to, that on some parts of Morvern with the advent of sheep the hill land was no longer shared by all those in the local community. Instead it was now used solely for grazing the tackmens'[54] sheep. This loss of the hill grazing meant that the small farmers were now forced to

---

[54] Tackmen held large areas of land from landowners for which they paid rent and then in turn sublet to other tenants.

keep fewer animals and thus they were very much poorer than they had been previously.

As they spoke, a young woman came in, saying that her grandmother was asking if Eilidh Ruadh, when she was finished in this house, would come and look at her leg which was paining her something sore and would not heal.

All the rest of that day Eilidh went from house to house looking at the sick and injured, setting an old injury here, cleaning a wound there or giving advice about a pregnancy that was going ill, or some other problem. All the while she was followed by all the local children who waited patiently outside each house for her to come out, then they would follow her to the next, jostling each other to see who could get the closest to her. And always there was an older child with a basin of water and another with a cup full of water and a mixture of herbs; as Eilidh insisted on washing her hands in these as she moved between houses. For there was no Doctor in Morvern.

By dusk she was finished. The little boy whom she had met earlier that day up on the hills now came to her with a message asking that she accompany him to his aunt's house to join them there at their evening meal.

After all had eaten they walked over to a neighbouring house to join many of the other villagers who had come to listen to the seannachie tell his tales and to sing some songs; though the death of the child made the mood of the gathering not one of merriment.

This house was much as the first she had entered that day, though in here there were two beds containing the meticulously clean sheets and the plain counterpane. At the bottom of each of the beds stood a chest and in one corner of the room was laid a pile of freshly cut peat and in another was a dresser containing bowls and plates. There was the usual fire in the middle of the clay floor, but the smoke that evening was drifting obligingly through the hole in the roof. Moreover this evening there were no wet drips descending from the roof for the rain had subsided. The cattle that would habitually have been present had been removed temporarily to a different location to make room for all the extra people, but a black rooster remained. He eyed the incomers calculatingly as he perched with his harem in the rafters. The room possessed a solitary window but this was at present stuffed with peat to keep out the cold. The only light was provided by a couple of small candles, set near the seannachie so all could see him as he spoke.

Despite her sadness at the death of the child, that evening for Eilidh was one that she cherished long for the memory it gave of warmth and love and friendship. Here amongst her own people she relaxed as she had done but seldom since the death of her father. Quietly and happily content she listened to the stories the seannachie told in the soft Gaelic tongue and heard the songs of her land sung in that same beautiful language as they had been sung generation after generation.

She herself did not sing that night preferring to listen, and despite their pleading with her to stay longer, she and Dawn and Liath Macha left the village as the villagers retired to their own cots.

She slept that night not far from there, sheltering amongst some shrubs in a small copse. Curled up next to Liath Macha and Dawn for warmth she slept sound as she had not slept for many a long night.

Chapter 18 The Spanish Princess

The sun was smiling brightly high up in a clear cloudless sky when Eilidh woke the next morning, after a dreamless night. This day she did not hurry, content just to be here traipsing amongst the hills she loved and knew so well, accompanied by her beloved Liatha Macha and Red Dawn.

As they rambled along they glimpsed the smoke of a number of small settlements rising and rising, mingling with the blue of the sky, far in the distance; but they did not choose to approach nearer. They trekked inland until she could no longer smell the sea, though the seagulls could still be heard squawking as they fought over the scraps they had found.

While she ambled thus happily alongside Dawn and Liath Macha a stray thought sidled into her mind abruptly shattering her serenity. Without warning the tale of the 'Spanish Princess' crashed into her awareness. The seannachie at Rahoy had related this story only the previous night in honour of her visit, for the story involved a kinsman of hers; one Lachlan Maclean of Duart.

For a moment she felt ice cold.

It was a legend she had heard many times before and thus whilst dozing comfortably amongst the people of Rahoy, listening contentedly to the seannachie tell a story whose very familiarity only added to her pleasure, she had failed to recognise the startling resemblance between the vision which had haunted the Spanish Princess, and her own recurrent visions. How could she not have noticed? She felt suddenly sick, dizzy.

Legend claimed that a certain Spanish princess called Clare Villo, whilst living in her father's palace, received a vision of a man she had never before seen, a man whose dress and language was different to that of her own countrymen.

Night after night Clare beheld the face of this man in her dreams and as the days went by his image gradually crept into all her waking hours.

Day by day her thoughts began to dwell more and more on this stranger whose form and visage she deemed to be the most comely she had ever beheld.

After some time she grew to imagine that she was in love with this bonny man whom she saw in these visions, and when visitors came to her father's court she awaited their arrival with great eagerness, hoping that one of them might be he who haunted her nights and disturbed her days.

The months passed by and still there came none to the court of the King of Spain who bore any resemblance to the fair stranger.

Clare began to despair of ever finding him. Then it was that she resolved that if he did not come to her then she must go herself and search unto the ends of the earth until she might discover him. With this in mind she ordered one of her father's frigates to be put ready to sail.

Princess Clare Villo of Spain travelled far and wide in search of her love. She and her staunch captain sailed in the Florida, their magnificent Spanish galleon, to numerous different countries, stopping at countless foreign harbours. As soon as they reached a new land Clare would have invitations sent out to all the young nobles in the surrounding area to come to dine with her on her ship; but never did any of her guests resemble the man in her dreams.

After many months of travelling she began to despair, to fear that her search was hopeless, that she would never find he who she was seeking for.

Eventually the great ship approached near to the Island of Mull, off the west coast of Scotland. Although she held no real hope that such a small island would contain her Love, the princess asked her captain to stop there. Then as soon as the Florida arrived in Tobermory harbour, as was her usual practice when anchoring off foreign shores, Princess Clare Villo sent out invitations to all the nobility on Mull.

Many came to answer the invitation of the Spanish Princess, for tales of her beauty had spread far and wide and all were eager to catch a glimpse of her fair face and form. As each man entered the ship her heart would leap and she would scan his face anxiously, hoping passionately that his would be the visage of he whom she was seeking.

When it seemed that all who had been invited had come, she turned away to join her guests who were waiting within, trying to mask her disappointment. Then she heard a tread on the deck, and a merry voice ask in a language she did not understand "Is it too late that I am come?"

She spun around on her heel and stopped and stared, for the face she beheld was that which she had been longing to see, the face for which she had left land and home to search for. As if in a daze she walked towards him and clasping her arms around his neck she kissed him.

The Maclean of Duart, for he it was who had arrived so tardily, was enraptured by the sight of Clare and he immediately forgot that he had a wife at home in Duart Castle. Many days he dwelt on the Florida, where much feasting and merriment was organised and enjoyed in celebration of the ending of the Princess's quest. For the Princess had found the embodiment of her dream in the form and person of the Sir Lachlan Mor, The Maclean of Duart.

Now Maclean of Duart's wife soon wondered why it was that her husband did not return, and she was exceedingly wrath when she learned of his visit to the galleon and his reported rapport with the lady within. The days went by and still her husband did not return, and fear began to grow in her heart; for it was whispered that the galleon was soon to leave and The Maclean would remain on board the day it sailed.

Lady Maclean set to plotting how she was going to extricate her husband from the coils of the foreign princess. Quickly her plans were made ready. Then she sent out a servant to the ship with an urgent message to her husband, such that he must leave the ship immediately.

As soon as Lachlan Mor had left the galleon one of Lady Maclean's servants set fire to the gunpowder which had been secreted on board the ship earlier that day.

There was a mighty explosion and then the Florida disappeared.

Only a small black dog, who gamely managed to swim to shore, survived, and it was said that it's pitiful whining could be heard for days along the coast of Mull.

Thus died Clare Villo, Princess of Spain, murdered by the jealous wife of her lover.

Lachlan Maclean ordered that a search be made for the body of his beloved princess. When it was eventually found on the shores of Morvern he had Clare Villo buried in a stone coffin in the churchyard of Kiel-Colum-kill.

The story did not end here though, but went on to tell of how the Princess's shade did not rest easy in her coffin in Morvern, and of how she persuaded a young man, Ewan of the Glen, to take her bones out of the coffin and wash them in the waters of a well in Kilmaluag in Lismore. Indeed to this day there is still a well on the Island of Lismore called Tobar[55] a Clar. It is alleged that this Ewan of the Glen then sailed to Spain with the Princess's bones which he duly returned to her father.

The King of Spain was exceedingly wrath when he heard of how his daughter had been murdered and he immediately ordered several warships of his armada to sail to Mull to enact his revenge.

Now great was the fear in the heart of Maclean of Duart when he heard of the coming of these vessels and he had scouts sent out around the island and up the coastline of the mainland to watch for the arrival of these wrathful, high masted Spanish warships.

At last the day came when he was sent tidings that these ships were fast approaching the island. Hurriedly he called for all the witches of Mull to come to his aid. He begged them to raise a wind such as would destroy and sink the ships before they could reach Mull.

The witches did as he requested and before long the winds began to howl and rage so fiercely that much of the armada was either sunk or blown so much off course that they were forced to turn tail and head back to Spain; that is all except that proud Spanish warship commanded by the dread Captain Forester.

Unfortunately for the plans of Maclean of Duart, magic stronger than that possessed by all the witches on Mull had Captain Forester. Thus all the wiles and spells of Mull's witches were rendered fruitless due to the strength of the Spanish captain's magic.

The witches of Mull, fearing greatly that they would fail in this task that Maclean of Duart had set, decided that they must send to the 'Great Gormshuil of Moy' for assistance.

---

[55] Well or spring.

One of the witches of Mull therefore immediately flew off to beg the help of this famed witch of Lochaber, whose powers were stronger than all the witches of Mull put together.

Gormshuil agreed to their request and set off at once for Mull.

As she flew nearer to Mull the winds blew yet fiercer and fiercer.

Captain Forester soon realised that a force stronger than even he himself was fast approaching, and he immediately resolved to turn and flee. Before he had time to act the great Gormshuil in the form of a cat had climbed onto the top of his mast. There she sat and sang a strong binding spell. In an instant the Captain Forester's ship and all her crew had sunk.

As with all myths and legends Eilidh knew that this one also had its basis in fact. There were stories other than this as to the reason the Florida was blown up and why the Spanish Armada was in this area and if the truth were told none of the stories reflected well on this particular Maclean of Duart. Fergus had told her that his kinsman the Duke of Argyle had a cannon reputedly belonging to the Florida on the lawn of Inverary Castle. Fergus had said that the local people affectionately call it the 'Glede Gun'[56].

However it was not the accuracy of this story that troubled her, but the fleeting fear that she had felt that perhaps the visions that she had been given augured her doom just as they had that of the Spanish Princess.

Then laughing at herself for even imagining anything so ridiculous she shrugged this idea away for she had no intention, indeed no desire to travel the country chasing the personage in her dream to the ends of the earth or beyond; moreover she

---

[56] 'Glede' means hawk.

knew the man in her vision to be unwed, with no wife to plot the demise of a rival out of jealousy.

She pushed away the fell thoughts of Clara Villo, whilst thinking wryly of how odd it was that Mull, so famed for its witches, should be the ancestral home of the chief of their clan; but yet she, who some believed to be a witch child, could not quite love this shadowy island with its mists and caverns and peculiar rock faces. A strange feel did Mull have but to there she was now journeying, both on her mother's account and on her own, for one of her father's closest friends lived there and she wished to bid him goodbye.

Chapter 19 Aulustin

As she battled to clear her head of her troubled musings Eilidh
turned her thoughts again to the impoverishment of the
settlement that she had visited the day before and how that
visit to Rahoy had rendered the horses' packs much smaller
than they had been when they had first set out. She had
expected this and had come well prepared, for the provisions
that she had brought with her had not been for her own use as
she required but little. She knew very well that the child who
had died the previous day would probably still be alive if it had
been better fed and that there were many other children in a
similar state throughout Morvern. Though, she thought sadly,
the pitiful amount she had been able to bring with her could
make little difference to the communities overall, but short
term to a few families it might bring a brief but welcome
respite.

Her father had told her that Morvern's population had
almost doubled in the past half century; a state of affairs that
served only to increase the severity of the impact of the recent
policy undertaken by many of the landlords in the area of
withdrawing from their tenants, who had previously just about
managed to scrape a meagre existence, the common grazing
rights that they had enjoyed for centuries. This practice was
unfortunately being adopted all over Scotland and not just here
on the land owned by George Campbell, The Duke of Argyle.

The reason for the new policy was profit. The tackmen
believed that they could get more of a return on their land by
grazing their own sheep on the common grazing where all the
community had previously grazed their hardy black cattle.

Whilst increasing the revenues of the landlord this loss of the
common grazing significantly decreased the prosperity and well-

167

being of those communities who had hitherto relied on it to feed their black cattle. As a direct consequence of this policy, those workmen and cottars living in the small settlements had now to reduce the number of cattle which they kept as they no longer had adequate grazing to raise the same numbers as before. They could no longer raise sufficient cattle to sell at market, and this considerably decreased the amount of money which the community could generate.

For a short time the production of kelp, from a type of yellow seaweed found on some of the shores in Morvern, had helped augment their income. When this yellow seaweed was burned a yellow ash called kelp was produced which was important for such manufacturing processes as the bleaching of linen and the making of glass and soap.

Eilidh remembered as a child going to the beach at Fiunary when her father went to visit the minister Norman MacLeod, and helping gather the seaweed there. She had found it fun searching for and then dragging the wet seaweed up the shore along with the other children. Now however she understood what hard, painful work it was collecting and carrying masses of slimy seaweed day after day.

On average twenty tons of seaweed had to be burned to produce just one ton of kelp. It was backbreaking work that left the hands rough and calloused; unpleasant when the prices were high, but when the prices were low that would render the work even more miserable, even intolerable, especially when it was wet, cold and windy and you possessed few clothes and came home to a small house whose roof leaked, where the wind blew its chill air through the windows and doors and chased the smoke round the room, smothering the fire; and where there was little food to fill the empty belly.

The beaches near Rahoy did not have such a plentiful supply of the right kind of seaweed as did some of the other beaches in Morvern but here too it had been a useful additional income. However now, when the price of kelp had fallen continuously over the past ten years, even this industry was failing to help in the battle to keep starvation at bay.

There was still the fish, but she well knew that despite the lochs hereabouts being teeming full with fish, they were only fished to fill the table of the fishermen's' own families and that fishing did not bring any extra income into the community.

Suddenly the merry sound of voices interrupted her ruminations.

"Eilidh Ruadh, Eilidh Ruadh! Seoras[57], a' Mhairi[58], its Eilidh Ruadh!"

Eilidh looked up and smiled and then laughing she ran to meet her childhood friends. Here she could be sure of a welcome always.

This was Aulustin, a small tenant farm in the vicinity of Drimnin and as such was let out directly from the owners of Drimnin, rather than sublet. It was still farmed in the traditional way, as a cooperative. The people of Aulustin therefore still retained control of their common grazing.

It was an ideal life, or so she felt, if that is you were content to have only the important things in life. The farm was shared between a number of families, who would each have their own tiny cottage, just like those in Rahoy. Like those families in Rahoy they also produced their food using the runrig system whereby the land was farmed in strips. Some of the strips, usually only the one nearest to the village, were farmed intensively year upon year, and all the fertiliser was used on

---

[57] George.
[58] Mary.

this. Strips of land further away from the settlement would be used for perhaps two or three years, until the ground was empty of goodness and then left to lie fallow for a few years, to grow whatever the earth chose to grow, and so the soil would regain its goodness, at which time it would be cultivated again. These strips of land were shared and alternated between the villagers so that they each got a share of the better strips of land.

However here, as had occurred in Rahoy previous to the enclosure of the common grazing, the cattle were grazed in the manner that her father had told her was called transhumance. This simply meant that the hill grazing was shared and in the spring the women, older people and children would take the animals up to the shielings[59], to the better grazing up in the hills, and live there in small round huts throughout the summer, only coming down in early autumn as the days grew shorter and colder. The men would remain behind mending the houses and tending the fields.

She knew the people at Aulustin would soon be preparing to make for the shielings. She smiled as she thought of the many happy times she had spent up there as a child when her father had taken her through Morvern on those long summer days.

Too short felt the time she stayed in this blessed place. Here, although there were the same blackened faces, the same ragged children, they were not quite so thin, nor the faces so gaunt or so worried. Here too she was called to see babies, but most often to admire, not to cure. There was the odd person who needed her skills, someone's granny, too old to move, had sores that needed looking at, and there was young Iain, who had broken his arm the other day, and could she just look to see if it had set right; then little Sheoras had a bad cough and there

---

[59] The shielings were better grazing land, usually up amongst the hills.

was Flora who had been married two years but as yet had no child who wondered shyly if perhaps Kai-Ying had told her of a cure for problems such as hers. The day passed too quickly, with everyone wanting a word with 'Our Eilidh'. Too soon it was evening.

Here also Eilidh left many of her parcels of food but much of these were used for that evening's party in honour of her visit, rather than stored carefully away to be used sparingly in their time of need to stave off starvation.

After the evening meal was finished and they were replete, all gathered round to listen to the stories.

The seannachie, on the prompting of the children who pressed close to Eilidh, told the very same story that herself had suggested old Padraig, her own seannachie, tell to her brothers only a short time before - the story of 'The Battle of the Birds'.

When this story was told someone lent Eilidh a clarsach and after much entreating she played for them and sang, but did not tell a story herself claiming that their seannachie was far more skilled than she.

Too soon and it was time to go. Despite much pleading, and many teasing threats as to what they would do to her if she refused to remain with them, still she would not stay. Instead she saddled Liath Macha and put her remaining packs on Dawn and by the light of the moon and stars she set off on her way, while the whole village stood by to wish her 'Gods speed'.

She spent that night much as she had spent the one before. Though little sleep she got, for it seemed that almost as soon as she closed her eyes the nightmares would come, but this time worse than ever before.

Each glimpse she had of him would dissolve into nightmare; she would get a sight of his face with its derisive smile or see him leaning idly against a wall talking to a companion, or watch him practice duelling, sword held lazily in his hand or working with his horses, driving them, riding them and then again standing close to a beautiful woman, too close, and picking up a lock of her hair, still with a mocking look on his face, and those cold, cold eyes. Eyes which warmed her heart, eased her loneliness yet filled her with an unnamed longing which she struggled to banish. Even as he bent to kiss the woman's neck, even then, even that scene dissolved and suddenly there was blood everywhere. Once more there he was lying on the ground, his face so deathly pale and there was blood everywhere……

Even the most seemingly innocuous, commonplace vision of him would dissolve thus.

She knew there were other people there, but she never saw them; just as she never saw his assailant's face, though somehow she knew it was the same man each and every time. Always they would fight, and she would watch maybe one or two throws and sometimes she even thought, for just a moment, that Hindley would win, but invariably it would end the same; though one time he might be strangled, another time his neck would be broken, the next his throat cut.

She knew all the throws she saw him use. Duncan had taught her. She was not as good as Hindley, but Duncan was. Duncan was better, far better than Hindley, for Duncan had learned the business the hard way.

Duncan had been a gypsy boy press ganged into the navy. There he had learned to fight; to fight even for his life. He escaped the rigors of the navy only to be forced to eke out his living as a prize fighter. That was when her father had found him, left to die after a fight he had lost, after those he had thought to be his friends had left the dying gypsy boy, believing that he was of no further use to them.

Duncan had remained with her father after he had nursed him back to health; first as his batman and then as his personal servant, and still later, back in Scotland, his friend and most loyal retainer.

He was good, this Hindley - but not good enough...... else he would not die.

Chapter 20 Dukes and Princes

Eilidh arose at dawn, intent on boarding that morning's first ferry to Mull, for this day she was going to visit one of her father's good friends, James Maxwell, Chamberlain to George Campbell, The Duke of Argyle. James Maxwell was responsible for the Duke's estates on Mull and Morvern, and one of the letters that her mother had charged her to deliver was addressed to him.

She grimaced as she thought of the Campbells. What was there about them she wondered, that had caused them, century after century, to stick so close to the most powerful in the land? They were Scots and Highlanders and yet somehow they chose to live much of their lives outside Scotland, seemingly ill content to act solely as the loyal supporters of their own nation and it's King, preferring instead to play the 'Game of Kings'.

Perhaps they did not see themselves as merely Scottish, perhaps their delight in power was greater than their love of their land or perhaps they felt their country better served through maintaining stronger links with England. She smiled wryly, perhaps it was just that the southern way of life suited them better than the less sophisticated ways of the north; certainly others more exalted even than they had made that same decision.

When their own King James VI of Scotland gained the English throne on the death of Queen Elizabeth I, thus becoming King James I[60] of England, he had rarely thereafter returned to his homeland; despite knowing that his own mother had been executed in his adopted country. His mother, Mary Queen of Scots, had been beheaded at the behest of second cousin[61]

---

[60] For the remainder of this chapter James I of England (James VI of Scotland), will be referred to as James I, where appropriate.

Elizabeth Tudor, Queen of England, who had feared that her Catholic enemies wished to supplant her, a Protestant queen, with the exiled Catholic Queen Mary.

What terrible troubles and torments were affected in the name of religion! Jesus commanded us to love one another[62]. How could those pertaining to be Christians fail to understand or obey the maxim that Saint Paul explained so clearly; 'For all the law is fulfilled in one word, even in this; Thou shalt love thy neighbour as thyself'?[63] If all followed this simple command then what turmoil and heartache would be prevented?

Jesus had not lied when he claimed that he had come 'not to send peace but a sword.' He had warned, 'For I am come to set a man at variance against his father and the daughter against her mother and the daughter in law against her mother in law. And a man's foes shall be they of his own household.'[64] Well had Jesus understood the hearts and minds of man, Eilidh thought wryly; but if all just obeyed that one basic commandment to love their neighbours as themselves, then there would be no need for the sword. For Jesus did not mean that he wished for war, only that he knew that man, being what he was, would fight for the interpretation of God's word that suited him best; rather than be prepared to humble himself and 'come to God as a little child'[65], as had been asked of him.

Eilidh thought suddenly of Queen Margaret, sister to the English King Henry VIII[66], who had been sent to Scotland to wed

---

[61] Queen Elizabeth's father, King Henry VIII, had a sister called Margaret who married the Scottish King James IV. Mary Queen of Scots was their grand-daughter, and hence Queen Elizabeth's second cousin.

[62] John chapter 15, verse 17.

[63] Galatians chapter 5, verse 14.

[64] Matthew chapter 10, verse 35.

[65] Mark chapter 10, verse 15.

James IV, King of Scotland, in the forlorn hope that their marriage would bring peace between the two warring nations. This wedding was perhaps arranged in the hope that it would help to promote the love that Jesus wished to see spread abroad; though, she reflected wryly, poor Margaret would likely have felt more fear than love when she was sent to marry this probable stranger in what to her would have seemed a barbaric country with a bewildering dialect. She wondered if that love for their nations had developed into kindness between the both of them and if indeed it had flourished into that love which can grow, in time, between a man and a woman.

Strange to think that this union should have resulted in the union of Scotland and England, a few generations later, when the childless Queen Elizabeth looked to Scotland's King James VI[67] , the son of her erstwhile rival Mary Queen of Scots, for her heir.

Queen Elizabeth's father, King Henry VIII, would have been less than pleased to learn that his sister Margaret had managed that which, with all his six wives, he had failed to do![68]

---

[66] Henry Tudor, son of King Henry VII.

[67] Margaret Tudor, daughter of the English King Henry VII, married King James IV of Scotland. Their son James V of Scotland's second marriage was to Mary, daughter of the Duke of Guise. The offspring of this marriage was Mary, who became Mary Queen of Scots when her father King James V died. James VI of Scotland (James I of England) was the fruit of Mary Queen of Scots second marriage to Henry Stuart (Lord Darnley).

[68] Henry VIII, King of England, sought to establish a dynasty of Tudor Kings; even going so far as to marry six different wives in order to affect this. However none of his three surviving children produced any progeny. When Queen Elizabeth I of England (King Henry VIII's last surviving child) died, the crown passed to King James VI of Scotland who became King James I of England. King James was the son of Mary Queen of Scots and thus was the great grandson of King Henry VIII's sister Margaret Tudor (wife of King James IV of Scotland).

It was strange also, she pondered, that the line of kings should continue time after time through the female line and not the male. Even the proud line of Bruce was carried on not through his son David, but via his daughter Margery. It was from this marriage of Robert the Bruce's daughter Margery to Walter Stewart, High Steward of Scotland, that the Stuart line of kings originated. Just as it was ultimately James I's daughter Elizabeth of Bohemia[69], rather than his son Charles I, from whom the present line of kings, the Hanoverians' came.

She thought how sad it was that despite their apparent liking for England the Stuart Kings had not prospered there. James I's son, Charles I[70], had been beheaded and for a time after his death there had been no king, and the country had instead been ruled by Oliver Cromwell, who became Lord Protector, and his Parliament.

After Cromwell's death this Protectorate had begun to crumble. The English had then decided that they wanted a king again, and turned to Charles II; the son of Charles I.

Unfortunately Charles II left no legitimate sons, so after his death his brother became King James II[71].

King James II's oldest daughter, Princess Mary, married William of Orange[72], the Protestant son of James II's eldest

---

[69] James I's daughter Elizabeth married Frederic (Elector of Palatine), and became known as Elizabeth of Bohemia. Elizabeth was the sister of King Charles I. Elizabeth's daughter Sophie married Ernest Augustus, (Elector of Hanover) and it is their son who became George I in 1714.

[70] Charles I had four sons and five daughters; two of his sons, Charles II and James II, became King of the British Isles.

[71] James II, (James VII of Scotland), had four sons and two daughters by his first wife, but only the daughters survived. He had two sons and five daughters by his second marriage.

[72] William of Orange was the son of Prince William II of Orange, Sadt Holder of the Netherlands, and Mary Henrietta, daughter of King

sister. When some years later, partly due to his leanings towards Catholicism, James II was forced into exile, it was James II's daughter, the Princess Mary, and her husband William of Orange who ascended to the throne in his stead; not his infant son Prince James who had been but recently born of his Catholic Queen.

When the childless William and Mary eventually died, it was Mary's sister Anne[73], and not their Catholic half-brother James[74], who gained the throne.

Anne in turn died without living progeny; and yet again it was not her half-brother, the Catholic James[75], who was offered the crown but the protestant George I[76], a great grandson of James I.

Thus began the line of kings that their new King George IV came from.

What troubles this decision had brought Scotland she thought sadly, for Scotland had not wanted this foreign king even though he came of the Stuart line by virtue of his mother.

Many Scots believed that James[77], the brother of Queen Mary and Queen Anne, should be King instead. To this end, in

---

Charles I. Mary Henrietta was the sister of both King Charles II and King James II.

[73] Anne was a daughter of King James II and sister to Queen Mary, the wife of William of Orange. She married George, the son of Frederick III of Denmark. They had no surviving children.

[74] James, 'The Old Pretender' was the legitimate son of James II and his second wife. He was half-brother to both Queen Mary and Queen Anne. His elder son was famously known as Bonnie Prince Charlie.

[75] The Old Pretender.

[76] King George I, was also Elector of Hanover. His grandmother Elizabeth of Bohemia was the daughter of King James Stuart (I of England and VI of Scotland). She was sister to King Charles I. James I (VI Scotland) was therefore George I's great grandfather.

[77] The Old Pretender; he would have been James VIII of Scotland (James III of England), should he have gained the throne. He died in

1715, a year after George I came to the throne, the Scots made a fruitless attempt to place their Stuart King, James, the 'Old Pretender' on the throne. About thirty years later their own Bonnie Prince Charlie[78] also made an attempt to gain the throne for his father, with disastrous consequences.

Though, she thought wistfully, many there were who even now, despite all the death, bloodshed and sorrow that had resulted from Prince Charlie's attempt to gain the crown, still wished that it was a Stuart King who sat on the throne rather than the despised Hanoverian who occupied it at present.

One family who had been instrumental in putting down both the 1715 and 1745 uprisings and who were very satisfied with their present King, as she knew only too well, were the Campbells. The Dukes of Argyle[79] had characteristically fought alongside the English King against the 'Young Pretender', Bonnie Prince Charlie. The Campbells thus had fought against many of their Highland neighbours; neighbours who were later to pay a high price for their attempts to return their Stuart King to his throne.

Though the Campbells themselves previous to this had paid dearly for their stance against the Stuart Kings. They had fought against Charles I, and thus against her hero Montrose[80], during

---

1766.

[78] Bonnie Prince Charlie was the son of the 'Old Pretender'. Bonnie Prince Charlie would have eventually become King Charles III of Scotland and also King Charles III of England if the 1745 Uprising had been successful and he had won the throne for his father, 'The Old Pretender'.

[79] The Duke of Argyle is the Chief of the Campbell Clan.

[80] The Marquis of Montrose started out on the side of the Covenanters but later reviewed his allegiance and became a loyal defender of King Charles I and was appointed King's Lieutenant in Scotland. He was a brilliant General. On the orders of Charles I, who had been captured by the Scottish Covenanting army, Montrose went into exile in France

the time of the Covenanters; that confused time during which Charles I lost his head and Cromwell took over the country. Archibald Campbell, The Marquis of Argyle, or King Campbell as some had called him, had in turn lost his head when Charles II eventually became King.

The son of the Marquis of Argyle, also had a taste for power, but he fared no better than his father, in that he was also executed; for his role in a plot to put James, Duke of Monmouth, the illegitimate son of Charles II, on the throne in place of Charles II's brother, James II.

Travelling to Mull did not usually cause her to recollect so much of the history of her country, Eilidh thought ruefully. Perhaps it was because her mother was marrying another Archibald Campbell that the fortunes of this family were brought to remembrance thus, but more likely it was because the present Duke was intent on selling off Morvern to pay for his debts.

The present Duke of Argyle was said to be a close friend of their new King George IV; his wife being the daughter of one of the King's most powerful mistresses, Lady Jersey. George

---

in 1646. Charles I was subsequently handed over by the Scots to the English Parliamentarians in 1647, and executed in January 1649. In 1650 Charles II sent Montrose back to Scotland to gather an army on his behalf. Montrose discovered little enthusiasm for a royalist uprising. In the meantime King Charles II had also opened up negotiations with the Scottish Covenanting army which he had sent Montrose out to fight against. Therefore, when Montrose was betrayed and captured by the Scots, King Charles II disowned him. The Marquis of Montrose was subsequently hanged in Edinburgh, as a traitor, and his head was placed on the City's Tollbooth. In January 1651 King Charles II was crowned at Scone, but he fled back into exile later that same year. Cromwell's Parliamentarian army then took control and 'Home Rule' in Scotland disappeared in 1653 when the Scottish General Assembly was disbanded.

Campbell, the 6th Duke of Argyle, as Adrianne had boasted to her more than once, was a good friend and relative of their future step-father. He was reputed to be a dandy, and to be hugely extravagant, running up vast debts, appearing to care nothing for the land or the people, only for the money that could be made from it. Morvern itself was now up for sale, ostensibly to fund his profligate life style.

She idly wondered what James Maxwell, his Chamberlain, thought of him. She had known James Maxwell as long as she could remember; her father had visited him frequently, supposedly to talk about farming but in reality just for the plain pleasure of friendship. James Maxwell was a good man and in his role of Chamberlain to the Duke of Argyle, tried hard to ease the lot of the people whose land he had charge of. The old Duke of Argyle had been a fine man too, even if he had been a Campbell and had fought on the wrong side at Culloden! Though at that time he had been but a young Colonel, and only a nephew of the then incumbent Duke of Argyle.

Maxwell uttered little in the way of criticism, but she knew it broke his heart to watch George Campbell destroy what his father, the 5th Duke of Argyle, had so much loved and what he had spent much of his life tending.

Chapter 21 The Mull Ferry

Eilidh had now reached the shoreline. On the other side of this stretch of water was the Isle of Mull.

Leaving the two horses to graze, whilst they waited for the Mull ferry to arrive, Eilidh walked slowly down to the shore to look for the sea creatures and pretty shells that could usually be found there. How she loved the sea, the fresh salty smell, the sound of the waves breaking on the shore! She smiled as she saw that the seals had already begun to gather to bid her welcome.

Walking along the shore Eilidh noted the glistening seaweed and grimaced. Ruefully she remembered the day that she had cut all the red out of her hair, leaving only the few strands of gold. The seaweed contained just those same reds and yellow as did her hair and who would wish for hair that looked like seaweed!

Her mother and sisters all had the most beautiful blonde hair ranging in tone from silver to golden blonde and she had so much wanted to have hair of that same colour, even if it were only a muddy blonde. To be honest she still wished it, wished that all her hair was of that one golden colour rather than being mostly auburn red with the odd streak of gold. No wonder her mother and sisters thought she was a freak!

Even now she always tried to arrange her hair so that the gold was hidden and only the red showed. She would have shown only the gold but there was not enough of it!

She remembered her father, so very gently, questioning her as to why she had cut it so, remembered how sad he had seemed when he had eventually understood that she had cut all the red, leaving only the golden hair, because she wished to look like her mother and sisters. Though now she wondered that he had not laughed, he must surely have been sorely tempted, for she must have looked so very strange with only a few strands of gold on an otherwise bald head!

Her father had made her promise never to cut her hair in this way again and had tried to persuade her to appreciate that her hair had its own beauty. He it was who had first suggested that it looked lovely and natural, just like the seaweed that lay so plentifully along these beaches. She sighed. She still failed to understand how he could have claimed that her hair was attractive. The seaweed she supposed was most splendid, if not rather slimy, when you saw it sparkling in the water or glistening on the shoreline; but to have hair that looked thus!

Her attention was momentarily diverted by a small hermit crab whose legs had suddenly peaked out from under its shell as it began to scuttle through the clear water. She smiled and crouched down to see it clearer and noticed the sea anemones sitting there gaily waving their tendrils in the air; they too were red, but all red, not piebald.

Eilidh sighed and stood up and as she did so she spied the Mull ferry approaching the shore. Reluctantly she began to make her way back up the shore to where Liath Macha and Red Dawn were still grazing eagerly.

She knew the ferrymen well having often made this journey.

"Ciamar a tha sibh?"[81] She called out to the ferry men as she, Liath Macha and Dawn approached the boat.

"O, Meadhanach math, meadhanach math, Eilidh, agus Ciamar a tha sibh fhein?"[82] replied one of the ferry men. While the other, his eyes alight, strode towards her crying, "Failte, Eilidh failte!"[83]

---

[81] How are you?
[82] Reasonably well, reasonably well, Eilidh; and how are you yourself?
[83] Welcome, Eilidh welcome.

The boat left almost as soon as she boarded, taking both her and her two horses swiftly across the water, though they were the sole occupants at this early hour of the morning. The ferrymen were very wary of Liath Macha, asking that she make sure he did not kick their boat to pieces.

Eilidh laughingly assured them that Liath Macha was on his best behaviour. She tried to ignore the wary look that the elder of the pair gave as he noticed that the seals were following the boat, coming all the time closer and in ever greater numbers; many more than he usually saw, unless of course it was Eilidh who they were taking across to Mull.

He would be making the sign against the evil eye Eilidh thought with a wry smile, knowing that his respect for her father and his enthralment with her looks warred with his instinct that something strange was happening. She knew that rumours of her mother's opinions about her would only grow stronger with time and wondered how long it would be before this prejudice outweighed the goodwill that the recommendations of her father and her own actions had gained her in times past.

They soon entered Tobermory Bay, that same Bay where the Florida had been blown to pieces and Captain Forester's ship had reputedly been sunk, and she shuddered as she remembered anew the Spanish Princess and her fated vision, and then suddenly there came before her again, unwanted, the vision of the face that habitually haunted her.

The seals stayed watching for some time after she and the horses had disembarked from the ferry. Eilidh took time to thank them for their company and bade farewell both to the seals and the ferrymen before continuing on her way.

This day she did not intend to visit Bloody Bay where Angus MacDonald had won a battle against his father John

MacDonald, Lord of the Isles[84]. This John MacDonald was the same man who had sent her forbear, Donald Maclean to punish The MacMaster for his insults, and gifted him Ardgour as a reward.

Her ancestor, Ewan Maclean, 2nd Laird of Ardgour, had been killed here. He was said to have been Master of the Household to the Lord of the Isles and as such must have fought for the Lord of the Isles in this sad battle of father against son.

---

[84] That Lord of the Isles who had made a treaty with the English King Edward IV against his Scottish King James III. Edward IV later betrayed this Lord of the Isles to the Scottish King. The eventual outcome of this betrayal was the ending of the power and autonomy of the Lordship of the Isles.

Chapter 22 John Maxwell, Chamberlain to the Duke of Argyle

Eilidh, Liath Macha and Dawn walked leisurely down the coast of Mull until they reached Aros Mains. Here Eilidh stopped and unsaddled both the horses, turning them loose, whilst leaving her possessions under a stubby tree. Liath Macha would not let anyone approach them as she well knew.

Aros Mains was where Maxwell had built his family home. It was situated near to Aros Castle, which had once been a seat of the Lord of the Isles, and overlooked Morvern. Eilidh could think of few places better in which to build a house than here where the smell of the sea was intoxicating, where you could almost feel the splash of the spray as, cavorting with the fresh sea breeze, it was blown inland. Though perhaps she herself, if she could choose, would prefer to situate her home where the Lords of the Isles had elected to place their castles; high up on a rock face, as was Aros Castle, with the sparkling sea deep down below, diffusing in almost every direction far and wide, where you could see the land stretching out behind for mile upon mile, as if unto the very ends of the earth.

Contentment touched her for a moment as she stood outside James Maxwell's house as the memories of happier times crowded in.

The next moment the man himself was suddenly there.

She had not thought she would be honoured thus by him coming out himself to meet her. She smiled ruefully to herself, she had not said that she would be coming, news it seemed travelled fast. James Maxwell would well know that if she was in these parts she would never pass by the door of his house.

She walked towards him smiling. "Ah it is the Sight that you have now to know the time it is that I am coming!"

A slight smile touched the edge of his mouth as he strode forward to greet her. "Eilidh Ruadh you are most welcome. I knew that ye would not leave without a visit. I left word that I should be told of your approach. It seems that there are still some that mind the word of James Maxwell." His eyes smiled as he said this.

He was a man above middle years, but hale and hearty as one much younger, with an autocratic look that might frighten if you missed the kindly lines around the eyes; eyes that now retained a hint of a strained, sad look that had not been there before.

There was a slight question in her eyes as she saw this, but she said nothing.

She was following him into his house, when suddenly he turned and straightened, fixing her with a stern look. "Eilidh!"

"Sir?"

"That black divil of yours, you have got him tied up have you not?"

She grinned back impishly. "I should by rights charge you stud fees. I had a wee glance at that filly your mare had last spring. She appears to be rather special."

He looked back at her sourly before replying, "That's as may be but I had no intention of breeding off her Dam when she was so young." He turned round and stomped forward saying as he went, "For your information I had all my mares taken in doors the moment I heard that your arrival was expected."

Eilidh laughed. "I see how it is now. How silly of me to imagine that it was my presence that you were making all these preparations for, that you were so prompt in coming to meet me because you were pleased to see me. I should have guessed should I not, that it was on Liath Macha's account that you were so anxious to be on the lookout for my coming!"

It was his turn to laugh as he turned into a cosy little room where a pretty young girl was standing with a tray, setting down refreshments. "Thank you Ada, that will be all."

Eilidh smiled at the girl as she made to leave, then she asked suddenly "Are you not David Cameron's daughter?"

"Yes Miss," replied the girl shyly.

"You have a likeness of your mother about you," said Eilidh. "How is she? Is her back better?"

"Yes Miss." The girl's eyes lit up for a moment before she lowered them again shyly.

"Tell her I was asking for her, give her my best wishes."

"Yes Miss," said the girl and went quickly out of the door.

"A nice girl that," said Maxwell, "good family, David Cameron has worked for me since he was a boy. His eldest son works for me now, good worker, can trust him to work even if there is no one around. The other men like him too. I have plans for the lad."

Eilidh asked intently, "You intend to stay on then even when Morvern is sold?"

"There is still Mull, not that I need the work. As you can see I am comfortably situated myself. No, I'll not move. I've lived here most of my life and I'd like to die here. The children are doing well," he said contentedly.

"B..."

"No buts," he said firmly as he sat down.

"Yet I think Sir that you are not as content as you were when last I visited," she retorted.

"You see too true Eilidh," Maxwell answered tiredly.

"The Duke?"

"The Duke," he admitted. "But nothing new," he sighed, "Just sadness for the people who will be affected by all these changes. The Landlords who will come will have no connection

188

to this land, no love for it or the people. Argyle at least is a Highlander himself, and this is after all the land of his fathers." He looked pensively out of the window for a moment before continuing. "I greatly fear Eilidh that many of the changes that are coming will not be for the better."

He poured Eilidh a drink and smiled at how her eyes widened as she saw the cakes that he offered. "I do not think that I ever met a female who enjoyed her food so well and ate so much cake as yourself," he said with a laugh in his voice.

"That is because all the females you know have a plentiful supply of such delicacies. I must have a talk with your cook!" she retorted. Then with a pretence at sadness continued, "Not that I could ever manage to produce something so good myself!"

There was quiet for a moment as Eilidh ate her cake, then she asked "It is not so bad though is it? Gregerson bought Ardtornish did he not?"

"Aye, that he did. He's a good man, there will not be too many changes at Ardtornish, but you of all people cannot think that the rest of the estate will go so sweetly. Think you that it will be only Highlanders that will buy? Mark my words Eilidh before many years have passed the place will be filled by Sassenachs! Moreover, Ardtornish itself will not belong to the Gregersons forever. Not all are blessed with sons like mine own; some like the late Duke are less fortunate." They were both quiet for a moment and then he continued "Imagine Ardtornish in the hands of those such as that factor on the Duke of Sutherlands Estate, Patrick Seller!"[85]

---

[85] Patrick Seller did in fact buy Ardtornish Estate in 1838. He was the factor responsible for much of the evictions on the Duke of Sutherland's estates.

189

Eilidh shuddered and then said wistfully, "It was not as I planned, not as I imagined, this visit to Morvern I mean. I thought it would give me comfort to think that though I was leaving, all this would still endure, the people, the land would still remain evermore the same, just as the Feinne somehow still dwell on the hills of Morvern, immortalised forever; just as they also continue to live on in the tales and stories of Ossian. These past few days though it was almost as if they had left, I could not see their shadows, imagine their paths." She sighed and looked up at him anxiously, before going on to say almost pleadingly, "It was as if they had gone, vanished or never been; and the glens," she continued in what was nearly a whisper, "The glens, I kept seeing them empty, empty of people, with the houses crumbled away to only the odd stone, and the sheep grazing where the children played." She was silent, eyes far away.

The old man listened and watched her silently before asking quietly "The Sight?"

She nodded, "I did not know that father told you of this."

"I knew he had it. He often said that he could not decide if it was a curse or a blessing. He did not tell me that you too possessed the 'gift'." He was quiet for a few moments before continuing almost brusquely. "I was at your father's funeral Eilidh. He was buried with almost indecent haste, as if she wanted to remove his presence from her sight as quickly as possible. I am sorry Eilidh but try as I might, and as beautiful as she undoubtedly is, I cannot like your mother. Anyway, that is as may be, but when you arrived as you did that day on Liath Macha, I guessed. I knew there was no other way you could have known of your father's death so soon, unless it was the Sight." He continued heavily, "I have not the Sight but I fear your vision is only too true."

"Sometime that which one sees in a vision can be changed," she said slowly, "But not this I think. The Sight was hazy, the visions crept in and then fled and then crept back. It was strange." She shook her head as if to shake the vision away. "There must be a will to make it different."

"And in this case the will is that the land becomes more profitable and for that the people will have to go," he continued for her. "Though in truth Eilidh lass I believe, and I have pondered and thought over this question for many a long hour; I think now that it will not be all bad."

She looked at him disbelievingly while he continued, "Things are changing Eilidh. While we love the land hereabouts, and the people and our ancient customs, not all are like us. Take for instance, Lord George Campbell, the present Duke of Argyle."

The image of Hindley sitting round the card table with the Duke of Argyle flashed before her and her heart contracted with a flurry of fear. While she had never met the present Duke of Argyle she had seen paintings of him. Her momentary distraction must have been obvious, for Maxwell misinterpreted it.

"Eilidh," he said gently, "he is not alone, most of the gentry hereabouts want a better way of life. They do not wish to remain up here in the Highlands in relative poverty. They want what the southerners have; luxuries, excitement, change, different opportunities. They are not interested in past traditions but in what they can get for themselves, now. Those that have been raised south will have little or no understanding of what they are losing of their cultural inheritance."

She still did not say anything, momentarily cold; though she listened intently as he continued, "Soon it will be the people as well as the gentry that will want more than what this land freely offers them. I remember when there were almost half the people in Morvern, and the land did not yield richly then. Now the people are going hungry."

"Only where they are denied their rights to graze their cattle on the hills, on the common grazing," she cried. "The hills that are needed by the people for their cattle are now used instead to fatten sheep, to further line the pockets of those whose pockets are already heavy with silver."

He looked at her quietly. "It saddens me too that the life on the shielings is going. Remember though that while the people of old scratched a living from the land, they and their animals still went hungry. The Old Duke and I planned that they gain wealth by having individual farming units, but the people were stubborn," he sighed. "The new owners will not be so patient with their tenants' inability to pay a rent. That same land Eilidh, when farmed by the tackmen using sheep rather than the old system, yields a lot more return for one's money. If the people had agreed to farm as we suggested, such as your father has implemented in Ardgour[86], they could have paid more rent and then perhaps there would have been less temptation to introduce the more radical changes. But still," he mused, "still I believe it would not be enough. The old people love the life they have Eilidh, but the young ones with hungry stomachs they will leave when they see that they may get more elsewhere."

"But they won't!" Eilidh exclaimed. "Not all of them gain a better way of life I mean. I have seen the beggars on the city streets, the children working in the factories, the women left

---

[86] The historical Alexander Maclean seems to have been a concerned and enthusiastic landlord. In order to prevent emigration, and to improve the standard of living of his tenants he divided up a number of farms, which had originally been farmed by a community, into individual small holdings, or crofts. Although he met initial resistance to these changes, the long term outcome seems to have been beneficial to the community as a whole.

with the bairns when men with no community to remind them of their responsibilities go off to pastures new leaving these young women, girls with little choice but to......" her voice fell away as she realised that she should not be talking of such things.

James Maxwell, compassion written in his eyes, on his wise face, replied gently, "I understand Eilidh. Is not my very own son-in-law Norman MacLeod busy trying to help those very people? Often times he has sat in that very same chair that you sit in now, saying much as you have just said. He believes that things will get worse yet and I pray that he has the strength of purpose and the strength of mind to continue in the work that he has chosen for himself. It is my little Agnes I feel for though. It is a good man she has chosen but she will not find it easy comforting him whilst managing alone when he is out and about at his good works."

Eilidh's face lit up, "And their bairns," she asked, "How are they?"

The old man looked proud, "Grand, right grand, and young Norman he is getting a great big chap, all of seven years he is. Like to be as good a man as his faither."

"And grandfaither," said Eilidh, her eyes laughing now.

"That old fellow over in Fuinary," returned Maxwell with a mock show of annoyance. Then he chuckled, "I suppose he could do worse than be like the old man." He turned to her concerned as he asked "Did you know that his sight was failing?"

"I should have said like both his grandfaithers," Eilidh acknowledged cheerfully, and then more seriously she added, "I did not know that the minister's sight was going. It is longer than I like since I last visited the manse[87]. I had planned to call in, to say my goodbyes, on my return journey to Ardgour."

"Tell young John that if he wishes to go to the youngsters' ball that they are holding for Adrianne before the wedding, then he can travel with me. I have promised to go to the wedding, though I like it ill; but Archibald Campbell is kin to the Duke and if there is no need to give offence…" He did not continue.

They were quiet for a moment, all the food was gone and Eilidh looked at her empty plate and sighed, "You are right of course."

James Maxwell stayed silent, but watched her intently as Eilidh continued.

"The food I have just eaten, those in the villages do not get such food. If they could choose between a diet such as you and I usually eat and such as they live on, why there is no contest. If they are lucky they may get potatoes for all three of their meals, with milk or dairy products from the cow, if she is in milk, and perhaps a wee bit of herring or some such on a good day! Then of course there are usually some small amounts of oatmeal for to bake scones or some such thing, or to add to the meal; though at times there is not even that. Some few may have meat occasionally, but only those who can afford to kill a sheep or a cow, and most cannot; while even then one cow has to last a family all winter!" She looked at him big eyes wide, "The family, the community, the stories, they will all go because the people need to eat. As you said, they too will begin to want what they feel the southerners have aplenty. Why should it be only the southerners that get the good living, can afford the luxuries in life? And those like you and I who have plenty of everything, why they will just want even more," continued Eilidh sadly.

"It is human nature Eilidh. The life here, the community, the friendship, the land, the sea, the air; I believe that though I went

---

[87] Vicarage.

194

to the ends of the earth I would find none better, but I am not hungry. You cannot blame the people for wanting to better themselves," said Maxwell kindly.

"No, not for wanting to fill their stomachs when they are empty; that I can understand. But to deprive others of their homes, of the land that they and their families have worked on over countless generations, solely for greed, this I find much less easy to forgive."

"I too Eilidh, but the land cannot continue to support more and more people. What if the crops fail, if the harvest is poor, what then? Something must happen, things are changing Eilidh. Why I heard only the other week about the ship that came to Liverpool, what was her name?"

"The Savannah," said Eilidh in a disinterested tone.

"Yes…, yes…, that's right, a steamship." His eyes lit up and there was a momentary excitement in his eyes. "To see a ship powered by steam!"

"She had sails too did she not?" said Eilidh shortly.

"She did, but do you not see Eilidh she is a start, change is coming whether we like it or not."

She sat up straighter suddenly, pain in her eyes, "Did you…, did you…?"

"Find out as to the mood of the authorities with regard to the radicals. What is there to expect Eilidh?" Maxwell said gently. "They are in no humour to stand any nonsense. They want a scapegoat, an example to show the people that they will react decisively and harshly in response to any trouble the people might be planning."

"Was not Peterloo harsh enough!"

"Peterloo was embarrassing to the government, but it also frightened them. They do not wish to chance any more trouble. The Six Acts are proof of that. Tell Ruairidh this, warn him that

195

the government is looking for any excuse to make an example of someone and they will not be lenient. Armed revolution is not the answer. Advise the young fool to use his head rather than his heart if he wants to make a difference to the lives of the common folk. Put him in touch with young Norman."

Eilidh's eyes brightened. "Now that is an idea!" She went quiet for a moment before saying pensively, "Peterloo……"

"Yes Eilidh," he said with mock longsuffering in his voice.

"Do you think that the people were right to want to reform the way in which the Members of Parliament are elected? At present, as in Argyle, the younger son of the local landed gentry automatically gets the seat or, if he does not wish to accept it, that area will be represented by someone who has had his seat bought for him, on the understanding that once elected he would be required to vote in the Commons in whatsoever way he was directed to by the person who paid for him to gain that seat in the first place."

"Lord John Campbell, the Duke's brother, will be elected unopposed at the elections here next month and 'tis said he never even takes his seat in Parliament! Would it not be better if every adult could vote for whosoever they wished to represent them in Parliament, if Argyle, for instance, were represented by someone who would speak up for our rights, our needs?"

Maxwell looked amused. "Think you that the body who was voted in by the people would be any the less likely to have his own self-interest at heart?"

"It would be more likely for one of the people, a representative of their own kind, to speak out for the needs of those of the ranks that he hailed from!"

"Think you that," Maxwell replied grimly. "I tell you Eilidh that once such a one tasted power he would be more inclined to try to imitate his betters and to do everything possible just to hold onto that position that he had gained, even if that entailed compromising his integrity, if ever he possessed such a thing in the first place. There are not many men so strong and upright that they can resist the allure of wealth and power, especially those who have never previously experienced it. It is a heady brew. Our Norman is perhaps one of the very few who understand the true responsibilities of power; but remember he has tasted the life of a gentleman and has supped a strong brew of morals with his mother's milk and been fed high principles with his father's preaching. He has thus maybe a small mite of protection from such corruption; but if you are born into poverty where do you find the strength to resist such temptations and avoid despising the dung heap you were born into?"

Eilidh looked to be about to interrupt but he went on regardless. "Furthermore, there are rich men who look to the lot of the less fortunate in society, wealthy philanthropists who try to help the poor and make laws for their protection. It is men such as these, such as Wilberforce, to whom we must look to protect those whose lot in life is more difficult than our own."

"True", Eilidh responded, "there are a few good honourable men who do what they can for those who have been born into less fortunate circumstances than they themselves. However more are they who would resist change, who will fight tooth and nail to keep those so called upstarts in their place so that they do not threaten their own position in society, than those who would and do strive to improve the lot of the common man. There is much injustice in our country sir. That is why the weavers of Glasgow, who grow hungry as they continue to be paid increasingly less for their work than was agreed by the law, are becoming unsettled; why they look for less peaceful means to create change."

"Were you not yourself complaining, just a few moments before, that change is coming? Eilidh, these are unsettling times, unsettling, but exciting; changes are coming, both for the better and for the worse. Let us pray that we do not get such change as happened in France when the people sought to take change into their own hands. However I have news of a more pleasant change Eilidh. Did you hear that Lord John Campbell, the Duke's younger brother, is to wed again this April, after the election is over? Not of course, as you so rightly pointed out, that there is the least chance of him losing his seat!"

Eilidh smiled now. "No I did not hear it. I knew of course that last year the Duchess's son by her first marriage had wed one of the daughters of Lady Charlotte, the Duke's sister. That was a strange marriage was it not; they would be what... step cousins?"

He laughed. "I suppose so, though there is no close blood link. Your sister Adrianne went to that wedding along with Archibald Campbell. Though I confess I was surprised to see her there as it was not long after the death of your father."

She smiled, "Adrianne enjoyed the ceremony very well I believe. Mother did not attend the wedding however but I assume she will be invited to Lord John's. Is his new wife more acceptable to the family than the last?"

"She appears to be quite unexceptional," he said calmly with a twinkle in his eye. "Lady Charlotte[88] also is very contented in her new marriage."

---

[88] Sister to the 6th Duke of Argyle and one time lady in waiting to Queen Caroline.

"Is the Princess Caroline[89], or should I call her Queen Caroline now, still asking her to accompany her on her travels around Europe?"

"I believe she still writes to her frequently, but understands that Lady Charlotte's new domestic arrangements preclude her visiting abroad. Now if she returns to England, in the unlikely event that King George will acknowledge her as his Queen, then she may be persuaded to accept a position in her household. However ......"

Eilidh looked at him sadly. "You think then that he will not have her as Queen. How could that be?"

"I believe he hates her. Since the death of their daughter Princess Charlotte she has lost any worth politically. He will do everything possible to ensure she is never acknowledged as his consort. Let us hope she remains abroad."

Eilidh was silent for a moment. "Poor woman."

"Poor woman indeed. However Eilidh, we cannot set the world to rights this morning. Come, I want to show you my horses, and then there is the garden. You have no idea the satisfaction I get from what comes out of the soil." He stood up and Eilidh uncoiling herself from the chair she had been sitting in, not unwillingly got up to follow him.

Eilidh did not leave Aros Main until after she had enjoyed a late lunch. She treasured every moment of the time spent in the company of James Maxwell. It was not often now that she benefited from time and conversation with such as he. When her father was alive it had been common place and not the occasional occurrence.

Eventually the time came for her to leave and as she called for her horses she laughed at Maxwell's mock horror at the sight of Liath Macha.

---

[89] The estranged wife of King George IV.

Eilidh hated goodbyes and left quickly, but it warmed her heart long did the remembrance of this visit, of Maxwell's reiteration that she would be at all times welcome here at Aros Mains, and his offer of sanctuary if ever the time came that her mother was no longer willing to provide for her. Eilidh knew that her mother would make quite sure she would be unable to accept this aid, but she also knew that the offer was genuine and for that she thanked him from the bottom of her heart.

Chapter 23 Lady Rock

Eilidh rode down from Aros Mains, through the pretty village of Salen, and then carried on travelling along the coastline until she arrived, in what seemed to be very little time, at Duart Castle, the traditional seat of Clan Maclean. Brigadier General Sir Fitzroy Maclean was the 24th Chief of Clan Maclean but so far as she was aware Duart Castle did not belong to him, nor did she know his present whereabouts, only that he had spent much of his life serving in the West Indies.

Eilidh stopped on a small hill that overlooked the castle, and then dismounted.

The castle was built high up on a rock, looking out over the water across to the mainland. It was ideally situated both defensively and strategically, and was set in an extremely picturesque position.

For some time Eilidh just sat there, staring at the ruins, as if to imprint the picture of them on her memory for ever.

Just over one hundred and thirty years ago, whilst Sir John Maclean of Duart[90] was away fighting for the Jacobite[91] cause at the Battle of Killicrankie[92], English warships had battered Duart Castle leaving it in such a state as to enable the Campbell's, shortly after, to demolish it further and to thus increase their grip on the erstwhile Maclean lands. The Jacobites had won this battle against William of Orange[93], but they may as well have lost as their leader 'Bonnie Dundee' was killed just as the battle ended. Their allegiance to the Stuart Kings cost the Macleans of Duart dear!

---

[90] 20th Clan Chief of Clan Maclean and 4th Baronet.
[91] Those who favoured the cause of King James II.
[92] Battle fought for the cause of James II against that of his daughter Queen Mary and her husband William of Orange in 1688.
[93] Became King when his father-in-law James II was driven into exile.

The Campbells now owned much of what had of old been Maclean territory, but they and the Maclean's had not always been enemies. There was a story about a time when they had been allies, when to further cement this friendship Lachlan Maclean of Duart, a different Lachlan to that of the story of 'The Spanish Princess', wed Catherine, sister to Campbell of Argyll.

The story however had an ill ending which tragically somewhat upset relations between the two clans; for according to the tale that she had heard, after the pair had been married a few years, Lachlan began to grow frustrated with Catherine's failure to produce for him an heir.

There is a rock just down from Duart Castle that can only be seen at low tide as it becomes submerged by water when the tide comes in. To this rock, late one evening Lachlan rowed Catherine and there he left her. When morning came his wife had gone and Lachlan Maclean, convinced that his plan had succeeded, sorrowfully reported to the Earl of Argyle that his sister had died. Unfortunately for him a well-meaning fisherman had not only rescued Catherine, but returned her to her brother. Lachlan Maclean was duly rewarded for this cowardly act when a number of years later the Campbells had their revenge and dirked him whilst he was in bed during a visit to Edinburgh.

The rock however was still named Lady Rock, in memory of this dishonourable deed.

Eilidh had to admit that this story somewhat lessened for her the allure of this particular castle, which was perhaps foolish as of course the numbers of brave and worthy chiefs far outweighed the dastardly ones. Despite this aversion to the castle, she determined to spend that night sleeping safe and dry amidst its stout walls.

She awoke at dawn unrefreshed and uneasy, for her slumbers had been troubled by strange recurrent images such as might have led her to wish she had slept elsewhere other than in the vicinity of Lady Rock with its memories of treachery waiting to bewitch her dreams.

It had seemed as if her eyes had but closed when she drifted off to sleep, only to be immediately met with the dream sight of Lady Rock. All night long the vision of that tiny landmass had pervaded her dreams.

Involuntarily she had witnessed it at low tide as it proudly displayed those of its attributes which it deemed suitable to exhibit; unwillingly she watched as the tide rose higher and higher, she observed the rock whilst slowly it appeared to diminish in size so that she was bound to note the exact point at which it finally disappeared from view, the point where it transformed from a familiar landmark into a hazard, most treacherous to the unwary sailor.

Then the scene would change and the rock would once more be in full sight for all to see, but now the winds roared and the waves crashed against the side of the lonesome little rock, one minute it was there and the next it was covered by a vast wave; and then all of a sudden all would be quiet again, all at peace and the sun shone and the sky was so blue and she could almost feel the heat and smell the fresh tang of the sea and hear the sound of the birds as they swept overhead glorying in the idyllic warmth of the soft sea breeze. A second later the skies would darken again and the scent of danger would fill the air. All night long, so it seemed to her, she had dreamed thus, spun moment to moment from delight to fear, compelled to observe the fate of the rock as it stood victim to all the elements.

Once or twice she thought that she had caught a glimpsed of a hazy figure lying on the rock as if drowned, while the rain fell and the thunder raged, but she was never quite sure if the figure were ever really there, if it had been but a trick of the light or her imagination.

Slowly Eilidh stood up. She would sleep no more this night. She walked carefully down to the sea line and then made her way slowly along the shore.

Lady Rock lay there in full view amongst the still waters and as she stood looking out at it she realised that last night's dreams had somehow rent from her all her previous dislike of the rock. Now she viewed it differently. Somehow she now understood that for Maclean's unhappy bride, that rock would have held bittersweet memories.

Left there all alone, exposed to die, she must have been in terror for her life, but paradoxically the rock had turned out to be the place of her earthly salvation. From that rock she had been rescued from imminent death and past misery and returned to her family. Would she not have cause to love, or at least remember with gratitude that place which had been the means of her redemption?

There was no sign of any life on Lady Rock, but yet Eilidh gazed for many a long moment looking out over the waters wondering at the strangeness of her dream, trying to discover the illusive detail that caused the Lady Rock that she had seen in her dream to seem to differ in some intangible way from the rock she beheld this moment before her. Trying to decipher what it was about the rock that had caused her, in those strange dreams, to fancy that it held some great treasure.

At last, after one final lingering look over the water, she turned and slowly retraced her steps, climbing pensively back up to where Red Dawn and Liath Macha yet remained contentedly grazing.

Chapter 24 Innis-nan-Druidhneach[94]

After a leisurely breakfast Eilidh remounted Liath Macha and, with Dawn ambling alongside, continued slowly on her way. Iona was where she was headed this morning, but she felt a strange reluctance to go there.

She had sailed past Iona earlier in the year but not stopped, despite the great temptation. Instead she had anchored just off Staffa, and then swum over to the island to spend a night in Fingal's Cave. Such a grand place to sit and dream was Staffa; a place where so many centuries before, the Feinne and their noble King Fingal would have visited, perhaps to hold secret meetings or maybe to hide. She had always believed that Fingal himself would have gone there when he wished to be alone or needed its seclusion, its tranquillity, to help him to think, to plan...... She sighed, a more simple age than this but fraught with the same passions, love, hate, honour, loyalty, treachery...

Iona had been her father's special place. He had always maintained there was something peculiar about this island, that the atmosphere there was quite unique; and indeed nowhere else had she ever felt that sense of peace that engulfed her when she stepped onto Iona. For the religious fervour and piety of generations of monks and nuns had indelibly left its mark. It wasn't the buildings, or the sense of history, nor the cemetery containing the bones of the ancient Scottish Kings that made Iona so special, but the centuries of worship. Man's devoted love and reverence to God, rigorously practiced and observed on this island century upon century, had engendered such an aura that it was ingrained, embedded in the very rocks themselves.

---

[94] Island of the Druids.

Invariably, just as soon as she returned home from those long winters in the lowlands, her father would take her with him to visit Iona, just for the joy of seeing the Island itself. Sometimes James Maxwell would accompany them for he, loving the land and its people as he did, loved Iona also. Her father however would also at times choose to visit Iona alone; when he felt unhappy, when some other worry weighed him down, on those occasions when his relationship with her mother became intolerable, then he would come to Iona in the hope that the peace and faith that Iona exuded would ease his tiredness and refresh his faith.

The Island was known by many of the local people as Innis-nan-Druidhneach, thus lending support to the idea that Iona had been a place of druidic worship even before St Columba built his abbey there all those hundreds of years ago.

Columba, or Colum Cille as he was known hereabouts, was said to have been a priest from an Irish royal family. Tradition told that Columba copied one of the manuscripts belonging to his mentor, Saint Finnian[95] with the intention of keeping it for his own use. When Saint Finnian disputed his right to retain this copy, Columba refused to return it. The disagreement escalated and, as both parties had many important friends, a battle soon ensued over who had the right to possess the manuscript. Many died in the conflict.

Eilidh smiled wryly as she thought of this. How could men be so foolish as to fight over a mere manuscript? True, if it contained God's word it was a very important document and needed to be shared, but surely God would expect a peaceful sharing of such information rather than a bloody battle for ownership of the script!

---

[95] St Finnian of Moville was a famous Irish Christian monk and teacher.

Some versions of this tale claimed that Columba was threatened with excommunication for his theft of the manuscript and for the ensuing violence, and that this punishment was later commuted to exile. Others told that when Columba realised the harm his pride and folly had caused he was much chastened and determined to exile himself from his beloved Ireland and thus he set forth with twelve companions vowing to settle on the first bit of land he came to where he could no longer see the country of his birth.

In some ways, she mused, it was similar to the story of Saint Paul, who spent the early part of his life persecuting Christians before he realised that he was lacking in his understanding of the role that God wanted him to perform in life. Both men initially inadvertently used their immense talents to do harm before undertaking a commission that would have them remembered down through the ages as colossal men of God. How right had Kai-Ying been when she taught that great ability was a double edged sword capable of use for ill as well as for good!

Columba was said to have been instrumental in spreading Christianity throughout Scotland. He and his monks travelled far and wide sowing the word of God wherever they went, reaching at least as far south as Lindisfarne where Saint Aidan, who came from Columba's monastery on Iona, established another monastery.

Columba only returned to Ireland once more when he was alive, and that was to found a new church. He died on Iona and was buried inside his abbey, but his remains were said to have been removed from there, perhaps to escape desecration by the marauding Vikings, and were eventually returned to Ireland, the land of his birth.

Her father had told her that the Vikings had come seeking to steal treasure from the monastery, which they eventually destroyed; but not before many of its relics, including the exquisite Book of Kells[96] had been removed to a place of safety. She had never seen the book but her father had often described to her the extraordinary artwork that the book contained, expressing his awe at its beauty and artistry and wondering at the belief of those who had helped in its creation.

Little now remained of Columba's old monastery that could be seen by human eyes, but another abbey had been built on Iona many years after Columba's death. Reginald[97], son of Somerled[98], built a Benedictine abbey and monastery and filled it with monks who would worship along the Roman Catholic lines rather than the traditional Celtic Christian faith[99]. Reginald also built a nunnery on the island. Both this abbey and the nunnery eventually became casualties of the Scottish Reformation[100] and were now in ruins.

---

[96] Ornate manuscript containing the four Gospels of the New Testament.

[97] Somerled's son; ancestor of the MacDonalds, who later became the Lords of the Isles.

[98] Somerled, King of the Isles, born around 1113 in Morvern. Some claim he was a descendent of Lulach, Macbeth's stepson, possibly also of Norse descent. He died in 1164 whilst attempting to raid Glasgow.

[99] Malcolm Canmore (Malcolm III), son of the King Duncan that Macbeth is reputed to have killed, and his wife Margaret (Saint Margaret), are said to have been instrumental in bringing the Catholic faith to Scotland.

[100] Reformation of the Church. In England the Protestant faith had gained ascendancy in the time of King Henry VIII. In Scotland, at about this same time, the preaching of John Knox amongst others began to introduce the Protestant doctrines. In 1560, on the death of the Catholic Mary of Guise, (who had been Regent in Scotland whilst her daughter, Mary Queen of Scots was a child), a Protestant Parliament took control of Scotland, to govern on behalf of her daughter Mary I

She loved to sit amongst the ruins of the nunnery, an Eaglais Dubh[101], wrapped in that spiritual peace which they had left behind as a gift for those to come throughout the ensuing centuries. As she sat she would imagine that the nunnery was still alive, with real nuns living and breathing within, and not just the memory of them, and make believe that they were all around her, going about their daily tasks. At times it would feel so real that she could almost hear the music that they must have made when they sang praise to God, or perhaps it was the music of the angels that she heard, for surely they would remain basking in the worship that somehow still exuded throughout the island.

One of her favourite tombs was that of the prioress Anna Maclean. Her tombstone was engraved with her image, and animals were depicted standing next to her, while an angel was placed at each side of her head. She had often sat next to this tomb imagining what the prioress had been like in life and wondering if she, like Saint Francis of Assisi, had loved all the wild animals, feeding them and caring for those that were injured or sick.

Another picturesque tombstone, thought to be that of a Maclean, was that of the 'Rider', who was portrayed mounted on a horse, sword in hand; on this tombstone there was also a carving of a pious lady. This tomb, along with those of many other of her forbears, was located in the Reilig Odhrain[102].

(Mary Queen of Scots) and her daughter's young husband 'Francis the Dauphin' (heir to the French throne). One of their first actions was to forbid the celebration of mass and to declare that the Popes would no longer have any authority in Scotland. This accelerated the Scottish Reformation. Mary Queen of Scots' son King James I of England (VI of Scotland) was raised a strong Protestant.

[101] The Black Church, so called because the Nuns, like the monks, wore black.

Iona was the resting place of numerous famous kings, such as the great Kenneth MacAlpine[103] and the much maligned Macbeth and thus she and her father had often wandered around these gravestones trying to make out the worn lettering. She remembered the game they had played of guessing the king or the noble who was interred within and then trying to remember his family tree, his claim to fame. Macabre possibly; but she realised now that her father had done it with the purpose of teaching her both family and Scottish history.

Another tomb that was special to her was that of Dr John Beaton, physician to the Maclean family. Her milk brother Ewan counted himself a direct descendant of this family which had produced many generations of learned men. However Ewan, much to his father's disappointment, did not look to follow in their footsteps. Not that he was unintelligent, but he lacked the interest. His was a fun-loving disposition. He preferred his horses to his books, preferred to learn sword skills rather than medicine.

Her face softened as she thought of Ewan, and suddenly a longing rose within in her to hurry home, for surely he would be there by now. How very much she wished to see him, for nothing upset Ewan, nothing got him down and he was always ready for any type of escapade. They were like as twins, he being but three days her elder and both having been nursed simultaneously by his mother. They had spent most of the first five years of their lives together, and much of the following years also; though Mairi his mother, who doted on Ewan, had resented her presence. She had been told that Lachlan had

---

[102] St Oran's Graveyard.
[103] King of Scotland; he unified many of the Scottish and Pictish tribes. He became King of Scotland in 841 AD and is thought to have died in 858 AD.

often taken her with him when he went to work in the stables so that Mairi, his wife, could enjoy time alone with Ewan; that she had spent many a night alone amongst the horses when Lachlan 'forgot' to take her home with him in the evening. But that also had worked out to the good because now Helen, the elder daughter of the proprietor of that stables, was as a sister to her.

Eilidh smiled to herself as she remembered the one time that Ewan had accompanied her father and herself to Iona. It was one of the very few times she had ever been annoyed with him.

The coming of a dead king to Iona must have been quite an occasion and she as child had loved to walk down along the Sraid nan Marbh[104], where countless processions had brought the coffins of the kings and chiefs up from Port nam Mairtear[105] to Reilig Odhrain, imagining the pageantry and pretending to be part of the wake of a long dead king. Ewan however had, most unusually, refused to play this game with her. Indeed he had stubbornly refused to have anything to do with what he called 'her morbid interest in those dead and long gone.'

Along the 'Street of the Dead' stood the reputedly ancient and elaborately carved Maclean's cross under which she and her father had often sat and talked for hours. For her it was a symbol of both the peace which Iona exuded coupled with a sense of the continuity of her family line down the generations.

Saint Odrain's cross was another of the magnificent crosses that had escaped destruction and there was also a chapel built in his name. She had been told that Saint Odrain's Chapel had been built by the great Somerled, one time 'King of the Isles' as a family burial place and had often wondered if his bones also were interred within.

---

[104] Street of the Dead.
[105] Port of the Martyrs

Legend said that this Saint Odrain was a cousin of Columba's and that he had volunteered to be buried alive to stop the walls of the first church from falling down. There was another story that claimed that Columba had asked that he be dug up again so that he could say a last goodbye to his friend and kinsman, but had quickly ordered him reburied due to the great amount of profanities and blasphemies he was uttering as to his vision of heaven and hell.

She had been quite horrified when she first heard this tale, but her father had merely laughed and said that it was probably a story that had got confused over time with some practice of the druids who had inhabited the island long before Columba arrived. She fervently hoped that this was the case.

Whatever the truth of the story, the following generations of monastic worship had obliterated any trace of such barbaric customs and replaced it with a feeling of sanctity such as could only have appeared after generations of pure worship to the one true God.

It seemed strange though that this island whose major purpose had been that of a burial ground should be the one to spread the message of salvation and so bring hope and the promise of everlasting life to so many.

She sighed as she thought that Kai-Ying would possibly have said that it was not really that strange in that we had to pass through death into everlasting life. She would have reminded her that in going through the waters of baptism one died to one's old sinful self and when one rose out of the water again it was into a new way of life with Christ. Baptism was a symbol of passing through death, as did Jesus when he died on the Cross for the forgiveness of our sin so that we might have life everlasting through his resurrection[106].

---

[106] Romans chapter 6, verses 3-11; Colossians chapter 2, verse 12.

She was still puzzling about this seeming paradox when she caught sight of the Island just as dusk was falling. She found a small copse just down from Fionnphort, some way from any human habitation, and quickly un-tacked Liath Macha and Dawn, placing her remaining packages amongst some bushes for protection from the weather. Then she brushed the two horses and fed them before turning them loose to graze.

Eilidh herself ate sparingly that evening. As she sat there quietly gazing out across the water, she was unable to rid herself of a feeling of deep unease. Mull with its strange shadows, mists and stone formations always made her uneasy, but this was different.

The night was dark, the moon was but young and the sky overcast. Then suddenly Eilidh heard the sound of the seals as they came from all around to welcome her. Immediately her spirits lifted and scrambling to her feet she ran straightaway into the water to meet them. She lost count of the time that they played but it was a tired and happy girl that dragged herself back onto the shore much later that night and settled contentedly to sleep alongside Liath Macha and Red Dawn.

Chapter 25 Fraoch nan Lannan Geura[107]

Eilidh awoke as the light began to appear again over the horizon. She awoke not at all refreshed for her dreams had been filled with the flight and fight of dragons and with their eventual, inevitable, fatal fall.

A huge black dragon had awoken her, swooping down on her, claws out, fire streaming out of his mouth, eyes cold and hard. She had immediately banished the vision and quickly fallen back asleep again only to be awoken with the sight of this same dragon bearing down on a lone man who stood on the shore armed with a knife in each hand. Somehow she knew that he had others stashed all over his body in readiness for just such an occasion; for thus carried she her knives.

In other dreams she woke to the vision of the dragon dying with multiple knife wounds and the man looking on healthy and victorious. Then in that last dream a girl had appeared running, mad with grief, who when she saw that the dragon was dead had lain down beside it and died of her sorrow. She had shared the agony and torment, the anguish and despair that the girl suffered at the loss of her beloved; she had watched as the girl died, much as, or so the lays of Ossian told, many of the women of the Fienne had perished through their utter desolation at the death of their lovers.

She knew the story, but somehow she had dreamed it wrong. It was a story well known on Mull, about a famous outlaw named Fraoch[108]. She had always though that 'Heather' was a strange name for an outlaw, she could only suppose that he was named this as he lived his life amongst the heather on

---

[107] 'Fraoch of the Sharp Blades'.
[108] Fraoch is the Gaelic word for 'heather'.

the hills; though the rest of his title was more reassuring in that he was called 'Fraoch nan Lannan Geura'.

When she was younger she had dreamed and made believe that she was this 'Fraoch of the Sharp Blades', for did she not also carry her blades with her wherever she went? She wore a dirk in her belt and a skian dubh[109] tucked away within each of her boots, the small mattucashlass[110] concealed under each armpit and another knife in a sheath under her shirt at her shoulder.

She had prided herself on her ability to throw and use a knife or dagger. Her father had been immensely proud when she had begun to even exceed him in this skill, and his skill was prodigious. She so dearly remembered that day when she had beaten him in one of their mock competitions for the first time. She remembered how her father had taken her back to the library at the Big House where he had taken out of a locked cupboard a quite exquisite set of knives. Then he had proceeded to tell her the tale of how he had won them off her maternal grandfather. He had told her previously that the only man better than him at throwing knives was her mother's father, now he related to her the story of the day in which he had bested her grandfather in a duel, the day that he won off him this beautiful set of nine knives, the day he stole away with her mother.

The set must have been worth a king's ransom. The handles were covered with miniscule carvings of seals and encrusted with tiny jewels, but so cleverly indented that they in no whit affected the balance of the knife, or its feel as one held it. She had always thought it slightly incongruous that on each of the blades was engraved one of the different nine fruits of the

---

[109] Small single edged knife.
[110] Small double edged dagger worn under the armpit.

Spirit: love, joy, peace, longsuffering, gentleness, goodness, faith, meekness, temperance. Kai-Ying had however explained to her that they were probably there to remind the owner that if he had to resort to fighting then he had failed, and that he must use these gifts of the Spirit fully to try to resolve any issue peacefully. Her father had given her the blade marked 'Joy' on this occasion, to mark his joy at her achievement. She now owned the full set.

She had always considered the story of her father's flight with her mother as a great romance and looked upon their marriage with awe and even a slight envy - to be loved enough to be fought over, to leave thus one's family for ever for the love of one man, surely it was like a fairy tale. It was only much later, in the summer before her father's death, that she had learned the full truth of the story.

Thus the tale of Fraoch and the Dragon was a favourite of hers. Perhaps she had dreamed it because she had slept that night just down from Bunessan Bay which was near to the dragon's island. As a child she had often pretended that she was Fraoch, though of course in her playacting she had inevitably won and the dragon had always been successfully killed. She supposed that must be why she had dreamed the story thus. The real story went otherwise.

Now on the Island of Mull, just down from Bunessan Bay lived a maiden who had eyes as bright as the stars and hair as gold as the new corn, and teeth like tiny pearls. One day as she was walking down by the tide, 'Fraoch nan lannan geura' spied her and his heart was smitten, and he had eyes for none other.

Many were the days that he came down to the shore to find her, and many were the hours that he would walk and talk with her. He soon found that she was as kind and gentle as she was beautiful and it was not long before her heart belonged to the handsome outlaw.

Unknown to Fraoch, Maeve, the girl's mother, had conceived a passion for the young outlaw. When she discovered that her love was unrequited and that the object of her desire was in love with her daughter she was wrath and resolved that if she could not get Fraoch then neither would her daughter.

Then one day Maeve's daughter became extremely ill. Fraoch much concerned, begged Maeve to tell him what he could do to ensure her recovery.

Now in Bunessan Bay, which was not far from where Maeve and her daughter lived, there was an island in which a dragon had his cave. Maeve told Fraoch that her daughter would only recover if she had some berries off one of the rowan trees on this island.

Fraoch duly swam over to the island and brought back a branch of the rowan tree covered in berries.

Maeve, furious that the young man had survived, now told him that a single branch was insufficient and that he must bring back the whole tree if he wished her daughter to be healed.

Much distressed over the failing health of his beloved, Fraoch immediately swam back to the island. Unfortunately for Fraoch the movement of the earth as he dug up the small rowan tree disturbed the dragon who rushed out of his cave to see who had troubled his repose.

Fraoch raced into the water as quickly as he could, not forgetting the rowan tree. He swam across the water and reached the shore with the dragon in full pursuit. The fight between the dragon and Fraoch was long and fierce, for Fraoch in his concern for his beloved, in his haste to recover the rowan tree for her, had forgotten his knives.

217

*Fraoch, so great a warrior was he, did not despair and
eventually he succeeded in thrusting his whole arm down the
dragon's throat and with his bare hands, he dragged out its
heart. As the dragon died so did Fraoch also fall to the ground,
mortally wounded.*

*Maeve sat in her house watching the battle on the shore,
gloating over the success of her scheming. Her daughter
hearing the noise of the battle and filled with a sense of
foreboding, with great effort arose from her bed and went to
the window to try to see what might be causing the disturbance.*

*In fear and horror she ran from the window, out of the door,
and raced full of anguish and terror down to the shore where
she found Fraoch lying close to death. Flinging herself down at
his side she embraced him and as the life left his body, so did
hers seep away and hand in hand their spirits danced away
together joyfully into the wind[111].*

She sat up ruefully remembering the child that she had been
and how she had gloried in the pleasure and excitement of
fighting the dragon; trying now to repress the shaking in her
body, to subdue the waves of nausea, to forget the deathly
anguish she had felt just moments before as the dragon in her
dreams died.

It began to rain and the winds were strengthening as once
more she saw the dragon rush towards her.

Hurriedly she arose.

The clouds came down and the winds rose even greater and
fiercer than before and the waves grew higher and higher, while
the rain hammered down torrentially in sheets. Soon the Isle of
Iona was hidden from view. Yet still the black dragons came!

---

[111] The place where Fraoch and the Dragon came ashore and had their
mortal battle is to this day called Camus na Cridhe or, The Bay of the
Heart.

One after the other they appeared out of the icy mist, teeth bared, eyes cold, so very cold, before disappearing, only to return again moments later.

Eilidh shuddered and turned away, turning blindly towards Liatha Macha knowing that this day she would not be visiting Iona, knowing in her heart of hearts that should she have gone ashore she might never have left. Realising that she would never have summoned the strength to have resisted the temptation to remain on Iona where she could delight in the enduring peace that it held and bask in the comfort of her memories; or at least she would not have left until it was too late, not until long after her mother wedding; by which time she would have contravened her mother's orders to journey south with Lachlan and Mairi. Thus she would have forfeited the protection of Lachlan's guardianship.

And so, as the ice dragons soared through the wind and rain barring her way to Iona, Eilidh quickly gathered her possessions together and readied Dawn and Liath Macha for that day's long trek. Resolutely turning her back to Iona, she commenced her journey to the Mull ferry and from hence onward onto the mainland into what increasingly seemed to be a most insecure and uncertain future.

Chapter 26 Fuinary

That next morning Eilidh awoke to the sound of waves crashing on rocks far below, to the smell of the fresh salty sea, and the comforting presence of the solid, ancient walls of Ardtornish castle. She stood up quickly and rushed to the window to say her good mornings to the seals that were playing joyfully outside, revelling in the disruption that the frolicsome wind made to the now turbulent sea. For the wind this day was fresh, lifting her hair as it lifted her spirits also.

These ruins of Ardtornish castle were one of her favourite places. The castle had been very well situated, built as it was on the mainland of Morvern, on a peninsula, high on a rocky outcrop overlooking Mull. From here The Lord of the Isles, whose castle this had been, would have been able to see the approach of friends or enemies from afar, whatever direction they might approach from. To one side of the castle lay a hidden harbour, within which the Lord of the Isles would have been able to hide his fleet of galleys. He would thus have been able to quickly send out ships in a surprise attack whenever any enemy was foolhardy enough to approach.

This was that same castle in which the Lord of the Isles gave her forebear, Donald Maclean, First Laird of Ardgour, leave to wrest Ardgour out of the hands of the MacMasters. Here also had that same Lord of the Isles agreed to open negotiations with the English King Edward IV.

Eilidh could not resist the call of the seals and spent much of the early part of the morning swimming and playing with them in the water. Then much rested and refreshed she set out eagerly to visit the old minister Norman MacLeod of Fuinary, whose son was wed to James Maxwell's daughter. Both horses were happy to remain behind, grazing contentedly on the lush plentiful grass beside the castle.

Fuinary was only a short distance for her to travel and Eilidh ran swiftly all the way there.

She was met at the door of the manse by a tall gangly youth who stood open mouthed for a moment when he saw who it was that had come to visit.

"Why John it is a grand tall fellow that you are become!" She took a step backwards to get a better look at him. "You look to be trying to get an unfair advantage on the rest of us poor folk, growing so high as ye are as if to get the nearer to heaven!" she said merrily.

"E…, Eilidh," he stammered. While from inside the house came the sound of another voice.

"Eilidh Ruadh, Eilidh Ruadh, come in, come in. Well, don't keep her waiting John, bring the lassie in from the cold."

She did not need to be shown the way to Norman MacLeod's study, from whence the voice had come.

She danced in and rushed over to him, stooping to kiss his forehead. He had been almost like a grandfather to her and she came to visit as often as she could, though the past year she had managed to visit but rarely. His wisdom and conversation were for her alike to good medicine. John his son was a year younger than she was and a firm friend sharing her love for the land, the people and sharing her staunch faith.

Norman MacLeod was an excellent scholar and many a long and happy evening had her father spent with him discussing varies points of theology and the classics, while she and John sat nearby listening. The talk was always in the language of the area, in the Gaelic, and he it was who had shown her Ewan MacLachlan's poems and his translations of Homer into the Gaelic.

221

When she had been much younger, and unable to read the Iliad in the original Greek, he had often read these translations to John and herself.

She had met the poet himself once only, for although he had been born in Lochaber he lived and worked in Aberdeen. He was a kindly man and so enthusiastic about the Gaelic literature, and the local bards. He had endeared himself to her further by his enthusiasm for and his love of the stories and poems of Ossian.

Today was little different to all the other visits she had made of yore, though she had arrived earlier in the day than she was want to do and left shortly after the midday meal. Here, as in the house of John Maxwell, she felt welcome and, more unusually for her, here she felt at home, safe. The old man well understood her fears and feelings of loss at leaving, telling her of how his son Norman also hated to leave Fuinary, though he loved his own home and the work that he did in the lowlands. Talk of the younger Norman soon led to talk of the grandchildren.

While the old man was talking with obvious pride of his fine young grandson Eilidh suddenly went quiet. The old minister, despite his growing blindness noticed immediately that something was not right with her and sent John out the room to fetch some more wood to build up the fire.

"What is it lass? What is it you See?"

She turned to him surprise on her face.

"I once saw your father look thus. He said it was the Sight; he told me that day that you too had been blessed with it."

"Blessed or cursed," Eilidh replied wryly, "but this at least is a blessing. I saw your sons as they might be twenty or so years hence. You can be proud. They will both be great men."

The old man sat silent not asking more.

Eilidh said softly, "'Tis said to tell of what one Sees can change the future. I would not wish to change this."

"Even to one who will not speak of it to those whose future it is?"

She smiled, "I do not know, but I think forbye that your sons are not changeable men. You have done your work well Sir. Your elder[112] will be great in the eyes of many in Scotland, him they will call, Caraid nan Gaidheal[113]. The younger will be a great man also, just as you are yourself. He too will gain a grand name[114], but will not I think venture so far afield.

"The Lord has blessed me greatly Eilidh with bringing you to me this day with such a prophesy. An old man like me dies the easier with such knowledge in his heart."

"You do not think then that the Sight is sent from the Devil?"

"Eilidh lass! How could ye think such a thing?"

"I see such things Sir, sometimes I fear from whence they come."

"It is a gift Eilidh, but like all such gifts it is to be used wisely. It is the choices we make rather than the gifts we are given that are important. My sons have great gifts of oratory, of intelligence and learning. If they use these God given gifts for evil then they could do much harm. If however they allow

---

[112] He became Moderator of the Church of Scotland General Assembly in 1836. His son Norman likewise became Moderator of the General Assembly in 1869. While his son, the old Norman MacLeod's great grandson, was to become 1st Baronet of Fiunary. The son of the 1st Baronet of Fiunary, George MacLeod, became the founder of the Iona Community and was created Lord MacLeod of Fuinary in 1967.

[113] Friend of the Gael.

[114] Became his father's assistant and on his father's death took over his parish. Said to have been 6 foot 9 inches in height. Became known as 'The High Priest of Morvern'; also became Moderator of the Church of Scotland.

themselves to listen to the guidance of the Holy Spirit, then they will perhaps instead use their gifts to do much that is good. So it is with the gift that you and your father were given. Use it wisely child, with much prayer."

"I saw glimpses of much that is not well in Morvern, glimpses of the harm that will be done by those who choose to worship mammon rather than God. Why Sir, why are your sons such goodly men while the sons of others, despite the manifold advantages they were born with, are otherwise?"

"Surely Eilidh you know the answer to that question without asking me," he said gently. "My wife and I look to the Holy Spirit for guidance in all that we do. We try to copy the life of our example on earth, our Lord Jesus; and we teach the children to do likewise. Do you not feel the presence of God when you enter our house Eilidh?"

"It wraps itself like a blanket around me when I enter your home," she whispered. "Forgive me Sir, but why…, but why is it that…, that…" she stumbled to a stop.

"What is it Lassie? Speak on."

She looked at him for a few moments before asking the question that was foremost in her heart. "Why is it that there is so much sorrow come to those that seem not to deserve it, such as the folk at Rahoy? Why they are almost starving through no fault of their own and, and the children die too easy!"

A solemn look came over his face, and he sighed. John had entered just as she asked the question and he now turned to his son, "John answer the lassie if you would."

The boy blushed and began to stammer a reply.

Understanding that his son's lack of clarity came not through lack of ability to answer the query, but rather that young as he was and despite their having been childhood friends he was overpowered by their visitor's beauty, he took pity on the lad.

"Hush then John, pour us some more of that tea and then sit yourself down by the fire and listen."

Then Norman MacLeod took onto his knee a large well-thumbed Bible from its accustomed place on a table at his side. This he opened carefully and then proceeded to read aloud, "Genesis, chapter two, verse seventeen, 'But of the tree of the knowledge of good and evil, thou shall not eat of it: for on the day that thou eatest thereof thou shalt surely die.'"

He looked up at the two young people and smiled. "As we all know, God made Adam and Eve to dwell in the Garden of Eden where every necessity for their life and happiness was provided. In addition they were blessed with the gift of immortality, but with one condition; that they did not touch the fruit of one particular tree in the garden."

"God also gifted them 'free will' whereby they could choose whether to obey or disobey his request, thereby rendering their love, loyalty and obedience of greater value. For is not love that is freely given more valuable than love that is given through coercion and enslavement?"

The two young people sat listening to him quietly as he continued sagely. "You both know the rest of the story but I will tell it anyway. As time went on Adam and Eve grew discontented with the fact that the fruit from this one tree was denied them and, as is the case with us all, that which is forbidden becomes increasingly alluring."

"Satan came to talk to them, fanning their desire to consume of this fruit and thereby taste what it is to know good and evil. The punishment for disobedience was death, but what did they know or understand of death, living as they did in the haven that is the Garden of Eden? Eventually, as we know, temptation won over obedience and Adam and Eve ate of the fruit of the tree."

225

"However death did not strike the moment that they ate the fruit. What they lost was their gift of immortality."

"Now Adam and Eve would have to go out into the world of men and become mortal. They had eaten of the forbidden fruit and now understood the difference between what was good and what was evil. This loss of innocence meant they could no longer live in the Garden of Eden, no more could they walk there freely and enjoy the presence of God," explained the old minister. "Sin had entered their soul and it was no longer pure. For them now to see God in all his Glory would be more than they could have endured. Their ejection from the Garden of Eden was therefore not so much enacted as a punishment by a wrathful God, but a consequence of their actions."

He went silent for a few moments as if contemplating anew the enormity of what their forebears had forsaken. Then he put down the Bible and continued more strongly. "If we were the perfect man we would understand the seasons and the mysteries of the earth, the sea and the heavens. Have you not seen how even the animals know if a storm approaches, how they know where the water is and when fire comes to consume the forests, long before man; who is as if blind and deaf to all these things?"

"Man is too caught up in the desires of his heart, or the desires of his loins to notice what is before him. Man rushes through the world ruled not by God but by the cravings of his mind and his body. His head and heart are full of his need to have, to gain, to maintain, that which he covets. He will not listen when his body tells him what it needs, he chooses instead to attend to his desires; thus his mind and his body and his spirit become out of balance and he becomes sick."

"Think you that man would have sickness if he listened to what his body told him, if he could keep himself in balance, if he could subdue his loud and furious emotions, if he were able to keep his mind and body under subjection to the will of God? However this is impossible for one who has eaten of the tree of knowledge."

"It is for this reason that evil things like famine, death, wars and sickness occur."

"God wishes us to choose rightly. He wants us to choose freely to love and obey him. As such, rather than compel us to obey him he gave us free will. Man however, time upon time, down through the ages has chosen to follow the lure of his own appetites, rather than following the dictates of God and thus the utopian state of the Garden of Eden passes further and further from his grasp."

"But you have chosen rightly Sir," said Eilidh.

"Indeed," he replied, "and were I perfect, and were all those around me perfect, then yes I and mine would no doubt never sicken nor die. However I am not a perfect man, nor are those around me. Unfortunately, the choices of those around us affect the wellbeing of others; such as you saw in Rahoy Eilidh."

He saw Eilidh about to speak but smiled and continued, "That is not to say that I believe that we are directly guilty of the death of our own children, nor indeed that God causes them to die as a punishment for our sins, only that the world that we are in contains physical sickness, caused ultimately by that greater sickness that is evil. We who live in the world suffer the results of the evil therein."

"God is not a God of chaos, he does not destroy the laws he himself set in progress for the ordering of the universe. That Eilidh is why despite his manifold protections such as we, who try to follow his teachings, suffer setbacks and sorrow, fall prey to the evil of the world that is brought about by the fall of man."

227

"I confess Eilidh, that even I have asked such questions of heaven as you have today asked me, when one of mine own, or another's child has passed away before his or her allotted three score years and ten." The sorrow was plain on the kind peaceful face of the old man as he continued sadly. "Even now my heart weeps for the life they have not experienced and for the time with them that we have lost. Indeed it is only the belief that their innocence will surely mean that when the 'Great Book of Life' is opened they will reign in heaven for ever; a guarantee that we who yet sin have not, despite our Lord Jesus dying so sorely for our sins."

He turned to the girl, and his eyes were full of love and trust, as he said, "I have always found however that even in the darkest of hours, if you hold fast to your faith in God and his protection, that he will always lead you safely out of that place of darkness, back into the light."

"As I grow older I can't help but wonder if perhaps that time of trial, though hideously unpleasant and painful, strengthens one; I also wonder if we would be less able to do the greater things that God hopes for us to do, if we do not first learn to deal with lesser adversities."

"I believe Eilidh that God has His hand on each and every one of His children, and that although we may be touched by the sorrows of this world they can never overcome us while we trust in Him."

"Sometimes it is difficult to have that blind faith, sometimes also it is difficult to remember that as we are in the world we cannot just sit back and expect God to sort things out for us, that we must ourselves respond to the situation we are in whilst at the same time allowing ourselves to listen to God as we make these choices. Did not Jesus say 'If ye have faith as a grain of mustard seed, ye shall say unto this mountain, Remove hence to yonder place; and it shall be removed; and nothing shall be impossible unto you.'" [115]

The old man turned to the girl smiling kindly as he said, "Eilidh, we cannot ever know someone else's true story, or fully understand why they have the life they have, why they have seemingly been blessed with life's fortunes or disasters. This knowledge God keeps to himself. It is only for us to know fully our own story."

"Suffice it is for us to know and believe that if we have faith in God and our Lord Jesus then we have the guarantee that out of darkness will come a future better than that which we, with our puny mortal eyes, could for ourselves ever have foreseen."

"He sent Jesus to us as an example of how we should live, if we choose to follow God's ways, and to show us the blessings that would happen if we could follow him perfectly," said John, growing more confident as talk moved on to the topics he had heard discussed time and time again both in his home and in the home of others. "But they chose to kill him rather than accept him as the Messiah. They chose not to listen to his words."

"Some though do choose to listen," said Eilidh softly, looking at her young friend.

"Yes", John replied, his eyes bright. "And so they receive the gift of the Holy Spirit so they might be guided at all times as to how they should speak and what they should do, that words of Jesus and his life might be at all times brought to their remembrance."

They sat silent after this for a few moments thinking about these words, then Eilidh turned to them and said quietly, "I thank you both, for your kindness. Your words will sustain me

---

[115] Matthew chapter 17, verse 20.

over the next few months as I leave these parts. It is a sore thing to do, to leave the people, the place one loves, perhaps for ever."

The old man looked at her kindly, "Those whom we truly love are never far away Eilidh, they are always with us in our hearts. You are young however. I can still remember how it was to feel the need of the warm touch of those that one loves, the desire to have them with one always. That need never really goes but patience, which I believe increases a little with age, tempers the need apace."

"The 'Fruits of the Spirit,'" said Eilidh with a smile, "why I believe you have grown a veritable orchard!"

"Still the odd fruit of the wrong variety needing to be pruned out, but I'm working hard on it," he replied with a wry smile.

The rest of the visit was jolly with both John and his father telling her the news of the place and of their family and neighbours and their own plans and dreams for the future. All too soon it was time for the midday meal.

After partaking of a hearty lunch Eilidh stayed firm in her resolve to set off on her journey home, despite much urgings and pleas from both the old man and his son that she stay longer.

As she stood up to leave, the Minister suddenly turned to his son saying, "John you know the words, sing that farewell song for the lass that your brother wrote, while I look out for her a copy of the words and music that she can take away with her."

Nothing loathe, shyness long gone, the young man complied. He had a beautiful voice, newly come, and he was rightfully proud of it. He sang the lovely song that his brother had written, 'Farewell to Fuinary,' with true feeling in his voice as he too imagined how he would feel if ever he had to leave this place he loved so well.

"'Eirich agus tiugainn O.'" [116] As Eilidh listened to the opening lines a lump stuck in her throat, and indeed, as the words of the song went on to say, her heart within her felt as if it would almost die 'at thought of leaving Fiunary'.

They were quiet for a moment after John finished singing. Then the old man returned and presented her with the words and music for the song. She did not leave before she had given John the message from John Maxwell; neither did she leave without many prayers being said for her future, and safe journeying.

John accompanied her back to Ardtornish and her waiting horses, giving a wary greeting to Liath Macha but petting Dawn and feeding her with the sugar and carrots he had brought specially.

Long was it after she rode out of sight that he remained there watching, before at last turning to disconsolately make his return journey home.

Eilidh also did not hurry on her journey from Ardtornish to Ardgour.

Never could she pass these parts without remembering that the troops of the Duke of Cumberland[117] had set fire to the area. All the barns and houses of the people here had been burned in revenge, as a punishment to the community of these parts for choosing to follow the 'Young Pretender' rather than the Hanoverian King George I. This part of the coast was still practically bare of trees because of this.

She had always felt it to be paradoxical that this land, which had been burned so badly by the army of King George I, had belonged to the Campbells, to the Duke of Argyle, who had

---

[116] 'We must up and haste away'.
[117] Younger brother of King George III.

chosen to fight for King George I rather than for the Jacobite cause and for Prince Charlie. The Campbells may have acquired the land, but you cannot buy people's hearts; although Argyle had gained the land, the people who lived there, she thought proudly, had remained loyal to the Macleans and the Camerons, whose chiefs in turn had kept loyal to their Stuart Kings.

She imagined that the then Duke of Argyle would have complained bitterly to Cumberland for his heavy handedness. Her father had told her that later, when the Jacobite Rebellion had been crushed, that it was Argyle's nephew, the father of the present Duke of Argyle, who had directed the disarming of Morvern and thus they had been largely spared the retribution that Cumberland's own troops delivered so harshly elsewhere after the Jacobites were defeated at Culloden.

From Ardtornish she followed the footsteps of young Donald Maclean of Ardgour as he left the Lord of the Isles to ride swiftly to the territory of his maternal grandfather Maclean of Kingairloch and then onwards, intent on the gaining of Ardgour.

Eilidh rode on slowly for she loved these hills and the wild black goats with their proud high heads and their huge horns, who ranged so free amongst them. She loved the way they could get into every crevasse and how they stood so arrogantly, high up on the rocky outcrops. She loved the heather clad hills and the deep glens and the waterfalls that sparkled and fell so gaily down the rocks and amongst the pebbles, as they meandered merrily down the mountain side. She loved the red deer who roamed majestically over the hills and amongst the valleys, and their loud cries as they roared their challenge out to one and all. She loved the flight of the eagle as it flew so free above its domain and the sight of the heron as it stood at the side of the loch, standing so still just like a sentinel as it watched and waited for its prey. Then there were the stoats and the weasels that scurried underground that one only glimpsed if one was silent and looked very carefully, and the shy wild cat who hid amongst the branches high in the trees but who was so ferocious if brought to bay, and the owl with its eerie call and oh so many other creatures that she would miss so much, and the smell of them, the scent of the sea and the wet earth, and the gorse after the rain fell......

She was not anxious to go home too quickly that day, wishing to savour each moment of this journey, to enjoy every sight, smell and sound of her beloved hills for as long as she could. And so it was nightfall before she reached her cave at Salachan where she immediately set the horses loose, leaving the tack in the cave, before setting off for her wee cottage at the side of the Castle Lochan.

Chapter 27 Old Friends Reunited

Eilidh savoured every moment of her trek to her little cottage at the side of the Castle Lochan, intensely aware of each and every sound that disturbed the quiet of this night, revelling in the different scents that she passed, in the fresh feel of the wind on her skin, on her unbound hair; treasuring these last few hours of freedom.

Both horses accompanied her as far as the stables at Ardgour House. Here Dawn left her, trotting eagerly into the yard, whinnying anxiously for her foal. Eilidh smiled as she heard the answering cry, knowing that Red Dawn would herself unbolt the door to the stall which held Sithfadda[118], her little filly.

Liath Macha exhibited little concern at his mother's defection, nor did he evince any interest in greeting his sister; choosing instead to accompany Eilidh.

They continued slowly on their way, enjoying the cold night air, walking as close as lovers. As they strolled along Liath Macha would from time to time rub his head on her shoulder and she, for a whiles, put her arm across his withers, wholly content to be walking thus, enchanted by the beauty of the clear night sky, humbled by the immensity and splendour of the heavens above. She marvelled anew that travellers and mariners alike would have used their knowledge of the dance of those same constellations to plot their unnumbered journeys over land and sea, for thousands upon thousands of years.

---

[118] Named after one of the horses that pulled Cuchullin's chariot. Sithfadda means long stride. He was also called Sulin-Sifadda. The other horse who pulled the chariot was Dusronnal.

After a while Liath Macha began to stray further away, grazing as they travelled; yet still it was as if they walked as one, as if each could hear the others thoughts.

Then, all of a sudden Liath Macha stilled. He stood poised, head lifted high, ears pricked, nostrils flared.

Eilidh knew at once that he had seen some of his own kind and smiling, bid him go.

She watched as he raced towards them, not prancing with ears pricked and neck arched and eyes light, but with head snaked out, ears slicked back, eyes slit and narrow, with a high pitched scream wrenched from his throat.

She watched until they had galloped out of sight, and then walked on alone, faster, eager now to be home.

As Eilidh approached nearer to her small cottage she noticed a light in one of its windows. Her face lit up with delight and she quickened her pace to a trot; for none but one would use thus her cottage at this time of night, one whom after Liath Macha and her brothers she loved most in all the world.

At the door she paused, suddenly aware that he was not alone; but after this initial hesitation she went in regardless.

"Ewan! You hound! What kind of a den is this that you are turning my poor wee cottage into? I'll warrant an all that it is my faither's good whisky ye are all a drinking!"

"Eilidh!" A tall youth with tight black curls stood up and taking her in his arms swung her round and kissed her soundly on both cheeks. "I said as you would come! That snivelling coward of a Campbell would have it that you would not return in time for our tryst in the morn, but Joe and I swore you would be here."

A harsh voice, which Eilidh did not recognise, interrupted abruptly "Fie Ruairidh[119]! Shame on ye! Whit hive o' iniquity hev ye brung me tae!"

235

"Ruairidh!" cried Eilidh delightedly, ignoring the complaint of the stranger, as she peered eagerly into the ill lit room, intent on welcoming her childhood companion and ally, John Boyd's son.

A thin youth with a serious face and bright eyes stood up and came quickly towards her.

"Ruairidh! Why if I had known that you would be here I would have hurried home the sooner! Your father mentioned that you might arrive in time for mother's wedding, but the weather is unco chancy at this time of the year, and I knew ye were busy, so I tried not to hope..."

"I wished it to be a surprise. Though I would now that I had left him south," Ruairidh added wryly, indicating the owner of the harsh voice, a thin faced man who stood in the corner staring at her with an outraged look on his face. "I will ask him to leave, if you wish."

"Let him 'bide," Eilidh replied smiling happily, her face alight at the unexpected sight of these, her friends. "My skin is over thick to be pierced so easily by the barbs of ignorance."

"Harlot!" Accused the stranger, who yet stood in the corner. "I'll hae nay tae dae w' the likes o' ye!"

Eilidh looked at the stranger quietly and then said slowly, "Any friend of Ruairidh is most welcome here." After which, her eyes alight with delight, she transferred her attention back to Ruairidh, smiling reassuringly at him to quieten his obvious agitation and embarrassment at his friend's comments.

Ruairidh sat back down uneasily on the chair he had moments earlier so eagerly vacated, curtly asking that his friend do likewise.

Eilidh was still standing at the door and the man would have to push past her to get out. This she knew he would be feared

---

[119] Rory.

to do, and as he still stood glaring in her direction she said to him lightly, "I would hazard a guess that ye are either priest or lawyer in the making." As she spoke the fire in the hearth began to blaze more fiercely and the light this cast lit up her face and for a moment the man could do nothing but stare open mouthed. She continued as if oblivious to his regard, "If a priest you might wish to recall our Lord's suggestion, that he that is without sins should cast the first stone[120]."

"Woman you wid dare tae preach tae me!" cried the other drawing himself up to his full height.

Eilidh took the scarf off her head and cast it and her cloak over the back of a chair and after tying up the loose strands of her hair, she walked over to the fire.

Then turning to the stranger, who was still staring at her as if he could not tear his eyes away, she said gently, "Sit yourself back down friend of Ruairidh. You have nothing to fear in this house and are most welcome."

"Whit is a body tae ken when he sees a bonnie lassie, such as thysel, gang in alain in tae a hoose filled wi' laddies wi' nae show o' modesty?" he returned heatedly. "Nane but a woman hae has lost sicht o' all that is Gawdly and chosen instead tae follow after the ways o' darkness would gang thus. I wid hae nae t' dae wi' the likes o' ye!"

Eilidh smiled kindly, "I fear that you misunderstand; Ewan here is my cousin, my milk brother, these others are my friends. Although I confess that you are correct, in that it does not create a good impression for a young single woman to wander abroad thus, I rather fear that you may be accustomed to being unnecessarily severe in your views. Women, as is the case with every blessing and gift on earth that man has been given, can be

---

[120] John chapter 8, verse 7.

used for ill, or treasured and succoured. If I understand you correctly, you fear that women are the cause of all temptation and immorality. I believe however that you err. It is not necessarily the woman who is at fault when a man's lack of understanding and control leads him to fall into temptation." She looked teasingly at her milk brother, "What say you Ewan?"

It was Ruairidh's friend however who interrupted, "Ye cannae mix salt and pure water," he replied scornfully. "If ye add rotten fruit tae a bowlful o' that which be fresh, ye will soon find them all rotted. 'Tis the same wi' immorality. I say ye should hae nay t' dae wi' they as follow after the ways o' the evil one if ye wish tae keep thysel pure, and walk i' the way o' the light."

"It is not so simple as you try to make it sound," Eilidh countered. "Most fall into sin such as you are insinuating, not through evil but through poverty, through foolishness, or through the fault of some man who is selfish and unprincipled. At the very least can you not, in charity, understand why a woman would prefer to risk eternal damnation on her own account if she might only continue to be able to provide bread for her child? Have you seen a child die for lack of bread or milk to fill his belly, heard his pitiful cry, seen the thin limbs and the enlarged stomach?" Eilidh accused with unaccustomed bitterness. "I have just come from the house of a minister whose son is also a minister, but a minister who seeks to aid those who live in poverty and sin and not judge them. He finds it enough to leave it to the Lord to judge them. It is sufficient also for him just to try to help, to comfort and support them. His other son, John, who is also going into the ministry, will be at my mother's wedding, Ruairidh here can introduce you if you wish."

"Whit ken ye o' such!" sneered the other.

"What indeed!" exclaimed a merry voice, "Alan, who would think it, not only a physician but a preacher too!"

Eilidh had sat down by the fire and taken out the griddle and some oatmeal whilst she had been talking to her unknown adversary. She now stood up. "Andrew!" Delight was in her voice. "Where have you been hiding? What brings you here? And if Andrew is here then George too!" she laughed. "Why I am most shamed to be seen here without my trews, for to my knowledge you have never seen me thus!" She looked unusually flushed and now turned to Ewan with laughing eyes, "Ewan you never said!"

"I did not know!" Ewan replied, laughing also. "I met the pair of them by chance the day before we were due to travel. When they heard that I was coming to see you they insisted on coming also. I had to explain though that you were other than you seemed, other than they believed you to be of yore," he continued awkwardly. "I hope you do not mind Eilidh."

"We were mighty relieved," interjected Andrew solemnly. "George and I were beginning to worry, feeling that we were becoming ower fond o' ye; to find you were but a lassie was very reassuring!" He said with a twinkle in his eye.

George still remained in the shadows, silent.

Eilidh lit another candle and walked towards him. "George have you brought any books?" she asked eagerly. "You must be almost qualified now." There was a touch of envy in her voice.

The other at the mention of the profession he loved lost his shyness and for a while the three of them talked of the studies they had been doing, for George and Andrew had brought her some of their textbooks, which she insisted on reimbursing them for, knowing that they could ill afford the extra books.

It was Ewan who interrupted, "Eilidh, I am so hungry for those bannocks that you had started on baking. If I had known that they would shamelessly take all you attention I would have refused to bring them. However," he declared his face alight with laughter, "I could not resist the opportunity of seeing George's face when he saw you thus!"

George laughed also, saying musingly, "You know Alan you are not so very different to how you were before, when one gets talking to you. I suspect it would surprise Ruairidh's prejudiced friend," he gave a sly look in the stranger's direction, "but it does not seem to have affected your intellect swopping your britches for some petticoats. You don't mind if I continue to call you Alan?"

"Alan, Eilidh, what matters? It is the same person." She smiled and returned to her post at the fire while the talk warmed up around her and Ewan stood up to refill the empty glasses.

It was some time after the bannocks were eaten and the fire replenished that Eilidh picked up her clarsach and sat in the seat that Ewan had vacated without asking.

"Are ye bard as well as priest an' blood-letter?" came the dry voice from the corner.

"Shall we throw him out for ye Alan?" George offered eagerly. He was not so quiet now.

Ruairidh did not know where to hide his face, so wrath was he with his friend.

"You might with my blessing George except that it is partly on his account that I wish to tell the story that I am about to tell." Eilidh then turned to the man in the corner to ask, "Friend, what name do ye go by?"

Ruairidh answered for his friend, "My apologies Eilidh, I should have explained. This is Findley Gordon. As you say, he is a friend of mine; he is studying with me at the University. Like me he is interested in the cause of the radicals. I am afraid he has very strong notions about the behaviour of women," he stated ruefully. "I..., I should have made clear to him that this was your cottage. I believe he thought that it belonged to Ewan. He did not expect to see any women here." He turned to Findley and explained, "Eilidh is the daughter of our late Laird; she is a friend of mine. My father John Boyd has been working closely with Eilidh to run this estate this past year on behalf of her younger brother. Unfortunately she is to leave directly after her mother's wedding to go south with Ewan and his parents."

"Thank you Ruairidh. The fault is mine; I should have introduced myself when I came in just as soon as I realised that there was a stranger with us. Only I was so pleased to see you all..." She fell silent for a moment before turning to Findley and saying seriously, "I am sorry Findley if my unexpected arrival distressed you, but I hope you will forgive me for the intrusion and enjoy the rest of your evening with us."

Then Eilidh turned to Joe asking with a smile, "Would you mind changing seats with Ruairidh, I will not have many days in which to talk with him and am most anxious to hear his news. Especially as to how the weavers are faring in Glasgow."

Ruairidh flushed anew at this comment. "Has father been talking to you Eilidh?" he asked. "It was not I that telt him but the faither of a friend o' mine."

"Another father worried about his too brave and enthusiastic son," Eilidh said with a smile. "I promised your father I would talk to you about it, but said that he should not worry over much as you have too much sense to make a fool of yourself. You know that he accepts that you are justified to be concerned about the injustices in our country. All he is worried about is the manner in which you intend to set about attempting to help right the wrongs that we see all around us.

He does not question that you should try." Eilidh was tuning her clarsach as she said this.

For a few moments all was quiet apart from the sound of the clarsach.

Then Eilidh looked up, "Throughout the ages there have been women so beautiful, so much desired by the men who saw them, that they have been the unwitting cause of bloodshed, of senseless war, of the tearing apart of friendship and kinship bonds, of all forms of wanton destruction. Such a one was Helen of Troy, another was Deirdre, the daughter of Felim, a seannachie of Ulster."

"Why have you omitted this tale of Deirdre from my education Eilidh?" Ewan interrupted teasingly. "I much prefer the stories of beautiful women to those of witches which you seem to delight in telling."

"This tale has no witches, but it does tell of a Druid", Eilidh returned seriously. "Indeed the story starts when this Druid receives a vision of Deirdre's birth and the doom that she carries with her."

"Starts wi' nonsense then," retorted Findley. "Hae wid believe that any could have a vision o' the future?"

"All of us Highlanders believe in the Sight," Joe answered curtly. "It is well known that amongst us there are some who have that gift."

"Nonsense," Fergus reiterated. "It is just fear an' superstition that makes folk tae believe such ungawdly things."

"Eilidh has the Sight, as did her father before her," Ewan countered lightly.

"She Saw the death of her faither," Ruairidh stated, looking at his friend. "I can vouch for that. She appeared at his funeral unannounced, unexpected, after riding fast all the way from

Fife. There would have been no time for any to have told her of it."

"She could hev been on her way hame, and hev heard o' his death on the way," the other man argued.

"She could have, but she didn't," retorted Ewan tartly. "She was staying with me and my parents at the time. She woke me and told me that her father had died, that she and Liatha Macha were just that minute setting out for home. That is how we ourselves learned of his death. We left shortly after, to follow in her tracks, but the Laird was long buried by the time that we arrived."

"There must be another explanation," Findley maintained stubbornly.

"I have known Alan, or should I say Eilidh, a good few years now and never known her lie, excepting that we thought her a lad and not a lassie." George looked at Eilidh, "Do you have this Sight?" he asked. "Do you see visions, of the past and the future?"

Eilidh shrugged, "It is as Joe says a common thing in the Highlands. My father had the Sight and I have had the dubious fortune to have it also. Often I have wondered if perhaps the gift of the Sight came from the Irish Tuatha du Danaan."

"Who?" asked George, his voice filled with curiosity.

"The fairy folk," Andrew answered with a glint in his eye. "My old nurse was Irish. She would often tell me tales of their mighty heroes."

"Have you Irish blood then?" George asked with interest.

"One of my grandparents was Irish. But it was my nurse who told me the old stories. She was one of the O'Neil's and extremely proud of this. Always she would be telling me how the blood of the Irish High King Niall of the Nine Hostages ran through her veins. As my family lineage only goes back to the time of Robert the Bruce you can imagine how insignificant and inconsequential this used to make me feel!"

Eilidh laughed. "I am sure she told you for the good of your soul! Though I suspect that she did not tell you that Niall of the Nine Hostages claimed direct descent from Ith, the uncle of Milesius."

"I confess that I have never even heard of Ith or Milesius," replied Andrew.

"Ith was the Uncle of Milesius, the leader of the Sixth and possibly the most successful, invasion into Ireland," Eilidh explained.

"The Sixth Invasion? I did not know there were any!" Andrew admitted.

"Perhaps that is because 'The Invasions' are as much legend as history. The First Invasion was said to be led by Cessair, Noah's grand-daughter, who finding no place on her grandfather's ark, acquired a large boat and in this she and a number of others sought to escape the flood. They sailed to Ireland, but sadly, despite being in this boat, most of Cessair's party drowned in the Deluge. All the invading groups claim relation to Japhet, son of Noah, one way or another." She paused.

"And the other 'Invasions', what of them? Andrew inquired.

"The Second Invasion was led by Nemed. When this failed Nemed's grandsons led the Nemedians' retreat in three different groups. Britan took his group to Britain, and as you might suspect from his name, he is believed by some to be an ancestor of the British.

"The other two parties are thought to have gone to Greece. The Fourth and the Fifth invaders, the Firbolg and the Danaan are reputedly descended from them."

"What about The Third Invasion?" prompted George.

244

"This was led by Nemed's nephew Parthalon who is thought to be the forebear of the Royal Line of Ulster. His grandson Ros Ruadh is credited with establishing the Red Branch Warriors that were so famous in the days of Deirdre. Conor Mac Nessa, the villain in my story, was King in those times. Though," added Eilidh musingly, "I have an additional reason to remember him, for had a sister called Feidhilm, and her son was one of the group of men who killed Cuchullin. It was his spear which was said to have wounded Liath Macha, Cuchullin's faithful horse."

"That would be Earc, King of Tara[121]," Joe concurred, then added, "Earc's son Murtagh became High King of Ireland and his other son Fergus is said to have invaded Scotland and there established the Kingdom of the Dal Riada[122]."

"Was it not that Fergus who borrowed the Stone of Scone[123] off his brother, the High King of Ireland, for his own coronation in Scotland and then refused to return it?" Ewan said mischievously.

"Trust you to remember that Ewan!" Eilidh laughingly concurred.

---

[121] Tara was thought to be the capital of the ancient High Kings of Ireland; Tara was originally called Temair; it's location near present day Dublin.

[122] A tribe who occupied the Argyle region of Scotland, which came originally from Ireland.

[123] Stone of Destiny, (Lia Fal), the Coronation Stone of the Kings of Scotland. Believed to have been Jacob's Pillow, (Genesis chapter 28, verses 11-22). In 1296 the Stone was captured by Edward I of England, and taken by him to Westminster Abbey where it became part of the Coronation Chair. The Stone left Westminster Abbey in 1996 to be returned to Scotland, and now resides in Edinburgh Castle. Though legend has it that some loyal Scots hid the real Stone of Scone, just before it was stolen by King Edward I, and replaced it with a piece of sandstone, and that the real Stone still lies hidden somewhere in Scotland.

"Some say that the Stone of Scone was brought to Ireland by Gaedheal Glas[124], he whom it is thought the Gaels are named after, and that Scotland is named after his mother Scota[125]," Joe added.

"Are you sure Joe?" Ewan asked. He turned to Eilidh "Did you not tell me that you it was a Hebrew princess who brought the Stone of Scone to Ireland and that it was her mother-in-law[126] who gave her name to Scotland?"

"So I did," Eilidh, acknowledged. "If you like I will tell you about her."

"What, and not tell us of the beauteous Deirdre!" Ewan protested laughingly.

"Have patience! I will tell of Deirdre later - after I have explained how a Hebrew princess fits into our Scottish history." She turned to Andrew "Before I tell the story of Ewan's Hebrew princess, would you mind telling us what you know of the Red Hand of Ulster?"

"What has the Red Hand of Ulster in common with a Hebrew princess?" Andrew asked quizzically.

"That you will find out when I tell her tale," she replied with a grin. "However if we start the story by you relating to us what your nurse told you of the Red Hand of Ulster, I think it will greatly add to our understanding of the legend as a whole."

"In that case I will see what I can remember of my nursery story." He thought for a few moments and then began, "A long time ago, in the dim and distant past when the world had just began, there lived an old and well beloved king who was the

---

[124] Said to be a forebear of the Milesians, who carried out The Sixth Invasion.
[125] Daughter of the Pharaoh Cingris, mother of Gaedheal Glas.
[126] Scota, daughter of the Pharaoh Nectanebus; the mother of King Eramon (who married the Hebrew Princess Tea Tethi).

246

ruler of a most ancient and magical place. Now this king was the most powerful in the land, all obeyed his every command, yet he lacked one thing. He had no child of his loins, no son to inherit his kingdom." Andrew looked across at Eilidh slyly as he continued, "He had not even been blessed with a daughter, who would perhaps have been sufficient, for a daughter would surely have born him a grandson!"

Eilidh glowered at him in mock anger, then laughed, and Andrew continued with his story.

"In desperation the old man put away his old wife and got himself a young bride, but still no child was born unto him, and within a year of the wedding the king was dead."

"I detect a few embellishments Andrew," commented Joe dryly.

Andrew grinned. "Tis true. I have no idea why the throne of Ulster was vacant, or who the king was who left it so, however the next part of the story is the bit my nan told me." He continued, "After much debate as to who would be the next king it was eventually decided to hold a boat race and leave the Throne of Ulster to the mercy of he who won this race. Toward the end of the race one very resourceful competitor began to fear that he would lose. Then in desperation he chopped off one of his hands and threw this bloody member to the shore and so claimed victory. I assume he was rewarded for his pain by being given the kingship. Though I always wondered if it was worth it," Andrew mused. "Myself I would have preferred the use of my hand."

"I suspect that he did not long remain King," George avowed. "From what little I know about those barbaric times, you did not get far if you could not handle a sword in good form."

"I would wager that he did not amputate the hand which he used to hold his sword," Andrew countered.

"Hae wid he hold his shield though?" Findley now joined the conversation.

Andrew laughed, "You may have a point friend. I have no idea how long he ruled. Have you any notion Alan…, er…, Eilidh?"

She laughed. "I have no idea how long he kept the Kingship of Ulster, though I believe that the Ui Neill Clan have held an important place in Ireland for many a long year."

"There is a red hand on your own coat of arms Eilidh, if I remember rightly. Do you know why this is?" asked Ewan curiously. "I had always wondered before if it was there because your family took Ardgour er…, rather forcibly, but hearing this tale of Andrew's makes me wonder if there is a different reason."

"The answer to that question Ewan should become clear when you have heard the story of your Hebrew Princess." Eilidh paused for a moment, then said slowly, "It was Kai-Ying who first told me the tale. Father used to collect ancient documents, many of which told of old legends and genealogies. He and Kai-Ying would spend hours poring over these manuscripts. Joe here would often be found with them, drooling over some exciting bit of information they had found to help solve some or other ancient puzzle."

Then she looked mischievously over at Findley "Have you perhaps heard of Tamar?"

Findley looked at her suspiciously, but made no answer.

"You will have heard of Judah, Jacob's son?"

Findley nodded curiously. "Aye. Who hasnae heard o' the twelve sons o' Jacob?"

"For the purpose of this story I shall call Jacob by the name given him by God. I shall call him Israel, for from his twelve sons

248

came the twelve tribes of Israel. To Israel was given the birth right and not his elder twin Esau."

"I had heard that he stole it," Findley grunted.

"Perhaps," she looked up at him her eyes twinkling with amusement. "The story I am about to tell makes mention of another set of twin boys."

"Eilidh, you do not want to tell that tale, not with him here," Joe indicated Findley.

"But I do, and he can say if he thinks the woman or the man more to blame for the situation that unfolds," Eilidh retorted with a grin,

"An' ye say she is a friend o' yourn," Findley said dryly to Ruairidh. "I wonder that ye are no' two feet high wi' yer nose dragging along the ground the way she seems tae love tae rub yer nose in it when she wants tae prove a point." There was a gleam in his eye as he said this.

Ruairidh laughed, relieved that his friend seemed to have relaxed and at last accepted Eilidh. "What of that great big gowk over there?" He indicated Ewan. "He has been crushed and oppressed since he was barely three days old, and yet he has still managed to grow to an indecently large height!"

"Much good it has done me, for all she is but a wee bit o' a thing!" Ewan cast a teasing look at Eilidh as he stood up and went over to where Eilidh's Bible lay. "To spare your blushes Eilidh I will volunteer to do the readings." He then sat down and rifled through the pages of the Bible until he found the verses he was looking for.

All gathered closer.

"Thank you Ewan," Eilidh said with a smile. Then after looking around at the rest of her audience she began to speak.

Chapter 28 A Hebrew Princess

"The story of Ewan's Hebrew Princess begins many centuries before her birth," Eilidh explained. "It begins with a wedding, the wedding of beautiful young woman named Tamar to Er, the eldest son of Judah, son of Israel[127]".

"Sadly, before they had been wed many months tragedy struck. Er unexpectedly died."

"As was the custom of those times, Er's younger brother, Onan, then received Tamar as his bride. Onan however was displeased with this marriage. He did not wish Tamar to have a child, for he knew that her first child would be regarded as the child of his elder brother Er, rather than his own[128]." Eilidh nodded to Ewan.

Ewan read, "Genesis thirty-eight, verse nine, 'And Onan knew that the seed should not, be his and it came to pass, when he went in unto his brother's wife, that he spilled it on the ground, lest that he should give seed to his brother.'"

Eilidh took up the story again. "Tamar was not long wed to this ungenerous husband, for Onan did not long survive his brother. Poor Tamar, twice widowed and now with the prospect of having Shelah, the third son of Judah, for a husband! Her first two husbands sound to have been rather selfish unpleasant young men. What was the likelihood of her finding love and companionship with their younger brother?"

"However Shelah was still only a child. So Tamar had no choice but to return to the house of her childhood, there to

---

[127] Israel was the name God gave to Jacob.
[128] On Er's death Onan, as the next most senior surviving brother would be his father's heir. However if Tamar bore Onan a son then this child would be regarded as Er's son, rather than Onan's ; in which case 'Er's son', instead of Onan, would receive Er's inheritance.

250

await the day when Shelah would be old enough to claim her as his wife."

"Many long years passed by and still Tamar remained in her father's house. Shelah grew into a handsome strong young man. Yet still Tamar remained in the house of her father."

"Then one day Tamar heard that Judah would be taking the road to Timnath to shear his sheep. She had long grown tired of waiting for Judah to keep his promise, and now decided on a desperate plan."

"Gathering together all her courage, Tamar rose up and dressed herself as one of the Canaanite temple prostitutes."

"Then she left the house of her father and made her way to the roadside where resolutely she seated herself, determined there to await the arrival of Judah's cavalcade."

"She did not have to wait long."

"As Judah approached with his entourage he caught sight of Tamar sitting by the wayside and was struck by her beauty. Mistaking her for one of the temple prostitutes he immediately ordered his servants to stop."

"Then he walked over to where she sat."

Eilidh turned to Ewan with a mischievous smile, "Would you like to read us what he said to Tamar?"

Ewan with a quick side glance at Findley read, "Genesis, chapter thirty-eight, verse sixteen to eighteen, 'And he turned unto her by the way, and said. Go to, I pray thee, let me come in, unto thee; (for he knew not that she was his daughter-in-law). And she said, What wilt thou give me, that thou mayest come in unto me? And he said, I will send thee a kid from the flock. And she said. Wilt thou give me a pledge, till thou send it? And he said, What pledge shall I give thee: And she said, Thy signet, and thy bracelets and thy staff that is in thine hand. And he gave it her, and came in unto her, and she conceived by him.'"

Eilidh took up the story again. "As soon as Judah bid her go, Tamar returned to her family home taking great care not to be seen by anyone she knew. Once home she quickly dressed herself once more in her widow's clothes and then carefully put the ring, bracelets and staff, which Judah had given her, in a safe hiding place."

"Meanwhile Judah, anxious to keep his promise to the prostitute, sent out his men to find her and give her the lamb. When they came back saying that there was no prostitute where he had said she would be discovered he was immensely puzzled. He had his men search high and low for the woman, but they failed to find any trace of her."

"As the months went by Judah forgot about the mystery of the missing temple prostitute."

"Then one day he heard some gossip that made him absolutely furious. His daughter-in-law Tamar was said to be with child! Full of righteous anger at the shame his daughter-in-law had brought upon him and his house he immediately ordered that she be brought before him to make answer for her sin, declaring...,"

"Genesis, thirty-four, verse twenty-four, 'Let her be burned,'" pronounced Ewan.

"A heavy penalty indeed!" Eilidh continued. "However when the beautiful Tamar arrived for her audience with Judah she gave no appearance of fear. She came to him, aglow with joy and health, her face full of peace and assurance as she confessed to Judah...,"

Ewan read, "'By the man, whose these are, am I with child: and she said, Discern, I pray thee, whose are these, the signet, and bracelets and staff. And Judah acknowledged them, and said, She hath been more righteous than I: because that I gave her not to Shelah my son. And he knew her again no more.'"

Eilidh looked over at Findley and asked "Who was to blame for Tamar conceiving out of wedlock? Tamar but dressed as a prostitute and put herself in the way of Judah; he did not need to give into temptation. Indeed he later admitted that he had been at fault in putting her in the situation whereby she had to look to her father-in-law to get a son for her dead husband Er."

Findley gave no answer, only looked thoughtful. So Eilidh continued, "But Tamar's story does not end here."

Eilidh looked over at Ewan and he obediently read, "Genesis thirty-eight, verses twenty-seven to thirty, 'And it came to pass, when she travailed, that the one put out his hand: and the midwife took and bound upon his hand a scarlet thread, saying, This came out first. And it came to pass, as he drew back his hand that, behold, his brother came out: and she said, How hast thou broken forth? This breach be upon thee: therefore his name was called Pharez. And afterwards came out his brother, that had the scarlet thread upon his hand: and his name was called Zarah.'"

Eilidh took up the story again. "It was eventually decided that Pharez was the first born and therefore the heir. From him runs the line of Judah down to King David and Solomon and through to our own Lord Jesus. His brother Zarah's ancestry cannot easily be traced for much more than three generations. However legend claims that his descendants left their brethren and journeyed into new lands, and that their emblem was a Red Hand encircled by a scarlet cord."

"Milesius[129], he who led The Sixth Invasion of Ireland, was reputedly of the line of Zarah. Milesius and his wife Scota[130]

---

[129] Also known as Galam or Galamh.

both died in this invasion but their son Eremon[131] eventually succeeded in chasing the previous occupants of Ireland into hiding, in the guise, so 'tis said, of fairies."

"The Tuatha de Danaan!" interjected Andrew. "You know Eilidh; I have to concur with you. It must be from them that you inherited the gift of the Sight if, that is, you have any Irish ancestry. There are many fine stories about the exploits of the Tuatha du Danaan," he added with a merry grin.

"Indeed there are!" Joe agreed, as his eyes lit up. "Though," he said reluctantly, "they had better wait until another day or Eilidh will never get this story told."

Eilidh smiled and continued. "At round about the same time as Eremon was busy contesting the Kingship of Ireland with his brothers, Nebuchadnezzar, King of Babylon was busy subduing his vassals, one of whom was Zedekiah, King of Judah."

"As retribution for Zedekiah having dared to challenge the might of Babylon, Nebuchadnezzar ruthlessly ordered the destruction of the City of Jerusalem. The walls of Jerusalem, the City of David, were demolished, its temple destroyed and its people taken into captivity. King Zedekiah was blinded and sent as a prisoner to Babylon. His sons were all put to death."

"Only a tiny remnant of penniless Jews remained behind to eke what living they could from the soil; and some few escaped transportation to Babylon by fleeing to Egypt and other outlying areas."

"Legend has it that one of those who escaped was Zedekiah's daughter, the Princess Tea Tethi, and that when she fled she took with her one of her people's most treasured possessions, Jacob's Pillow, known more familiarly to us as 'The

---

[130] Daughter of the Pharaoh Nectanebus. Some believe Scotland to have been named after her.
[131] Also known as Heremon or Eochaidh.

254

Stone of Scone'; to prevent it from falling into the hands of her enemies."

"Perhaps she was taken initially to Egypt, as was the prophet Jeremiah. Whatever her initial escape route, it is written in the ancient manuscripts that Princess Tea Tethi, daughter of King Zedekiah, accompanied some say by the prophet Jeremiah himself, eventually arrived in Ireland. There she met and married King Eremon, son of Milesius and Scota."

"Tea Tethi is the Hebrew Princess who is sometimes credited with bringing the Stone of Scone to Ireland, and she enjoys one other lasting memorial."

"Legend tells that her husband Eremon named his capital city, the place that we now know as Tara, after her. The original name for Tara was Temair[132], and the alternative rendering of Tea Tethi's name is Tamar which, as I am sure you all recall, is the same name as that of the mother of Zarah and Pharez."

"Eremon reputedly came of the line of Zarah, while his wife Tea Tethi, being the daughter of Zedekiah, would have come of the line of Zarah's twin brother Pharez. If that is the case then their marriage would unite once more the families of Tamar's twin sons."

"Two of the ancient heraldic symbols of Ireland would appear to have originated from the separate lines of Tamar's twins; one emblem being the Red Hand[133], the other the royal harp of King David," concluded Eilidh.

"You said earlier that you of the Western Highlands trace your lineage from the Dal Riada[134] of Ireland," George stated.

---

[132] Temair is the old name for Tara, the ancient seat of the High Kings of Ireland, located near present day Dublin.

[133] The Red Hand encircled by a scarlet cord was at one time the official emblem of the Kingdom of Ulster.

[134] An Irish tribe from part of Ulster who came over and populated the

255

Eilidh nodded, and so George continued, "It sounds to me as if those of the Dal Riada who came over from Ireland to Scotland may have brought with them the emblem of the Red Hand of Zarah." He added thoughtfully "You have it on your wall over there Eilidh; that is the Maclean coat of arms is it not? In one of the quarters there is a red hand clutching a cross."

Eilidh nodded. "That is what my father also suspected. The Dal Riada settled in the West of Scotland. Fergus, he who borrowed the Stone of Scone off his brother the High King of Ireland and failed to return it, he was reputedly of the Dal Riada."

"And you Eilidh," George asked curiously "What do you think? It sounds an unlikely story to me. Do you think it is based on fact?"

Eilidh hesitated for a moment before answering, "I believe that all legends are based on fact in some way or other. This tale of a beautiful Hebrew princess whose family all perish in the hands of a cruel invader, who is then forced to flee the country of her birth but eventually finds love in the form of a handsome king in a far flung land is a wonderful story, is it not? It is a tale of love and hope, of triumph over disaster, a story that could belong to any age. For me it does not really matter how historically accurate the stories are. They are still an important part of our heritage. They tell us something of the beliefs of our forebears; give them some sort of identity. It seems to me that in some way they are all parables, for they teach us of the important things in life, show us examples of beauty, of integrity, of morality and terrible evil. They tell of the depths of inhumanity to which man is capably of falling but also his capacity for greatness. The story of Deirdre which I am

North West of Scotland.

going to tell you next is just the same, it tells a story within a story."

"How so Eilidh, I confess I saw no such thing in this tale of the two Tamars," George stated. "Though," he added, "I did wonder if perhaps you told it to show Findley here that one should not judge a situation based solely on its outward appearance."

She laughed. "No, it was just chance that the story taught that. Have a think though about Pharez and Zarah. Ask yourself who should have been chosen as the first born? Put yourself in their situation. If one does that one can imagine the bitterness Zarah would have experienced when it was finally decided that Pharez was the first born. For was not Zarah's hand born first, like the hand of the O'Neil that won the boat race? Only Zarah's hand did not win, for his brother pushed him out of the way, his hand was retracted and Pharez won that race. One can imagine how the resentment grew amongst Zarah's offspring as the children of Pharez were favoured over those of Zarah. One can imagine the jealousy that Zarah felt when his twin Pharez eventually took the leadership of the tribe; how this disgruntlement grew and grew until eventually those of Zarah's camp decided to leave and seek their fortunes elsewhere."

"To me the story of Eremon and Tea Tethi is primarily a tale of reconciliation. The marriage of the son of the tribe of Zarah with the daughter of the tribe of Pharez united the twins once more in harmony. It healed the rift between their two families that had been there century upon century. That is why I love this story. Then she turned to Ruairidh and asked, "Are you all right Ruairidh? You are unusually quiet."

Ruairidh sighed, "I am sorry Eilidh; it is just that I have been thinking about the story which you started to tell us before and wondering what on earth this tale of Deirdre could possibly have to do with the plight of the weavers, and the poverty and injustice that is rife within our country."

Still looking concerned Eilidh picked up her clarsach and with a lop sided smile said, "I'd better try to explain then hadn't I?"

Chapter 29 Revolution or Education?

The haunting music of the clarsach filled the cottage, its refrain chillingly eerie, full of foreboding, leaving the listeners with a feeling of intense unease.

As the last lingering notes died away Eilidh put down her clarsach and began to speak.

"It was late one night that Cathbad[135] the Druid, received warning of a terrible catastrophe that was to come upon his beloved Ireland; vision after vision passed through his eyes, scenes of horrific bloodshed, of war, dishonour, treachery and strife. Night after night his dreams were tormented by visions of the destruction to be begotten because of Deirdre[136], the daughter of Felim the seannachie.

Cathbad decided to set out at once in search of this seannachie.

Felim was bard to Connor mac Nessa, and it was soon that Cathbad found him.

Delighted to be given the opportunity to show off his exquisite baby daughter, Felim proudly sent for her to be brought before the druid; but when Cathbad saw Deirdre, fear constricted his heart. At first he could do nothing but stare. He had three daughters of his own, but none had looked such as this when they were so young. Deirdre seemed almost ethereal,

---

[135] Cathbad the druid wed Maga, the daughter of Aonghus Og the God of love and beauty, and they were blessed by the birth of three daughters, Dechtire, Elbha and Findchaem. Their daughter Dechtire became the mother of Cuchullin the greatest of all the Red Branch champions. Elbha wed Uisneach and bore Naoise, Ardan and Ainle, and Findchaem wed the Druid Amergin and they were blessed by the birth of Conol of the Victories. All these five grandsons of Cathbad and Maga became Red Branch Champions.

[136] Deirdre is remembered for being the most beautiful woman that Ireland, and possibly Scotland, has ever seen.

with masses of hair the colour of the sun on a bright summer day, porcelain cream skin brushed with the red of roses, and eyes as blue as cornflowers, and when she smiled she was even more enchanting.

Understanding now the 'Doom' that Deirdre unwittingly carried, Cathbad set out immediately for the Court of King Conor mac Nessa[137] to ask that the child be killed.

Conor however laughed at his fears, dismissed his visions with scorn. However could a girl child cause destruction such as Cathbad talked of? How could a mewling female infant harm his legendary Red Branch Warriors[138]?

Cathbad then appealed to the other warriors of the house for support. They immediately and unreservedly urged Conor to agree to Cathbad's demand.

Yet Conor was immovable, and Deirdre was allowed to live.

As the years went by, Deirdre, unaware of the Doom she carried, grew more and more lovely, and her disposition was just as charming and delightful as her appearance.

Then one day King Conor chanced upon her whilst he was walking in Felim's garden. He watched as Deirdre and her nurse picked roses, entranced by her grace, captivated by her beauty.

---

[137]Cathbad the Druid (Maga's second husband), was actually Conor's biological father. Conor's mother was Nessa, the wife of Fachtna Fathach, the poet King, (Fachtna was Maga's son by her previous husband King Ross Ruadh of Ulster, - hence his name - Conor mac Nessa (Connor, son of Nessa)). King Fachtna however brought Conor mac Nessa up as his own son.

[138] Body of warriors set up by Ross Ruadh, King of Ulster. Ross Ruadh was the first husband of Maga (Maga, later wed Cathbad the Druid). Boys as young as seven years of age came to be trained as Red Branch Champions, the greatest of which was Cuchullin. The Red Branch warriors were a bit like King Arthur's Knights of the Round Table, and were at their greatest in the time of Conor mac Nessa; who as Fachtna's adopted son was therefore Ross Ruadh's adopted grandson.

Conor's wife Maeve had recently left him and he had begun to tire of the company of Maeve's equally demanding sisters, all of whom were extraordinarily beautiful passionate women, but feisty, tempestuous. He contrasted Deirdre's gentleness and sweetness of nature, her peerless beauty that far surpassed that of any other woman that he had seen and decided that this was the wife for him; a wife who would bring him contentment and ease of heart and spirit and refresh him with the purity of her loveliness and innocence.

Felim was not unaware of the honour that would attend the marriage of his daughter to the King, but he loved his little Deirdre well and did not wish her to go too young into the arms of this seasoned warrior king. Therefore although he reluctantly gave his permission for the union, he stipulated that it could not take place until the girl had reached sixteen years of age.

Conor mac Nessa however was not happy. He feared greatly that someone else would hear of Deirdre's astonishing beauty and seek to steal her off him. Had not his own wife recently left him for another and had not Lugh, of the Tuatha du Danaan, stolen his sister Dechtire from her husband Sultaim Mac Roth on their wedding night, the result of which had been the birth of his nephew Cuchullin? He did not wish to risk one of the Tuatha du Danaan, or any other, stealing this jewel from him.

Therefore Conor removed Deirdre from the house of her father Felim and took her to live out the years of her maidenhood in a high fortress, hidden deep in the middle of one of his thick dark forests, far, far away from any prying eyes. He gave her into the care of Lavercam, his maidservant, until the day when she should reach the age at which her father had given consent for her to be wed.

Despite Conor's best efforts to keep the matter secret, word soon got out as to his high handed treatment of Felim's

beautiful daughter. His abduction of Deirdre rather increased
the curiosity of all who heard of her; for she must be incredibly
handsome for Conor to feel the need to hide her away.

One of those whose curiosity was wetted was Conor's own
nephew Naoise, one of the sons of Uisneach[139], grandson of the
Druid Cathbad, great grandson of Aonghus Og, the God of love
and beauty.

Night and day were the dreams of Naoise filled with pictures
of the mysterious girl that King Conor mac Nessa had hidden
away and soon she became an obsession. He must catch a
glimpse of this daughter of Felim before she became his queen.
He must judge for himself whether she wished to wed Conor
mac Nessa, or would prefer instead the company of a man
nearer to her in age. His brothers Ainle and Arden willingly
aided him in his search. They thought it fine sport to seek for
the hidden bride of their King.

Then one day, whilst Naoise was out hunting alone, he found
himself deep in a part of a forest which he did not remember
having chanced upon before. Unconcerned he continued after

---

[139] Around 300 AD the sons of Uisneach left Ireland for Scotland; yet they clearly left their mark on the Scottish Highlands. The names of the sons of Uisneach are Naoise, Ardan and Ainle. Adoman, the ninth bishop of Iona, in his manuscript about the Life of Columba, mentions that whilst journeying to Loch Ness to visit the King of the Picts, Columba passed by the flumen (stream) Nesae and travelled through the districts of Arcardan and Cainle. Indeed some believe that Loch Ness itself is named after Naoise. Likewise in the vicinity of Loch Ness there are a couple of old forts called Dun-dheardhuil's, perhaps named after Deirdre herself; whilst near Oban there is, Dun(Castle or Fort) mhic Uisneach. Another fort connected to the children of Uisneach, is Dun Scathaig on the Isle of Skye, the home of Scathaig, the warrior princess said to have trained, amongst others, Cuchullin, the greatest of all the Red Branch Champions, and the sons of Uisneach, in the warrior arts.

his dogs for they were hot on a scent; then suddenly his way was bared by a thick hedge full of briars and sweet smelling roses.

Annoyed at have his hunt disrupted just as his dogs were about to close in upon their prey, Naoise searched eagerly for a way through or round the hedge. Soon though he began to wonder what was enclosed within this wall of thorns, and, losing interest in the hunt, called his dogs to him. Then, his curiosity growing, he climbed high up in a tree. To his great surprise he beheld a tower. As excitedly he inspected it, his eyes met those of the most beauteous maiden he had ever seen in his life, who was sat at the window of the tower, and his heart was lost. The next moment she was gone.

Naoise had found that which he had been looking for and she was even more beautiful than his wildest imaginings. Deirdre had also caught a glimpse of Naoise, and he was much more like the husband of her dreams than was the middle aged king, Conor mac Nessa.

To cut a long story short, after much persistence Naoise managed to persuade Lavercam, Deirdre's maid, to allow him to visit Deirdre, and it was not long before the two young people, so much in love, decided to risk their King's wrath and flee together to Scotland. Lavercam who loved Deirdre as if she were her own daughter went with them, as did Naoise's brothers.

One can imagine the wrath of Conor mac Nessa when he discovered that his bride, the most beautiful woman in all Ireland, had flown, had run away with his own nephew!

He had his warriors search far and wide for Naoise and Deirdre. Only when he found that they had sought refuge in Scotland did he call off his men.

Deirdre and the children of Uisneach lived for many years in the Highlands of Scotland. Here they prospered and were happy. Yet Naoise could never forget his homeland.

Similarly Conor mac Nessa could never forget the bride he had lost.

As the years crept by Conor's fury grew ever greater at the theft of Felim's daughter by the sons of Uisneach. Continually gnawing at his mind was the knowledge that the beautiful Deirdre yet lay in the arms of another. The thought that the traitor who had abducted her still roamed free infuriated him more and more as time crept by. Increasingly he brooded over his loss and he began to search for a means to gain revenge on the sons of Uisneach and have Deirdre returned to him.

Then at last he remembered Cathbad the druid and the warning that he had been given of the Doom that Deirdre would bring on Ulster.

Conor at once called Cathbad to him.

Cathbad however did not believe the protestations of his King that he desired reconciliation with the sons of Uisneach. Instead he advised Conor not to send for the sons of Uisneach, reminding him of the vision that he had received on the night of Deirdre's birth. Cathbad warned Conor mac Nessa that should he invite Deirdre to the shores of Ireland, her Doom would come upon her and upon the people of Ulster.

But Conor would not listen, so maddened was he by his desire for Deirdre and his hatred of Naoise. He asked Cuchullin to take a message to the sons of Uisneach begging them to come and promising them clemency, honour and great gifts, but Cuchullin, not trusting the mood of his King, refused to go. For Cuchullin loved the sons of Uisneach like as brothers. Often had he been to visit them in Scotland and knew that they prospered there and that Deirdre was happy and did not wish to return to Ireland.

Conor asked many of his warriors to deliver the message to Naoise and Deirdre, but all refused to go as messenger, for none believed Conor mac Nessa when he avowed that he had relinquished his desire to have Deirdre as his wife.

Finally he requested that great champion, Fergus mac Roth the husband of his mother Nessa, to go to Scotland to see if he could persuade the children of Uisneach to return to Ireland.

Now Fergus loved the sons of Uisneach as his own sons, and he dearly wished for their return. So after first obtained Conor's oath that no harm would come upon them should they set foot on the shores of Ireland, he set out immediately for Scotland.

When Fergus arrived in Scotland laden down with all sorts of gifts from the King he was given an enormous welcome by the sons of Uisneach; and when Naoise heard of the offer of Conor mac Nessa he was delighted.

Although Deirdre and the sons of Uisneach had indeed thrived amongst the glens and hills of Scotland, Naoise had always felt enclosed, stifled among the high mountains. Often had he longed for the lush green valleys of Ireland. Despite his great love for Deirdre he still dreamed of returning to the land of his birth to feast and fight once more with his companions, the warriors of the Red Branch, to see once more his family and friends, to walk again the hills and valleys of his childhood. To him Ireland would always be his homeland, his country, however many long and happy years he might live in Scotland. Eagerly he agreed to Conor's offer of forgiveness, of land in Ireland, of a position at court.

Deirdre however was distraught when she heard of her husband's intention of returning to Ireland. She loved the land of her marriage, remembering Ireland only for her imprisonment and Conor only as her jailor. She did not wish to leave this land where her children had been born, where she had hoped to live long and happily until the day of her death.

She did not trust the promises of this King. How could her husband believe that Conor Mac Nessa wished to reward him for the theft of his bride, to honour him for deeds he had done far from his shores, to praise him for having succeeded in gaining a successful happy life with the woman he loved when he himself had coveted that same woman? She begged Naoise not to go, not to believe the words of his King, not to believe the words of Fergus Mac Roth, for had not Fergus once before believed the word of this King, and found it flawed; thereby relinquishing the throne of Ulster[140].

Fergus might believe Conor's promise that no harm would come to the sons of Uisneach, but she, Deirdre, was not so trusting. Once they set foot on Ireland she believed that Conor would forget that he had ever promised clemency to the sons of Uisneach and remember only his hatred of them, remember his fury that they had tricked him out of his bride, had stolen the woman he coveted.

Naoise refused to listen. He had long dreamed of returning to Ireland. Now his dreams were coming true.

---

[140] When Ross Ruadh died his eldest son Fachtna was given the throne of Ulster. When Fachtna in turn died the throne then went to Fachtna's half-brother, Fergus mac Roth, rather than Fachtna's 'son' Conor mac Nessa. After Fergus had been King for some years he found himself enamoured of Nessa, his brother Fachtna's widow. Initially she refused to wed him, but after some time she agreed to marry Fergus on one condition, that Fergus relinquish the throne of Ulster to her son Conor mac Nessa for one year. After a year the throne would be returned to him. Fergus mac Roth agreed to these terms and wed Nessa. However, Conor mac Nessa, despite his sworn oath to return the throne to Fergus at the end of the year refused to relinquish it.

Fergus and his entourage were feasted and feted while preparations were made for their journey.

Only Deirdre did not rejoice.

As they boarded the ship bound for Ireland the wind blew strong and in the sound of the wind Deirdre heard the voices of her ancestors crying out to her that she must persuade Naoise to turn back, they whispered of treachery, of Conor's hatred, of the army of men awaiting them on their return to the shores of Ireland.

But Naoise would not listen.

For Naoise, Arden and Ainle this journey was one of unadulterated joy. Deirdre also put off her sad looks, dressing herself in her best clothes, anxious that these last days with her husband be pleasurable, happy times; determined that when he died his last memory of her would be that of a loving, beautiful wife.

As they drew near the shores of Ireland a messenger came to meet them saying that Fergus was urgently required in some distant part of the Island. Fergus, suspecting nothing, took his leave of Deirdre and the sons of Uisneach, urging them to make haste to the court of Conor where he would see them again upon his return.

Naoise however suddenly now became cautious, thinking it strange that Fergus should be called away at such a time. Too late he remembered that Conor was not one to enjoy having his will crossed. Too late he realised that Deirdre, though a decade older than before, was if anything more beautiful than she had been in her youth. As fingers of ice began wrapping themselves around his heart he remembered anew that the King had wished to wed his wife, and suddenly he began to fear for her safety. With this in mind he warned Deirdre to remain on board the ship until such time that he should return for her. He left many men with her on the ship so as to guard her and their children, ordering the captain of the ship to anchor some way out from shore - as a precaution.

Nevertheless as the sons of Uisneach set foot on dry land and began their journey to the court of Conor mac Nessa, their spirits rose once more for under their feet was the grass of Ireland, and the smell of its flowers was in the air, and they were riding to meet the companions of their youth.

On that first day's journey they saw no sign of armed men, encountered no problems, and as the night came they settled down with a light heart, posting only a few guards.

Conversely that evening in the depths of her cabin Deirdre lamented sorely as vision after vision showed her that the hour of her husband's death was drawing closer.

Naoise and his brothers slept soundly that night, their faces etched with happiness and contentment. Then suddenly they were awoken by the sound of steel against steel as one after another the warriors of Conor mac Nessa rushed in upon the sons of Uisneach and their men.

Naoise and his brothers rose up, fury in their hearts at this cold blooded treachery, and charged out to enjoin battle with their attackers.

Many fierce, stout and valiant warriors they killed that night, but however many of their assailants fell under their hands, many more rushed in to take their place.

Then, as sorrow filled the heart of Naoise, for he has seen his brothers fall around him and weariness now made his arm grow heavy, then Conor himself came upon him, and with his heart intent on revenge he plunged his spear into Naoise.

Deirdre in a vision saw her beloved fall, and weakened by sorrow and grief, not wishing to live in a land where Naoise was *no more, her breathe left her and her spirit departed to join he whom she loved more than life itself.*

Even now the spirits of Naoise and Deirdre, together forever, still wander over these very hills and glens that we ourselves roam. Their mortal remains are long gone but never forgotten.

And so the Doom that Cathbad 'Saw' in a vision on the night that Deirdre was born came to pass.

Many brave men died because of Deirdre, many families lost father, sons, brothers and lovers all because of the beautiful Deirdre. Because of Deirdre the Company of the Red Branch became troubled and divided, no more did men trust the word of Conor Mac Nessa, for he had pledged his word on the safety of the sons of Uisneach and betrayed his promise.

Fergus Mac Roth went into exile, furious at the treachery, for Conor's betrayal also besmirched his good name.

In revenge for the death of the sons of Uisneach their cousin, Conol of the Victories, killed Fiachra, one of King Conor mac Nessa's sons.

Conor also lost the support of the druid Cathbad. For Cathbad was wrath at Conor's treachery and sore with grief at the loss of his strong, courageous grandsons, the three proud stalwart, valiant sons of Uisneach.

As for Deirdre and Naoise's children, well, Aonghus Og took his great grandchildren to live with the Tuatha du Danaan, where they would be able to grow up protected from the vitriol and venom of Conor mac Nessa.

To this day the mountains, rivers, lochans and stones throughout the Highlands remember Deirdre and the sons of Uisneach, and we too should remember the story of Deirdre, who through no fault of her own brought death and injury to many men; causing the wreckage of many family and friendship bonds and severely weakening the land of Ulster."

"She should hae wed the King as she was bid," Findley offered, "and then nane o' the trouble would hae happened."

Eilidh looked at him quietly for a few moments without answering. Then she said. "Would Deirdre have escaped her Doom if she had wed Conor mac Nessa rather than Naoise? I do not know. However if you consider her tale in the light of that of Lancelot and Queen Guinevere it might suggest not. For it is said that Guinevere continued faithful to King Arthur all the days of her life and that Lancelot was ever her true knight; yet despite this their love was blamed in part for the demise of the Knights of the Round Table. We shall never know what would have happened if Deirdre had not run away with Naoise."

"However I did not tell the story because of Deirdre, but because of the treachery of Conor mac Nessa."

"What happened then is happening now. Those who choose to challenge Kings or, in our case, Parliament still put themselves in the way of being crushed; destroyed by fair means or foul."

"Not much has changed since the time of Deirdre and Naoise. We still have our hero's, men of passion and ability who desire to do what is right and honourable. So also do we still have men in power who do not like to have their will crossed, who will stoop to any depths to remain in power and obtain what they want."

She paused for a moment before continuing sadly, "I have walked through Morvern these past few days, through the very glens where Naoise once strode and Deirdre rode, those same glens where not so very long ago Cumberland's troops destroyed the homes and crops of those whose families chose to fight for Bonnie Prince Charlie rather than the victorious army of King George I. The people of Morvern were punished because they got betwixt and between the games of Kings, just as did poor Deirdre and her husband Naoise."

"That land which Cumberland's men put to the torch is still bare of woodland, perhaps as a lasting memory to our Bonnie Prince." Eilidh turned to Ruairidh and with an apparent change of subject asked "Did you know that Maxwell's lass wed the son of the minister Norman MacLeod?"

Ruairidh nodded, but said nothing.

Eilidh continued, "I was talking to Maxwell about the problems that will arise from the machines coming in and taking the work from the people and the bringing in of the sheep, also in place of the people. Well, you know how he knows many folk in high places on account of his being Argyle's Chamberlain. He claims to have heard that the government is extremely worried as it believes that there are many in our country who are not happy, that they fear that there are those who wish to follow the example of the French and overthrow its rule."

Andrew had pulled his chair nearer to listen to the story, he now, eyes bright and face intent, said "After that fiasco at Peterloo, is it surprising?"

Ruairidh's friend Findley now joined in the conversation. "Were ye there?"

"No indeed!" Andrew answered somewhat impatiently.

"I wis though," stated Findley grimly.

Eilidh looked at him considering for a few moments before avowing, "It must have been very frightening when it became apparent that there was going to be trouble."

Findley, by this time seemed to have accepted Eilidh, for nothing loathe he replied sadly, "When the soldiers came aye, but no at first. Ye should hae seen all the marchin' in the days afore the meetin'! Those as had fought at Waterloo, they had us all marchin fir days afore. No a bit o' trouble wis there, all o'

271

us wishin' tae state peaceably tae the government that we were awishin' tae change the way folks are elected tae Parliament. We were wantin' tae tell the government that we should all hae a voice, that each and every man should hae a vote. Then the government wid represent all the people and no just they as is wealthy. If we choose hae we send tae the Parliament, if we can choose hae will speak for us common folk, then we can pit an end tae all the injustice an poverty that we see all around."

"Ah" he continued bitterly, "a grand sight it was, all those folk a standin' the gether in unity w' all their banners a flyin', wi' all the bands, the horses and all those flags, why ye niver saw such a braw sight! It was fair wonderful," he mused. "The wimin were there tae," his face changed and he looked sick.

"It wis the wimin hae suffered when all the cavalry charged. I mean…, I…, I tried tae help…, there they were a, a lyin' there……, there wis this lassie, a…, a saw her a lyin' there, bleedin', after some brute o' a sodjer had used his sabre on her, an'…, an' her bairn, I saw it fall oot o' her airms as she fell doon."

He paused, visibly shaken by his memories. Then grimly he continued, "I saw others trampled by their horses. I…, I meself was hit by a truncheon."

He turned and looked at Ruairidh, the pain in his voice was written all across his face as he continued, "When those there cavalry charged it was all I could dae no tae run."

"I helped a man, hardly maer than a lad he wis, I helped him tae gang hame after he was shot; shot like a dog he wis! A' nay ken if he survived or no."

Findley went quiet for a moment, before asking bitterly "Whit kind o' a government treats their folks in such a way when all that the people wished was tae say that they want work so as tae put bread into the bellies o' their bairns? Whit kind o' a tyrant treats its people in such a way when all they are trying tae dae is tell the government what changes they should make so that the country as a whole becomes a better place tae live, a country fair tae the rich an' poor alike? Is it any wonder that when there are fools like as yon Liverpool our Prime Minister in the government, an when we have such a King as we have just fallen heir tae, that some o' us wish for revolution such as had the French no so very many years ago."

"All that marching and posturing that led up to Peterloo only served to frighten the government into believing it was outright revolution that was being planned, rather than peaceful protest such as was intended," Andrew stated calmly.

George added, "Aye, the tragedy of Peterloo was that for all the good intentions of the people and the organisers of the demonstration, all that it succeeded in doing was to induce the government to act more repressively. Consider the injustice of those Six Acts which have just been brought in to attempt to prevent a repeat of what happened at Peterloo."

"To prevent the people grouping together in large groups to petition for reform, and to stop people writing about ideas which they deem to be too radical," Ruairidh interjected angrily.

"Maxwell says that there is talk that the government has sent out spies to encourage pockets of resistance," said Eilidh. "He says that the government are looking to make examples of a few to try to discourage subsequent disturbances by greater numbers. Indeed he believes that if people are unwilling to put their neck in the noose voluntarily then they will gently be encouraged by these spies, by false promises, to do so. Then once this small orchestrated rebellion has begun it will be crushed unmercifully and the ring leaders made examples of." She turned to Findley and smiled, "But remember, my friend is getting aged and will have a poor memory for having been telt or having told about such things."

"Yir freind," asked Findley "has he heard that the Lowlands will rise?"

"He has heard that the government would wish the Lowlands to rise soon so that they will get the chance to crush any minor rebellion and hang a few of the instigators, or dupes, as an example to try to discourage anyone else from being foolhardy enough to openly oppose them in this way," Eilidh replied.

"Did he mention that the government have just foiled a plan to murder the Prime Minister, some of the Cabinet ministers and overthrow the government itself?" George asked dryly.

It was Eilidh's turn to stare. "He did not."

Andrew it was who explained, "It was in all the papers the day we travelled up. They were arrested in Cato Street by a band of Bow Street Runners, 'twas said that some of the conspirators escaped, but I doubt they will remain free for long."

"Poor men," said Eilidh with some feeling.

"Think you Eilidh that now the government is already frightened, that a rebellion of the people is the more likely to succeed?" Ruairidh asked eagerly.

"You and I don't remember the 'Forty Five' when our Prince came with empty French promises. None of us here were born at the time nor did we see how many of our men, women and children died," Eilidh replied. "Here in Ardgour, the Laird was too young to be punished for Jacobite affiliations; it was not so in other places."

"Look at Lochiel for example, or indeed Maclean of Duart. They lost their lands for a generation and more. And for what?"

"The Jacobites had a Prince[141] to lead them and many Lairds and noblemen came out in support, bringing their liele men to fight[142], but it came to nothing but the sorry murder of many innocent men."

"Or consider what happened even more recently in France when they murdered their royal family and goodness knows how many ordinary decent folk. What did the people of France then receive as a reward for their alleged thirst for liberty and equality other than a power hungry Emperor and more war, death and destruction; and now they have returned to a monarchy again! All that pain and suffering - for what purpose, for whose gain?"

"Think you that our King and his nobles will easily give up their wealth and power to the people? Think you that the people will win what they wish through bloodshed, when our government can call on trained soldiers to put down any rebellion?"

"And if by chance a leader arose who could induce all the people to rise up with him, and if those who rebelled outnumbered the soldiers who were sent to subdue the rebellion, what would be the price in blood and death? What happened at Peterloo would be as nothing compared to the tragedies that would be enacted then!"

"We have already had our share of regicide have we not?" observed Joe lazily. "Did we not behead King Charles I, just as the French guillotined their King Louis XVI? We had a few years in which Cromwell and the Parliament ruled without the aid of a monarch, but when Cromwell died Charles I's son Charles II was invited to take the throne. In this also did France imitate us, for the French likewise discovered that life with no King was no

---

[141] Bonnie Prince Charlie.
[142] The Jacobite Rebellion of 1745.

better, indeed possibly worse, than life with a King on the throne."

"We invited back the son of our murdered King; they have now on their throne the younger brother of their murdered King. It seems to me that armed rebellion gains little in either the short or long term except sorrow and bloodshed, even where great armies are involved," Joe concluded.

"Except," said Ewan," that Louis XVIII is said to be trying to limit the power of the nobles and to keep much of the sensible laws of government that Napoleon laid down. If he does this then surely it means that all the murders and atrocities that occurred during the revolution were not done totally in vain."

"If they had used more peaceable means to instigate change then the people would, at some stage, have obtained more say in how they wished to be governed without incurring all that death and bloodshed," retorted Joe. "I remember Eilidh's father telling me once that Louis XVI had already been induced to give up much of his power, even before he was sent to the guillotine; the implication being that the Revolution would have been rendered unnecessary if people had been less greedy for power and been content instead to let time and due process win for them justice and freedom. Patience and consistent working with the King to maintain and obtain progress towards a more enlightened government would have been a more sure and painless way to achieve change."

Eilidh looked sadly at Ruairidh as she asked "How think you that a few weavers and the like can overturn the whole government in England and by force seek to return a Parliament to Scotland, to make anew a Scottish government separate from that of our Hanoverian King? Remember Naoise who was tricked into returning to the land he loved so he could be vanquished. Think you that our King, our government will not stoop to use similar means to crush those who seek to rebel, to supress those who seek, for all sorts of reasons, to have Scotland regain its independence."

"You surely do not suggest that we should sit back quietly and accept the rot that is in our government, the unfairness of our franchise? Should we sit back and applaud our fat, lecherous, debt ridden King as he sits on his throne in comfort while the people that he is supposed to care for starve?" Ruairidh cried.

"I believe it is well educated, compassionate, principled people such as young MacLeod, who work to improve the lot of the people, who speak up against the injustices in our society, who will make a difference to our country. I believe that rather than planning armed insurrection we should be working towards, preparing the way for, and dreaming of sending people such as yourself Ruairidh into Parliament, people who understand what the common people want, so that they can pass laws that will help those who have no voice. Gaining independence from England, or removing the King and nobility from power, if it were possible, will not of itself produce the utopia you dream of."

"Bloodshed breeds bloodshed," Eilidh continued. "It is education and the willingness of God-fearing men to go out and serve the people that will help bring wealth and power within the reach of everyone, not just the few who are lucky enough to be born into the right families and who have the abilities to either gain wealth and power or hold onto that which they have been born to."

"Such as we," affirmed George with his charming smile, "we who will give freely of the use of our skills and seek the health and welfare of our neighbours rather than solely the health and welfare of ourselves, eh Andrew! We have to be part of that voice of change" he avowed, as he grinned at his friend. "And such as this curly haired chap," he indicated Ewan, "who has inherited, so I have just learned, estates from his grandfather and a large pot of the ready."

"Only if I survive a term or two at Oxford," replied Ewan with a grimace, "And aye, Eilidh would not allow me to be ought other than the benevolent landlord. I believe she would come in the night and dirk me herself if she thought I was not comforting the widows and orphans on my lands!" He shot her a mischievous look.

George laughed and then he looked at Eilidh curiously. "If you don't mind my asking Alan, just what age are ye?"

She shrugged her shoulders and then replied casually, "Ewan here has three days more than me."

Andrew looked measuring at Ewan, "If ye are to go up to Oxford in the autumn my guess is that ye must turn eighteen sometime this year." He turned to Eilidh. "What age were ye when you started at the University?"

"Perhaps I may have had thirteen years on me," she responded offhandedly. Then picking up her clarsach she asked "Who's for a song?"

Ewan refilled the glasses as Eilidh started up a well-known air.

They remained at Eilidh's cottage until the early hours of the morning, talking, playing card games, singing and telling stories; and left only with great reluctance after Eilidh maintained that she herself wanted a couple of hours of sleep before their assignation with Fergus at dawn, and that she knew that Ewan could not be wakened unless he slept for a least three or four hours.

They left quickly and quietly after that, even Findley managed a civil farewell. All of them made her promise to write to them; whilst Ruairidh assured her that he had listened "right well" to her message and would attend more seriously to his studies on his return south and look to avoid the traps and lures sent out by any present day Conor mac Nessa.

Chapter 30 Eilean nan Craobh

The sun's rays had just begun to peep through the rising mist to glisten on the water below and the birds were singing merrily on what promised to be a fine late winter's day as Fergus Campbell made his reluctant way down to the shoreline. A seagull squawked loudly overhead and Fergus scowled, irritated by its raucous clamor, oblivious to both the fresh smell of the sea and the wind's gentle caress as it carried the spray over the land to kiss his face in welcome.

Annoyance prickled at the edge of his awareness as he suddenly noticed a youth, dressed much as he was himself, standing down on the shore next to a small rowing boat. Fergus could think of no occasion to account for the presence of a stranger at this hour in the morning and wondered with renewed irascibility how he could persuade the youth to leave the area before Eilidh arrived. He suspicioned that her mother did not know of today's outing and would not approve if she did.

He was about to question the youngster when another figure came into view and the merry voice of the unknown youth rang out.

"Failte, Ewan! I had feared that you would be late."

"I would have been," replied Ewan, "but yon fiend," he indicated his companion who now appeared hurrying behind him, "came with fearsome threats so that I was feart to linger; especially as he reminded me of your promise of a drouking should I be late!"

"Ah, Joe, well done!" the unknown youth exclaimed to the 'fiend'. Then the youth turned to Fergus and in that same annoyingly cheery voice exclaimed "I see that Fergus also is not laggard!"

Fergus, who had now joined the other three, stared at the stranger, ignoring the others for a few moments. Then his heart began to hammer violently, "E... E... Eilidh!" he stammered.

Ewan looked at him scornfully. "Who else would it be?"

Joe also looked slighting. "Ye havne seen herself dressed thus afore have ye? How did ye reckon she would gang to Achnacarry? Ye didnae think she wore the petticoats when she sailed yon boat. It's no a boat that's right easy for a body t' sail alain niver mind ane hae wears the petticoats!" He said this in the broad accent that Fergus knew he affected at times solely to annoy.

Fergus did not answer for a moment, then he blurted "Eilidh, it is not suitable! It is not necessary that you take me. Your mother..."

"Would not approve, but she need not know. Who is to tell her? If you did not recognise me then who will who is not loyal to me? Besides you do need to go to Achnacarry. Moreover I have promised Iona we are coming, she is expecting us and I do so much wish to see her myself. Come Fergus," Eilidh said coaxingly, "I often dressed thus when father was alive. I thought you knew that the nephew who occasionally accompanied him as his secretary was really me."

Fergus looked unhappy.

Eilidh stepped into the rowing boat saying as she did so, "Joe if I row you and Fergus over to where Cuchullin is anchored would you mind returning for Ewan whilst I get Cuchullin ready to sail?"

Joe indicated his readiness to do this and very reluctantly Fergus followed Joe into the boat. Fergus then offered to row, as Joe did not, and was laughingly refused. At this he sank back on his seat in petulant silence at the perceived slight to his ability; though indeed he had little skill with the oars, only he misliked to see a female row whilst he sat back idle. He also misliked the superior way that Joe smirked at him.

Eilidh's sailing boat Cuchullin was anchored just out from the shore and within minutes Eilidh was aboard and requesting that Fergus climb up into the boat also. This he did with some awkwardness and embarrassment, not helped by Joe's undisguised impatience to make a start on the return journey to collect Ewan.

Joe soon returned with Ewan who seemed in high spirits, and before long the rowing boat was secured, the sails made ready, the anchor pulled in and they were off.

Fergus had been asked if he wanted to sit within the tiny cabin, but this he had refused. He was not a good sailor but preferred to be in a place from which, if they did capsize, he would have some chance of swimming to shore. He now sat where, as he ruefully recognised, he would be out of the way. Ewan soon joined him there, whilst Joe stood with Eilidh at the tiller.

It was an Eilidh he did not recognise. She was always joyful and blithe, but here she looked somehow different, and not just in her apparel. As she stood there with her head high, gazing out across the water, tranquil, seemingly oblivious of the uneven motion of the boat as it rose and fell with the swell of the waves, heedless of the strong gusts of winds that blew behind; it was it almost as if she were a part of the very wind and sea, an Elemental[143] or a Naiad[144] come out of legend.

---

[143] Mythological being of which there are four types each belonging to one of the four elements (earth, water, fire and wind).

[144] Naiads are a type of female nymph. Naiads are associated with fresh water just as Oceanids are associated with salt water. Nymphs are minor deities who are linked to different aspects of nature, for example: water, land, plants, the heavens and the underworld. They are usually believed to take the form of beautiful maidens.

As he watched her standing there looking so at peace as the boat sped through the water, chased by the wind, with the spray rising and the light rain falling, it came to him that this was where she belonged; and then she turned to look at him and smiled. All the angry feelings that had clouded his head since he first awoke so very early that morning, just drifted away. He watched as she gave the tiller to Joe and walked over.

"Is it not grand? Thank you for coming Fergus," Eilidh said as she approached, still smiling.

"You don't thank me," interjected Ewan, "and me forced from my bed with a dirk half an inch from my heart!"

"My! You must have been sleepy Ewan! Did I not say you would suffer from the theft of my faither's good whisky?"

Ewan groaned in mock sorrow and pain. Then said craftily "What were you doing sitting on such a fine hoard when you claim not to touch the stuff?"

Eilidh laughed. "I've given it to John Boyd, so that will be the last you taste of it if you are false to Ealasaid." She noticed the seals and her face lit up as she went over to talk to them. Then, after a few minutes, she returned to where Joe was standing and regained the tiller.

"Do they always come when she sails?" asked Fergus when she had gone.

"Always, or so Joe tells me. I rarely sail with Eilidh; though she has a small boat anchored off the coast of Fife for when she comes to stay with us. I confess I am not fond of the water and sailing with Eilidh is a chancy business at times as she is as often in the water as out of it and she expects me to follow. I have discovered that it is best not to get into the boat in the first place rather than attempt the impossible task of trying to persuade Eilidh that I do not wish to enter the freezing sea, even if she does. She is more understanding now, but when we

283

were children she could not conceive how I could possibly not share her passion and I was too proud to confess my terror."

"You must swim well then!"

"Very well," Ewan grimaced. "I *think* she would not have let me drown, but I was never convinced that she would remember that I could not hold my breath as long as she. Often it was a seal that noticed that I was tiring, before she did. I grew quite fond of the creatures. One in particular, a youngster so Eilidh said, would always stay close to me when I was in the water. Eilidh claimed that this seal was fond of me and for a time I believed her. I'm not so sure now, and suspect that Eilidh told her to keep a look out for me."

"She can speak to the creatures?"

"She seems to," Ewan replied. "She says she can't but if you watch them..."

Joe came over to join them, and there was a moment of silence. Joe's grim visage told its own story and Fergus suspected that he also did not feel comfortable with their companions.

All three sat silently watching the lone figure who stood before them; small and trim, dressed more for riding than for sailing, with her hair hidden under her hat, standing there all alone looking far out ahead with the sails billowing around her. All three sat watching quietly, engrossed in their own thoughts, while casting occasional surreptitious glances at their companions who still swam loyally alongside the craft.

It did not seem long before the shores of An Gearestan[145] could be glimpsed in the distance. To Fergus's surprise they sailed on by without stopping. Then before they had travelled much further, Fergus spotted a few small islands just ahead of them.

---

[145] Fort William.

Eilidh turned to where they were seated saying, "Fergus, one of these islands was once the home of the Chief of the Locheils."

Fergus pulled a wry face. "Their name then is imaginative if they are named after the Loch which their original home was on."

"Indeed, and do not all the chiefs call themselves after some bit of land important to them? Look there it is, Eilean nan Craobh[146]."

They sailed past the tiny island as they made their way towards the shore of the mainland.

"We will anchor over at Corpach where there is a grand little bay," commented Eilidh. "No one will disturb Cuchullin there and it is a fairly straight path up from Corpach to Achnacarry. Joe has arranged for some horses to be waiting for us, and there is a croft nearby where we can leave the horses later tonight; someone will collect them in the morn."

This time it was Joe who rowed Fergus and Ewan to the shore and then returned for Eilidh.

Fergus savoured those few short minutes sitting alone with Eilidh on the shore, basking in the early morning sunshine while they waited for Joe and Ewan to fetch the horses. Eilidh seemed somehow more relaxed, more forthcoming than he had ever known her to be. Always before he had got the impression that she was trying to get away as soon as possible, and there had been an almost invisible constraint in her manner, but now, here, she somehow seemed to be more at ease and it was as if time were not an issue.

All too soon however a third member of their party came into view.

---

[146] Island of the Trees.

As Ewan approached them, Eilidh asked musingly "Do you remember Ewan when you came with father and I to Iona?"

Ewan pulled a face. "Do I not! A right awful place it was, cold and windy and full of gravestones and streets of the dead and the like." He laughed, "I remember that you were right mad at me for refusing to pretend to follow the wake of Kenneth MacAlpin[147] or some such monarch!"

Eilidh grinned "I was an' all! Anyway you will no doubt also be just as delighted to learn that Corpach, where we are sat just now, is one of the places where many of those kings and noblemen are said to have been temporarily interred whilst they waited for the winds to change so they could continue their journey to..."

Ewan with mock seriousness finished the sentence for her, "embark on their final journey to that sacred Isle, there to enjoy their eternal slumber!"

Eilidh laughed, "I see that the visit was not entirely wasted on you Ewan, even if you did show a lamentable lack of curiosity in Iona itself and displayed not a particle of interest in the fact that many of your most prestigious forebears are buried there!"

"If Eilidh, your ancestors were forever raised up before you as the embodiment of all that is good and desirable, and if you perpetually had the accusation thrown up at you, that your idleness would preclude you from ever enjoying the same eminence that they had achieved, then you also would not wish to eulogise over that further confirmation of their fame and success!"

"Come Ewan," said Fergus lazily. "Do not seek to gammon us that you are in the least bit affected by such comparisons. It

---

[147] King sometime in the 9th century. He was of the Dalriadic people, but also became King of most of the other tribes in Scotland.

seems to me that you are most content with your situation in life!"

Ewan grinned and said confidingly, "I only say it to try to get Eilidh to feel sorry for me. Believe me she is much easier to live with then, much less demanding!"

"So that is how you manage to stay on such good terms with Eilidh! Perhaps I should try it," Fergus said giving a sly look in Eilidh's direction.

Ignoring this Ewan raised his eyebrows and looked at Eilidh mischievously "Is it not a mite insensitive to be talking about an island where ancient kings are buried when we go to visit your friend who carries the same name?"

Eilidh lay back against the rock she was leaning against and put her arms behind her head. "Ewan! Who but you would think of such a thing! It is a name to be proud of!"

Joe arrived as she said this and his eyes lit up. "Aye, Iona is a grand name for a woman to carry. What could be better than to be named after an island with such an honourable history? An island honoured by both kings and priests from whom the message of our Saviour has gone out throughout the length and breadth of Scotland and beyond. Just as Iona is a precious jewel amongst islands, so is Iona Cameron, a pearl among females."

"Very poetic Joe! Why, I do believe that you must entertain a secret fondness for the girl. If you think so highly of her why do you not wed her yourself?" challenged Fergus lightly.

"I am not so fickle as some," responded Joe curtly.

Fergus was about to retort angrily when Ewan interjected with a mischievous look "What about that very pretty girl in London, Joe? The one who follows you everywhere when you are visiting the family and looks to me as if she has no intention of letting you run far!"

"Katherine Lyon is nought but the daughter of my father's business partner!" returned Joe quickly. "She and Eilidh are as sisters, so Katherine and I could not be other than close friends, as well you know Ewan Beaton!"

"It is not as a sister that she looks on either you or Eilidh," commented Ewan with unusual dryness!

Fergus, his face alight with amusement, joined in the baiting. "Well Joe, this is news to me. I did not know you had a sweetheart. Is she very pretty? I wonder if you would speak of her as highly as you do of Miss Cameron? If not I might suggest that you are merely trifling with the poor girl's affections!"

Joe it was now who had a martial look in his eye but it was Ewan who spoke first. "Katherine has not the quality of Miss Cameron, nor indeed of her own elder sister Helen, though she is much prettier than either of them. What say you Eilidh?" Ewan asked.

"Katherine is indeed remarkably pretty," Eilidh returned simply. "However this conversation, interesting as it is, does not get us any nearer to Achnacarry. It is time we set off." She then turned to Joe, "My thanks Joe for speaking so kindly and so honestly about my friend, for it is true Iona Cameron is as wise as she is kind and true."

Chapter 31 Journey to Achnacarry

As they made ready to mount their borrowed steeds and set off on their way Fergus's serenity was once more disrupted. Seeing Eilidh riding astride, dressed like a boy, laughing and larking around with Ewan, flooded him with a myriad of opposing emotions. True, he was used to seeing Eilidh ride astride, for even when she wore petticoats she wore britches underneath and had the skirts fashioned so she could ride thus with little hindrance and no loss of modesty, but he could not feel happy seeing her dressed in male attire. Indeed he found it uncomfortable even to look at her dressed thus, found it impossible to unravel his mixed emotions at the sight of her in this guise.

He noticed that Joe also rode silent and guessed that he likewise did not like the change, did not like the ease of her friendship with her milk brother; her cousin, if the gossip was to be believed.

They had not gone far however when Eilidh and Ewan stopped to wait for Fergus and Joe. Then, turning to Fergus, Eilidh said, "We are near to a place called Kilmallie. There are a couple of churches there with an interesting history. One of them was built by someone who they call 'The Black Son of the Bones'. Have you read Walter Scott's poem 'The Lady of the Lake'?"

"I have indeed," Fergus replied with a smile.

"Well, I met Walter Scott once when I was a child in Fife, one of his relatives was a friend of mine, a little girl called Marjorie Fleming[148]; anyway when he heard tell of where I hailed from he

---

[148] 'Pet' Marjorie Fleming (1803 -1811) was a child writer and poet. H.B. Farnie published her diary in 1858; her poems have also been published. A copy of all her writings is kept in the National Library of

told me that he had based one of his characters, that of Brian the Hermit, on 'The Black Son of the Bones' of Kilmallie on account of his reputedly strange birth. I don't recall much else about him," she mused, "which is hardly surprising I suppose as I must have been very young at the time because Marjorie died when she was only eight years old and I was younger than she. Marjorie was already writing fine poetry even at that age. 'Tis a pity she died so young," Eilidh said wistfully. "It was never quite the same returning to Fife after she had died."

She went silent, and after a few moments Fergus stated quietly, "You mentioned that there were two interesting churches."

She looked at him for a few moments and then as suddenly smiled. "You don't ask to be told the story of 'The Black Son of the Bones'!" she retorted. There was an impish light in her eyes. "In that case I shall leave you to ask Iona about the local legend, and then you can see for yourself the similarities between the local tale and that told in the poem."

Before Fergus could respond, for his brows had begun to lower into a more set look at that last comment, Eilidh continued, "Of the other church there is now no sign except perhaps a few stones in the old cemetery, much as is the case in Cille Mhaodain. Do you recall the graveyard where my father is buried?"

Fergus answered in the affirmative and so Eilidh resumed her story. "Well, next to that graveyard there are some old ruins that are said to be that of an old church dedicated to Saint Mhaodain. It is thought to have been constructed by one of the Camerons; Ailean nan Creach[149] they called him and he was the 12th Chief of Lochiel. Apparently he was a very bad man and

---

Scotland. She died of post measles meningitis.
[149] Alan of the 'Forays'.

plundered land and cattle and other possessions from his neighbours."

"I thought that was the usual practice hereabouts," interjected Ewan. "Did they not all try to steal cattle off one other?"

"Indeed and you have the rights of it Ewan, but this Ailean nan Creach apparently committed all sorts of atrocities and murders in the process, more than would be expected in the normal practice of such reaving. There were reputed to have been *seven* of these 'Forays' that were particularly notable. So wicked was he that it was even murmured that he was in league in the devil."

"And this is an ancestor of Miss Campbell?" asked Fergus dryly.

"Indeed, that he is. Would you like me to tell you the tale?"

It was Ewan who answered "I have been wracking my brains to think what it is about you Eilidh that I have missed all these months, and now I have realised that it is your stories which I have been pining for!"

"And no my fair self?" Eilidh countered teasingly. "Well I believe that this story is one that ye deserve to be telt!" she said with mock severity.

They all crowded close to listen to the story.

"'Tis a pity it's not your black divil ye are riding th' day Eilidh!" joked Ewan. "For he'd not let anyone near and thus spare us the tale!"

She laughed, and then began to speak:

"As Ailean nan Creach began to feel his age, he started to give some thought to his immortal soul and to fear that his repose in the next world would be less than peaceful. The thought that he might receive eternal damnation as a payment for his unsavoury actions began to worry at the edge of his mind

291

causing him to agonize for many a long hour as to what he could do to gain forgiveness for all the acts of atrocity that he had committed.

Eventually he decided to go to Gormshuil, the witch of Moy, to ask her advice. After some thought Gormshuil suggested that he should consult the oracle of the Tau Gairm[150] and instructed him as to the rites that he would need to enact to gain the counsel that he sought.

Wasting no time Ailean built himself a hut in a small meadow. Late one evening, shortly after this was built, he and an old faithful servant of his made their way to this small dwelling taking with them a cat.

There was a fire in the hut made ready to be lit and above this stood a spit such as was used for the roasting of meat. On entering the hut Ailean immediately instructed the servant to light the fire.

As soon as the fire had begun to burn fiercely Ailean took hold of the cat and pierced its side with the spit. The cat was not yet dead and…"

Eilidh grinned as she saw the look of disgust that appeared on Fergus's face and said mischievously "You can imagine the noise the creature made!" Then before Fergus could reply she continued with her story.

"He next ordered his servant to turn the spit so that the cat would be slowly roasted alive. Ailean not in the least sympathetic to the animal's agony now strode to the door of the hut with his claymore in his hand to guard against possible intruders.

---

[150] Invocation of the Tau; the Tau was often considered to be a symbol of redemption.

292

Before long, attracted by the noise of their compatriot, strange cats started to arrive outside the hut and soon the clamour outside began to be worse than that inside.

Now, the performance of the Tau Gairm had given the cats the power to speak and they soon began to threaten Ailean with all kind of torment should he not desist from torturing his prisoner.

However he paid no heed to their threats to tear him limb from limb merely instructing his servant to:

'Ciod air bith a chi, no chual thu

Cuir mu'n cuirt an cat'[151]

As he spoke a large black cat entered the hut. This enormous creature turned to the cats outside and ordered them to be quiet. Then he directed his cold blue eye upon the old chief demanding of him the reason for his torturing one of his people and bidding him to free the unfortunate cat immediately.

Ailean, no whit impressed by this display of authority, informed the black cat that should he wish the cat to be freed from the spit he must first divulged to him what he must needs do to save his soul and gain reparation for his sins.

The black cat, after considering for a few moments, replied that to gain forgiveness for all the wrong he had done throughout his life Ailean nan Creach must build seven churches, one for each of the terrible forays that he had enacted.

On receipt of this answer Aileen immediately commanded his servant to free the cat; whereupon that animal instantly and with a great squawk leaped up and rushed out of the house with all the other hoard of cats at his heels streaking straight down the brae to where the River Lochy ran.

The half roasted cat jumped into the water followed by the others and swimming across they all soon disappeared from

---

[151] 'Hear you this, see you that. Round the spit, and turn the cat'.

sight. To this day there is a deep pool on the river Lochy called the Cat Pool."[152]

"What a charming story," commented Fergus dryly.

Eilidh laughed "It is an' all! A good one to tell to frighten the children into behaving!"

Fergus looked horrified.

"Only joking! I do not believe in scaring children into obedience. Moreover, I am not sure who would be most frightening, Ailean nan Creach, the Great Black Cat, or Gormshuil herself!"

"I'd settle for Gormshuil," interjected Ewan. "There are too many tales about her powers for my liking! Though I don't recall that you ever told me that story Eilidh!" said Ewan.

"I must have done!" Eilidh exclaimed. "The trouble is Ewan that since you have been with me since the day of my birth I often assume that you know all the things that I know also."

Ewan pretended to shudder, "You can't know me that well if you think that I know all what's in those books that you, Andrew and George forever have your eyes in. Can you believe it? All the way up from Fife all they talked about was different diseases and different parts of the bodies that they had cut up; but I confess I drew the line when Andrew attempted to describe in great detail a tumour that he had seen one of his teachers discover in one of the bodies he had been hacking at!"

"Did not your mother have something to say about such talk?" asked Eilidh looking amused.

"Oh she was riding well behind with father. I'm afraid she did not enjoy the journey over much. It was a miserable journey Eilidh. What with your friends talking about nothing

---

[152] There are other stories about why the seven churches were built, and indeed some versions give the credit for the building of the churches to Ailean's son Ewan, the 13th Lochiel.

other than the contents and workings of the insides of folk, and mother complaining all the way! I had to do most of the work an' all, as mother was too unwell, father was busy with looking after her and George and Andrew, although most willing, were not at all used to rough living! And all for a wedding that none of us wished to go to!"

"It must have been terrible cold too!" Eilidh commiserated. "Your poor mother Ewan! Could she not have stayed behind? Especially since she will have to make the return journey in a few days' time!"

They had almost reached the channel where the Caledonian Canal commenced, and before Ewan could respond Eilidh suddenly turned to Fergus and asked "Did you know Fergus that a battle between the Camerons and my own kinsman Hector Bui Maclean was fought between here and the River Lochy?"

"I know little of the history of my clan and still less of the history local to this area," returned Fergus. "Though I confess that I feel ashamed to admit this as my mother was like you Eilidh in that she loved the history of this country; for all she was an Englishwoman."

"You will regret having acknowledged that!" warned Ewan. "I'll warrant Eilidh will now proceed to tell you what took place on every single blade of grass that we pass over on our journey to Achnacarry!"

Eilidh laughed and turned to Fergus admitting ruefully, "He speaks true I fear. For as I walk the hills hereabouts it somehow makes me feel more part of the land to remember just a few of those countless stories that the rocks could tell if we could but understand their speech. I am therefore perfectly willing Fergus to aid in your education and help resolve your feelings of guilt by telling the tale of that battle that my unfortunate kinsman lost." Fergus indicated his willingness to learn and so Eilidh continued with her story.

"Donald Dubh was Chief of the Camerons at this time and he and this Hector had long fought over who should be chief in Lochaber. As I understand it, they had been fighting near Loch Ness and had come to a stalemate, and then Hector executed one of his prisoners, a Cameron. In return Donald Dubh hanged two of Hector's sons whom he had taken prisoner. Hector naturally wanted vengeance and came down here to Corpach where they fought again. However Hector, my kinsman, lost on this occasion. I used to always feel that it was most unfair that he was unable to enact vengeance for the murder of his sons."

"I would imagine Eilidh that the life of that unfortunate Cameron who your kinsman executed first would be just as valuable and as sorely missed as that of the Maclean's sons," retorted Fergus. "I would further suppose that this battle did not conclusively end all the battles over this territory. Indeed I wonder that you wish to know such history! Perhaps it were better that the rocks keep their secrets."

"That would be like saying that we should walk around with our eyes and ears closed for fear that we might discover something unpleasant. Instead we should learn from our past history so that we and our nation do not repeat the mistakes of our forefathers!" Eilidh countered.

Then when Fergus forbore to reply she continued quietly. "Some however of what you say is true, in that the life of the Cameron was as important as that of the Maclean's sons. Like you I am persuaded that retribution, a life for a life is as pointless as it is futile. It is this desire for revenge that leads to conflict between families and clans; conflict that continues generation after generation, for no sensible reason. How much better it would be to effect reconciliation rather than vengeance as a means to assuage grief and loss. It is also true that this little skirmish was of itself relatively unimportant. However I believe that we forget the ancient sagas, the history of our land at our peril. Rather should we fear to forget those stories that tell of our heroes, of valour, of loyalty and honour."

"Those tales have remained with us throughout the centuries giving courage to those of us who are less brave and hope to those whose existence is repressed and unhappy and who long for and pray for the day that a great man shall arise who will deliver them out of their misery. Such men live on long in our memories, continuing to inspire. Because of such tales of valour some will be imbued with the courage and inspiration to also attempt great deeds, while for others it is enough that the memory of past brave men will encourage them just to continue, to hold on in the face of adversity or despair. Men such Fingal, Cuchullin, King Arthur, William Wallace, Robert the Bruce and even Somerled, and men such as the Marquis of Montrose, shine out as a light to keep the darkness at bay. You have heard, have you not Fergus, that great tale of Montrose's[153] march from Glen Roy through to Inverlochy?"

"Not for the Campbells was it a great tale!" interjected Ewan grinning. "If I am not mistaken they lost that particular fight and if I remember rightly the battle itself was fought not far from here."

"Aye, you are correct Ewan. It was fought at Inverlochy and indeed the name of that Campbell[154], he who came up against the Marquis of Montrose on that day, does not sound well to

---

[153] General James Graham, Marquis of Montrose, fought for King Charles I, but was later betrayed by his son King Charles II and was executed by his adversaries as a traitor and his head attached to the Tollbooth in Edinburgh.

[154] Archibald Campbell, the Marquis of Argyle. A forbear of the present Duke of Argyle.

those who remember his subsequent treacherous betrayal of Montrose." Eilidh smiled at Fergus as she said this to lessen the bite of the comment. Then she asked "Did you know that at some point between Blarmachfoldach and Loch Lundavra there stands a large stone called 'Clach nan Caimbeulach'[155]? A cairn stands nearby to mark the spot where this stone stands and 'tis said that those who support the Campbells remove a stone from this cairn as they pass it by, while the supporters of Montrose add one."

"Remember Eilidh, MacCailean Mor[156] himself died on the scaffold not many years after Montrose," interjected Joe.

"'Twas so, indeed Joe. 'Twas MacCailean Mor's head which replaced Montrose's on the Tollbooth in Edinburgh, after Charles II had him beheaded for treason."

Eilidh then turned to Fergus, and with a teasing look she asked, "Did you hear the song that the Bard, Iain Lom[157], wrote about that fight at Inverlochy between the armies of the Marquis of Argyle and those of the Marquis of Montrose?"

"I have not had that pleasure," returned Fergus warily.

"Well it goes something like this when one translates it into the English," she said with a merry look:

"Fallen race of Diarmid! Disloyal, - untrue,
No harp in the Highlands will sorrow for you:
But the birds of Loch Eil are wheeling on high,
And the Badenoch wolves hear the Camerons' cry,
Come feast ye! Come feast, where the false-hearted lie!"

---

[155] The Stone of the Campbells.
[156] Gaelic name for the Chief of the Campbells. In this case the Marquis of Argyle.
[157] Ian Lom MacDonald was the Keppoch Bard. He was said to have later been appointed Poet Laureate by King Charles II.

"If you were really the sex that you dress as today, I would challenge you for that Eilidh!" Fergus stated harshly.

Ewan excitedly called out "A mill! A mill!"

Thus earning him an angry look from Fergus.

Eilidh, her face alight with mischief, avowed with a grin, "Nothing personal was meant Fergus, but pray do not mind the fact that I am female. I would be quite happy to accept your challenge; but only for a friendly bout!"

Fergus looked quite horrified at this. He was unsure whether to reply to Eilidh, or berate Ewan for his laughter and encouragement.

"Inverlochy Castle is close to here and it also has a claim to fame," interjected Joe hurriedly, seeing the ugly look on Fergus's face. "Charlemagne[158] was reputed to have gone there once to sign treaties with some Pictish King."

Eilidh, ignoring Fergus's confusion, answered Joe, "I also have heard it said thus. Though I wonder as to what treaties they would have made in those ancient times. Perhaps Charlemagne thought to add Scotland to his Empire!"

"Inverlochy Castle is also of interest in that it was once the home of the Comyn's when they were the Lords of Lochaber and Badenoch," continued Joe determinedly, "Indeed one of the ruined towers is still called Comyns tower."

"Was it not one of these Comyns that Bruce murdered in that church in Dumfries?" interjected Ewan looking amused. "'Twas a rather spectacular way to end the controversy as to

---

[158] Charlemagne (Charles the Great), King of the Franks and Christian Emperor of the West was born around 750 AD near Liège in modern day Belgium. Pope Leo III crowned Charlemagne Emperor of the Romans in 800 AD. The immense territories that he conquered became known as the Carolingian Empire. He consolidated Christianity throughout his kingdom and established a new library of Christian and Classical books. He is thought to have died in 814 AD.

whether Bruce or the Red Comyn should be King after John Balliol!"

"A dishonourable start to a great reign!" Eilidh retorted.

"'Tis said that Bruce should have had the throne over Balliol in the first place," Joe countered defensively.

"Perhaps, but that does not excuse him committing murder whether on holy ground or not!" Eilidh stated seriously. "Though it is claimed that he was ever sorry for the deed, if not the outcome!"

"Walter Scott told of it in his poem, 'The Lord of the Isles.' You know, that part where he relates the tale of the Brooch of Lorn[159]," Joe offered.

> *"Vain was then the Douglas brand*
> *Vain the Campbell's vaunted band*
> *Vain Kirkpatrick's bloody dirk*
> *Making sure of the murder's work."*

Recited Ewan cheerfully, before continuing, "I wonder if Kilpatrick really did rush into the church to stab the Red Comyn again to ensure that the job had been done properly!"

Eilidh grimaced, "I suppose I can understand why he might have done such a thing. I can even almost see the sense in it, but still that does not make it any the more honourable." Then looking at Fergus she added with a smile, "If Walter Scott's tale tells true Bruce had a Campbell as a close friend," and without attempting further to coax Fergus out of the sullens, she rode on ahead with Ewan, since he had just challenged her to a race.

---

[159] The Brooch of Lorn is said to have belonged to Robert the Bruce and he wore it as a fastening for his cloak. The then Lord of Lorn, the Chief of the MacDougals and a supporter of the Comyn, was said to have gained it in a fight with Bruce when Bruce's cloak was torn off as he attempted successfully to escape.

Joe's eyes had lit up at Eilidh's mention of this particular Campbell and, making no attempt to follow her and Ewan, he turned to Fergus to ask if he knew whether, and if so how, he was related to this particular Campbell. He was still discussing the topic as Eilidh and Ewan returned, "...if it be Sir Neill Campbell of Lochawe that the poem tells of then he was rewarded very well by Bruce for his friendship and loyalty. He was given the hand of Bruce's sister Mary no less. I am fairly certain that he also gained a large share of the forfeited lands of the House of Lorn; that same family that gained the Brooch of Lorn from The Bruce himself..."

"'Thence in triumph wert thou torn, By the victor hand of Lorn[160],'" interjected Ewan with a grin, looking pleased with himself as he and Eilidh trotted back to join the others. Turning to Eilidh he asserted generously, "Fortunately for me it was not that black devil of yours that you were riding." Then he teasingly asked "You are sure Eilidh that it is a bull and not a horse up in Lundavra Lochan? Eilidh will never say who the sire of Dawn's twins is," Ewan explained to Fergus. "I have always suspected that it was some kelpie[161] or other."

Eilidh laughed, but said nothing to either refute or agree with the accusation, merely riding on.

Fergus, suddenly embarrassed by his churlishness, hurried his horse forward to catch up with her. "What is this water bull or horse?"

---

[160] From the poem 'The Lord of the Isles' written by Sir Walter Scott.
[161] Kelpies ,or water kelpies, were thought to be shape changers, sometimes taking the form of an old grey man or a handsome young man but most usually appearing as a horse. They are thought to take their victims down into the water and so drown them. They were also thought to breed with horses, producing exceptionally swift and strong offspring.

She smiled, "Legend has it that one of the lochans on the Blarmachfoldach, Loch Lundavra, near to that 'Stone of the Campbell's' that I was telling you of, is said to contain a water-bull. It is reputed to come out and graze on the side of the lochan along with the other cattle to lure the cattle to a watery death. Calves born with a chancy temperament are believed to be the offspring of such bulls! Water horses are similar. Some stories tell of one in Loch Ness and another is thought to dwell in Loch Tulloch, they are thought similarly to lure humans to their death."

"I would have thought then the kelpie would then be more interested in you Eilidh than in Dawn!" interjected Joe who had just ridden up with Ewan to join them.

Eilidh laughed, "But I would be more interested in him as a horse than if he shape changed into a handsome young man!"

"'Tis sad for us," said Ewan mock sorrowful, "that you are more interested in your horses than us poor fellows who lie grovelling at your feet."

"Why Ewan, you grovel! I must have missed it!" returned Eilidh disbelievingly.

"These water horses are they thought to be related to the hippocampi[162]?" Fergus asked Joe, but it was Eilidh who answered.

"Related to the horses of Poseidon[163]! I doubt these kelpie would pull his chariot so willingly, being as they are shape shifters and not true water beasts as are the hippocampi; kelpie come out onto the land to entice their prey into the water. Though there is a legend that one day all the Scottish fairies will

---

[162] One of the sea horses of Poseidon, said to have the tail of a fish or dolphin.

[163] Poseidon (who's Roman equivalent was Neptune) was the Greek god of the sea, earthquakes and of horses.

put a bridle on the kelpies and that riding such strong and fearless steeds and led by Thomas the Rymer[164], or some such hero, they will have an enormous battle and rid Scotland of all the English and thus Scotland will once more be *free* again. Lundevra Loch though has one other claim to fame has it not Joe?" Eilidh prompted.

"Aye," Joe's eyes lit up, for he shared Eilidh's love of their countries history and legends. "Macbeth is said to have had his abode on one of its islands. Indeed 'tis said by some that it was there that he died. You may remember Fergus that Banquo, was thane of Lochaber; we pass quite close to Tor castle, which is reputed to have been his residence, as we journey to Achnacarry."

"Yes indeed," said Eilidh enthusiastically, "Tor Castle is situated high on a rock on the banks of the River Lochy, and there is a beautiful avenue of trees just north of the Castle called Banquo's walk. However that which was Banquo's Castle is long gone and the ruins of the Tor Castle that now stands in its place were built by Ewan Cameron, the 13th Chief of the Lochiels and son of that Ailean nan Creach that I told of before. There is a little clearing called Dail a Chait[165], situated close by to the Castle." She gave Fergus a laughing look before going on to say, "Moreover, the 'Cat's Pool' that the tortured cat jumped into to cool his roasted flesh lies in the part of the River Lochy that sits just beneath Tor Castle, close to a lovely little island that you can always be sure to find herons on."

"I am not too sure I would wish to venture there alone on a dark night!" Ewan joked.

---

[164] Thomas Rymer was said have visited fairyland; he was also a prophet and a poet.
[165] Cat Field.

They had been riding for some time along a track that followed approximately the path of the Caledonian Canal[166], which in turn was winding its way alongside of the sparkling waters of the River Lochy which burbled and danced down its customary course on its way to join with Loch Lochy.

Before long their track met that of the River Loy and here Eilidh rode up alongside Fergus to ask, "One of father's good friends lives near here, Colonel Sir Alan Cameron. Do you know him Fergus?"

"Cameron of Erracht, did he not command the regiments of the Cameron Highlanders?" Fergus replied.

"Indeed and raised them," Eilidh said proudly.

"He doesnae right get on with Lochiel though does he?" Joe observed playfully.

"Why ever not? Fergus demanded.

"They only argued over who should be clan chief! Lochiel as you know was made Chief but there are many believe it should have gone to Erracht," retorted Joe.

"Your father Eilidh, what did he think?" asked Fergus.

"Oh he was friends with the both of them. He did not take sides," she answered fleetingly, her attention obviously elsewhere.

They rode on in silence.

It was not long though before Eilidh stopped suddenly at the side of the canal. "This is Moy. You may have noticed that here the canal no longer follows a straight line but bends slightly off course. Near here is the small churchyard where Gormshuil the witch is said to be buried and 'tis said that the reason the canal takes this slight detour here is that the builders of it preferred to build a bend in the canal rather than risk disturbing the Moy graveyard on account of Gormshuil. She is in much of the local

[166] Built by the pioneering engineer Thomas Telford opened in 1822.

folklore and if you ask Iona, she will tell you the story of the time that Gormshuil saved one of the Lochiels from the treachery of a neighbour." As she said this Eilidh rode on again.

Fergus hurried his mount on to join her.

"You love this country don't you Eilidh?"

For a moment she looked sombre and then answered shortly "Who could not?"

"Does your friend feel as you do about the place?"

"Iona? Why of course! When you know your ancestors have lived in a place so long and that they have played such a proud part in its history it feels like one is connected to, that one is somehow part of the land."

"Yet the other night you seemed to be apologising for the first Maclean of Ardgour."

"Did I? It was not meant so. In those times that was how things were done. They ruled by the strength of their arm, and by guile. The rulers had absolute authority until someone stronger came along. No, I am proud of my ancestors, such as acted honourably by the rules of the times. Donald Maclean by all accounts was a very capable gentleman and he married, so I understand, one of Lochiel's daughters."

"So you are a cousin of Miss Cameron?"

"I am indeed, and closer even than that. I understand that the Eighth Maclean married a daughter of Lochiel as did the Tenth. All the local families are very much interconnected. You must find the same in your family?"

Fergus laughed, "Yes, it is so, but I have been away a lot and our estates are spread all over the country and we do not have a family seat as long established as yours, so perhaps I do not feel so strongly about such things as you seem to. My grandfather was a younger son who married money and who used it wisely, as did my father which is why he is now in a position to tempt your mother into marriage with him."

Eilidh turned to him concerned, noticing the slightly bitter tone of his speech.

"You worry that this marriage will affect your inheritance?"

"Indeed, if my father will not curb her spending, and if she bear a son, then yes I believe there will be need to worry. Your mother is young still is she not?"

Eilidh was silent for a moment, thoughtful. "She has been denied for many years the life she says she was brought up to, but I believe that even should she wish to be extravagant that your father, so used to being wise in the ways of his money, will not long keep his purse open wide."

"You do not know the hold she has on him. My father is not a strong man; his stringencies are as much due to his lack of passion as wisdom. Always it has been your mother that he has dreamed of, worked for."

"My mother and not yours!" Eilidh exclaimed.

Fergus nodded his head grimly. "I used to visit with him here when I was but a child. I believe I have always been aware of his fascination with your mother Eilidh, but never once have I seen her even attempt to discourage him from his devoted attendance on her, not even in the presence of your father. He has always doted on her rather like a fond lapdog," he concluded derisively.

Eilidh was silent for a time before saying quietly, "Perhaps she is genuinely attached to him and he to her." Then she changed the subject. "You are not then cross at me now Fergus for riding out dressed in these clothes?"

He laughed harshly "Would it make any difference if I was?"

"'T would make me sad."

"Then I am not cross," Fergus said gently. "Though I confess I do not find it easy to see you thus."

"No, nor does Joe, though he is well used to it. Ewan does not mind though," at this she smiled. "Come, I will race you. Do you see yon copse of trees?" And she was away and he, nothing loathe, followed suite.

It was some time later that they entered a small beech avenue and Eilidh was explaining how the Gentle Lochiel had been planting these trees on the day that he had heard that the Young Prince[167] had landed.

"I am entering into the house of my erstwhile enemy am I not Eilidh, with the 'Forty Five' Rebellion still so strong in the minds of those hereabouts," Fergus said ruefully.

Eilidh laughed, "Your ancestors had a habit of picking the 'different' side to fight on. However when I was in Morvern this past week, I wondered if perhaps the people there were fortunate that the Duke of Argyle had fought for the English, that perhaps they had been less severely punished than people in many other locations, through his being their landowner." She sighed and was silent for a few moments before continuing pensively, "Though conceivably if your family and some of your allies had fought with Lochiel, rather than against him, we might now have a different king."

"Aye and perhaps the fight would have gone on longer, and more would have been killed. You surely would not wish for a papish king?"

"I might have wished for one who was not a gambler and rake," she retorted.

Fergus did not answer this. He himself had little interest in politics, though he would have countered that it was now Parliament rather than the King who was of import, and that by

---

[167] Bonnie Prince Charlie.

all accounts James II had been guilty of his share of intrigues; but they were now almost at the doors of Achnacarry itself, the seat of the Lochiels.

Chapter 32 Achnacarry

An elderly man walked unhurriedly over to intercept Eilidh and her three companions as they entered the forecourt of Achnacarry house.

"Oh, it is yourself Miss Eilidh. We were expecting ye. Miss Iona said for ye to go right up if ye would. I'll see t' the other gentlemen. Himself asked that he be telt when ye arrive as he wishes to come and greet ye all."

Eilidh jumped down from her horse immediately, giving the reins to a waiting groom.

"My thanks Alisdair."

They watched as she walked quickly up to the house and saw that she was intercepted by a man dressed in the regalia of a Highland gentleman. He spoke briefly to Eilidh and then came purposefully towards the trio who had in the meantime dismounted, and were standing waiting.

"Welcome, welcome," he said as he approached. "It has been quite a while since I last saw young Eilidh, and yourself Joe." He turned to Ewan, "Lachlan's son, I presume. I have heard a lot about you, not all favourable I must admit, though Eilidh assures me you will improve. Heard your grandfather has left you rather well off."

"Only if I first spend some time up at Oxford, Sir," returned Ewan respectfully. For this was Lochiel himself come to greet them.

The older man laughed, "And so you should, do you good. He had the rights of it!"

Lochiel then turned to the third member of the party. "Eilidh has told me a lot about you, she speaks well of you. Good sound common sense has that lass. If she says well of you then that is enough for me. You will join us for lunch after you return from your ride I hope. My niece has spent half of this morning in the kitchen organising it and the other half in her room deciding what she and Eilidh are to wear," he laughed shortly, amused.

"I would be loath to disappoint your niece," Fergus replied with a slight bow. "I understand that Eilidh is concerned that we return at a time when the tide will be favourable for our journey home. So long as our stay does not interfere with this then I, and I believe my companions also," he looked at them as he said this, "would be delighted to accept your invitation Sir."

Lochiel smiled, "Eilidh has explained to me the need for haste, but has agreed to the meal. Now if you will excuse me, I will leave you for now in the capable hands of Alisdair who will see to any need you may have for refreshments or such while you await the ladies. I would ask you in, but I fear that this might but serve to delay you all."

As Lochiel made his way back to his house, Alisdair conducted the three young men to a seated area and set about providing them with much appreciated refreshments to engender their wait the more palatable.

Fergus had eaten little that morning, due to the early hour that they had set out, but it was not until he saw the food that he realised how very hungry he was. He had just sat back in his chair relaxed and replete when he noticed his companions, who had been talking quietly together until now, suddenly still. He looked in the direction of their gaze and his heart suddenly started to quicken alarmingly.

He had been cogitating on the difference between the Eilidh he knew and the one he had seen on the journey, the laughing, lively teasing 'boy', so much the same yet subtly different, more alive, wilder than the confident joyful creature he was used to. He wondered which was real, and it crossed his mind briefly that he could almost understand Caroline Maclean's wish to hide her away in an asylum. He no longer doubted that she could with ease put forward the case that Eilidh, so unusual in many ways, should be locked away. Then he immediately pushed away in horror this abhorrent thought. That anyone so alive, so loving, so beautiful could be treated in such a manner! And he remembered anew why it was that he loved her.

Now he almost forgot to breathe, could not take his eyes off the slighter of the two figures that approached.

Chapter 33 Iona Cameron

The two girls, so intent on their conversation, appeared completely oblivious of their audience. They were dressed in very fashionable matching riding habits and were about the same height; but there the resemblance ended.

Iona Cameron had mousy brown hair, was just below medium height with a slightly stocky build but a very pleasing figure. Although you might hesitate to call her pretty, when you saw her closely and noticed her beautiful kind blue eyes, her fresh complexion, the dimples that leapt out of her face as she smiled, and if you caught a glimpse of that merry look and noted its intelligence, you would have to admit she was an extremely attractive girl; but next to her companion she seemed plain and gauche. Her friend was dainty as a fairy, with huge brown almond shaped eyes and delicate eyebrows that looked painted on her exquisite face. Her hair, gold and red glistened and framed that almost ethereal countenance, the red of her lips contrasting with the olive skin, so she looked almost exotic.

For a moment Fergus failed to recognise her, for a moment he forgot to breathe. Then abruptly, rage flooded through him. It felt as if his whole being had exploded with fury; fury at Eilidh that she should torment him by dressing thus after she had refused him with such finality. Dimly, as if through a haze, he looked at her. It seemed as if time itself stood still.

Slowly, as his heart beat slowed, she came back into focus. Sharp pain seared through his awareness, and with this pain came the realisation that she was quite, quite unaware of the picture she made. He felt suddenly bereft, as if he had lost something important, and looking at his companions he saw a similar yearning on both their faces and knew that they likewise wished beyond anything that she could be theirs, that they knew, just as he did at that minute, that such as she was not for him and there flashed through his head the hope that that bastard Hindley would never see her, that neither he nor any of his ilk would ever get near her; and fear for the future her mother planned for her suddenly constricted his chest further so that he wished, such as he had never wished before, that he had it in his power to force her to run away with him to safety.

"Well Iona, did I not say that I would bring you three handsome men to visit," exclaimed Eilidh happily.

"You said you would bring three of those whom you loved as much as if they were your brothers, you did not mention anything as to their looks," the other girl returned laughing.

"Well, do you recognise any?" demanded Eilidh

"Joe of course I know. Though I believe Joe that I have not seen you for many a long year!" said Iona.

"Ye were a little girl in pigtails last time I saw ye Miss Cameron," replied Joe with a smile.

"Oh, call me Iona as you did before Joe, unless that is, you wish for me to call you Mr Beaton."

Joe flushed and mumbled that he would rather she called him by his Christian name as not.

Fergus now wrenched his eyes off Eilidh and looked at her companion for the first time. He saw the kind eyes, the natural manner, and was amazed that one so young should be so confident. Neither was she at all brash nor he noticed did she seem to mind in the slightest that her companion so outshone her in looks.

He noticed likewise that Joe seemed hardly able to look at Eilidh, that his discomfort did not come from the meeting with Miss Cameron alone. He was therefore not at all surprised when he heard Eilidh say quietly to Joe, "Joe I am sorry to appear dressed thus. I should have warned you. Iona she

313

bullies me so and swore she would only come down and ride with us if I dressed as she bade me."

"Do you think I would be allowed to go gallivanting around the countryside with four young men that I barely know?" cried Iona. "I had to have one female with me. Besides, I wished Eilidh for you to ride Trojan, my new horse!"

"You are a most confounded minx Iona Cameron!" Eilidh retorted. "You threaten me first with the slowest horse in the stable and now you suggest I ride your wildest mount in the hope that you may be amused by my discomfiture when he runs off with me!"

"Or you fall off!" Iona countered slyly. "Like you did when you rode uncle's horse."

"I was only about eight when I did that!" returned Eilidh laughing. Then she accused "I bet you have not ridden Trojan in days and have been feeding him on oats!"

"But of course!" replied the other unrepentant. She looked curiously at Eilidh's other companions before saying thoughtfully, "The tall dark one must be Ewan Dubh. Ewan, failte! I have heard so much about you. Though indeed Eilidh, I must complain for you have not praised your milk brother nearly enough!"

Ewan bowed with a flourish. "Eilidh you did not tell me that your friend had such wisdom as well as beauty!"

"Indeed I told you that she read Latin and Greek better than you do yourself," Eilidh countered, "but I would not have said so much about her sense if I had thought her so easily taken in by your pretty face and ready tongue," she continued with mock annoyance. Then she turned eagerly back to her friend, "Now Iona, you have correctly guessed two out of three, what of my third brother?"

Iona looked at the other for a moment before replying, "One who mislikes your calling him brother if I read him aright."

"I believe that the three of us are very proud to claim the affection that the relationship implies," replied Fergus smoothly, "I thank you for your welcome Miss Cameron, Eilidh has extolled your virtues at great length and I can see, even from such a short acquaintance that she has not lied."

Iona looked at him measuredly, "Any friend or brother of my sister is welcome here, though I understand that it is a few days yet until the day that you are her brother other than in affection."

Before he could answer everyone's attention was drawn, by the sound of hoof beats, to a groom leading out some prime horses. Fergus stared with absolute amazement at the side saddles that the horses wore. To his experienced eyes neither of the horses were a suitable ride for a lady, especially the dappled grey. He was very handsome but too lively, moreover he looked to be a green youngster. He looked pensively at the two girls, and realised that he did not know if Eilidh even rode side saddle. He had seen her ride astride often enough, but usually on Liath Macha, and he knew that Liath Macha would never unseat her. He had to admit though that she had handled the strange horse that she had ridden today with ease.

He was about to protest when he heard Eilidh laugh and say ruefully "I see that you do mean to have the last laugh today Iona! First you bully me into wearing this ridiculous skirt and then you expect me to ride that wild beast. I know you," Eilidh teased, "it is that you hope that he keeps me busy so that you can have all my brothers to yourself!"

Iona blushed at this while Eilidh, her eyes twinkling exclaimed "Ah, caught out!" She then merrily turned to the others and suggested, "It might be sensible if everybody mounts up quickly so that Pegasus here won't have to wait around too long!"

"Which horses do you want the men to ride Eilidh?" asked Iona quietly.

Eilidh turned to look at the three fine specimens that had just arrived in the yard before saying, "Fergus can choose; he has a steady head on his shoulders." Then she walked over and began to pet Iona's pretty chestnut mare.

Fergus wondered if it was a test. He looked at the three horses thoughtfully. There was a youngster amongst them who looked to be by far the best piece of horseflesh and if he had felt any need to show off his riding ability he would have chosen to ride him himself. However he wanted to watch, to talk to the ladies, he did not want to be distracted by a young nervous horse. Therefore he allocated this horse to Joe deciding that it would serve to keep Joe busy, and Joe did indeed look as though he needed something to take his mind off his troubles! Ewan was the biggest of the three men and to him he gave the largest of the horses.

He chose the sensible bay for himself and looking inadvertently at Eilidh he saw her smile in approbation. He noted that Iona was already mounted and that she had an extremely good seat, and then he saw Eilidh walk towards the mounting block and his heart jumped into his mouth with fear. He made his way quickly over to where Ewan was standing holding the reins of his large black gelding.

"You don't mean to let her ride that thing do you?" Fergus demanded of Ewan.

"Why ever not?" asked Ewan disparagingly.

Fergus was just about to retort angrily in reply when he heard the old calm voice of Alasdair, Lochiel's Head Groom.

"If it be Miss Eilidh ye are feart for, ye need nay," Alasdair said reassuringly. "She can ride ought w' four legs so she can. I've known her since she were a nipper and only the once have I seen her take a fall," he chortled. "We all thought she had deid. His Lordship had been trying a new horse over a couple of fences, he'd dismounted sae he cuild take a peek at sumitt he had spied in one o' the hedges. Miss Eilidh, well as soon as she kenned Lochiel's horse was loose she sneaked in, wee rogue that she was, and somehae scrambled aboard and set him tae the larger o' the fences. She had nay a bit o' bother wi' the first o' the fences, it wis on the way tae the second that the *bee* struck."

"The *bee*?" asked Ewan looking amused.

"Aye, the horse went fair wild! She stayed on fir a lang time but she was such a wee bit o' a thing and the horse wisnay sma'; she was cast off, went high up in the air and then tumbled doon tae the groond. She lay there so quiet that we awe thought the wurst, but she was up and awaw afore we got tae her, after catching the beastie she was aw fir tryin' it at that there fence again. She got into a sore bit o' trouble that day. I niver saw Himself so white, and her faither as weil!"

"You say she rides often with Miss Cameron dressed thus?" asked Fergus, ignoring the story while Ewan stood there laughing.

"She never told me that tale," interjected Ewan still chortling.

"Like as no she forgot, she was maybe all of six years old at the time and that wild! Why even Miss Iona, used tae get mad at her! But there's no seperatin' them now when Miss Eilidh comes tae visit. Miss Iona if she buys a new habit fir hersel', she alus gets ane the exact same fir Miss Eilidh. 'Tis right sad that Miss Eilidh has no been here since her faither deid, poor lassie."

317

Whilst they had been talking Eilidh had apparently got tired of waiting and when they next looked up she was mounted, and the grey looked to be as quiet as a kitten.

The old man noting the direction of Fergus's gaze and his stupefied look, said, "Aye, they are all like that wi' Miss Eilidh, gentle as a lamb. Ye wid niver think to look at yon that he had ony notion in his head but tae walk and trot quiet as ye like," he chuckled, and as he walked off he said as if to himself, "Must be all that there mare's milk they say she supped as a bairn."

The girls had already set off, as had Ewan, and Fergus quickly followed suit leaving Joe to struggle with his recalcitrant mount.

"What do you think he meant by that?" Fergus asked of Ewan as he rode up alongside him.

Ewan did not answer for a moment so Fergus pulled his horse to a stop and turned to face him. "Do you know what that old fellow meant?" he demanded.

Ewan shrugged, "It is of no moment." Fergus did not move, only waited for an explanation and so Ewan continued reluctantly, "He only meant that Eilidh was literally brought up on the stuff."

"What mean you?" demanded Fergus.

"I only hesitate as it reflects ill on my mother. You may not know but when Eilidh and I were very small my parents moved to London and, as Eilidh's mother adamantly refused to have her in the house, Eilidh came with us; we were brought up almost as twins. My father used to work at a large livery stables in London which, as I understand it, Eilidh's father had a part ownership in; he left his part share in the stables to Duncan when he died. It is at these stables that Joe is to work when they travel south. Anyway, my mother resented having to look after Eilidh; I was her first child after a long, childless wait, and, moreover a son. Father used to regularly leave Eilidh in the

318

stables in a box with a mare and young foal, a different mare each day; and since he left Eilidh no food, she became accustomed to supping milk alongside the foal. Eilidh could not walk, could barely crawl, so I have been told, when first he left her thus. Father once told me that he had hoped she would die; my mother did not want her and neither did her own mother and he felt that the babe drove a further wedge between the old Laird, Eilidh's father that is, and his wife."

"Eilidh's mother, so they say," murmured Fergus.

"Oh there is no doubt at all about that," countered Ewan easily, "Mother says that Eilidh is the image of her maternal grandfather, but who he is she will not say. My mother, so I understand, is related to your step-mother to be in some way, again I do not know how." He grinned and then said "I suppose that that means we will also become kin after your father's marriage!"

They were both silent for a few moments then Ewan suggested "Shall we catch the girls up? Joe is fine on his own," he grinned maliciously. "May I tender my sincere thanks that you did not put that idiotic youngster my way, not, may I hasten to point out," he added merrily, "that he would be anything more than a nuisance!"

To Fergus's surprise Eilidh hung back to speak to him, leaving Ewan and Iona to ride on together, and he could hear Iona's laughter, as nothing loathe, Ewan set about the task of charming her. Ewan liked female company and was very much aware of the effect he generally had on the female heart.

As they rode, Eilidh enthusiastically explained to Fergus how the old Achnacarry had been destroyed after the defeat of Bonnie Prince Charlie's army at Culloden and how the present Lochiel, grandson of the Gentle Lochiel[168] who had died in exile

---

[168] Major supporter of Bonnie Prince Charlie when he came over from

in France with his prince, had rebuilt Achnacarry in its present position.

They rode on thus chatting quietly together, until they came to the Caig Falls where they halted, the better to admire the waterfall. While they waited, Iona told them the tale of the witch who was reputed to have fallen to her death there whilst trying to escape from her pursuers in the shape of a cat. She explained that the pool at the bottom of the waterfall was now known as the Witch's Pool or the Witch's Cauldron in memory of that same witch.

"There are over many witches around here Miss Cameron!" stated Ewan lazily. "Eilidh has been telling us about Gormshuil and your kinsman Alan of the Forays."

Iona pulled a face and turning to Eilidh asked "Could you not have told them a more flattering tale as you walked by Tor Castle? Perhaps boasted to them that the First Lochiel was said to have wed Banquo's sister." Then, her eyes dancing, she continued "After which if you were really being a kind sister to me you could have explained how we claim kinship with the line of the Stuart kings! Told them the story of Banquo's son Fleance[169] and the Welsh princess!"

"My apologies sister dear!" Eilidh laughed. "I will make amends!" Shall we dismount and take a seat next to the

---

France to try to claim the support on behalf of his father. His estates and lands were declared forfeit after the battle of Culloden. If Cameron of Lochiel had not declared his support for Charles Edward Stewart (Bonnie Prince Charlie) the 1745 Rebellion may never have begun.

[169] Warned that he was in danger, Fleance, some say with the aid of the Lochiels, escaped and fled to Wales. There he fell in love with a Welsh princess and a son was born to them. From this son it was believed came the line that led to the birth of Walter, Stewart of Scotland in the time of Robert the Bruce, who went on to wed Bruce's daughter Margerie and so found the Stuart line of Kings.

Witch's Pool whilst I tell the tale? It is an appropriate place to tell it in that it begins with a witch."

"Not more witches!" groaned Ewan.

"At least it's not Gormshuil!" giggled Iona, as she jumped down and led her pretty mare over to tie her to a tree.

The others swiftly followed her example.

Soon they were all five seated on the rocks near to the waterfall waiting to hear Eilidh's story.

"I would that I had my clarsach with me," declared Eilidh with a smile. Then she grinned at Ewan. "Things are about to get worse Ewan. There are three witches in my story, rather than the customary one!"

Ewan groaned in mock distress. Then grinning brightly he quoted, *"When shall we three meet again? In thunder, lightning, or in rain?"*[170]

"'When the hurly-burly's done, When the battle's lost and won.'" Joe piped up straight faced.

Fergus sighed but not to be outdone added his mite while Iona sat there giggling.

"'That will be ere the set of sun.'"

Eilidh laughed. "Stop giggling Iona! Your turn next! I say 'Macbeth has come' and you can say the weird sisters lines!"

"No indeed that would be most unfair!" countered Iona excitedly. "There are three of them and three witches! They can say the words together, I will say Macbeth's lines and then you can tell Banquo's story!"

"Very well Iona," said Eilidh laughing. "We are at your command!" She looked at the three young men saying with mock severity, "I hope that you can all remember your lines!"

They looked at each other, nodded and to the accompaniment of Iona's giggles they quoted in unison:

---

[170] From Macbeth, Shakespeare's play of the same name.

321

"'The weird Sisters, hand in hand,
Posters of the sea and land,
Thus do go, out and about;
Thrice to thine and thrice to mine.
And thrice again to make up nine.
Peace! The charm's wound up.'"

Iona still giggling managed to gasp out, *"'So foul and fair a day I have not seen.'"* Then she collapsed giggling on the grass.

Eilidh cast her a look of mock disgust, before saying, "While Macbeth recovers from hearing our three witches speak so beautifully, I will set the scene to our story. King Malcolm II has recently died without male issue and with him dies the name MacAlpine, as the name of the ruling Kings. With only daughters the succession now is in dispute. The kingdom can either go to one of Malcolm II's grandsons or a grand-daughter of his cousin, the previous King, King Kenneth III. Duncan and Macbeth are both grandsons of King Malcolm II, but Macbeth is also wed to King Kenneth III's grand-daughter and so has a second claim to the throne. Despite this Duncan is chosen as king. Macbeth only becomes King subsequent to Duncan's death in battle. He had reputedly a long, benevolent and successful reign, until he was in turn killed, many years later, by Duncan's son Malcolm Canmore. However I am running ahead of myself!"

"On the day this story begins, Macbeth and his neighbour Banquo were aiding King Duncan I in his fight against the Danes. They were riding home to Lochaber, after having celebrated a spectacular victory, when they were met by three wizened crones who greeted Macbeth; each addressing him with an honourable title."

Eilidh looked at the three young men with a grin indicating that they help her out.

Ewan stood up with a flourish, and bowed to Iona before proclaiming "'All hail Macbeth! Hail to thee Thane of Glamis.'" Then he sat down again.

Eilidh laughed, "Thane of Glamis was a title Macbeth had just inherited from his recently deceased father."

Then she looked to Joe, who although he did not stand obediently quoted "'All hail, Macbeth! Hail to thee Thane of Cawdor!'"

Eilidh looked next to Fergus and he nothing unwilling also stood and bowing to the giggling Iona proclaimed "'All hail, Macbeth, that shalt be King hereafter!'" Fergus then sat down grinning.

"As one might suppose Macbeth was rather pleased with these prophesies, while Banquo was somewhat irritated that all the promises should go to Macbeth and he therefore demanded of the witches that they read him his future." She broke off and looked to her audience for assistance. "Fergus you are the third witch. Can you remember her prophesy concerning Banquo?

Fergus stood up with a flourish, bowed and proclaimed loudly, "'Though shalt get kings, though thou be none.'"

Iona was giggling again and so Eilidh pretended to frown at her before continuing with her story. "Well as you might imagine, both men were delighted with these promises, and it was not long before they were given proof as to the veracity of the second witch's prophesy when King Duncan gifted Macbeth the lands and title of Thane of Cawdor as a reward for his brilliant generalship and success in the recent battles. After some time however Macbeth began to be troubled by what he held to be Duncan's ineptitude, and by the fact that Duncan's sons were growing older and being brought to prominence. He began to fear that his chances of becoming King were diminishing; that the third prophesy might never be realised."

"Eventually the rivalry between the cousins, Duncan and Macbeth, came to a head. A battle was fought in which Duncan was killed and Macbeth, as the witches had promised, became King of Scotland."

"As the years passed by Macbeth began to worry about who would be King after him. His wife, although she had born him no children, had a son, Lulach, from her previous marriage. Lulach had a claim to the throne through the bloodline of his mother and so Macbeth determined that Lulach, the son of his heart, though not of his loins, would be King after him. Then he remembered the three witches. He remembered how their prophesies about him had come true, and his heart smote him as he recalled their prophesies to Banquo."

Eilidh paused and smiled at Fergus who obediently quoted, "'Thou shalt get kings though thou be none.'"

Eilidh continued the story, "Macbeth remembered that Banquo, unlike him, did have a son and at once determined to ensure that this son would not live long enough to allow this prophesy to come to pass. No son of Banquo's would steal the throne off Lulach, his wife's son. To this end he ordered that both Banquo and his son Fleance be disposed of. Banquo's murder was swiftly achieved, but Fleance his son was warned of Macbeth's treachery and fled to Wales were he fell in love with a Welsh princess."

"Now the father of the Welsh princess was exceedingly wrath when he learned of her attachment to this exiled Scot and would not agree to their marriage. She however refused to give up her love and when her father found out that she carried Fleance's child he banished her from his court, and refused thereafter to have her name mentioned again in his lands. The father of the Welsh princess then captured Fleance and executed him for his crime."

"The story does however have a happy ending. Some kind and goodly man must have taken pity on the princess and taken her in and looked after her and brought up Fleance's son as his own; for the child grew and thrived. Fleance's son lived to have sons of his own and those sons in turn begat other sons, until one was born named Walter who became High Steward to our own most renowned King Robert the Bruce. So valuable and noble and loyal did the King find his Steward to be that he rewarded him with that which he held most precious, his daughter Princess Marjorie. So it was that Walter Stewart of the line of Banquo wed the Princess Marjorie of Scotland. As time passed they were blessed with a son who was to fulfil that prophesy made to Banquo all those years before. King Robert II, son of Walter Stewart, grandson of King Robert I[171], was the founder of the great Stuart dynasty, just as the three witches had foretold!"

Ewan entering into the fun bowed slightly to Iona as he said, "And so the proud line of Banquo founded two great dynasties, Banquo founding the line of our Stuart Kings and therefore ultimately our most noble and magnificent present monarch King George IV, and his sister founding the honourable family of The Lochiels."

"Thus while Banquo lived high up along the banks of the River Lochy, his sister dwelt on Eilean nan Craobh, on Loch Eil," added Fergus not to be outdone. He turned to Eilidh with a grin "See, I have been listening throughout to all of my history lessons!"

"You are a quick learner!" said Eilidh admiringly with a twinkle in her eye. "Iona can further educate you as to the history or this area if she can refrain for a moment from boasting about her illustrious lineage," she continued teasingly.

---

[171] Robert the Bruce.

Iona laughed, "Don't worry for me Eilidh, you forget that I will be sure to point out that he who was secluded so tenderly in the cave was a relative of mine, albeit rather distant!" She turned to Fergus then and said, "What Eilidh wishes me to tell you is that there is a cave near here where Prince Charlie is said to have hidden after Culloden. Have we time to go there Eilidh?"

"Not today I think Iona," replied Eilidh regretfully.

"I wonder if this relationship between your family and the Stuarts influenced your strong allegiance to the Young Pretender?" Fergus asked curiously.

Iona looked thoughtful for a few moments then smiled at Fergus. "I would doubt it since it is so long ago in our family history, and so wrapped up in legend. You must ask my uncle for his view point at lunch however. It is claimed though that it was Lochiel who helped Banquo's son Fleance to escape the fate that befell his father."

Fergus smiled, "Just as Lochiel helped Charles Edward Stuart[172] to escape from Cumberland's troops after Culloden. I begin to understand a little your, Eilidh's and Joe's fascination and love of the history, legends and folklore of this area. However, I must say that there is a strange feel about this place!"

"It is especially spooky here at dusk when one is returning home late from a visit to Clunes along the Dark Mile," said Iona lightly.

"The Dark Mile?" queried Fergus.

"Yes, that is what they call the following section of this trail." Iona explained, "Very little light gets through as the path is so heavily overhung by trees and thus it always seems shadowy and murky. It makes travelling through there feel unsafe as well as unpleasantly creepy."

---

[172] Bonnie Prince Charlie.

"You should talk to Ruairidh, Iona when you see him at the wedding," suggested Ewan suddenly. "Tell him just what their attempt to put a different king on the throne has cost your family. You might make him see the consequences of his dreams of revolution. Tell him what your family have suffered and if they have gained anything from that rebellion."

Iona looked concerned, and so Eilidh interceded.

"It is a good idea Ewan but Ruairidh would be less than pleased I believe, to think that we had discussed his affairs with a stranger; for you must remember he does not know Iona neither does he have your charm and confidence where women are concerned. You worry about him, as indeed I do, but he is no fool; neither I believe is his hot headed friend. We will just have to pray that he thinks well before he acts."

Joe glowered "You should have let us wash his mouth out for him!"

Eilidh laughed and said, "Ruairidh? Why I do not see how that would help him!" affecting to misunderstand.

Ewan grinned and turning to Iona explained, "Ruairidh returned home with a friend from the university he studies at. This friend engendered Joe's ire as he was less than polite to Eilidh when he first saw her. Let us hope he goes south a trifle wiser!"

"You must not blame Findley too severely," Eilidh said soberly, "I did come upon him unawares. Furthermore he sounds to have been rather badly shocked and thrown off his balance from having observed the bloodshed and violence at Peterloo. I could discern no actual harm in him and indeed much good. Findley means well and I believe that if he gets in touch with someone like Norman MacLeod and takes hold of their purpose that he will devote his life to doing much that is good." Then changing the subject she added, "However I fear that we must make ready to resume our journey as there is still some way to go to Clunes and we have promised to get back to Achnacarry in time for lunch. We do not wish to keep Lochiel waiting and the tide waits for no man."

They all obediently stood up and went to collect their horses, quickly mounting.

As they continued on their way Iona explained that Clunes was another Cameron stronghold that had been destroyed after the Rebellion, but that it had been rebuilt before Lochiel's own residence.

They did not stop at Clunes, instead picking up the pace after they had reached this point, as they were all feeling eager for their lunch and Fergus and Ewan felt that they had ridden far enough for that day.

On their return they were met by Lochiel himself who forbore to comment on it being Fergus and Iona who arrived first, some way ahead of the threesome who trailed along merrily behind. They washed quickly and the girls changed their attire before meeting the gentlemen in the dining room. This time however Eilidh had changed back into her travelling clothes and it was she who hurried the meal, for as she explained she was anxious not to miss the tide.

It was a tearful farewell on Iona's part as she said good bye to Eilidh, as neither of them knew when they would meet again. And it was many a mile of their return journey that Eilidh remained silent, while the others talked quietly amongst themselves.

It was just before they reached Corpach that Fergus rode up beside her and said awkwardly, "My thanks Eilidh."

She turned and beamed at him, all trace of sadness gone from her face. "It is sorry that I am Fergus to have been so quiet on the road. I mislike goodbyes." She was silent again for a moment, before adding soberly "Iona Cameron, she is an exceptional girl is she not?"

"I have accepted an invitation from Lochiel to stay at Achnacarry for a few days after the wedding, after father has gone south with his new bride," Fergus's face twisted as he said this.

"I am pleased," Eilidh said simply.

Ewan and Joe came up to join them and the remainder of the ride was spent pleasantly, in conversation.

They left the horses in a field at Corpach and their homeward trip aboard Cuchullin was uneventful; the seals had waited for them and they accompanied them throughout their return journey.

They did not drop anchor at the Corran narrows, from whence they had set out earlier that day, for Eilidh did not wish anyone to observe her passengers. Instead she set them ashore at Salachan and then sailed on through the night alone.

Chapter 34 Gruoch

The rain battered down on the roof of the cave, unremittingly, but Eilidh slept snug inside. She slept unusually soundly for one whose every waking thought was troubled by the pain of loss, rent with anguish at the prospect of leaving the land she so much loved, perhaps never to return. Not even the nightmares had disturbed her repose this night.

Cuchullin was now anchored off Strontian and there the sailing boat would remain until Malcolm MacLeod came to claim her. Eilidh had felt unwilling to leave the craft here in Ardgour, where the eyes of her mother might glimpse it and order a fate for the boat other than that which she had decided on. John Boyd had a letter which authorised him to transfer ownership of the boat to Malcolm MacLeod; but she did not want any unnecessary aggravation before she left, did not want her mother to suddenly decide that she would refuse Eilidh this journey south; as her fury would know no bounds should she ever learned to whom she had gifted Cuchullin. John Boyd would see that Malcolm gained possession of Cuchullin once her mother had left for her new home on the Campbell estates.

Eilidh hated goodbyes; but goodbyes that were perhaps forever were the worst of all. She had said all her goodbyes except one and that was to a child she had not as yet met. It was the knowledge that this task lay ahead of her that caused her to wake now at dawn on the morning of her mother's wedding.

She dressed hurriedly but carefully, for she had no wish to frighten the child who would possibly have heard all sorts of strange things about her. Fergus though, Fergus would tell her she had nothing to fear; for reputedly the child adored Fergus and he always spoke very fondly of his sister Gruoch, who was fifteen years his junior.

Eilidh emerged from the cave, wrapped tight in her plaid for warmth, to find Liath Macha patiently waiting for her. She grimaced as she saw how the rain fell relentlessly in sheets all around, for the sky told that it would be long before the rain eased that day. Quickly she saddled Liath Macha and then set off down the road that led to Ardgour House, where Dawn's latest foal Sithfadda was stabled. Eilidh did not intend to take the yearling filly with her when she travelled south, instead she hoped to give her as a gift to Fergus's sister Gruoch.

After unsaddling Liath Macha, rubbing him down and leaving him in a spacious loose box with a plentiful supply of fresh hay and a goodly measure of oats, Eilidh went in to see the little filly. There was no sign yet of Fergus but she knew that he would not forget his promise to bring his sister to her this morning, despite the early time of their meeting.

The rain continued to fall as Eilidh waited patiently, happy to be here with the pretty little Palomino filly, Sithfadda, who was all gold and cream and as dainty as her lovely mother. She was busy crooning to her and brushing her when she heard the welcome sounds that told her someone was coming. She arose and walked out of the stall, carefully closing the gate behind her, and made her way out into the yard.

Fergus was waiting for her there, sombre for once, and behind him looking both frightened and stubborn trailed a small girl, her unbrushed hair in lumps around her face, sleep still in her eyes.

"Eilidh you are here...? I am sorry I am late, but I had the utmost difficulty in persuading Gruoch...," he trailed off staring at Eilidh as he saw her in the shadows. She was not dressed as severely as she usually did and the hair which was usually bound tightly about her head and then covered with a hat or scarf was now tied in two thick plaits that came over her shoulder, she looked younger, almost like a child herself and he caught his breath and the regret he felt at what he could not have passed anew across his face.

"My thanks Fergus. I know that you and Gruoch have both a very busy day ahead of you." She turned to the little girl who, peeping out behind her brother, was staring at her, eyes wide.

"I am sure Gruoch that you did not wish to get up so early on such a morning as this is, so wet and cold. Poor mother to have her wedding on such a day!"

The child said nothing but continued to stare. She was very slight and quite small in stature with wispy fair hair and a thin, pale, elfin face, but there was that about her features that held the promise of latent beauty and she did not look unintelligent.

Eilidh continued, "It is sorry I am that you have had to leave your bed so early, but I so much wished to see my newest sister."

The child suddenly stood out from behind her brother and cried "You are not my sister! Adrianne is not either. I hate her. Everyone says you are a witch!"

Eilidh laughed. "They said that of my foster mother also but I can assure you that she was the loveliest person imaginable. Gruoch you will learn one day not to believe all that people say of others until you have seen enough of them to judge for yourself. People often call those they do not understand bad names like 'witch'. Perhaps there are real witches but I for one have never seen such a person." She paused for a moment and then asked simply "Do I look like a witch Gruoch?"

The child said nothing and so Eilidh continued "Where are the warts, the crooked nose, the whiskers?"

Fergus it was who laughed now "Eilidh whatever have you done with your black cat and your broomstick?"

"How silly of me I must have forgotten to bring them. Oh dear and I forgot my cauldron too!" Eilidh said with a giggle.

Gruoch still looked uncertain.

"I promise you Gruoch, Eilidh is lovely and no witch, or at least not the evil kind," Fergus said wryly. His face had a slightly hurt look on it as he said slowly, "Gruoch, if she would but agree I would wed her tomorrow."

"Then I hate her for making you unhappy!" the child said and was about to turn and run.

"Gruoch," said Eilidh softly, "don't go, wait a bit, please, and I will explain."

The child stopped and turned slowly and came again to stand close to Fergus, not looking at Eilidh.

"Gruoch, it is very loyal of you to be so cross that I cause your brother pain by refusing him. You will not understand now, but he would not be happy if he were wed to me. He will I hope wed another who I know and love and who will make him very happy such as I would not; though I confess I do love your brother most dearly. He is a fine man, a brother to be proud of. Often he has talked to me of you, told me how clever you are, and how pretty. He has also told me that he has promised that if you are unhappy living with my mother then you and your nurse can live with him; but you Gruoch, you must tell your brother if you are unhappy or he will not know." Eilidh looked at Fergus anxiously "You will explain to her will you not?"

"I am not a baby!" a cross little voice said. "Of course I will tell Fergus if I am not happy. I tell Fergus *everything*!"

A look of relief appeared on Eilidh's face and she smiled, "Then I shall try not to worry about you." She hesitated again for a moment before continuing carefully, "Gruoch, I asked

Fergus to bring you to see me this morning as I am to go away in the morrow and I may never have another chance to meet you and wanted to see for myself the little sister who Fergus has talked of so much. I wished to see you for another reason also. You see there is someone small who I love very much that I have to leave behind when I go, someone who needs looking after and loving. Her mother is coming with me when I leave, while she must remain behind and so she will be lonely."

Eilidh went quiet for a few moments before asking the little girl "Shall I show you that which I wish to give you as a present?"

Gruoch looked less stiff and you could tell that curiosity was warring with her suspicion.

"At least come and look," Eilidh coaxed.

The little girl did not move and her face became set once more.

"Show me Eilidh," said Fergus, "I would like very much to see what it is that you wish to give my sister. I am quite intrigued." He turned to Gruoch, "Eilidh has steadfastly refused to tell me what your present is."

"I feared that you would refuse," Eilidh stated soberly. "Come and I will show you Fergus. Gruoch please come, you will like it I promise!" she pleaded.

Fergus took the child's hand, but she stubbornly refused to move so Eilidh said lightly, "Wait here then, I will bring it out," and she quickly returned back the way she had come while Fergus, mortified, tried to remonstrate with his obstinate little sister.

It was seconds later when Eilidh returned with the filly.

"Eilidh, you can't!" exclaimed Fergus. "She is worth a king's ransom!"

But Eilidh had eyes only for Gruoch who was staring open mouthed, entranced by the beautiful little filly.

"Is she not pretty? Come, she is very kind, gentle. Come stroke her," Eilidh coaxed. The child all other thoughts chased out of her mind approached slowly, wondrously, and soon she had the filly's lead rope in one hand and in the other hand were bits of apple which the filly was devouring delightedly. Eilidh moved over to stand next to Fergus and they both watched as child and filly fell in love.

"I have not seen her smile like that for, well, not ever," said Fergus slowly as he watched his sister. "She is a sad lonely child, that is why she reacted thus so suspiciously with you Eilidh. But you should not Eilidh, it is too much!"

Eilidh smiled eyes still on the entranced child. "It is to my benefit. Sithfadda was a worry to me. She needs someone who will love her, care for her, play with her. She has a very loving nature, like her mother. When you said how lonely your sister was I immediately thought that it would benefit both her and me if she would take Sithfadda as her own." She turned away from gazing at the child and filly and now looked anxiously at Fergus "But you will see that Gruoch does look after Sithfadda, won't you Fergus? If your sister should tire of her, please ensure that she goes to Duncan he will know what to do with her."

"She will not tire of her, this I can promise you. She is already an intrepid horsewoman, as I told you, unlike my poor mother who preferred her books. Gruoch, she loves her books too...," he suddenly looked worried.

"You will see that she gets to continue her studies will you not Fergus, and that Sithfadda goes with her when they go south?" Eilidh urged earnestly.

335

He laughed quietly, "Eilidh! With all the concerns that you must have and yet you still have time to worry over my sister whom you do not even know! Rest assured I will see that both Gruoch and Sithfadda stay well cared for and safe."

"But you do not know my mother Fergus; I tell you the child is more at risk now than she has ever been. You promised me Fergus that you would look out for her, take her away if she seems more unhappy than usual. Mother I know will be only too pleased not to have the care of her, and you said your father..."

"Father sees not what she will be; only that she is a girl and small, quiet and obstinate and sometimes rude. He sees not her intelligence, her spirit, her loving nature; besides she reminds him of my mother. No, father will not complain if she were to come with me. I would take her now only..."

"Only you have no wife and feel it would be awkward," she smiled. "I hope that will soon be remedied." Then before he could reply she said suddenly, "You had best take the child away Fergus. They will want her washed and dressed soon, ready so that she does not impede the preparations for the wedding."

"Will..., will I...," he said awkwardly "will I see you again?"

"If God wills, but wherever you go remember, my thoughts, my thanks go with you."

"Eilidh," he stammered, "if ever you have need of ought, of help, you know you have only to ask."

"I know," she said quietly. Then she walked over to the child and gently asked "How do you like my present? Will you accept it do you think?"

The child lifted glowing eyes to Eilidh and as suddenly looked away as she whispered "What is her name?"

"Sithfadda. Her Dam is called Red Dawn and her Sire Golden Sunset. She has a brother called Dubh Sainglainn and another called Liath Macha. She is I think the prettiest of them all. I think Gruoch and Sithfadda go well together do you not?"

The child looked at her seriously and then said, "I do not think you are a witch. You're beautiful!"

"Thank you child and so I think will you be when you are full grown; as was your namesake," Eilidh replied gently.

"Adrianne says Gruoch was the name of Lady Macbeth and that she was a murderess. She said my mother must have hated me to give me such a name!" the little girl said fiercely.

"Adrianne does not know her history Gruoch; she should tend more to her studies. Have you read Shakespeare's story of Macbeth?" The little girl, still determinedly looking down at the ground, shook her head ignoring the filly who was nudging her shoulder for more food. "Fergus will give it to you to read later today so that you learn where Adrianne gets her false information from. There is a copy of the play in the library. It is in itself a good story, but mostly untrue for Macbeth was really a very good king. Gruoch was his wife and was a grand-daughter of Kenneth III of Scotland. King Duncan was not murdered by Macbeth but killed in battle, and many years later King Duncan's son, Malcolm Canmore, in turn killed Macbeth in battle, becoming King himself some years later. Such was the way of things in those times. Fergus tells me that your mother loved the old tales of Scotland and its history; that is why she named you after Macbeth's queen. So Gruoch you have a name to be proud of, for if Macbeth was a good King she must have been a good Queen and he must have loved her well, for when he died it was Gruoch's son Lulach, by a previous marriage, who became King; for Macbeth sadly had no sons of his own. Though Lulach did not reign long and it was after he was killed that Malcolm Canmore became King Malcolm III. Did you follow that?" Eilidh asked the child.

Gruoch nodded shyly, eyes wide open now as she looked at the beautiful lady. "Malcolm Canmore was married to Queen Margeret who was a saint; so nurse told me," she declared proudly.

It was Eilidh's turn to look surprised, but before she could comment Fergus joined the conversation, "Mother was lovely Gruoch; kind, loving. She named you thus because she loved you. I know this. If Adrianne or anyone else say such hurtful things in future Gruoch, then you must tell me so that I can explain to you what is true. However, Eilidh is right it is time for us to go and get ready for the wedding. You and I have a busy day ahead of us. Say thank you to Eilidh for her priceless gift. Remember she is to leave for the south in the morn."

Gruoch whispered 'thank you', then gave the filly a hug, before clutching her brother's hand and turning away resolutely. Fergus also thanked Eilidh then sadly and reluctantly he returned to the house with his sister.

Eilidh watched until the pair had passed out of sight, her hand clutched tight to the little filly's lead rope.

Chapter 35 After the Wedding

Black heavy clouds amassed over the small village of Clovullin and its neighbouring areas the morning after the wedding of Mrs Caroline Maclean and Mr Archibald Campbell. Showing no favouritism, they thickly blanketed the high hills of Ardgour and the majestic mountains of Glen Nevis as they dipped down to condole with the thick vapour which draped over the subdued waters of Loch Linnie.

This dense fog served to conceal the ferry that even now, was being made ready to meet the small party of travellers who, shrouded by this dank miserable mist, awaited its arrival

The ferrymen, irrespective of their personal feelings with regard to the bride and groom, had joined with much enthusiasm in the celebration of the previous day's wedding of their old Laird's widow to her long term suitor Archibald Campbell. Having partaken abundantly of the free food and drink that had been made available in one of the barns in the village nothing but their fondness for the old Laird's little lass would have roused them from their homes this early on such a morn. Even the hard words of a wife none too sympathetic to self-imposed ills would have failed to eject them from their beds when their heads were pounding as if the smith's hammer were being laid to it, and not softly at that!

Whilst affection for the lass did not in itself dispel the short temper usually attendant on such a reluctant awakening with a head both cloudy and painful, the look on Eilidh's face that morning caused them, despite the tricky weather, to work apace to make the boat ready to bear her swiftly across the waters of Loch Linnie.

She had asked that no one be there to see them off, for she did not like goodbyes did Eilidh Maclean. Not even the seals were there to watch her leave. It was as if they somehow knew that today it would hurt the more to see them than not.

There were but five people and one horse who awaited so patiently the arrival of the ferry; for Duncan, his wife and youngest son, although expected, had not arrived in Ardgour in time for the wedding. Instead Eilidh and her companions would meet up with them in Fife.

Mairi was seated on a small rock on the shore, tight faced and wrapped up in a warm shawl, unhappy and dispirited at the thought of undertaking again, so soon, the cold, long hard journey betwixt Lochaber and Fife. Next to her sat her husband Lachlan, speaking to her comfortingly, encouragingly, assuring her that even now he could see signs that the sun was pushing its way through the clouds, that the mists would lift soon enough for their journey across the water to be safe from the risk of their boat foundering on some unseen rock. Their son Ewan was seated nearby talking quietly to Joe, while Eilidh sat a short distance away from the other four, close to Liatha Macha, her face white, unable for once to manage even a glimmer of a smile. It was she however who first caught sight of the ghostly presence of the small craft as it emerged out of the gloom.

Leaving Liatha Macha to graze on the shore Eilidh immediately stood up and made her way towards the slipway so, if necessary, she could catch the thrown rope and thus aid the passage of the boat to the shore; for none knew better than she how difficult it was to sail in such hazardous weather.

As soon as the boat was tied up on the slipway, Eilidh's four fellow travellers stood up and quickly made their way towards the vessel, greeting the ferrymen with many proffers of thanks for their efforts on their behalf. All of them well knew that the ferrymen would not have left their beds this early on such a driech morning if it were not for the kindness of their hearts.

340

For the ultimatum given by the widow of the old Laird to Eilidh, that if she wished to travel south with her friends then she must be gone the morning after the wedding, was well known to them all.

Joe had been busy the day before and all the horses were now across on the other side of Loch Linnie, all that is excepting Liath Macha, and now the ferry men eyed him askance knowing well his reputation.

"You will make sure that black hearted kelpie o' yourn shows a proper respect for my boat, will you no lass?" one of the ferry men demanded as Eilidh led Liath Macha down to where the ferryboat awaited its passengers.

The ready twinkle came into her eyes as she gratefully responded to his banter.

"Aye Douglas, I have spoken most firmly to Liatha Macha. Indeed and I have pointed out to him that it would be not at all the thing, indeed most ungrateful, to attempt to kick anyone or even to take the gentlest of bites. I cannot however promise as to the cleanliness of the craft by the time we reach the other side."

"Well," Douglas grumbled "just so long as he doesnae cause us all to join the fishes below. I suppose that will be a mercy!"

Eilidh grinned, "If you fall in I'll send Liatha Macha after you so you can ride him to the shore."

"Heaven preserve us lassie, I doubt I'd rather swim than take my chances with yon mad divil!"

Eilidh laughed and then began to lead the horse aboard. Liath Macha walked on regally, head held high, showing neither fear nor trepidation and as Eilidh walked so close beside him, it was as if it were he that gave her the comfort and not the other way around.

The two ferrymen noticing this went about their work swiftly, silently, sympathy in every glance. Likewise, during the crossing, they talked quietly to the rest of the party leaving Eilidh to her thoughts, and to whatever comfort she got from Liatha Macha.

A couple of men awaited them on the shore, and with them were the fine horses belonging to the five travellers and some well laden packhorses, just as Joe had arranged.

Eilidh and her companions quickly mounted, and after a brief leave taking of these two men and of the ferry men, and accompanied by many good wishes for their safe journey and prayers for their future they set off on their way.

It was a slow road they travelled that morn. They rode through Onich where the waters of Eilidh's beloved Loch Linnie began to mix with those of Loch Leven, and from hence they continued their journey until they got to Ballachulish. Here along the shores of Loch Leven they waited for yet another ferry boat.

Never could Eilidh cross over to South Ballachulish without remembering the deplorable, undeserved execution of James Stewart of the Glen for the murder of Colin Campbell of Glenure. A murder he almost certainly had not committed[173].

However this morning as they rode past the knoll on which James of the Glen had been so unjustly hung it was not James of the Glen who she saw standing beside the gibbet with the noose around his neck, but Hindley.

---

[173] Glenure had by all accounts been appointed by the Crown to collect rents and order the running of the estates that had been taken off their rightful owners as punishment for them having taken up arms against King George I in the 1745 Rebellion in support of Bonnie Prince Charlie. Not surprisingly these 'tax collectors' were unpopular as most of the clansmen and tenants were still loyal to the original owners of the land.

Not the Hindley of her recent visions, but a youngster, clean, scrubbed and smartly and fashionably dressed; but so thin and pale. Eilidh knew at once that this was a vision of Hindley as he had been as a youth, knew that she saw him now as he would have looked on the morning set for his own execution; though the place appointed for Hindley's execution would have been somewhere in England and not here on the side of Loch Leven. Likewise she knew that, unlike in the case of Stewart of the Glen, Hindley relatives had managed to obtain a stay of execution and eventually produced new evidence which put in question the original verdict.

What she did not know was whether it was the original or the subsequent verdict which was the correct one. Was Hindley, like James of the Glen, innocent of the crimes he was accused of?

As if in a dream she scanned his face, she could detected no signs of fear, nor indeed of any emotion. It was as if all trace of self were gone, disappeared somewhere far inside, buried out of sight where it could not be hurt; or if it could where none would see, not even perhaps himself. She wondered if that Self had ever fully reappeared.

As she resolutely turned her face away from the knoll, the vision as quickly vanished, leaving her with a continued feeling of deep unease.

She knew that the next section of their journey would bring her but little comfort, for the path out from Ballachulish led directly to Glencoe where the very rocks themselves still cried aloud their fury and anguish over the wanton massacre of the MacDonalds of Glencoe so many years before.

It was said that the Chief of the MacDonalds of Glencoe had been a staunch Jacobite, and as such he had arrived late to swear his allegiances to King William and Queen Mary[174]; but

343

better late than never; and why punish the rest of the clan for their chief's dilatoriness! Why order Captain Robert Campbell of Glenlyon, of the Earl of Argyle's Regiment, to 'put all to the sword under seventy'?[175]

However not all the stories about the massacre were shameful, some told of acts of integrity, of resourcefulness and courage in the face of adversity; there were heart-warming stories told of the reluctance of many of the soldiers to carry out their orders. The story that she liked best was that of a soldier called Henderson.

After Henderson and the men had eaten their fill in the house of one of the MacDonald's of Glencoe, Henderson asked his host if he would mind taking a turn with him around the village for he could do with a walk before he slept that night. Ever sensible of the responsibilities of hospitality, his host agreed, though he would fain have preferred to sit there warm by his hearth, with his plump little wife and bairns.

To the MacDonald's surprise Henderson did not just walk around the houses but walked some way out beyond the village until he came to a large stone which stood on its own out in the open far away from any human habitation or trees. Henderson stopped next to this stone and explained to his host that it was not just for the pleasure of his company nor for the sake of his stomach that he had trekked all the way out here on such a bitterly cold evening. Rather he had come to this place because he had a very important message to deliver to this particular boulder.

---

[174] William of Orange and Mary ascended the English throne in February 1689 in place of Mary's father King James II

[175] The massacre took place in 1692; final papers authorising the 'Massacre of Glencoe' were signed in Fort William.

Henderson then proceeded to inform the boulder as to the details of the orders given to Captain Robert Campbell of Glenlyon and his unfortunate regiment.

Henderson's soldier's oath forbad him from warning his host directly of the coming treachery but the tale he told to the stone was said to have been enough for the Chief's two sons to remain awake that night and ensured that they and others were able to escape when the massacre began.

Eilidh smiled, albeit sadly as she thought of Henderson's ingenuity. 'Twas just a shame that it had been necessary and that more had not been spared!

As Eilidh and her companions passed by Sgorr na Ciche[176], that small mountain that stood as if to guard the very entrance to the Pass of Glencoe, the sun at last managed to break through the heavy cloud. Yet even this failed to lift Eilidh's spirits for she felt as though they were passing through a gateway that led out of the land she so loved.

Soon they had reached the Clachaig Inn. Here Mairi insisted that they halt so that they could have a hot meal before continuing their journey through the Pass of Glencoe. However Lachlan would not allow them to tarry long and sooner than Mairi would have wished they had left the Inn and were riding alongside the River Coe.

Not far from the Inn the River Coe widened as it joined with Loch Achtriochatan, which was thought by many to be the home of a water bull. Here at last Eilidh's heart began to lighten somewhat for the bard Ossian was said to have been born here on the banks of Loch Achtriochatan.

To one side of this lochan stood the great mountain Aonach Dubh[177], where Ossians's cave hid high up in its ramparts. Joe

---

[176] Pap of Glencoe.

[177] The first of the Three Sisters of Glencoe. The others are Gearr

now rode over to Eilidh "Do ye remember Eilidh that day that we climbed yon peak?"

"Who could forget? Though I would not wish to climb it on a day like today; not that is unless I knew the path like the back of my hand!"

"Indeed not," he agreed, "for I warrant that there will be more than a smattering of snow yet remaining up there. However 'tis a pity we have not time to traverse the hidden valley."

Ewan had been listening and his eyes lit up at this. "What valley is it that you speak of?"

"If you walk between Aonach Dubh and her sister Gearr Aonach you come across a beautiful little valley," Joe explained.

Ewan his eyes alight with mischief said "A fine place to hide cattle not your own!"

"A fine place indeed!" Eilidh returned with a grin. Then she said musingly, "I would not like to be part of an army that tried to fight or trace fugitives over these hills, especially if the fugitives knew the hills well, knew where to hide, knew the best places to place an ambush and the best spot to start a rock or snow fall."

"No one is likely to invade here now Eilidh," retorted Joe curtly. "For who would want it! It is beautiful, grand, majestic but apart from the gift of freedom, it contains naught that would be worth fighting for!"

"True," she replied sadly. "Though there was a time, not that long ago when it was enough just to own the land itself. But as you say, things are changing. The world grows smaller and the means to gather wealth is changing also. I wonder how long it will be before the wealth that these glens contain in

---

Aonach and Beinn Fhadda.

abundance will no longer be seen or appreciated, thanks to the blindness that mammon brings in its wake."

Eilidh fell silent after she said this, and her companions recognising her wish for solitude rode off ahead talking quietly amongst themselves.

The glimmer of sunshine, that had met them as they entered the Pass, had been quickly vanquished and the cloud thereafter remained low, allowing them little view of the mountains which surrounded them.

As they passed by the third sister, Beinn Fhadda, the land began to climb more and more steeply and the higher they climbed the greater grew the feeling that the clouds themselves were pressing in on them. In silence they slowly trudged on up the hill, and soon the quiet itself began to feel oppressive. Yet still they continued their journey onward and upwards into the thickening mist.

Shattering the desolate still Mairi's voice intruded, frightened, querulous; for often had she trod this path and well she knew the treacherous drop that the unwary could fall victim to. Lachlan's calm, soothing tones instantly followed before the eerie hush was reclaimed again.

Thus cocooned they rode past Buachaille Etive Beag[178], travelling until they arrived alongside Buachaille Etive Mor[179] where at long last, and much to Mairi's relief, they came upon a narrow road[180].

How Eilidh longed to follow that rough road up and over the Devil's Staircase homewards towards Fort William[181]! But instead she must follow it south.

---

[178] Mountain called The Little Herdsman of Etive.
[179] Mountain called The Big Herdsman of Etive; a ridge with four principal tops.
[180] 1725 General Wade began building his roads in the Highlands.

This road had originally been built by General Wade to enable soldiers to be marched quickly into the Highlands so that subsequent insurrections by the Jacobites could be quickly suppressed. Eilidh wondered if it was his building of this road to help protect[182] the English from the wild Highland savages that had awarded General Wade the dubious honour of being mentioned in the English National Anthem[183]! Was it any wonder the Scots did not love this Anthem, nor indeed love the English whose National Song contained such verses as those which mentioned Wade!

General Wade's road followed the line of the Buachaille Etive Mor, and as they traversed its path the uncanny quietness continued to follow them, broken only by the calm tones of Lachlan as he sought to soothe and encourage his wife, still nervous despite the fact that their course was now a lot more definite and easy to make out; for now they were travelling downhill and Mairi feared a fall should her mount stumble as it performed its cautious decent.

They stopped for a while at the feet of Stob Dearg[184], that high peak which signals to the traveller that he would shortly be

---

[181] 1690 Old garrison strengthened on orders of William of Orange (King William III) and renamed Fort William.

[182] Born 1673 and died 1748. He was replaced as Army Commander in Chief in 1745 by Prince William Augustus, Duke of Cumberland.

[183] 'Lord grant that Marshal Wade
May by thy mighty aid Victory bring
May he sedition hush
And like a torrent rush
Rebellious Scots to crush
God save the King.'
First performed in 1745; additional verse, not used much after 1745 and did not appear in the official published version.

[184] Stob Dearg, one of the four tops of the mountain Buachaille Etive Mor.

leaving the Pass of Glencoe to venture forth onto the desolate slopes of the Rannoch Moor. Here Mairi was too tired to do ought except lie on the ground and rest, and it was not enough for her to have Lachlan alone to comfort her, but she must have Ewan also beside her to render her what encouragement and reassurance that he could.

Thus it was left to Eilidh and Joe to see to the horses and unpack and make ready the provisions, and Joe made a small fire to heat some water so that they could at least drink something warm, for the cold mist seemed to seep into their very bones.

Eilidh though felt not the cold, nor was she unduly bothered by the gloom, for she could see further than the others and was content to sit surrounded by those high mountains whose presence never ceased to fill her with awe. Although this day she could not see the extent of their majesty, for her it was sufficient to be amongst them, to be able to smell the countless different intoxicating scents and glory in the intense silence, savouring each and every moment that she remained in this land.

She comforted herself with the thought that even should she never set foot again on these hills her memories would never leave her, nor would the stories. Her memories would stay with her wherever she went, a comfort in times of loneliness, of sorrow or hardship. Her recollections would not endure as long as did those held by these ancient rocks, or those broad majestic mountains, but they would endure so long as she did, which would be quite long enough for her.

Eilidh marvelled at the thought of Stob Dearg, that ancient sentinel who in addition to signposting the Pass of Glencoe also guards the path into Glen Etive, the home of 'Deirdre of the Sorrows' and her husband Naoise. What scenes he must have seen in his immense lifetime. How strange to think that Deirdre and Naoise had ridden and walked these very same hills that she did now. The grief that Deirdre felt on leaving these beloved hills and glens would be more even than her own, for Deirdre knew she would never return, and that her beloved husband rode out of this land to his death; tricked by her jealous former suitor.

How odd, she mused, that the tale of 'Deirdre of the Sorrows' should have been passed by word of mouth down through all those centuries. Perhaps though it was not really so surprising, for everyone enjoyed love stories, even those which ended so sadly as had this one. Perhaps it was so memorable because of the romantic beginning of their story and because Naoise and Deirdre had remained true to each other always. Deirdre had remained loving and loyal to Naoise regardless of his disregarding her advice, in spite of his foolishness in trusting the jealous King, even though he uprooted her unwillingly from a home, a land she loved. Their love had survived despite desperate circumstances, despite hardship, had indeed survived beyond the grave. As Eilidh wondered at the strength of the love between Naoise and Deirdre, unbidden Hindley's mocking face flashed before her. Resolutely she banished it.

She stood up determined also to drive out, to shake off this dragging sense of melancholy that had pursued her since the day of her mother's wedding. As she began to repack their provisions in preparation for the continuation of their journey her heart lightened as suddenly she realised that she had been free of the nightmares since the day that she had left Cuchullin at anchor that last time. Perhaps, she thought hopefully as she made to get the horses ready to ride those last few miles of their first day's travel, perhaps that meant that the harbinger of the nightmares was pleased, content with the direction of her journey.

As Eilidh walked over to join Joe and Ewan, she noticed their faces brighten at her approach, and this served further to encourage her to firmly expel those feelings of desolation, of anguish, which had erstwhile preyed on her. Now she began to feel almost as if she could try to smile at the familiar sound of Marie's complaints and Lachlan's soothing reassurances as they too made ready to continue the last few miles of their journey to Kings House, that old inn which sat alone on the edge of the bleak but awesomely beautiful wilds of Rannoch Moor. There they would find a fine Highland welcome, as had centuries of travellers before them.

Chapter 36 Interlude at Kings House

The welcoming sight of a huge and hearty fire roaring blithely on the hearth was awaiting them at Kings House and, after first seeing to the horses, Eilidh was well pleased to settle as close to this as possible.

Dozing contentedly she sat amidst her companions as they waited hungrily for their meal, relaxing in the comfort of the warmth, listening unwearyingly to Ewan's mother Mairi as she fussed and worried, complaining of the dirt on the floor, the dampness of the sheets and the time they were taking to bring the food and drink; while Lachlan tried patiently and gently to sooth her, to distract her from the discomforts of the journey and their present abode and Joe sat quietly in the corner carefully repairing a torn part on a leather bridle. Eilidh, smiled to herself as she heard Ewan's noncommittal, wary answers to his mother's peevish queries and demands. Observing her amused look, Ewan raised his eyes to the heavens, gave her a grin, then respectfully answered yet another of his mother's querulous questions.

Before long this homely scene was troubled by a cold silence, resulting from Ewan having refusing his mother's request that he go and determine the reason for the delayed arrival of their food. This quiet did not long remain, it was soon shattered as Mairi's voice began to rise; the thin reedy tones filled with complaints as to her son's lack of compassion on refusing so simple an appeal, especially when she was feeling so weak and tired after the manifold trials and discomfort of the previous day's wedding and the exhausting exertions of that day's cold arduous ride.

Hearing in her foster mother's voice the tired irritable tone that told that this tirade was barely started, Eilidh rose quickly, saying that she would go to ask after their meal, as she knew the innkeeper and his wife of old.

Kings House on the Rannoch Moor was indeed a place which Eilidh knew well. Many times as a child had she and her father crossed the Rannoch Moor and always they would stop by the Kings House for a meal and very occasionally they had stayed a night or two and Una, the lady of the house, had developed an affection for her over the years and had been want to spoil her, and indeed had continued to do so as she grew older.

Eilidh likewise was very fond of both Sheoras and his wife Una, and would have visited earlier were it not that she had not wished to disturb them at this the busiest part of their evening. She knew well that for them life was not always easy, living as they did in such an isolated position, especially with the harsh winter weather they had to endure. Most travellers passing their door would interrupt their journey for a bite to eat, and a chance to sit by the fire, and many would stop there for food and lodgings for the night. Thus the innkeeper and his wife had the difficult task of maintaining a good supply of victuals. Due to their location they could grow little themselves and so much of their provisions had to be obtained from outside the local area. This meant that at certain times of the year good fresh food would arrive only at irregular intervals.

Now as she made her way down to where she knew the kitchen to be she heard the strident voice of the innkeeper's wife, "That's ower much peat ye are a takin' to they in the lounge. Fir if that's no a rare powerful blizzard that'll be on us in the morn my name is no Una Macpherson! An' they folk will hae tae bide wi' us fir mair thin ane nicht. If we are no careful wi' the fire, we will hae nae peat fir oursel', nivermind yon grousing biddy that is sat in there wi' a face soor enough tae curdle the cream an' a tongue sharper than this here knife. Just you let half o' that kindling bide where it is!"

Eilidh grinned as she heard her say this for she knew that the hard voice belied a heart of gold. "Mither and it is freezing that ye must wish us to be to deny us a wee bit o' warmth at the hearth that ye reckon to be fit fir nane but oor braw bonny King, an' that after the trek we have had through yon freezing mist, wi' the cold wind biting into oor viry bones over mony a long and teerible rough mile!"

The woman turned quickly and stared for a few seconds before walking over and enveloping Eilidh in her arms. "Why an' if it isn't our Eilidh! Gawd be praised. Welcome! Welcome! Come away in with ye, and sit yirsel' down."

Then she turned to berate her husband "How was it that ye never telt me that it was Ardgour's lass as had arrived? If I had kenned I would have got out our best meat fir thim rather than this poor thin broth!"

She looked back at Eilidh saying, "Ah but it is too late to be a-makin' ought else ready for thee this nicht, ye will just have tae sup that as is in this here pot. Ye must be fair famished poor chiel. I'll mak' sure though that ye have plenty tae tak' wi' ye in the morn, that an' I will."

As she said this she turned to her husband saying, "Now Sheoras be sure tae tak plenty o' that there wood up fir the lassies folks, an' stoke the big fire up fine and warm for them the now. Mind an' tell them that their dinner will be wi' them shortly, just as soon as I can manage!"

Then turning back to Eilidh, just as though she had been talking to her all along, she warned, "Though I have a bad feeling about the weather, Eilidh lass, a very bad feeling, such as I would that ye stayed wi' us another night rather than travel abroad in the morn."

354

Eilidh moved over to where the bread was baking, so she could better enjoy the heat. "Ah, this smells so good Una, I am right looking forward to our meal, whatever it is that you have cooking in that there pot." She sat down and leaned back in her chair smiling at the woman, before saying seriously, "I have never known you wrong about the weather neither and I will tell Lachlan about your warning, but I doubt he will listen for his wife is wearied of travelling. She is most desirous of getting home as quickly as possible and will be extremely reluctant to tarry here."

Una turned to the Eilidh and stood up the straighter and with her hands on her hips stated sourly, "And I suppose that if ye have Lachlan wi' ye then ye also have wi' ye that thieving, black headed rascal o' a .... " A tall, merry person came round the corner interrupting Una in mid flow. Eilidh's eyes lit up as she saw him, whilst Una exclaimed caustically, "Speak o' the Divil!"

"Una! I was sure that it was your merry voice that I heard, and I thought..." It was Ewan, come to escape from his mother's complaints and recriminations as to his being an unfilial son.

"Ye thought only tae help yoursel' tae my bakin'!" retorted the woman tartly.

"Why, Una, how could you accuse me of such a thing, when it is but to get a glimpse of your bonny blue eyes that I am come?" Ewan replied with a grin.

Una laughed, "I knew if our Eilidh wis here ye wouldne be far away, with all yir sweet talkin' and yir empty stomach. Ye will have to wait though fir the food for I hiv a great amount of folk to cook fir this night and..."

"... and my mother is somewhat particular," finished Ewan for her.

Una raised her eyebrows. "That is yer mother! Well ye can thank the Good Lord that it is yer faither that ye favour. Though I dare say ye had yer wild hair and those wicked dark eyes of yorn offen she that bore ye," she added reluctantly before proceeding to open up a large container and cut both Ewan and Eilidh a slice of cake. She then kindly but firmly attempted to shoo them away.

Ewan went off to see to the horses, but Eilidh insisted on staying to help prepare the meal and spent much of the early evening chatting with the staff of the inn and helping with the chores, before going to while away the later part of the evening with Liatha Macha and Dawn.

Chapter 37 The Road to Inveroran

It was with a strange feeling of unreality, that Eilidh made her preparations to leave Kings House early the next morning. Lachlan had, as she had expected, chosen to disregard Una's dire warning of the imminent threat of atrocious weather.

When they realised the impossibility of changing Lachlan's mind, Una and Sheoras urged on them more provisions for their journey than they could possibly have spared, but Eilidh thanking them kindly for their concern managed to refuse much of the food without giving any offence.

The innkeeper and his wife accompanied them to where their horses awaited and after anxiously surveying the sky Una once more beseeched Lachlan to tarry with them for just one more day.

Lachlan after politely thanking her for her on-going concern merely continued with his preparations for their journey. Upon which Una threw Eilidh an imploring look, but Eilidh only shrugged her shoulders; then as Una still remained agitated Eilidh jumped off Liatha Macha and came over to give her a hug. "Don't you worry Una, we will be just fine. Liatha Macha has a sixth sense, he will see us safe!"

"Come on Eilidh, I too do not like the look of those clouds, the quicker we leave the sooner we arrive at Inveroran," Lachlan urged sharply. "Our thanks Sheoras and Una for your hospitality and may many blessings be upon your house and all they who enter." He bowed shortly and then quickly walked over to his wife to help her to mount up on her kind pretty grey mare.

Eilidh immediately returned to Liatha Macha and remounted.

Quietly all the others of the partly likewise mounted, with many a surreptitious glance at the sky. Then with their pack horses in tow, and after calling their thanks and goodbyes to Sheoras and Una, they set out for Inveroran Inn.

Una returned slowly to the inn grumbling all the while to Sheoras about the pig headedness of some people, and how she reckoned that they would all be discovered in a few weeks' time frozen to death, with their bones picked clean by the crows!

Liath Macha for once seemed content to amble behind the others, snatching a blade of grass here and there, for Eilidh made no attempt to guide him, content to let him follow as he willed.

Lachlan however set a fast pace that morning, even being short with Mairi when she attempted to remonstrate with him, for despite his earlier assurances to Una, he misliked the feel of the weather.

It grew darker and darker. It became quieter and yet quieter so that even Mairi grew silent. Soon the hush had intensified until it had become almost deafening. The air had an uneasy eerie feel to it.

Lachlan's anxiety became almost palpable - though this day Eilidh did not feel it.

For Eilidh loved the loneliness of the Rannoch Moor with its vast bleak stretch of heather clad moorland interspersed with hills and rocks and secretive, magical lochans. She loved the austereness of the Rannoch Moor, its stark driech wild beauty; for despite its apparent barrenness the Rannoch Moor was filled to bursting with wildlife and usually as one travelled over this wilderness one came across vast herds of grazing red deer, sometimes it was the dainty little hinds that were there and at other times one would see gatherings of kingly stags, many with the most magnificent of antlers. Then there were all the different varieties of birds that hid among the heather or dived for fish in the lochans to watch out for, to marvel anew at the sight of their diverse plumage and glory in the freedom and joy of their flight.

This morning the mist had lifted somewhat and although the sky was now filled with heavy dark clouds Eilidh rode on utterly engrossed in the sounds and sights that hit her senses, determined to enjoy every last moment of her journey, enraptured rather than uneasy by the menacing mustering of the brooding black clouds and the ominous change in the light and sound and the feel of the air all around.

She was just lifting her eyes to scan the horizon in search of an eagle or some such bird of prey when suddenly her awareness was flooded by a vision:

The room was large with flowers draped all around, even on walls and ceiling, so that almost it could have been mistaken for a garden were it not for the costly drapes and the multitudinous candles that lit up the room. She could hear music and other sounds of merriment; gradually into focus there came the spectacle of pretty dresses, beautiful women and well-dressed gentlemen, talking, laughing and dancing. So many, that it was initially difficult to distinguish one from another.

Her glance was drawn to two young men standing to one side who looked, at first sight, to be brothers. Both were tall with jet black hair, thin aquiline features and piercing blue eyes, both were dressed in the most expensive and well cut attire.

As the picture cleared she could see that the larger of the two looked to be a kindly man, for his eyes held a gentle almost childlike look, and although he seemed to have put both time and thought into his attire he did not adopt the flamboyant fashion of the dandies of these times. Nor did he dress in the severe manner favoured by his companion, whose sardonic eyes were icy cold; who, clothed fastidiously in black, bore an air of frosty indifference.

"Charles...," said the more heavily built of the two, rather diffidently. Then he hesitated while the other looked on discouragingly.

"My sister...," the larger man continued resolutely, and then flushed, looked awkward.

His companion gave him no encouragement, and indeed conveyed the impression of being slightly bored. Determinedly he stumbled on, "You have not yet, so far as I can recollect, met my sister Bryony. She is most anxious to become acquainted with her cousin," the bigger man finally managed to state, almost defiantly.

"You astonish me Freddy," returned the black clad individual lazily.

"You declined your invitation to Bryony's coming out ball," Freddy accused. "She is your cousin Charles! It would seem strange should she never be introduced to you, if you fail to even acknowledge her."

Charles put his quizzing glass to his eye and looked over to where the girl sat with her mother. "She looks to be tolerably pretty I suppose," he said languidly. "However I am afraid that I quite fail to understand what possible advantage my society would be to her. I am certain that your father will be able to endow her with a considerable fortune in her own right. That should be sufficient inducement, if any were needed, to ensure that she does not long remain unwed. My addition to her court would serve no purpose, other than to fill me with a slight ennui," he continued indifferently. "Now, if you will excuse me," he added, bowing slightly.

The other flushed at this speech but swallowed his annoyance and persevered manfully, "Charles, our grandmother, she wishes the introduction, as does my mother. Though God knows why!" His anger flared briefly but was as quickly crushed. "Our grandmother considers that it is time you were leg shackled and that Bryony..."

A look of derision passed over Charles's face "And Bryony is to be sacrificed on the altar of our grandmother's ambitions!"

"She looks on you as some sort of romantic hero, so yes, Bryony is excited to meet her infamous cousin," affirmed Freddy, ignoring his companion's jibe. "My sister is no fool Charles," he continued staunchly, "she knows her Homer and Horace almost as well as I; she paints, plays the harpsichord beautifully and sings tolerably well. Moreover she can ride anything..."

"Worse and worse," pronounced Charles scathingly. "I am disappointed Fredrick! I felt sure that you would have recalled that clever women are one of my pet hates. I consider them to be just as useless as a dancing bear and far less entertaining. Neither, now I consider it," he continued broodingly, "do I particularly like debutants, so gauche, so unappealing; like and unripe pear, no succulence, pretty to look at but unpleasant to taste. Tell our mutual and much revered grandmother to fatten the child up; she is too undernourished to tempt my palate and much too lively. Though I suppose she has at least the one saving grace in that unlike our dearly beloved grandmother, she does not suffer from the blight of red hair, Now that would indeed be a failing! I cannot abide red heads. Indeed I'm not altogether sure that I like women at all," he mused. "I hesitate to confess," he concluded disinterestedly, "that from my not inconsiderable experience, I find them to be rather too grasping, too cloying and demanding; and rather fear that this renders the transient pleasure too dearly bought."

"You seem to be able to overcome your distaste tolerably well by all accounts!" Freddy accused bleakly.

"Ah, that reminds me Frederick," drawled Charles with a glint of amusement in his eye. "Whatever were you and Barney thinking of by trying to bid for Lizzie? She told me all about it you know, even claimed that poor Barney's father threatened to disinherit him if he established her. I understand that our inestimable uncle was worried that Barney, by showing such an uncharacteristic interest in the

High Fliers[185], was now bent on a career of ruin and debauchery. So unlike the Barney that I used to know, it seemed quite, quite unthinkable!"

"Just like yourself when we first knew you in fact!" Freddy retorted.

"Why yes indeed," Charles returned mockingly. "So unexpected of your insipid, spiritless cousin was it not! I must have appeared a veritable wolf in sheep's clothing! However to return to Lizzie. She was I can assure you most entertained! I take it that my other dear Uncle, your inestimable father, Frederick, was more tolerant. If I might advise you..."

"You wouldn't understand," retorted Freddy shortly, head down.

"Oh, but there is very little that I do not understand when it comes to the Pretty Horse Breakers Frederick, very little indeed," Charles replied softly. Then he bowed again, ever so slightly. His smile twisted as with studied patience he maintained, "Now I really must go Frederick, I believe I have suddenly remembered a most urgent assignation in the card room."

"Eilidh! Eilidh! Are you all right?" It was Joe. Bemused, it took her a few moments to work out where she was.

Then all of a sudden she was awake. Aware of danger! The clouds had darkened. The winds were gathering. Fear was in the air.

"Eilidh do you think you can get us to the old drovers' inn at Inveroran?" It was Lachlan who asked, worry etched on every line of his face.

She hesitated for a moment, looking around, trying to work out where they were, what was happening to the weather.

"Eilidh," he said impatience in his voice. "There is not much time!"

---

[185] A courtesan.

Suddenly she grinned and you could see Lachlan's face palpably relax.

"We will need to rope up," Eilidh replied lightly her face screwed up as she tried to look out on the horizon.

Joe jumped down and strode over to one of the pack horses and got the rope. "How do you want us to do it?"

"Lachlan at the back with two of the pack horses; then Mairi, and if you would lead your mother's horse Ewan, the third pack horse can go in front of you and Joe can take her lead rope. Dawn will be no trouble, she can come next as she will be quite content behind myself and Liatha Macha," she replied immediately.

They got to work quickly.

"Lachlan, what are you thinking of!" It was Mairi. "She will have us all killed!"

"We have a choice Mairi," explained Lachlan gently, "we either trust Eilidh and Liath Macha or we dig ourselves in here and wait this blizzard out. For myself I would rather be warm in an inn than out in this. It is threatening to be a wild night Mairi lass. Eilidh and Liatha Macha seem to have a sixth sense for the terrain and always know where they are. I believe they are the best chance we have."

At this the woman slumped back miserably on her saddle, while Lachlan made ready for the onslaught of the incoming snow, helping her don an extra cloak and scarf and then did the same for himself, before accepting the lead ropes for the pack horses.

Eilidh too brought her scarf over her face not so much for the cold but to protect her eyes from the snow. Then it began to fall and the wind picked up and Liatha Macha, unperturbed walked forward, ears pinned back, nose to the wind.

The howl of the wind rose so that you could not hear the speech even of the one behind. Its fury snarled all around them, encircling them all, tugging at their clothing, pulling and wrenching at the horse's manes, their forelocks, fetlocks and the packs that they carried, while the horses tails sailed behind them like banners as they struggled against the onslaught of the elements. They rode on, barely able to see even the tail of the horse in front, bent forward over their horses' necks as the horses inched slowly forward, heads down into the storm.

For Eilidh it was as if the very land was crying out against her departure, as if the sky wept large white tears and the wind blew so violently as if it were attempting to forcibly prevent her exit from this land of her birth.

Liath Macha however marched on as if oblivious to the blizzard, ever sure footed and confident as they walked into the eye of the storm.

It was as if time stood still, as if there were only the two of them there as they rode out across the Black Mount. Just the two of them in the whole world! Just Eilidh and Liatha Macha alone. A strange peace came over her. On and on they stepped, sure and steady, though she could barely see anything beyond Liatha Macha's ears; while the snow continued to fall. On and on they trekked while the snow piled up deeper and ever deeper around. Fully aware that the lives of the others were at her mercy Eilidh entertained not even the slightest doubt that they would arrive safe at their destination. She was utterly confident that Liatha Macha would notice any danger in the terrain before it could affect them and she knew that she was never lost and trusted that her foresight would warn her before disaster struck.

It was not long before they reached Loch Tulla, but to Eilidh it was almost an unwelcome sight for it signalled that their destination was approaching, and she had treasured every moment that she and Liath Macha had spent together cocooned within the snow storm.

Then just as the cheery sight of the lights of Inveroran Inn materialized in the horizon, for the first time that day fear suddenly flooded through her being and her heart began to thump and her mouth became dry and her eyes widened, for as abruptly as they had appeared out of the gloom the warm welcoming lights vanished and in their stead out of the pitch blackness there came tiny moving lights and she heard whispers, and then the indistinct figures became clearer and she *Saw* hooded men sneaking along dark city streets carrying something in their hands. She *Saw* them nail the poster to the wall and then run away.

The scene suddenly changed and the sky lightened and she instinctively knew that it was now dawn. People were beginning to come out into the street, then more came and then more and soon there seemed to be hundreds of men, women and children standing around a poster. It seemed as if they were all talking at once; then a voice came forth loud and clear and began to read:

"Friends and Countrymen........." She listened with growing horror, for she had no other option but to hear, however great might be her reluctance. The voice continued:

"......... reduced us to take up arms for the redress of our Common Grievances...... Equality of Rights (not of Property) is the object for which we contend,

LIBERTY or DEATH is our Motto, and we have sworn to return home in triumph - or return no more!

And We hereby give notice to all those who shall be found carrying arms against those who intend to regenerate their Country and restore its INHABITANTS to their NATIVE Dignity;

365

We shall consider them as TRAITORS to their Country, and ENEMIES to their King, and treat them as such.

By order of the Committee of Organisation for forming a PROVISIONAL GOVERNMENT, Glasgow."

Proof

Made in the USA
Charleston, SC
19 October 2013